Romantic Suspense

Danger. Passion. Drama.

Hunting Colton's Witness
Anna J. Stewart

Last Mission
Lisa Childs

MILLS & BOON

Anna J. Stewart is acknowledged as the author of this work
HUNTING COLTON'S WITNESS
© 2024 by Harlequin Enterprises ULC
Philippine Copyright 2024
Australian Copyright 2024
New Zealand Copyright 2024

First Published 2024
First Australian Paperback Edition 2024
ISBN 978 1 038 91746 1

LAST MISSION
© 2024 by Lisa Childs
Philippine Copyright 2024
Australian Copyright 2024
New Zealand Copyright 2024

First Published 2024
First Australian Paperback Edition 2024
ISBN 978 1 038 91746 1

MIX
Paper | Supporting
responsible forestry
FSC® C001695
www.fsc.org

Published by
Harlequin Mills & Boon
An imprint of Harlequin Enterprises (Australia) Pty Limited
(ABN 47 001 180 918), a subsidiary of HarperCollins
Publishers Australia Pty Limited
(ABN 36 009 913 517)
Level 19, 201 Elizabeth Street
SYDNEY NSW 2000 AUSTRALIA

Cover art used by arrangement with Harlequin Books S.A.. All rights reserved.

Printed and bound in Australia by McPherson's Printing Group

Hunting Colton's Witness
Anna J. Stewart

MILLS & BOON

Bestselling author **Anna J. Stewart** honestly believes she was born with a book in her hand. After growing up devouring every story she could get her hands on, now she gets to make her living making up stories and fulfilling happily-ever-afters of her own. Her dreams have most definitely come true. Anna lives in Northern California (only a ninety-minute flight from Disneyland, her favourite place on earth) with two monstrous, devious, adorable cats named Sherlock and Rosie.

Visit the Author Profile page
at millsandboon.com.au for more titles.

Dear Reader,

Writing a Colton book has become one of my favourite things to do as an author. Being a part of this series always feels like a bonus of sorts. The puzzling together of the stories and characters, bringing yet another branch of this family tree to readers? It just makes me happy.

Hunting Colton's Witness features Nathan Colton, an honorable police detective faced with a lot of unexpected family drama. His life's been turned upside down with the death of his father and the secrets that death has exposed. Of course that makes it the not-so-perfect time to fall in love, but that's what happens almost from the moment he sees Vivian Maylor from across a crowded restaurant and bar. Before they even speak a word to one another, sparks fly. And then, so do bullets.

Vivian's been talked into taking some chances with her social life. She had no idea accepting a date with an online match could result in every aspect of her life being upended. She barely leaves the house! What is she doing in the middle of a dangerous mystery? She's so far out of her comfort zone and experience, and yet...Nathan Colton seems the perfect hero to see her through.

I hope you enjoy Nathan and Vivian's journey to happily-ever-after. They've got a lot of work to do to get there, but by the end, it'll be the perfect holiday romance that I hope warms your heart.

Happy reading,

Anna J.

DEDICATION

For the legions of Colton fans.
This one's for you.

Chapter 1

"Can I get you another drink, Nate?"

Detective Nate Colton stifled a disheartened sigh and glanced at his club soda with lime. "No, thanks, Seb." He flashed a tight smile at the bartender/co-owner of Madariaga's before casting an even quicker glance into the mirror. Leave it to scam artist Dean Wexler to turn his free Friday night into one of alcohol-free surveillance duty. "I'm still nursing this one."

"Working, huh?" Seb's sympathetic expression did nothing to ease Nate's irritation.

"Afraid so." Nate paused, considered. He glanced around, trying to take some pleasure in the plethora of Christmas lights strung around, through and over the crisscrossing beams covering the ceiling. "Question, Seb."

"Shoot." The middle-aged man whipped a hand towel over the shoulder of his festive red vest. "Sorry." He grinned and had Nate chuckling. "Not a lot of cops come in here. Don't get many opportunities to use my well-honed humor. What's up?"

"This guy." Nate inclined his head toward the table at his left. The thirtysomething man wore simple jeans and a dark T-shirt beneath a black leather jacket. His hands flexed and relaxed in a kind of rhythm that had him alternating between grasping his half-filled beer glass and slicking back his straw-blond hair. "You see him in here before?"

"Don't think so." The gray in Seb's hair and full beard shimmered beneath the dim recessed lighting when he shook his head. "Why?"

Telling Seb the man in question was a convicted scammer and con artist probably wasn't the way to go. Instead, Nate shrugged. "He looks jittery."

"My guess? First date. Probably a blind one." Seb reached for a glass on the drying rack and set it aside. "Ever since we implemented our safe dating protocol, we get a lot of them."

"Safe...?" Nate shook his head.

"We put up a notice in the ladies' room," Seb told him. "They order a certain drink, we know they need help." Seb inclined his chin down the hall on the other side of the room that led to an emergency exit. "We call for a car, and they get picked up at the back of the building. Date's none the wiser, and the lady gets home safe and sound."

"Nice." Nate grabbed a pair of olives and tossed them in his mouth. "More restaurants need that kind of policy."

"It's definitely upped our business," Seb said. "Speaking of business, haven't seen you in here in a while."

"Been busy. Work and, you know..." Nate paused, ate another olive, this one stuffed with an almond. "Family."

He was still adjusting to the fallout of recent Colton family events and revelations. While he and his sister had always known of their too-close-for-comfort connection to the Colton line branching out of Owl Creek, that part of the family hadn't known either he or Sarah existed at all. Until recently, that is. The emotional fallout on both sides was still being assessed. It was one thing to know he had other siblings living not too far away. It was another to have to deal with them. And the role his mother played in the situation.

That needle-sharp prick of disdain caught as it always did and lodged like a bullet in his chest. Leave it to his mother to set off a familial bomb that resulted in near cataclysmic repercussions. Jessie Colton's calculated actions, as usual, bordered on cruel. But what bothered Nate most was that she never, ever did something like this without a bigger agenda in mind.

His mother was up to something. Something big enough to warrant blowing up a near thirty-year-old family secret.

Part of him didn't want to think about what was coming next. But he needed to do just that, if for no other reason than to protect his sister. He swallowed hard. Plus all ten of the half-brothers and sisters he now openly counted as family.

"Let me know when you're ready for another." Seb offered a sympathetic smile before he moved off to serve a pair of newcomers waiting at the bar for their table.

Pinning his gaze on the mirror to keep track of his target, Nate's stomach rumbled around the teasing promise of food. He'd made a mistake skipping lunch, but he'd been neck deep in planning how to deal with Dean Wexler, the aforementioned table dweller who seemed to grow increasingly fidgety as time passed. Well, Nate thought, he'd followed worse leads and trusted sketchier sources.

He took a deep breath and filled his senses with the familiar and intoxicating aroma of garlic, smoky paprika and saffron, which carried the sweetest hint of honey. The combination increased his crankiness and his hunger.

No one cooked a rib eye like the chefs at Madariaga's, but he couldn't count on Wexler sticking around long enough for him to finish eating. He'd have to make do with the selection of spiced olives and… He raised off his stool enough to grab a dish of mixed nuts farther down the counter. Judging by the way Wexler kept checking his phone for what Nate assumed was the time—or a message from his soon-to-arrive date—it was either going to be a quick wrap-up or a long, long evening. Either way, Nate was in it to the end.

Wexler was the closest thing he had to a lead when it came to his extortion and racketeering case against Marty DeBaccian. Since his release from prison two years ago, DeBaccian had been making his way up the criminal-element food chain here in Boise. Nate, along with a number of his fellow detectives, were determined to stop him before he got anywhere close to the top. Which was where Wexler—a smaller, less careful fish— came in. Nate had been working this case for going on six months. He was getting as antsy as Wexler appeared to be. He wanted this case closed. Now.

"Totally explains how you're spending your Friday night," Nate muttered to himself.

Friday nights on the Basque Block, an area of downtown Boise dedicated to the mix of French and Spanish culture, were notoriously crowded and energetic. The brisk December cold blowing through the city triggered temptations of warm, comforting food and drinks within the welcoming confines of the community. The streets were lined with countless lights and lanterns, windows displayed various images of the seasons, holiday sale signs were abundant and welcoming.

Add in extended Happy Hour at Madariaga's, a restaurant known for their clams Portuguese and in-house brews, and there were numerous festivities in which to partake. The snow had been somewhat gentle on his way in, but he could smell a storm coming.

As he lived a short distance away, Nate often found himself sitting right in this very spot, listening to various musicians performing on the small circular stage in the center of the dining room. Tonight, the usual weekend percussive sounds of drums, tambourines and flutes had been replaced by a solitary guitarist, who, if Nate was honest with himself, conjured a deep-seated envy as she plucked out familiar Christmas music with a finger-flying Spanish-inspired flair.

His lips twitched in unexpected humor. Growing up, he'd loved the idea of becoming a musician, but it soon became obvious the only talent he possessed where a guitar was concerned was stashing it in the back of his closet.

As entertaining as the place was, Nate bit back a self-pitying sigh as he rotated his glass. He'd really been looking forward to a night in, slugging down more than a few bottles of beer and binge-watching the latest in a series of ridiculous, over-the-top, high-speed vehicular action movies.

Seated on a corner stool at the bar, Nate ran through Wexler's rap sheet in his head to keep himself occupied and, more importantly, focused. There wasn't much Wexler hadn't been accused of in his thirty-three years. His first adult arrest had come two days after he'd turned eighteen.

Wexler's juvie record was sealed, but Nate would bet a year's salary the guy spent a significant amount of time locked down from a very early age. Now the guy had a tendency to mix things up and expand into whatever worked best for him. These days, burglaries seemed to be his preferred method of income. After going over numerous victim statements and reports, Nate strongly suspected Wexler was behind the rash of thefts that had relieved nearly a dozen single women of a significant amount of cash and property.

A streak like that had to have caught DeBaccian's attention, which gave Nate some solid leverage. Wexler's spine was as solid as straw. He'd bend over and kiss whatever backside he needed to keep himself out of prison. Or off DeBaccian's hit list. Nate planned on being the person who could make both those things happen. For a price.

Exhaustion crept up his spine. He hadn't had a good night's sleep since he'd gotten back from Owl Creek. Whatever switch that turned his brain off had been overridden by stress, circumstance and what probably amounted to an unhealthy amount of professional obsession.

"Heads up." Seb crouched to retrieve a trayful of clean glasses. When he popped back up, he jutted his chin toward the front door. "Your boy just went on full alert."

Nate's gaze shifted not so subtly to Wexler, who had indeed straightened up and was looking toward the door, which clicked shut.

Wexler's nerves didn't abate, Nate noticed. Instead, they intensified to the point of vibration. Like a cheetah poised to pounce on unsuspecting prey. Wexler stood, lifted an arm, and only then did Nate see the gleam of relief—or was it calculation?—on the man's face. Whatever it was, Wexler definitely had Nate's full attention.

Or at least he did until Nate looked to the door and saw her.

Her back was to him at first as she hung her coat on a hook. She wore a knee-skimming black dress and matching short-sleeved sweater. Her long, dark brown hair draped beautifully down her back. The knee-high boots spoke of practicality where an Idaho winter was concerned. She had curves where he preferred them and not an angle in sight. She was, Nate thought as she turned around and displayed a face worthy of a classical sculptor, the kind of woman who conjured carnal thoughts of endless nights spent in front of a fire while a winter storm raged outside their door.

"Beautiful," he murmured in a way that had him glancing around to confirm he hadn't been overheard. Impulse had his hands curled into fists before reality knocked him back down. He wasn't here for her.

But he wanted to be.

The woman paused, ran her hands down the front of her dress in a motion that spoke to her own bout of nerves. A thin gold chain around her neck displayed a solitary charm that, from a distance, Nate couldn't decipher. Rather than makeup, it was the cold that tinted her cheeks. Her full lips pressed together until they disappeared. Nate could all but hear the pep talk she was giving herself before she stepped shakily over to the hostess desk.

It seemed a cruel trick, or maybe it was a stroke of luck, when she was escorted to Dean Wexler's table.

Nate inclined his head, unable to pull his attention away. She stood beside her chair and offered her hand to Wexler, who immediately grasped it. He could see her mouth move, but couldn't, with the music and conversation bouncing around the restaurant, hear what she said. Her smile seemed strained when she pulled her chair back to sit. Polite. Reserved.

Nate gave Wexler's chances of a second date a whole one out of ten when the idiot neglected to play the chivalry card and pull out her chair for her. *Typical*, Nate thought with a silent snort. Why would Wexler act on something he probably couldn't spell?

Nate was so caught up in that observation he didn't realize she was looking directly at him.

Their gazes locked, and he couldn't, for what seemed like a full minute, find his breath. His smile came without thought, and he felt a chill of accomplishment when she offered him one in return. Maybe he was fooling himself, but this smile, unlike the one she'd offered Wexler, appeared genuine. A flash of uncertainty illuminated her candlelit hazel eyes before she turned her attention to Wexler and the menu he handed her. Reaching into her purse, she pulled out a pair of round glasses.

Nate glanced away, cursing himself for being tempted

to forget about the case and keep her in his sights. Darn if those glasses didn't add to her appeal. He'd never been into the librarian look. Oh, how wrong he'd been.

Focus, Nate told himself. If Wexler's pattern held, this woman could very well be his next burglary victim. Nate's hand tightened around his glass at the thought of anyone—Wexler in particular—taking advantage of her. Of eroding the trust and shadowy optimism he saw in those amazing eyes of hers.

"Seb!" As if taken over by someone else, Nate signaled for another drink. He couldn't risk surrendering to temptation and instead fixed his gaze on the mirror image of her.

Guilt had him shifting uncomfortably on his stool. He hoped he didn't look as pathetic as he felt. He needed to think about someone, anyone else, another woman he'd dated, met, talked with who had intrigued him more than this woman did. But it was a no-go. It was as if this woman, simply by walking into view, had erased every other woman from his memory.

"So?" Seb said. "What do you think?"

Nate took a too large sip of his club soda. "About what?" he choked out.

"Them." Seb tilted his head. "You think they'll make it to a second date?"

"No." Nate lifted his glass, toasted Seb with it. "I do not."

If only because Nate planned on having Wexler behind bars in the next few hours.

Vivian Maylor's head was spinning, and not in a good way. Why, oh why, had she let Lizzy talk her into online dating? Because Lizzy was her best friend and had rarely steered her wrong. Clearly there was a first time for everything.

Vivian's vision blurred as she tried to focus on the open menu in her trembling hands. Anxiety had grabbed hold, not when she climbed into her car or even when she'd parked a few blocks away. Oh, no, her old heart-stuttering friend had locked its twisty, suffocating bands around her back when she'd first clicked Accept on the online dating profile.

"Just jump in and rip the Band-Aid off," Lizzy Colton had told her a few weeks ago when Vivian made the mistake of lamenting feeling lonely out loud. "Just go out on one date and see what happens!" This from the woman who less than a month ago had been trapped in a blizzard only to be rescued by a man who may as well have stepped right out of one of Vivian's romance novels.

Of course, Lizzy's headline-making kidnapping around the same time had no doubt left her searching for an outlet for the residual trauma. As happy as Vivian was to serve as a support for her friend, she hadn't anticipated having to agree to a date in order to make Lizzy smile again. But she had. And Lizzy seemed relieved. About that at least.

"Leaving you to rip off the Band-Aid," Vivian muttered then suddenly realized she'd spoken out loud. She peeked over the top edge of her menu and smiled at her date. "Sorry." She forced a smile before reaching for the ice water their server had delivered. "I live alone, so I talk to myself." She took a big swallow. "A lot."

"Who doesn't?" her date teased. But the glint in his brown eyes didn't lessen her unease. She had the feeling he was trying too hard. "Have you been here before, Vivian?"

"Ah, kind of?" She set the menu down and did her best to ignore the tingling racing down her spine. There was this—she didn't know how else to describe it—this force, pulsing out at her from the bar. Not the bar, she corrected quickly and glanced to her left and saw him looking at her again. But the man sitting there. She pushed her glasses higher up her nose, a nervous habit she had when uncertainty descended. He looked familiar, but she couldn't for the life of her figure out why. "I live a little ways away, but I've ordered from their delivery menu." She needed to focus on her date. He was, after all, why she'd made the white-knuckle drive into town. "So. Sam." She needed to give this an authentic chance. "Is that short for Samuel?"

"Nope." His eyes flashed. "Just Sam. Sam Gabriel."

"Right." She shook her head. "Sam Gabriel." Truth be told, she'd only retained a modicum of the information that had been listed on his profile. While she was at the top of her game in the PR department, socializing outside of work wasn't her thing. She wasn't…outgoing. Or adventurous. But loneliness was a surefire trigger to pushing someone outside their comfort zone.

She supposed it was a good idea to leave the house for something other than getting her mail. Since her cat Toby died last month, she'd spent an inordinate amount of time feeding the strays in her neighborhood, an activity that was quickly earning her loony cat-lady status. All that was missing was the bumper sticker on her car declaring herself a cat mom. Best to get out in the world before that became a reality.

She'd have thought all the cheery holiday decor lining the downtown Boise streets would have elevated her mood, but instead, it only reminded her of how alone she truly was. "You're a teacher, aren't you, Sam? What was it? Third grade?"

"Second." He leaned his arms on the table and grinned so wide she could see the fillings in his molars. He was good-looking enough, she supposed, but that smile. She couldn't help but suspect there was something else lurking behind it. "I just love kids, don't you?"

"I haven't spent enough time around them to say, honestly." She looked back at the dinner offerings, telling herself not to be paranoid. His questions were normal for a first date. Her instincts were out of practice and headed into overdrive. It was a simple dinner date. Nothing more. She was the fish out of water here, not Sam. "I think I'm just going to get the panzanella." Her stomach rumbled at the very idea. She'd been so nervous all day she hadn't had much to eat. The idea of a bread salad hit all the right notes. "How about you?"

"Haven't decided yet." He reached over and pulled her menu down with one crooked finger. "You don't have to be nervous, Vivian."

"It's my natural state." Her smile felt stiff this time, and that voice in the back of her head was definitely crying out more loudly to be listened to. She shouldn't have done this. Taking chances, doing the unexpected—that was Lizzy's way of doing things, not hers. Vivian shoved her hands under her legs and scrunched her fingers, felt the wood against her nails. "So, um." She glanced around, did her best not to let her gaze drift anywhere near the man at the bar. Even as her mind raced to place him. Thankfully, their server arrived and took their orders. The few minutes gave her enough time to get at least some questions lined up in her overactive brain.

The guitarist had taken a break, and to be honest, Vivian welcomed the silence. Or at least as much silence as the crowded restaurant allowed. A solitary votive candle flickered in a deep vessel, sprigs of rosemary pressed up against the glass, casting wintery shadows on the red tablecloth. "So, how long have you been using the dating app?" she asked when they were alone again.

"Not long." He was back to leaning on the table, a semi-smirking expression on his face now. "I like how it gets all the tedious stuff out of the way. I saw on your profile you're in PR. You own your own business, don't you?"

"Yes." She tucked her hair behind her ear. "PR Perfection. I represent a number of clients from various industries. I focus a lot on authors and entertainment figures."

"Sounds interesting."

It must, given the sudden spark in his eyes. "Social media is a big part of what I do," she said. "I guess a dating app didn't seem out of the norm by comparison." If only she was as good at talking about herself as she was discussing her clients. So far, the only word that came to mind regarding this date was *excruciating*. "It can be pretty long hours, unexpected work hours sometimes." A few of her clients had run into some rather scandalous situations as of late. How she'd handled them had earned her a few more clients in return. "But I like the challenge of staying on top of things for my clients and helping them expand their reach."

"I bet that pays pretty well."

The man at the bar coughed and shifted on his stool. Vivian couldn't help it. She glanced over and found him looking at her again. This time, the pretty blue eyes carried a bit of a warning. Vivian straightened in her chair. Was he... Was he listening to them? Her stomach knotted to the point of pain.

"I do okay," she said. "What made you go into teaching?"

Sam's smile widened. "I liked the idea of helping shape the minds of the future."

Vivian frowned. That sounded so rehearsed she could almost see a script sticking out of his pocket. "Second grade is, what, ten years old?"

"Thereabouts." Sam leaned back as his second beer was delivered. "So, this place is a favorite of yours, then?" He looked around. "It has a nice vibe."

"It has good food." It was one thing she indulged in. Some people had a weakness for aged whiskey or bookstores. Vivian held an affinity for cuisine. It was a safe way to be adventurous, especially these days with so many restaurants offering delivery service. "How long have you been teaching?"

"A few years." He picked up his beer. "Do you travel much?"

"No. Do you?"

"When I can. Gets a bit costly on a teacher's salary."

Vivian nodded, making note of the fact that that was the second time he'd mentioned money. Was it her imagination or was this guy digging for something? It didn't feel like a normal date. Not that she knew what that felt like. She couldn't recall the last actual date she'd gone on. She had to be overthinking this. She looked to the man at the bar, who offered an encouraging smile before he looked away again.

She silently sighed and tried to return her focus to Sam. He was currently talking up a storm, about what she couldn't really say, but the man at the bar? He hadn't said a word, yet she had this unsettling desire to sit beside him and strike up a conversation.

Vivian slid her gaze to the mirror behind the bar, found him watching her again. But instead of making her feel uncomfortable or targeted, that *whoomph* of a force field seemed to pulse in tempting rhythm.

Those eyes of his were so bright against the light brown of his hair. She'd never been one to like messy hair before, but on him it worked. She couldn't see much more than his face, hunched over his drink the way he was. He had wide shoulders, though. Strong shoulders, she imagined, and a broad chest to match. Beneath the long sleeves of his navy shirt, muscles bunched and tightened in a way that left her feeling a bit foggy-headed. She liked his smile. A lot.

"Vivian?" Sam caught her hand in his and gave her fingers a gentle squeeze. "You still with me?"

"Um, yes, of course." She waited for a spark, for some kind of confirmation that there was something between her and Sam. Instead, she had the sudden urge to retreat and pull back into her town house of a shell. Whatever she might have said next was scrapped when their dinner was delivered.

Relieved, she picked up her fork and quickly filled her mouth in order to avoid any other comment. Or any temptation to look back at the stranger who made her feel things she honestly hadn't thought possible.

Despite her intention to speed things up, dinner passed at an excruciatingly slow rate. She had to give Sam points for trying. Her date was nothing if not persistent with the questions and attempts to discover common ground. But there wasn't any. And there certainly wasn't heat between them, not even a spark.

They both reached for the check at the same time.

"I insist," Sam said with a bit of an edge in his voice.

So did she. "We'll split it." Vivian kept her voice light. "I think we can both admit this isn't going anywhere."

"Maybe we just haven't hit the right moment yet." His smile was tight as he reached into his back pocket for his wallet. He flagged down their server and waved off her determined offer to add cash to cover her meal. "Tell you what," Sam said. "There's a great little dessert café a couple blocks away. Let's take a walk, get some fresh air and you can treat. They have a great chocolate peanut-butter lava cake."

Proof he'd read her profile. She'd mentioned a weakness for anything chocolate. She did the calculations in her head. Twenty or thirty minutes more in exchange for lava cake? She shrugged, her sweet tooth activated. Seemed an appropriate price to pay for dessert. "All right."

She clutched her hands in her lap, her knees bouncing as she watched him fill out the tip amount on the credit card receipt. He clicked the pen shut and stood up.

"I'm just going to visit the ladies' room before we head out." She pointed toward the back of the restaurant. "I'll meet you out front?"

"You aren't going to go scampering out the back door, are you?" Sam teased.

She'd be lying if she said the thought hadn't crossed her mind. "I'll meet you out front." When he moved off, she dug into her purse, pulled out a couple of twenty-dollar bills and slid them into the bill folder just as their server reappeared to retrieve it. "Thank you for lovely service," she told him. "Sorry about his tip."

"I'm sorry about your date," the young man said with an understanding smile.

"Thanks." When she stood, she couldn't help but give in to temptation one last time.

The corner barstool was empty.

The man with the blue eyes was gone.

"Of course he is." On a scale of one to ten, she was hovering at about a minus two at this point where tonight was concerned.

Since the ladies' room was just an excuse to make up for the anemic tip Sam left—clearly her date had never worked in the service industry—it wasn't long before Vivian retrieved her jacket from the hook by the door and shrugged into it.

Regret over having agreed to dessert surged as she joined Sam outside. She really just wanted to go home and forget tonight had ever happened.

Sam was standing by the valet parking stand, looking at his cell, when she emerged. He straightened when he saw her, shoved it into his pocket in a motion that had her earlier suspicions resurfacing. She did a quick scan of the street in both directions and noticed a number of people around. The windows of other restaurants displayed plenty of customers amidst the holiday decor of garlands, lights and glistening, colorful ornaments.

Sam's smile was back in place, but his eyes were a

bit jumpy, looking over his shoulder before he stepped closer. "All set?"

"Sure." Worst case, she'd head back to Madariaga's and use the escape hatch she'd seen posted in the bathroom. "How far is it?" She pointed behind her as he led her down the street at a rather hurried pace. "I'm parked in the other direction."

"Two, maybe three blocks?" He didn't sound nearly as sure of himself as he had inside the restaurant. He dropped a hand to her back to hurry her along. "I promise this cake is totally worth it."

"Mmm." It would have to be a pretty fantastic dessert to get her to put tonight behind her. Snow drifted gently to the ground. Her lined boots kept her suddenly scrunching toes warm, and she grabbed the lapels of her brown down jacket. She'd forgotten to wear gloves, but the coffee she planned to order should take the chill off her fingers. Her boots clicked against the sidewalk as they walked. "I hope your next date goes better than this one," she said as a peace offering.

"This one isn't over yet." Sam, hands shoved into the front pockets of his jacket, gave her an encouraging smile. "But if you're looking for sparks, yeah." He sighed. "Looks like we're out of luck in that department."

Sparks like what she'd felt when she'd looked at the man at the bar? "I'm afraid so. Is that the place?" She pointed ahead to the lighted café sign two blocks on the left. At nearly nine on a Friday night, traffic was still humming alongside them. The rumble of engines cut through that winter silence she'd been longing for. If she never answered another question in her life, it would be too soon.

"Look, Vivian."

Sam stopped and reached out, caught her arm and brought her to a halt. The display cases in the jewelry store beside them showed off a modicum of offerings that glinted under spotlight bulbs. Sprays of holly and tinsel decorated the windows, along with spray-on snow creating a framed effect.

In the street, a beige car occupied by two men drove by at a crawl. The passenger in front slid down, almost in slow motion as she glanced over her shoulder.

"Maybe we should give this another try?" Sam suggested. "This could have just been first-date jitters, and, well—" His eyes went wide as a pop sounded in the air. She jumped, looked toward the car. Something gold glinted in the back seat. The sound of breaking glass tinkled in the air followed by another pop. And another.

Sam caught her around the waist and knocked her to the ground, driving the air out of her lungs. She hit shoulder first. Her head bounced against the cement. Her glasses snapped, the jagged edge cutting into her face. Whatever scream she might have offered was caught by the whoosh of Sam's body landing heavily on top of her. Now that she could, she couldn't form the thought to cry out.

The weight of Sam's body pushed down on her to the point she could feel the ground pressing against her side.

More glass tinkled, another pop echoed. An alarm went off, blaring into the night as people cried out and tires screeched. Footsteps raced past and around her. Unintelligible conversation picked up speed to the point it became white noise.

Vivian lay there, frozen, the cold of the ground soaking through her jacket and making her shiver. A sob caught in her throat as she tried to move and got one hand up to her shoulder in order to shove Sam away. She kicked her legs in an attempt to extricate herself. "Sam, get up. Get off." She shoved again, only he didn't move. She felt an odd warmth trickle down her neck and spread beneath her jacket. "Sam?" She pushed harder.

The growing crowd didn't seem to know what to do any more than she did. "Help, please," she cried, her voice muffled by Sam's shoulder. "Someone…help!"

"Back! Everyone stand back!" The male voice that exploded through the crowd brought her an unexpected moment of relief before Sam was rolled off her.

Suddenly feeling as if she could breathe again, Vivian tried to sit up. When she did, she saw the man from the bar, crouched behind her, that handsome face of his marred with controlled fear and concern. She lifted a hand to where her glasses had been, where her face hurt. "You." It was the only word that came to mind. The only thing she could think to say. Her ears were ringing, and her head throbbed. She lifted her fingers to her temple. "What are you—?"

"Are you all right?" The man shifted slightly, reached into his pocket for his cell. "Don't move too much."

"I'm—fine." Her mind raced, trying to catch up with whatever had just happened. She looked around. The parked car didn't have windows anymore. Shattered glass littered the sidewalk. She clutched her hands to her chest, took comfort in the hand resting on her shoulder.

"That's not your blood?" The man asked in such an urgent way he left her blinking.

"Blood?" She looked down, saw the glistening red liquid coating her jacket and her neck. She touched a hand to her skin, drew away sticky red fingers. "N-no. It's not mine." Realization shot through her, and she felt her face grow cold. "Sam." She scrambled onto her knees, but the man from the bar shifted to keep her where she was. "Is he hurt? Why isn't he—?"

"Yeah, this is Detective Nate Colton, Boise Police." The man spoke into his phone. He clicked the speaker feature on, placed the phone on the ground beside him. "Stay right there," he ordered Vivian, who could only nod and stare. He turned his back on her, but the second she could move, she was on her knees beside him.

"You're a policeman?" she asked the detective as he pulled open Sam's jacket, pressed two fingers against the side of Sam's blood-spattered neck.

"Dispatch," Nate continued as if she hadn't spoken. "Requesting backup and patrol. And an ambulance to…" He glanced around and recited the address. "I've got a gunshot victim, at least two to the chest. Rapid pulse, but he's alive. I need to keep him that way. Over."

"Request received, Detective Colton. Assistance is on the way. Over."

"Great." He reached out a bloodied hand and clicked off the speaker. A number of people raced out of a nearby restaurant. "You!" Nate yelled over the heads of the crowd creeping closer. "I need towels or tablecloths or napkins, something to help stanch the bleeding."

"I can—" Vivian started to stand, but her knees folded immediately.

"You stay right there," Detective Colton ordered. "And you all, turn those stupid phones off," he snapped at the crowd, who all but ignored his order. "This isn't anything that needs to be shared."

Vivian shivered and tried to breathe regularly. Her head spun. Her stomach churned. For a moment, she feared she might throw up. She pressed a hand against her mouth and tasted bile in the back of her throat.

"Hey." Detective Colton nudged her knee with his foot. "You're okay, right? You still with me?"

"Yes." She nodded, feeling both useless and helpless, which only irritated her. "I don't know what happened. One thing we're walking down the street, and the next thing I know he knocked me down."

The detective gave her a blank look, but if he was going to ask her anything, he was prevented by the restaurant employees returning with a stack of towels and napkins.

"Great, thanks." Detective Colton inclined his head. "Grab some of those will you?" he told Vivian. "And keep one for yourself." He nodded to her face. "You're cut. From your glasses probably."

Her glasses. She looked around but couldn't focus enough to see where they might have ended up. She'd have to get her spare pair from home. Her hands shook as she accepted the offerings and quickly handed the detective one so he could slip it between his blood-soaked hands and Sam's open wounds. "Don't you die on me, Wexler."

"His name is Sam," Vivian corrected. "Sam Gabriel."

The detective leaned forward, pressed down so hard with his hands Vivian winced. "I need you to stay quiet right now," he told her, looking as if he didn't want to be saying what he had. "Just…trust me, okay? I'll explain everything I can soon, but not now."

It was a request Vivian often had trouble with. Trust was a big reason why she lived alone. Why she worked alone. But with this man… She couldn't explain it. "Okay." She said it in a whisper and reached for another towel. "Yeah." She swallowed hard. "I trust you."

Chapter 2

Nate had long ago lost track of the number of nights he'd spent in a Boise emergency room.

His years as a uniformed officer had made visits an almost daily occurrence, from getting unhoused people looked after to overseeing the transport of accident victims, or overdose victims in a sometimes futile effort to get them help before they succumbed to their addictions. Early on, he'd developed that necessary emotional detachment that kicked in every time he stepped through the swinging doors, whether trailing behind a gurney or having hauled someone out of the back of his patrol car. Nate had always been able to keep himself detached and logical in a crisis.

Tonight, however? Tonight was a very different, not to mention unnerving, story.

He'd left the restaurant the second Wexler's date reached for the check. Seemed an apt signal of the end of his target's dinner, and Nate hadn't bothered to dismiss the relief he felt at the encounter tanking. He needed his focus on what Wexler could do for his case, not what plans the scam artist might have for his date.

After signaling good-night to Seb, he'd made his way

outside and waited in the alley between Madariaga's and the dry-cleaning business next door. Out of sight. But close enough to pick Wexler up as soon as he was on his own, once his suspect finished the cell call he accepted.

Only Wexler wasn't on his own. Somehow, he'd managed to convince her to join him for coffee and dessert.

That odd, primal wave of protection surged as Wexler and his date walked past. There had been enough distance between the two that Nate could take comfort in the knowledge there wasn't anything close to a love match. Not that that mattered. That wasn't any of his business.

He needed Wexler to talk, which meant Nate needed to keep his target in sight, approach when he could be assured of privacy. He'd stepped out from the alley, waited until they'd crossed the first street before following.

Even now, Nate was kicking himself for not noticing the beige sedan creeping slowly up the street just behind the pair. He'd increased his pace, was only a little ways behind when the passenger window rolled down and the gun appeared.

What was happening should have dawned on him sooner and not after the first shot shattered the parked car's driver's-side window.

He was running as the second shot sounded and the jewelry store window exploded. Wexler dived forward as glass rained down like a deafening winter snowstorm. More shots. Tires screeched, and Nate leaped into the street to try to catch a glimpse of the plate number as the car raced around the corner and disappeared from sight.

Shouts of shock and terror reverberated before Nate gave up and shoved his way through the instantly forming crowd. He couldn't hear anything other than a low, dull buzzing in his ears. He thought for sure she was dead. She had to be, his mind screamed at him as he'd dropped beside them. For an instant, he let himself feel the fear and the dread, accepting, however reluctantly, the truth of what had happened.

Wexler was on top of her, unmoving. Blood seeped out and spread across the glistening frozen pavement.

His heart stopped. She'd moved. Only a little at first, then with enough of a determined cry he dared to hope...

He rolled Wexler off her. Seeing her blink up at him settled the unfamiliar panic that had surged inside him. She was covered in Wexler's blood as she pushed herself up. Her eyes were glassy with shock, and she was shaking so hard he was afraid her bones might snap, but she was alive.

And so, miraculously, was Wexler.

Now, standing outside the second pair of double swinging doors in the ER, Nate stared through the glass window. He flexed his tight, blood-stained hands. It felt as if he were wearing gloves. His heart pounded. He should have drawn his gun. He should have fired at the car, but there were so many people around and the car had been speeding so fast, it was just as well he hadn't.

"Detective?" A nurse from the registration desk approached. She was older, her silver-streaked hair worn in a long braid down her back. The badge she wore identified her as the duty nurse. "Are you all right?"

"I'm fine." The statement didn't sound like it came from him. "What's his status?"

"We won't know for a while. Why don't you come with me?" She took him by the shoulder and led him behind the desk. "You can use the locker room to clean up. I'll let you know when the doctor's available to speak with you."

Nate stopped outside the door as if he'd hit a wall. "There's a woman who was brought in. Pretty. Dark hair, brown jacket. She's being checked for injuries."

"I'll see what I can find out. Please." She motioned to the door. "Take your time. I'll make sure there's some coffee waiting for you."

Nate almost laughed at the idea of adding caffeine to the situation.

It was only when he was standing at the sink looking at himself in the mirror that he realized why the nurse was so intent on getting him out of sight. His hands, the front of his shirt, even part of his face were covered in blood. At least the dark fabric would hide most of it, once it was dry anyway, but the clothes and probably his jacket were toast after today.

He gave his hands a quick scrub, dried off, then cleaned off his phone and the wallet he'd dragged free to show his badge when the ambulance and other cops had arrived.

By the time he thought himself presentable, his anxiety over Wexler surged afresh. As selfish as it sounded, he really needed the guy to pull through. He needed him. His case against DeBaccian couldn't be made without him.

The nurse was back at the station when he walked past.

"Detective." She held up a large paper cup. "Dr. Billings can speak with you in a few minutes. In the meantime, the woman you asked about, she's being examined right now." She inclined her head toward the hall. "Third room, second bed on the right."

"Thanks. Can you..." He paused. "Did you happen to get her name?"

"Vivian Maylor." The nurse smiled as if understanding something he didn't. "And just so you know..." She leaned forward and lowered her voice, a soft smile on her lips. "She asked about you, too."

He moved away, ducking his head before she or anyone else saw the heat in his cheeks. Just what his evening needed, a matchmaking nurse.

Rehearsing what he was going to say to her would be a lesson in futility. There wasn't anything he could utter that would make any kind of sense, at least not yet. Right now, all he cared about was seeing that she was all right.

He stood outside the drawn curtain, heard her soft murmur of a voice. It was the same murmur he'd listened intently to and for at the restaurant. He closed his eyes, blotting out the words she spoke but listening to the tone. It was a tone that comforted him in a way he'd never quite experienced before.

The curtain was ripped open, and a woman stepped out. She wore blue scrubs and her blond hair up in a messy knot on the top of her head. "Ah. Hello. Dr. Preston." She held out her hand. "You must be Detective Colton."

"I must be." The sooner he got his sense of humor back on track the better. "Is she okay?"

"Near as we can tell." Dr. Preston nodded. "She has a bruised shoulder, so we're waiting on X-rays, and she got a pretty good knock on the side of her head, but no signs of a concussion. We took care of the cut near her eye." She reached up and grabbed hold of the stethoscope hanging around her neck. She'd clipped a sparkly harp-playing angel to the metal center. "She'll be sore for a couple of days and probably have a headache, but other than that, she's okay. I'm going to get her discharge paperwork started for once we see the X-ray's clear." She stepped aside. "Go on in."

"Thanks." Nate didn't know what was more embarrassing—the nurse's romantic coddling earlier or the fact he felt like a teenager picking up his first date.

He peeked around the edge of the curtain. She sat there, sitting up in the mechanical bed, her gaze pinned on him the second he stepped clear of the fabric. They'd put a small butterfly bandage on the cut by her right eye. Dried blood coated part of her face and the side of her neck. Her eyes seemed slightly dazed, the shock no doubt. Even with all that and very pale skin, she still struck him as beautiful. He felt like he could breathe again and yet...not. "Hey."

"Hey, yourself." Her smile was quick and more than a little confused. "Detective." She eyed the cup in his hand with the ferocity and longing of a fellow caffeine addict. "Is that coffee?"

"Supposedly." His first sip hadn't been promising. He removed the plastic lid and handed it to her.

"My hero." She accepted the cup with both hands and drank nearly half of it down. "For the second time tonight." With a sigh, she sat back. "How's Sam?" Nate hesitated long enough for her to roll her eyes. "His name isn't Sam, is it?" The calm acceptance had him frowning. "That might be one thing about tonight that actually makes sense."

"Bad date?" He blinked in feigned innocence, but that only earned him a judgmental glare.

"You know it was." She eyed him dubiously. "You called him Wexler back on the street. Who is he really?"

"Not anyone you need to be concerned with from here on." Nate came into the cubicle and reached for the metal-frame chair in the corner. "Is it okay if I sit?"

"Sure." She shifted on the squeaking mattress. "Trust me, you're getting the better end of the comfort deal." She tugged at the collar of the pale hospital gown. The monitor in the corner beeped out her vitals, which, in Nate's limited experience, still seemed a little high. "My butt's already asleep. You didn't answer my question. Is what's-his-name okay?"

"I'm waiting to hear." From his vantage point, he could see the hallway and the thin bits of tinsel strung in the hall. "Your doctor says you're fine."

"Oh, I'm just great," Vivian said with more sass than he expected. "But I think I'm officially off online dating." She laughed, but it sounded more pained than amused. Her hands were shaking, just enough to signal the shock hadn't yet fully set in. "As if I wasn't already inclined to swear it off completely. I don't think there's ever been a bigger first-date disaster on record."

He sat back and chuckled in an effort to put her at ease. "I once had a date that ended with me mistaking her brother for a burglar. Planted the guy face-first into her refrigerator. Broke his nose," he admitted. "And about a dozen butterfly magnets."

She looked doubtful, but there was a glimmer of amusement in her hazel eyes. "You're making that up."

"Oh, how I wish I was." Funny. For the life of him, he could not recall that woman's name.

"Verbal first aid for the heart. Who knew that was a thing?" She took another drink of coffee before handing it back to him. "Thanks. That jolt should be enough to get me home." Her eyes went wide. "Eventually. My glasses." Her sigh was heavy and resigned. "They broke back on the street." And she hadn't had the wherewithal to attempt to locate them.

"Where is home?"

"Here we go with questions again," she muttered. "Must be inquisition Friday and no one told me. I live about halfway between here and Owl Creek. Am I supposed to give a statement or something? That always happens on cop shows."

"One of the few things they get right," Nate observed wryly. Oh, if he could only list his pet peeves on that front. "There will be another detective to take yours."

"Not you?"

Maybe it was his exhaustion talking, but she sounded disappointed. "I was there, so no, not me." He would, however, have to give his own account.

"Well, I'm not going anywhere for a while, so." She pointed to a sign that listed how long various tests took to complete. X-rays averaged two hours. Vivian sighed in evident frustration. "Let's have it. Tell me exactly who it was I had dinner with tonight. How bad is he?"

"I don't think—"

"You can follow that tidbit of information with why you were running surveillance on my date," she said as if he hadn't spoken.

"I wasn't running surveillance on your date. Exactly," he added at his own doubt. "I didn't intend to, anyway."

"Yeah, well, lucky for me your intentions changed." She was getting fidgety, plucking at imaginary threads on her sweater and trying to keep her hands occupied.

Nate often played fast and loose with the truth. Faking out suspects, questioning witnesses and putting them at ease was necessary in his job. So was assuring people who had witnessed something borderline horrific that there was nothing for them to worry about. He possessed a talent for skirting that thin line of truth that most people only crossed in desperate times.

But there was something about the way Vivian Maylor looked at him that snuffed out that natural tendency and left him uttering the truth. "Long story short?"

"Don't shorten it on my account." She looked completely resigned to hearing the absolute worst. "Going to be here awhile."

"Your date's real name is Dean Wexler. He's a convicted con artist. His last stretch in prison was eighteen months for stealing an elderly woman's life savings shortly after she was put into a nursing home."

Vivian sat up, wide eyes filling with something akin to rage. "Nu-uh."

"Afraid so." He cringed. "He's currently a suspect in a string of burglaries targeting successful single women using various dating apps."

"Of course he is." She leaned her head back and sighed. "So that's why you were following him? To get an eye on his next victim?"

"No, actually." He looked down at his almost empty coffee cup. "That's not my case, unfortunately. But I've got a few leads that link him to another one I've been working on." He might be feeling chatty, but he wasn't about to add to her already overburdened and bruised shoulders by telling her about Marty DeBaccian. "Suffice it to say, I have reason to believe he's connected to a much nastier individual." He spotted the nurse from earlier standing in the doorway. She leaned over, caught his eye and waved him out. "I'll be back in just a minute."

"Sure. Gives me some time to absorb all that." Her tone was completely indecipherable as Nate left to meet the nurse in the hall.

"Dr. Billings has an update for you." She led him back to the nurse's station, where a rather rotund, middle-aged man tapped his finger on a tablet computer. "Dr. Billings?"

The doctor looked up, shifted his gaze from the nurse to Nate. "Detective Colton. Dr. David Billings. I'm a trauma specialist here in the ER." He set his tablet down and held out a hand. "Thanks, Lorna."

"You bet." Nurse Lorna shot them both a smile before ducking around the desk.

"Is Wexler alive?" Nate forewent any pretense. It was the only question that mattered at the moment.

"He is." Dr. Billings nodded slowly. "There's no guarantee he'll stay that way, however. Two bullets caught him in the chest. One went straight through, the other's lodged so close to his heart it's a miracle he's still breathing."

"Any chance I can question him?"

"Not for a good while. We've had to put him in a medically induced coma. Could be days or even weeks before it's safe to bring him out of it. He's semi-stable for now. He won't wake up again until after we get that bullet out. And for that, we need to wait."

"Right." Nate scrubbed a tired hand across his forehead. "Okay. I'd like to be kept apprised of his condition. And I'm going to see about assigning an officer to his room."

Dr. Billings frowned. "Is that really necessary?"

"Someone drove by and opened fire on him in the middle of a crowd," Nate said as he pulled out one of his cards and passed it across the counter to Lorna. "It's a miracle no one else was seriously injured." Last he'd heard, there were some minor injuries, bumps, bruises, scrapes and cuts from flying glass. "That tells me they hit their target. If word gets out he's still alive—"

"Say no more." Dr. Billings held up both hands. "We'll cooperate however we can."

"Is there a room you can put him, away from emergency exits? How's your security system?" Nate took a quick look in both directions. The round rotating cameras gave him some peace of mind. "Recent update?"

"Last year," Dr. Billings confirmed. "I'll alert our security office to pay close attention to the area around Mr. Wexler's room. One last question, Detective."

"Sure."

"Other than an ID for Sam Gabriel, we didn't find any other information or ID on him. Regarding his next of kin, do you happen to know—"

"He doesn't have any that I know of," Nate said. "I'll double check the file we have on him once I'm back at the station." Criminal or not, Wexler deserved someone to be responsible for him. "In the meantime, put me down as a contact."

* * *

Vivian really, really needed to stop watching so many cop shows. Obviously, they'd implanted shockingly unrealistic expectations in her psyche. Or dulled her to the realities of actual crime. Was that even possible?

It had been a shooting. Had to have been. All the broken glass and panicked racing about, not to mention the gunshot wounds in Sam—Dean's chest; there wasn't any other explanation.

"Wait until I tell Lizzy about this," she whispered and heard the growing hysteria in her ragged voice. "One date in four years and *bam!* I get shot at." She shook her head, thinking of her childhood friend. Well, her *only* friend. "She'll probably think I'm making it up to get out of trying again. Who doesn't pretend to be shot at to get out of dating?"

Was she ever not going to feel as if she wanted to jump out of her own skin?

Vivian's mind raced like a broken-down sports car, speeding up one minute, stuttering and stalling the next. Thoughts didn't seem to be completing themselves before another started, and they all sent her down winding, dead-end roads of panic and fear.

The coffee had probably been a mistake. She looked down at her trembling hands, feeling as if somehow, she was hovering above her own body, unwilling to retake possession in order to cope with the fact she'd nearly been killed. She squeezed her fingers into fists, tried to focus on the sensation of her nails digging into her palms.

How funny was it that the only thing that seemed to be holding her together was the thought Detective Nate Colton would be returning to her bedside?

Detective Colton, who had been the first person she'd beheld after the shooting. Handsome, messy-haired, blue-eyed Detective Nate Colton, who, when he'd peeked around that ER curtain, had acted as an instant balm and a kind of unexpected refuge.

Refuge. She squeezed her eyes shut, shook her head. What on earth was going on in her head that she even thought to use that word where he was—?

"Ms. Maylor?"

She nearly sighed at the sound of his voice. In that instant, the jagged edges of her thoughts smoothed, and she opened her eyes, unclenched her fists. "Vivian, please. Detective."

"Nate." His smile was easy.

"Nate." She must have knocked her head harder than even the doctors thought. Just saying his name made her feel better.

His hands were now devoid of the coffee cup. Probably a good thing with the way her heart was racing. Not that she could hide that, given the monitors that kept *beep-beep-beeping* overhead. And the good-looking detective wasn't helping. "Did you find out anything about..." She nearly got his name wrong again. "Dean Wexler?"

"He's alive," Nate said. "They've put him in a coma until he's strong enough for surgery. It could go either way."

"Oh." She didn't know how to feel about that. As off as the date had been, as suspicious as she'd been about Sam, Dean, whatever his name was, she certainly didn't wish anything like this on him. Or on anyone. "That's just...horrible. Do you know who—"

"Not yet," Nate said, then stepped back and motioned

to someone behind him. "Vivian, this is Detective Jim Sullivan. We work together in the Boise PD. He's been assigned to the case."

"Ms. Maylor." Detective Sullivan gave her a friendly nod. He was on the short and stocky side—nowhere near as tall or fit as Nate—and had ginger red hair. She figured him to be about forty years old with a cool, almost jaded awareness in his eyes. "I'd like to ask you a few questions about the incident tonight if you don't mind?"

Incident? So that was what they were calling a drive-by shooting? "Yeah, sure." She pushed her hair behind her ear and managed a flickering smile. That headache the doctor had warned her about was beginning to pound, dully, loudly, on both sides of her head. "I want to help however I can."

"I'll just leave you two—"

"No, stay," Vivian said, cutting Nate off and reaching out a hand that she immediately tugged back and held against her chest. "Please. If it's okay?" she asked the other detective. "He was there. He probably saw a lot of things I didn't." It made her feel slightly less dependent to make an excuse for him to be there. Other than her just wanting him to stay.

Sullivan didn't look particularly pleased at the request. "Sure." He motioned to the chair, but Nate urged him to take it while he leaned back against the cabinet of medical supplies beside the bed. After Sullivan took down her information—full name, phone number, address, occupation—he started in. "How do you know Dean Wexler, Ms. Maylor?"

"Vivian's fine," she said. "And I don't really know him. We connected on a dating app. We messaged a couple of times. A friend of mine told me to take a chance and say yes to a date. So I did." She smoothed her hands across the strangely rough and heavy blanket. "I don't think I'll be taking her dating advice again."

"Detective Colton said you know him under a different name?"

"Sam Gabriel." She rattled off the name of the dating app they'd used. "I'm thinking their vetting process isn't as secure as they state in their ads." How stupid could she have been, putting her faith in anything connected to the internet? Stupid, naive. Her mouth twisted. Lonely. She'd just become a statistic in the lonely to desperate ratio. "We agreed to meet for dinner at Madariaga's. He'd never been there, but I order from them occasionally when I want to treat myself. And I knew it would be crowded."

"Smart thinking," Detective Sullivan said as he scribbled in his small notepad.

"I was thinking it was a good test for temper," she said. "You know, how irritated someone gets around noise and chaos. I wanted to see if he was quick to trigger."

"Never would have thought of that," Nate said.

"You're not a single woman," Vivian said, but rather than the comment sounding or feeling snarky, it felt more conversational. "You've never had to. I'm not a big dater. Honestly, tonight was a complete fluke." One she was probably never going to forget. "Felt more like a game of truth or dare, and I stupidly chose dare."

"There's nothing stupid about going out on a date," Nate said.

"Seriously?" Vivian arched a brow and looked at Nate. "You're a cop, and you're going to say that, in this day and age? I let myself forget the world is full of psychopathic whackadoodles."

"Sneaking past defenses is what people like Wexler do," Detective Sullivan said. "An attitude like yours tends to be a pretty good shield these days."

"Always the exception to the rule. Anyway." She took a deep breath and sighed. "He let me choose the restaurant, which I took as a good sign. I arrived on time—"

"Did you see anything out of the ordinary before you went into Madariaga's?" Sullivan asked. "Anyone lurking or a strange car parked somewhere?"

"No." She shook her head and thought back. "But then I wouldn't have known if they were strange, would I? I parked in the lot across the street. I remember thinking it looked like it was going to storm and that I hoped to get home before it got going." She hesitated. "I don't like driving, especially at night. Add in the weather, and..." She was already dreading the drive once she got out of the hospital. "Honestly, it was just a simple, no-go date."

"Any particular reason it failed?"

"He didn't pull her chair out for her," Nate muttered.

Vivian's gaze flew back to his, and she saw in the way his cheeks tinted pink that he hadn't meant to say that out loud. "No, he didn't. I don't know that I expected him to, but..." She lost her train of thought. "You noticed that?"

"I noticed a lot of things," Nate said, then, after a look from Sullivan, he shrugged. "Sorry. I'll keep quiet."

"He lied to me. S— Dean," Vivian told Sullivan. "Almost from the start. About his job. He told me he taught second grade, but then said his students were ten years old."

Sullivan's brow arched. "Second graders are seven or eight. Good catch."

"It was a little thing," Vivian said. "But it was so strange. If you lie about small things—"

"What's to stop him from lying about bigger things?" Nate held up both hands. "Sorry. Last time."

Sullivan frowned, as if he didn't quite understand Nate's behavior. "Anything else strike you as odd?"

"He kept mentioning money in different ways," Vivian said. "That I must make a really good living with my business. That he liked to travel, but it costs too much. And a lot of what he said just felt rehearsed. Like he had a script."

Sullivan nodded, made another note. "You aren't the first woman we've heard this from about him. Looks like your instincts about Wexler were right, Nate." He poked his pen into the paper and glanced up at Nate. "I'm going to recommend we look deeper into Wexler in connection with those burglaries."

"As long as I get first shot at him for my case." Nate winced. "Wow. Sorry. Really bad choice of word."

"Walk me through after you left the restaurant, if you can," Sullivan prodded Vivian.

She shrugged. "He talked me into going down for a dessert at a café," Vivian said, wanting to get this over and done with. "A few blocks from the restaurant. Proof I'll do just about anything for chocolate," she admitted quietly. "We were maybe two blocks from Madariaga's when he stopped me. I heard what I thought was a kind of pop." She narrowed her eyes, tried to recall exactly what had happened. "I heard the glass in the car break before I realized what it was. I remember looking over my shoulder in the direction it came from and seeing this car. Light brown, like beige maybe? I remember thinking that the headlights were strange. The shape of them. More angular than round. And there was this face—"

"Face? You saw the shooter's face?"

She squeezed her eyes shut. "I'm not sure if it was the shooter or the driver? Sorry." She shrugged. "I didn't realize that was what I was seeing at the time. I remember seeing something bright, shiny. Something that glinted. Then there was another pop, and another. The next thing I knew, Sam, I mean Dean, knocked me to the ground. I remember being irritated because my glasses broke." She lifted a hand to her temple and rubbed it with her fingers.

Nate cursed, and Sullivan shot him a look of irritation.

"How about a description of the man you remember seeing?" Sullivan asked.

"Dark hair, weird…something." Vivian considered. "I feel like there's something odd about him? But it's not there. Not yet anyway. Maybe it'll come back."

"You said Wexler knocked you to the ground," Nate said. "Are you sure about that?"

"Absolutely." She nodded, a chill racing down her spine. "At the time, I was asking myself what he thought he was doing, then I realized…" She looked back to Nate. "The full weight of him landed on me. He was so still. I tried to shove him off of me, and then he was gone, and I was all…wet." She swiped her hand across her neck, which one of the nurses had scrubbed clean. "Oh." Her stomach rolled. "This was his blood."

Nate reached out and pulled her hand down. "It's gone now. Worry about that later."

"Easy for you to say." Vivian shuddered. She'd never wanted a shower more urgently in her life.

"Sounds like Wexler might have saved your life," Sullivan said.

"Yeah," she whispered in fear and awe. "I think maybe he did."

"And you?" Sullivan turned his attention to Nate. "How much of this did you see?"

"After the date? Beige car, late model." He almost snapped out the words. "No plates on the back. The quick look I got at the gun, I'd say 9 mm."

"Techs recovered a 9 mm bullet from the broken glass of the jewelry store window," Sullivan confirmed. "It had blood on it."

"Probably hit Wexler," Nate said. "The doctor said one shot was a through and through."

"We'll get it tested at the lab to be sure. If I put you in touch with our department sketch artist," Sullivan said to Vivian, "would you be willing to come in and work with her? Get an image together? She's good at helping people remember details they think they can't."

"Oh." She blinked, processing. "Sure, yeah. I could do that." Was it wrong to think that was kind of cool? She'd seen artists used before on TV, of course. And read about the process in books. What did that mean about her that she was anxious to see how it worked in real life?

"You don't have to do that," Nate said cautiously.

Sullivan cleared his throat and glared.

"I'm just saying—" Nate tried again.

"I know what you're saying," Sullivan said sharply. "Vivian? You up for it?"

"Yes." While she appreciated Nate's attempt to protect

her, she was going to do everything she could to catch the person responsible for such a brazen act. "I want to help find whoever did this."

"Okay, then. I'll give you a call in the morning." Sullivan stood and set the chair aside. "Nate? Can I have a word before I leave?"

"Sure."

Vivian didn't know anything about Detective Nate Colton, but that one-word answer, to her at least, seemed to convey both dread and irritation. The combination fascinated her. "Could you get me some more coffee?" she asked Nate when he started to follow Sullivan.

"If you can wait," he said, "how about I get you one once you're released?"

"Oh. I thought maybe you'd be—"

"I'm off duty. Kind of. Unless there's someone you'd like me to call?"

She shook her head and thought of all the people he might be considering. Parents, siblings, friends... "There's no one."

"Well, someone needs to get you to your car. That lucky person is me." That smile was back, and she wondered if he was aware of the power it held. "Don't go anywhere."

"Okay." She nodded and breathed easier. Not so long ago, heck, even yesterday, the idea of sitting back and letting a man show even the slightest amount of care for her would have left her laughing in dismay. Instead, she found herself counting the seconds until Detective Nate Colton returned to her.

Chapter 3

"Here you go, Detective."

Nate, keeping one hand at the small of Vivian's back as he escorted her out of the ER, caught the keys the patrol officer standing at the sliding glass doors tossed to him.

"Thanks, Coop." The younger officer, with only two years on the job so far, was one he'd met during a training seminar at the academy. Since then, Nate had found himself as his unofficial on-the-job mentor. Cooper was definitely in the breaking-in stages. The job hadn't tarnished that one-time debate team captain shine yet. Sometimes the kid smiled so brightly it was like he was made of sunshine.

"Your car's in drop-off parking," Coop said. "Thanks for recommending me for guard duty."

"Don't thank me yet," Nate told him as they passed by. "Cool it on the coffee, or you'll spend most of your time in the bathroom. No one but doctors or nurses with ID get in to see Wexler, okay? Learn their faces and their names. Anyone unfamiliar, don't hesitate to question. And remember to look at their shoes."

Cooper's light blond hair fell over his eyes when he nodded. "Got it."

"Shoes?" Vivian asked once they stepped outside.

"Doctors and nurses wear certain kinds of shoes. Soft soled. Practical."

"And someone coming in off the street probably would wear something different." Vivian nodded. "Interesting." She wrapped her arms around her torso and shivered.

"Here." Nate shrugged out of his jacket and draped it over her shoulders. He felt the need to remind her that chivalry did still exist in the world. Besides, he could practically hear her teeth chattering. "Sorry we took yours for evidence."

"Not like I wanted it after tonight." She touched fingertips to her chest and the edge of her dress. "I guess I should be grateful you didn't take everything. I'd hate to have to drive home in my underwear."

Nate felt that comment all the way to his toes. "Yeah," he managed on a slightly strangled note. "Wouldn't want that." The second they stepped clear of the ambulance bay, Nate cringed. "Looks like you were right about that storm." The snow was coming down in steady curtains now. Not blizzard conditions, not yet at least, but that could change on a dime.

"The perfect end to the perfect night. Even without the storm, I'd have been stuck. Can't drive at night without my glasses." She drew the lapels of his jacket close. Something about the way she turned her face into the lining, as if she were breathing him in, had parts of him tightening into complete discomfort. "I think there's a motel near the restaurant. I'll grab a room—"

"You can stay with me." The offer came out of nowhere and apparently surprised both of them. He inclined his chin toward the dark SUV parked in the second space over. "We can talk about it inside. Come on."

"Ohhh…kay…" Her drawn-out response indicated both reluctance and curiosity. He could definitely push back on one of those emotions.

Sullivan had made it clear he believed Nate had a bit of a conflict of interest with this case. Nate couldn't blame him. He'd been vocally protective of Vivian—without really thinking about it. It had just been… instinctual. Arguing would have only made the situation more difficult, so he'd silently agreed to disagree if only to be kept in the loop moving forward.

Once inside, Nate turned on the engine so he could raise the heat up to full blast. At least with the snow the temperatures would calm a bit and the cold wouldn't feel quite so biting. "I've got a guest room," he said without preamble. "Nothing fancy, but it has its own bathroom. You can shower and get some sleep. Sullivan's going to try to get the sketch artist in tomorrow. Might as well get it all over and done with before you head home."

She leaned back in her seat and slid her arms into his jacket. When she flipped her hair free of the collar, he had to stop himself from reaching out to see if her hair was as soft as he imagined. "Part of me is thinking this could be an extension of my bad decision-making tendencies for the evening," she said and looked out his snow-covered windshield.

"Or it's the chance to start making good ones," he suggested. "I promise, you'll be in safe hands. That I can keep to myself—"

She leaned across the console and pressed her mouth to his.

Nate wasn't a man prone to surprises. He prided himself on being able to expect just about anything that could possibly come flying at him. But Vivian Maylor proved yet again she was capable of sneaking past his defenses and straight into his heart.

Her lips trembled against his, as if she hadn't quite thought things through. When he angled his head and moved to deepen the kiss, he felt her hesitancy. Right before her hand slid up the front of his chest and grabbed hold of his shirt.

With the engine rumbling, he slipped his hand up to grasp the back of her neck, held her against him as he dipped his tongue in to taste her, tempt her. Tease her. The curving of her lips had him almost cheering in triumph, but that would mean releasing her, and as he continued the kiss, he couldn't imagine a time he would want to stop.

When he did pull back, it was only far enough to press his forehead against hers. She was breathing heavier than before. She licked her lips, pressed them together as if trying to capture the taste of him.

"Well." He slipped his hand to her face, stroked a finger down her cheek as something unfamiliar and strangely welcomed bloomed inside him.

"I've spent a good part of the night trying to remember where I've seen you before."

"Oh?" Panic swirled, but he kept his gaze steady and even. He could only imagine where she'd seen his name, or even his picture over the past few months. Being outed as one of Robert Colton's illegitimate heirs was something no one would want on their bingo card. "Figured it out yet?"

"No. But then I'm having trouble deciding if kissing you was another bad decision," she murmured, her brow knitting slightly in confusion. "Or a good one. Maybe my brain was a bit scrambled tonight."

"You can think on it for a while." It would be easy, he thought, so easy to make one gentle push that would probably topple her right into his bed. But tonight wasn't the night. For either of them.

She was going to experience the emotional upheaval that always followed a traumatic event, and he had no doubt it would hit with both barrels. While he... He took a deep breath and inhaled the faint fragrance of flowers drifting off her skin. When the time came for him to partake in what he had no doubt was the wonder of Vivian Maylor, he wanted to be fully present, awake, and...prepared.

"So, my place or would you like me to find a hotel for you for the night?"

"So long as I can get home in time tomorrow for an online meeting with one of my clients." Her smile curved her swollen lips and almost reached her eyes.

"What time would that be?" he teased.

"After lunch. One thirty."

"That should be doable," he assured her.

"Then I will accept your offer of the guest room. If that's really o—"

He kissed her this time. A quick one, just fast enough to convince her he understood but also give her a hint of what a promise between them might hold. "That's perfectly fine. And before you ask..." He hit the windshield wipers and cleared the view. "I have more than enough coffee to get both of us through to tomorrow."

"How did you know, Detective?"

He chuckled and shifted the car into Reverse. "Lucky guess."

As Nate pulled his SUV into the driveway of a darling little cottage of a house on the very edge of Boise, Vivian realized she might be attempting to deal with the evening's events by diving into something even more outrageous than a blind date.

But there was no need to rationalize Nate's invitation to use his guest room for the remainder of the night. It was closing in on one in the morning. The first dose of OTC painkillers the nurse had given her before she had been discharged was already wearing off. She'd felt a bit of a buzz the second she'd stepped outside into the cold December air. Almost as if she'd been given a second lease on life. Whatever else had happened, she'd literally dodged a bullet, and for the next few hours at least, she was giving herself permission to go with impulse.

Impulse had worked well so far and helped her to answer the one question that had been floating around in her mind since she'd first seen Nate Colton sitting at that bar: what would it be like to kiss him?

She pressed her lips together again. Well, she had her answer.

The only problem was she wanted to ask the question again. And again.

Some inquiries took multiple investigations to come to the correct and accurate conclusion, she decided and had to cover her mouth to stop herself from giggling. Man, she was really out of it.

"Well, here we are." Nate turned off the engine and

rested his hands on the steering wheel. "Ready to make a mad dash?" He leaned forward to examine the snow that had consistently fallen during their drive. "No," he said when she started to shrug out of his jacket. "Wait until we get inside. I'm used to the cold."

"Okay." It seemed to be her favorite word around him. Was there some kind of cosmic force at work? Even before they'd spoken a word to one another, she'd felt comfortable with him. As if she instinctively knew he was someone safe. But how was that possible? He was a stranger.

A stranger with a badge, but a stranger nonetheless.

Once she got some sleep and some distance from everything that had happened, she was probably going to come to a different conclusion or admit that her irrational reactions and actions were nothing more than spur-of-the-moment coping mechanisms. That said, there was nothing wrong with enjoying the moment, was there? Chances were that after tomorrow, she'd probably never see him again.

She wasn't the least bit surprised that, after climbing out of the car, he hurried around to open her door. Vivian couldn't shake the feeling of intimacy that struck her when he slipped his hand into hers and tugged her toward his front porch.

In the dim light of the porch lamp, she couldn't get a good look at or feel for the interior of his home. It seemed the second he opened the door the sky opened up and dropped a full blanket of continuous snowfall.

Once inside, a blast of warmth set her frozen cheeks to stinging as he drew the jacket off her and hung it on a hook by the door.

"Hang on. Let me get the lights." He left her in the entryway as he moved down the hall. A moment later, light blazed to life. Nate leaned out and waved her back. "I'll get the coffee going. Unless it's too late for you?"

"I have stratospheric caffeine tolerance," she said. It might make her jittery at times, but it rarely kept her awake. Especially when an adrenaline crash was coming. She strode down the short hallway to the kitchen, which she found surprisingly comfortable and practical. "Nice place."

"Yeah?" He shot her a surprised smile as he set his coffee machine to gurgling. "It serves a purpose. I'm fixing things up as I go along. Only been here a couple of years."

"Handy around the house, are you?"

"Well, I wield a mean paintbrush. The little touches are more my sister's doing. She's much more attuned to things than I am."

"Sister, huh?" She hugged her arms around herself as she wandered across the marble tile, nodding approvingly at the shiny black appliances and gold-flecked black marble countertops. "Younger or older?"

"Younger." He retrieved one mug from the dish rack by the sink and another from a cabinet. "We had a kind of complicated upbringing, but one thing we always had was each other. How about you? Brothers and sisters?"

Regret and that all-too-familiar pang of loneliness chimed inside her. She pulled out one of the two barstools at the counter and sat while he rummaged around in the refrigerator. "I was an only child. And not the best at socializing."

"Doesn't seem that way to me." He set a sealed container on the counter before going back in. "Let's see. I've got some leftover pizza in here. And some salad that…" He popped off the lid, then grimaced. "Okay, yeah, that might send you back to the hospital."

Vivian laughed. "Pizza sounds great, actually. And what's this?" She pointed to the first container.

"A neighbor across the street uses me as a guinea pig for his baking experiments. I thought you might appreciate them since you didn't get your promised dessert. Go ahead." He gestured for her to open it.

She did and felt some of the tension she'd been struggling with ease. "Chocolate chip cookies?"

"Double chocolate chip cookies," Nate corrected. "He has a secret ingredient."

"Espresso powder?" Vivian guessed and earned an arched brow. "I might not be the best baker, but I read a lot of books about food. The espresso's supposed to enhance the chocolate. I'll know for sure when I eat one. Later." She left the lid off and slid it out of reach. "Chocolate's best at room temp."

"Funny." The cardboard pizza box replaced the cookies as he went to get plates. "I've never been patient enough to prove that theory. Anything for your coffee?"

"Straight's fine." She could feel her energy beginning to drain. That adrenaline crash was barreling straight for her, no doubt coming on faster because of how comfortable she felt, both with Nate and in his house. "Can I ask you why you were following Wexler tonight?"

"You can ask me anything." He bit into an ice-cold piece of pizza, the corners of his eyes crinkling as he chewed and swallowed. "Doesn't mean I'll tell you."

"Why not?"

"Because you've had enough to deal with, and—honestly? I don't want you any more involved in this situation than you already are."

"So you're protecting me." Should that idea both appeal to and annoy her?

"Yes."

"I'd argue that I can take care of myself, but considering I couldn't find the courage to drive myself home tonight, I guess that argument's moot." She didn't think she could convey how relieved she'd been not to have to get behind the wheel of her car in the dead of night.

"You must have had high hopes for your date if you made the drive into Boise."

"Not high hopes." Surrendering to the rumbling in her stomach and wanting to give her pain pills somewhere to land when she took them, she reached for a slice. "But I did have a friend who wouldn't let me back out. Can't wait to tell Lizzy how wrong she was." That, at least, would be one silver lining to the night. She nearly had the pizza to her lips when the thought struck. The pizza clattered on her plate with a disturbing stale thunk. "Colton. Your last name is Colton."

"Yes." Nate frowned, concern rising in his eyes. "Are we starting over?" He reached out, touched a finger to her bandage and looked into her eyes. "Your head okay?"

"My head's fine." But her heart was racing so fast it nearly jumped out of her chest. "Nate Colton. Boise PD. Are you..." She swallowed hard as certain pieces fell into place. "Your sister's name? Is it Lizzy?"

His face went blank for an instant, as if her question had flipped a kind of switch. He gave a halfhearted nod and ducked his head. "One of them is."

"Oh, wow." She leaned back on the barstool, relief and shock tumbling through her. She laughed, pressed her hands against her cheeks before she jumped off the stool and raced around the counter. "This explains it." She grabbed hold of his arms and turned him to her. "Oh, my gosh. This... I don't know, this thing I feel with you. This ease. This..."

"Spark?" Nate said in a way that had her wondering if he'd heard that part of her conversation with Dean Wexler.

"How many Lizzy Coltons could there be?" Vivian challenged.

"Hopefully, only one," Nate said. "She's a bit of a firecracker, for want of a better term."

"You're her brother." She grabbed his face between her hands and looked more deeply into those blue eyes of his. "The brother she only just found out about. I don't know if I can see it, but I can feel it."

"Can you?" He looked a bit flummoxed at her comment. "What do I feel like?"

"Lizzy's the best friend I've ever had. Ever since grade school, she's just... She's always been there for me. No matter what. She's solid, you know?"

"Can't really agree or disagree." The humor in his eyes had been replaced by what she could only describe as pain. "I don't know her well enough to say."

"Oh." It was only then she remembered what Lizzy had said. "You and your sister." Her mind searched for the right name. "Your other sister, Sarah. You and she share the same mother with Lizzy and her brothers."

"Yep. Good old Jessie Colton. Fracturing families and setting the whole root system on fire." He extricated himself from her hold and ducked down into a lower cabinet. "Suddenly, I'm feeling the need for something stronger than coffee." He added a big splash of bourbon to his mug.

"I'm sorry." She didn't like the expression on his face, the way his entire body had tightened up, as if her realization had somehow unlocked a secret part of him he wasn't interested in sharing. "I should have realized the media coverage and fallout must have been horrible for you. Lizzy said things were complicated. *You* said they were. I'm prying. I'm sorry." She stepped away from him.

"No reason for you to be." Was his response more obligatory than polite? "Didn't think I'd be traversing that particular minefield of family history tonight is all. I'm glad Lizzy's your friend. I can call her if you want? I bet she'd be happy to—"

"No, please." Vivian held up both hands. "With everything that happened to her recently, I don't want to be another thing for her to have to worry about. Besides, last I heard, Ajay was taking her away for a little while to help her…decompress." Was that the right word when it came to being kidnapped?

"Good." Nate nodded and looked relieved. "That's good to hear."

"This is so strange." She returned to the chair. "From the second I saw you at the bar, I couldn't shake this feeling like I knew you. Even though I don't. Didn't. Does that make sense?"

"I'm going to say yes and leave it at that."

"Right. You don't want to talk about it."

"It's not that." Confusion filled his voice. "It's more… I don't know how to talk about all that, actually. I'm assuming Lizzy told you about me and Sarah and our... place in the family."

She nodded. "Yes. A few weeks ago, I think? She was trying to process finding out she had two siblings she knew nothing about."

"Yeah, well, Sarah and I always knew," Nate said, and it was then she was able to decipher what it was she was seeing on his face. In his eyes. It was definitely pain. But also sadness. "That whole Coltons of Owl Creek, the branches of the family who built that town into something greater than anyone believed it could ever be? Sarah and I found out a long time ago that we're related. So we've had a bit more time to adjust to the idea than Lizzy and her brothers and cousins. There's still a bit of...tension among us."

"You said you've had time, but you haven't adjusted," Vivian observed. "Have you?"

"Don't get me wrong." He started to play with his pizza rather than continuing to eat. "I've met most of them now, and I like them all well enough. They're good people. They have every reason to distrust us, especially given who our mother is. Maybe I can see a time in the future when we're closer." He shrugged. "But not now. I spent a good portion of my life accepting the fact I was never going to be one of them. It's a hard shift to make when you're suddenly presented with an opportunity you didn't think you'd ever have."

"I'm sorry." She reached out, grabbed hold of his hand and squeezed. "And here I am going all cheerleader on the situation."

That smile of his returned, if not a bit less bright than

before. "I'm sorry, but there's no way you were ever a cheerleader."

She laughed and squeezed harder. "See? You know that about me already. I'm thinking we were most definitely destined to meet." She surprised herself by yawning. Her eyes went wide as her cheeks went hot with embarrassment. "Oh, geez. Sorry." She covered her mouth, shook her head and pulled her hand free. But not before he clung to her for a few seconds more.

"I'm going to take that as a hint to show you the guest room. Give me just a sec."

"Okay." She nibbled on her pizza after he disappeared, then quickly cleaned up and put things back in the fridge and finished her coffee. She wandered around a bit, cookie in hand, looking for the bits and bobs of character that turned a house into a home. He didn't seem to be a collector type of person. Everything she saw projected a lifestyle of practicality and purpose.

Photographs were sparse. There was no mistaking the people in the few she found—one of whom she'd bet good money was his sister Sarah. The affection between them was palpable and made her smile. The man she'd been dealing with tonight seemed no different than the one in the picture. Whatever niggling doubt she might have regarding her current situation vanished.

"Okay, bedroom's good to go," Nate said from where he lounged in the door frame, watching her examine the photographs on the TV stand in the living room. "I set out some towels for you, and there should be other things like a toothbrush and stuff in the cabinet drawers. Sarah left a load of laundry last time she stayed here. T-shirts and stuff. You're about the same size, so take your pick."

"Thanks." That urge to shower returned with an unexpected ferocity as she finished what she had to agree was a pretty great double chocolate chip cookie.

"Help yourself to anything in the kitchen. I'm a light sleeper, so if you need anything, just knock on the door." He pointed to the one on the other side of the living room. "I'm usually up around six."

"Me, too." Nerves she thought she'd banked surged afresh. "Ah, I really am sorry. Bringing up all that stuff about your family."

"It's fine, Vivian." There was no animosity in his eyes. "I should probably take it as a sign that it's time to start dealing with it all head-on. They're family after all."

"Yes, they are." Vivian felt a pang of envy so sharp she nearly lost her breath. "Grab hold of it, of them, Nate. Trust me. I've been alone most of my life. There's nothing more important than being a part of something that's bigger than you are."

"As much as I'd like to continue this conversation," Nate said, "I think you're questioned out by now. For tonight, at least."

"I really am." The last thing she wanted to do was unload her particular tales of woe. "Whatever else you're struggling with…" She walked over to him, rested a hand on his chest and curled her fingers under ever so slightly. She wasn't certain if it was she who shivered, or if it was him. "You're a good man. That's what I picked up on when I walked in the bar. You radiate it. You glow with it." She lifted her other hand to his cheek. "Believe me, that is a very rare trait indeed."

She resisted the urge to kiss him again. Afraid that if she did, it would lead to something neither of them was ready for. "I'll see you in the morning." She moved past him, forcing herself to look straight ahead and avoid looking at him again as she closed the door.

Chapter 4

Nate lied. He wasn't up at six.

He was up at five thirty. Getting through today on a whole three hours of sleep was going to be so much fun. It wouldn't have been so bad if those three hours had given him a degree of rest. Truth was, he tossed and turned, his mind racing first around his options surrounding Dean Wexler, and then around the fact that Vivian Maylor slept only a few steps down the hall from his bedroom.

He couldn't recall the last time he'd started his day with an icy cold shower, but since first seeing Vivian, he'd been doing—and thinking—a lot of things he wasn't used to.

What were the odds that this woman would consider Nate's half sister to be her best friend? He shook his head as he set a fresh pot of coffee to brew. The universe must be having a serious laugh at his expense. Clearly, he hadn't been paying enough attention to the shift in his family dynamic. His stomach tightened. What would Lizzy think when Vivian told her about their meeting?

It was obvious his siblings hadn't decided if he was guilty by association just yet—his mother's antics and actions, including her recent involvement with the Ever

After Church and its leader, Markus Acker, had been the cause of much of the distress the Colton family was going through.

If he were to look at things from his siblings' side, he'd definitely be suspicious, not to mention cautious. Whatever he might be feeling about the situation, their reserved behavior had hurt Sarah more than anyone. His sister had always longed to belong to a big family, and it had been difficult when they'd discovered they had one that they couldn't reach out to. Wanting Sarah to have that now meant Nate would do what he needed to make that happen.

"Morning."

The sound of Vivian's sleep-husky voice triggered a smile Nate couldn't have stopped even if he'd wanted to.

"Morning." He turned and his knees went weak at the sight of her standing in the doorway, clad only in a rainbow-centric T-shirt that skimmed the tops of her thighs. "You, um, sleep okay?" His voice sounded a bit choked. He cleared his throat, tried to reboot himself into thinking clearly.

He'd spent a big portion of the night not imagining what her legs looked like. Now that they were on full display—those long, toned legs—he was forced to admit his imagination hadn't come close. Never in the history of the female form had a woman filled a T-shirt to the absolute perfection of Vivian Maylor. Judging from the slightly dazed expression on her face, she didn't have the first clue as to the effect she had on him. And the effect was…for want of a better word, *stimulating*.

"I slept great, thanks." Sleepy-eyed, she walked toward him. "Coffee going already?"

"First thing." He shoved his hands into the back pockets of his jeans, rocked forward, his bare feet scrunching into the hardwood floor. "Wanted it ready for you when you got up."

"Sweet." She touched a hand to his arm but didn't, as expected, come over to watch the coffee appear. Instead, she popped open the container of cookies. "My first shot of the day." She bit in and closed her eyes, sighed in a way that left Nate feeling oddly jealous of a chocolate chip cookie. "That shower in your guest room worked wonders." She leaned back against the cabinets.

"Glad to hear it." He cleared his throat again and distracted himself by putting away the dishes from the drainer.

Those kisses they'd shared in his car last night had been a pressure release, a way of coping with an adrenaline-spiking event neither of them could have prepared for. At this point, it would be unprofessional of him to pursue any kind of relationship or push for a quick encounter that could, in the end, cause her more emotional harm. It wasn't the time.

Or the place.

"Everything okay?" Vivian asked.

"Everything's fine." He'd never felt so grateful to hear his cell phone go off. He all but dived to where it sat on the counter across the room, skimmed the text message. "It's Detective Sullivan. He said he texted you, but you haven't answered."

"Oh!" Her eyes went wide. "I totally forgot to charge it when I got here. Geez." Muttering to herself, she hurried out of the kitchen, the T-shirt skimming higher up the backs of her thighs with every step.

"Heaven help me," Nate muttered to himself even as his jeans became increasingly uncomfortable. "I'm not going to make it another hour with her around."

"Did you say something?" She was already back, cell phone in hand. That wide-eyed, innocent expression on her face was more alluring to him than a classic femme fatale's come-hither look.

"Nope. Not a thing."

"I've got the message." She squinted at the screen. "I really need my glasses." She sighed. "Can you read it?" She held out her phone.

"Sure." Their fingers brushed when he accepted her cell. A zing of energy shot through him, from his fingers, straight down to his toes, then back up to where it settled significantly south of his heart. "Ah, he says the sketch artist can come in this morning. Time's up to you. She's free until noon."

"That makes two of us," Vivian said. "How about… nine?"

"How about eight?" The sooner he got her out of his house, the better. The longer she was here, the more his thoughts circled things other than work. Inappropriate things. She was his witness. He needed to remember that. "We can stop for breakfast on the way. This early, we'll miss the main weekend crowd."

"Sick of leftover pizza?" she teased.

"Something like that." He answered the message, then texted Sullivan on his own phone confirming the time. The message he received back was a simple smirk emoji that told Nate he was in for some serious ribbing from his fellow detectives and officers. "Okay, eight's good. There's a twenty-four-hour diner on the way, one of my favorite places, actually." But that didn't stop him from pouring them each a cup of coffee. "You hungry?"

"Always." Accepting the mug, she smiled and tilted her head, which sent her hair cascading out of its loose knot down around her shoulders. "I'll be quick." She grinned over her shoulder at him as she walked away. "Promise."

She'd done something wrong. Sitting in the passenger seat of Nate's SUV quicker than promised, she nibbled on her thumbnail. What was it? He'd been acting nervous from the jump today, like every word she said grated on his nerves. The tension radiating off him had been alluring at first, tempting. Even seductive, but the way he'd all but danced and dived away from her to get to his phone had left her wondering if last night's interaction had been a fluke. She hadn't dreamed kissing him, had she? Or that he'd kissed her back?

Oh. She frowned, panic grabbing hold of her heart. Last night hadn't been some weird hallucination. Or had it?

"Hey." Nate's voice broke through her circling doubt. "You okay?"

"Yeah, sure." She rested her hand against her stomach. His sister Sarah had a fun, quirky sense of fashion, at least when it came to her casual clothes. The bright, colorful T-shirt collection had given her a surprising choice. The jeans she found in the dresser were on the snug side, but at least the zipper had gone up.

Vivian's favorite all-purpose black dress was wadded up in his bathroom trash can. The second she'd tried to wash out the blood, the red in the water had set her head to spinning and her chest to throbbing. She'd never be able to wear it again without remembering the shooting. Best to toss it and move on.

"Why?" she asked Nate impulsively. "Everything okay with you?"

"Yeah, sure."

She caught her lower lip in her teeth and might have gnawed straight through if she hadn't stopped herself. "I appreciate everything you've done for me." She hugged her purse against her chest. "I'll be out of your hair pretty soon."

"You're not in my hair, Vivian."

"Tell that to your face." She'd meant it to be a joke, but even to her own ears it didn't sound like one.

He pulled into the parking lot of a throwback diner. Vinnie's boasted twenty-four-hour breakfast and a selection of cakes and pies that were, supposedly, second to none. The fact he had to circle the lot to find a space spoke of a dedicated clientele. She considered that an acceptable endorsement. As if it had a mind of its own, her stomach growled.

Once parked, Vivian scrambled to grab hold of the handle. The sooner she had a fork in her hand and food in her face, the faster she'd put some distance between them. She didn't jump when he gently grabbed her arm. But she did sigh silently at the way her body wanted to melt toward him.

"Vivian." He tugged her back before she could open the door. "I'm sorry if I'm making you uncomfortable."

"I think I'm the one doing that," she argued, determined not to look at him. She promised herself to stare out the window or at the floor. Anywhere that wouldn't force her to admit to the embarrassment flooding through her. "I'm sorry I kissed you last night."

"I'm not." His response sent chills racing down the arm he still held in his strong fingers.

"I didn't mean to—"

"I spent most of the night wishing I didn't have a guest room."

Her lips twitched and hope flared.

"The thing is…"

"Right." She sank back against the seat, and this time her sigh couldn't be stopped. "Of course there's a thing."

"I don't do well mixing business with pleasure. You're part of a case, however indirectly, and honestly, I'm worried I won't be able to do my job if I'm distracted by… you. And if I don't do my job, people get hurt. I definitely don't want one of those people to be you."

She blinked. Then frowned. His words soaked in, but she didn't quite accept them. "I distract you?" She broke her promise to herself and looked at him, unable to hide her disbelief. No one, certainly no man, had ever said that to her before.

"From the second you walked into Madariaga's." Nate released her and rested his arms on his steering wheel. "This can't come as a surprise. I didn't stop staring at you all through your dinner."

Her face warmed. So she hadn't imagined it.

"Add to that you're friends with Lizzy and I'm not entirely sure how she'd feel about us…connecting."

"Considering she encouraged me to go out with a con artist," Vivian observed, "I think me liking you would be an upgrade."

"Yeah, one would hope."

It was the first time she heard disappointment in his voice. Whether it was about her or his newly formed relationship with his siblings, Vivian couldn't be sure.

"For now, we have to keep things professional," Nate insisted. "I can't taint my case, and I don't want you getting more involved in something that could hurt you."

"What about after? Your case," she added when he seemed confused. "Can we see each other after you close it?"

"I—" Another shrug. "Well, yeah. I don't see why not."

"Be still my heart," she muttered. "What every woman longs to hear." But still she smiled. If only because she'd struck a nerve with him—a raw one, it seemed. And that was something that left her feeling more than a little bit powerful. "Okay. I'll leave it up to you if and when we... reconnect. Later."

"What every man longs to hear," he echoed with that charming smile of his. "You still hungry?"

"If I can't have you, at least I can have..." She leaned over and scanned the writing on the bank of windows. "A bacon buttermilk waffle with real Vermont maple syrup. Shall we?" She pushed out of the door before he could stop her again.

Or before she attempted to seal their pseudo-friendship deal with another kiss.

"Eight on the dot." Detective Sullivan was waiting for them at the Sergeant's desk on the first floor of the Boise Police Department. The fluorescently lit lobby boasted uniformed officers pinballing their way from door to door to staircase to elevators, some offering Nate a wave of welcome. Shoes squeaked on the linoleum floor that had probably been installed decades before he was born. "Looks like you got some sleep, Vivian."

"I did, actually. Thanks."

Nate hadn't known Vivian for long, yet he couldn't help but think she'd offered the other detective one of the most forced smiles he'd ever seen on anyone's face.

They stepped out of the way of a pair of officers dragging in a barely responsive suspect. Weekends might slow things down for everyone else, but for law enforcement, they went into overdrive.

"Thought you'd want to know," Detective Sullivan said to Nate, "patrol found a car about three hours ago, few miles away from the shooting. Burned out, but the VIN comes back to a beige sedan reported stolen two days ago in Conners."

"You think it's the one used in the shooting?" Nate asked.

"Fits the description, and it was completely torched. Whoever did it knew how to do it effectively. And they didn't try to hide it. We've taken it into evidence, but we aren't holding out any hope for prints or DNA."

"Right." Nate shook his head. Professional or not, like Sullivan implied, they'd probably done it before. "Hopefully, there's something to be gleaned from Vivian's sketch."

"Sure hope so. You ready to do this?" Sullivan asked Vivian.

"More than ready," Vivian confirmed. "Let's get it over with. Thanks for breakfast, Nate. And the guest room."

"Ah. Sure." Nate started to follow, but Vivian turned, held up a hand and shook her head. "I'm good from here.

Thanks for everything." She looked down at her T-shirt. "I'll get Sarah's clothes back to you as soon as I can."

"No rush. Let me know when you're done. I'll drive you back to your car." It hadn't taken him long to realize he'd completely messed things up. True to form when it came to women he cared about, he'd stuck his foot in his mouth. Only in Vivian's instance it seemed as if he'd wedged both feet—along with half his shoes—into the mix.

"That's okay. I don't want to be a bother."

"I can have a patrol car drop you off," Detective Sullivan offered.

"Perfect," Vivian accepted immediately. "We're all set then."

"We can have a patrol car follow you, just to be on the safe side." Nate wasn't ready to say goodbye. "Are you sure you don't want me to—"

"I'm sure." Her too bright smile was back in place. She did surprise him by rising up on her toes and brushing her lips against his cheek. "I'll be fine. Thanks for everything."

He had no response. Instead, he stood there, in the middle of the lobby, and watched Detective Sullivan hold the elevator door open for her. Nate was still trying to ease his disappointment when he got up to the third-floor bullpen where the criminal investigation department was housed.

"Colton!"

Nate turned as Lieutenant Luke Haig stepped out of his office. His commanding officer held up two fingers and circled them in the air to indicate Nate's presence was requested.

Just as well. He could already smell the over-brewed coffee spiking its way out of the break room. Peak distribution time had passed him by, probably back when he'd been trying to salvage something positive out of his time with Vivian. The fact he was already regretting how he'd handled things did not bode well for the rest of his day. Or weekend.

"Close the door," his superior officer suggested and gestured to one of the two hard-backed chairs on one side of his desk. The shelves behind his desk were lined with photographs of his superior, most of which showcased his close-knit ties to the community at large.

His focus on the Armenian community, the community he'd grown up in, connected him to various neighborhoods in ways other officers couldn't replicate. His successful years working undercover in the criminal investigation unit had given him his choice of commands and he'd chosen to remain here, in Boise. His home.

That said, his detectives called him the Mob Whisperer, and not only behind his back. The fiftysomething immigrant considered the moniker a badge of honor. "The desk sergeant tells me you requested Officer Cooper for protective detail at Boise General."

"Yes, sir." Because it was expected, he sat, even though the last thing he felt like doing was staying still. "Dean Wexler's condition is unchanged. There were enough cell phones recording the scene last night that it wouldn't be difficult for someone to assume he may still be alive."

"You're convinced someone will come after him?"

"Whoever shot him was willing to make a very public

attempt to take him out," Nate said. "If they think there's a chance to finish the job, we should be ready for it."

Haig nodded. "Agreed. And any progress connecting him to DeBaccian?"

"I'm going to do some more digging," Nate said. "But everything I've found so far leads to a connection versus not. Wexler's been maneuvering his way up the criminal success ladder for years here in Boise. If what we're hearing about DeBaccian is true, DeBaccian would have his eye on him. Wexler can't get any further without going through him. Debaccian takes a percentage from most career criminals working the Boise area. Considering Wexler's less than subtle tendencies when it comes to his targets—"

"And this woman from last night, this…" Haig leaned forward, his chair squeaking beneath his six-foot-six-inch height and significant muscle mass and checked his notes. "…Vivian Maylor, was Wexler's latest target."

"She fits the victimology." Just saying that word made him cringe. He didn't like to think of Vivian as any kind of victim. "I know Sullivan and his team are taking a closer look at the women already on file. But Vivian matches up in a number of ways, not the least of which is she met him through a dating app. She's a successful businesswoman, owns her own home. Is financially secure." He couldn't attest to any belongings that might appeal to a burglar with more fences than a prison yard, but then neither could Wexler. "Their date was a bust. Wexler was trying to save it, but she saw through him. He slipped up a few times. She knew something was off." She'd have ditched him at the restaurant if it hadn't been for that promise of chocolate. *Something to keep in mind*, Nate thought, then mentally kicked himself.

Nate had burned that bridge. Best to stop trying to rebuild it.

"If only everyone had such radar," Lieutenant Haig said. "Sullivan's report stated she thinks she saw a driver and one passenger. He's setting her up with Stacy? Putting a sketch together?"

"As we speak, sir." If anyone could get Vivian to remember the micro-details of what she'd seen last night, it was Stacy Crum. The woman was a talented artist, but her degree in psychology often aided in guided exercises that enhanced victims' recall. Put the two things together, and she was one of the best weapons the Boise PD had at their disposal. "But that's Sullivan's case." Time to cut the cord.

Haig eyed him with unveiled skepticism. "Is there anything I need to be apprised of in regard to Ms. Maylor?"

"Only that she spent the night in my guest room. Alone," he added just to make certain his boss understood. "Her glasses broke during the shooting, and with the storm, she didn't feel safe driving home."

"Glad you were there to lend your...support." Haig gave a nod of dismissal. "Okay, then. Keep me apprised."

"Yes, sir." It always amazed him, Nate thought as he returned to his desk, how a simple conversation with his superior felt like an interrogation session. The man was as no-nonsense as they came, but he was also cognizant of the fact that every detective in his unit approached the job in varying ways. He gave a lot of rope to his people and rarely, if ever, did they hang themselves with it. "Give me time," Nate muttered as he surrendered to temptation and headed into the break room for coffee.

Considering the way Vivian Maylor had been seared into his brain, chances were he wasn't remotely done with the fallout of having met her.

"So, I'm going to have you close your eyes, Vivian." Stacy, the sketch artist Detective Sullivan had put her in an interview room with, had placed Vivian in a chair directly in front of her. No table between them. Almost to the point of their knees touching. Stacy's red hair was pulled back from her face, and tiny springy curls bounced free to frame her bright eyes.

The large sketch pad sat on the table beside them, a series of sharpened pencils in easy reach. Vivian wasn't surprised by the nerves that struck, or that her hands were twisting themselves together like a frenetic acrobat troupe. She'd had a lifetime of learning to manage the anxiety that descended with any new situation. Anxiety that hadn't come close to appearing whenever Nate Colton was around.

She locked her jaw, shoved that thought out of her mind before it took hold. His explanation for backing off made complete sense. As disappointed as she was, she couldn't blame him. She could only imagine the dedication and single-mindedness it took to be a detective in this day and age. Becoming a clinging vine definitely wouldn't earn her any points.

"Why do I think this is going to be like one of my therapy sessions?" Vivian caught a quick smile on the woman's face before she closed her eyes.

"It's specialized therapy." Stacy's voice was calm,

even and gentle. "I've found this technique works really well when there isn't too much trauma involved. You seem relatively well-recovered from last night."

"It feels like it happened to someone else, actually." She focused on keeping her hands still and evening out her breathing. Truth be told, she was a master compartmentalizer. She hadn't let herself really dwell on anything that had happened last night, except her interactions with Nate.

"That may very well work to our advantage," Stacy said. "Did Detective Sullivan give you the information for our victim assistance department?"

"Detective Colton did." The card was wedged into the front pocket of her purse.

"I'd heard he was on-site right after this happened." The affection in Stacy's voice caught Vivian off guard. "He's a good one to have around in a crisis. Level-headed, cautious and a straight shooter. You always know where you stand with Nate."

"So I'm learning." The comment slipped out before she thought to stop it. She cleared her throat, shifted in her chair. "Do you know him well?"

"Well enough to have him on speed dial in case of an emergency." She paused. "Nate makes a habit of looking after strays. He doesn't limit his big-brother behavior to Sarah."

Vivian didn't know how to respond to that.

"Okay, so let's take some deep breaths and try to clear your mind," Stacy told her. "I'm going to talk to you for a little while, just to help you relax, and then we'll take small steps in getting you back to last night, okay?"

"Mmm-hmm." Vivian resisted the urge to nod. All

she wanted was to get this over with, put the entire incident last night behind her and move on with her life.

"Great. You're doing great, Vivian. Just keep listening to my voice, all right? There're no wrong answers. Everything is fixable. Details are my specialty, so I'm one of the few humans who likes change. Deep breath in, and out. In…and out."

Vivian instinctively focused on Stacy's voice and let herself fall into that space between full alertness and the brink of sleep. Stacy's questions gently guided her back, putting the memories into a kind of slow motion, but also kept Vivian separate from the action.

She walked behind herself and Dean Wexler. Her boots struck at the same place as her other self, and Vivian followed her motions, moving the same way. When Stacy asked what she saw, she talked about the store windows, the holiday decorations. The thick pine garlands winding up and around the lampposts accented with alternating tinsel bells and angel wings.

Her heart rate kicked up when she heard the car behind them. She turned in unison with her other self, seeing the bare details of the car.

"Tell me what you see, Vivian."

In the distance, Vivian heard the scratch of a pencil on paper. The sound was oddly soothing, she found. As if evidence of progress. Vivian knew as much about cars as she did NASCAR, meaning next to nothing. So color, the number of doors and the odd shape of the headlights were the only things she could mention.

"Who is in the car?" Stacy asked.

"Two men. Dark hair. Round faces." She squeezed her eyes tighter. "I don't know what I should say."

"Anything and everything that comes to mind."

"Right. Okay."

"Can you see them both?"

Vivian nodded. She hadn't realized that before. It was only now that she could see she'd originally merged her description into one person. "There's an older one driving. The passenger looks darker somehow. Meaner. Cruel. Sorry." Her lips twitched in apology. "I work in PR. I tend to pick up on personalities and intentions, even silent ones."

"That's good," Stacy encouraged. "Like I said, there's no wrong way to go about this. I want you to do something for me, okay? I want you to pretend to take a snapshot with your mind. Just like you do with your cell phone. Just click and store it for later. Can you do that?"

"I think so?" *Odd*, Vivian thought as she did just that. She even tried to zoom in and find more details that could help. A medal of some kind hung from the rearview mirror. A parking lot stub was wedged on top of the dashboard. The bucket seats were dark, almost black, and in the back seat...

Vivian gasped. Her eyes shot open. It took a moment to focus again, but when her vision cleared, she went wide-eyed when she looked to Stacy.

"What did you see?" Stacy asked.

"A third man." Her voice nearly broke from the tension winding through her body. "There was a third man in the back seat. He was wearing this big gold ring. That's what was glinting." He'd looked at Vivian and

Dean when the gun fired. For an instant—a blink of one—she'd looked him directly in the eyes.

"Did you see his face, too?"

"Yes." She whispered now, tried to ignore the shiver racing down her spine. "Yes, I saw him." She swallowed hard. "I saw all of them."

Chapter 5

As glorious as Nate's updated waterfall shower had been in the early hours of the morning, the first thing Vivian planned to do when she got home was jump into hers and wash that man right out of her hair.

"That man. Last night. And everything in between." She cranked up the throwback '80s station on her satellite radio. It was obvious from the moment Detective Sullivan had joined her and Stacy in the interview room that Vivian's description of not one, not two, but the three men from the car in the drive-by had exceeded everyone's expectations.

Detective Sullivan had tried to hide his surprise, and there was a flash of anger that glinted before he covered it. But she'd seen it. It had sent chills down her spine.

He'd always been polite. But his more solicitous attitude when he'd escorted her back downstairs and handed her off to a pair of uniformed officers who'd driven her back to her car had definitely left her feeling both accomplished and unnerved.

Almost as unnerved as the trio of dark, dangerous eyes that all but glowed from inside that car. She shuddered, gave herself a hard mental shake and took a cleansing breath. Getting all those details out and into Stacy's talented hands had offloaded a lot of the anxiety that had been churning inside her. But not all of it.

A glance at her watch eased a bit of her anxiety. She had plenty of time to make the half-hour drive to Owl Creek, get cleaned up and jump on her call with Harlow Jones, a rather ebullient relationship-expert client who always managed to lift Vivian's spirits.

Taking the back roads always gave Vivian a bit of comfort. Getting behind the wheel was one of her least favorite activities, but a necessary one. Not that she'd be making her way into Boise again anytime soon. Detective Sullivan had insisted that should he have any follow-up questions, he was happy to come to her. Again, that solicitous attitude seemed a bit of a stretch from the no-nonsense detective she'd first met at the hospital in the middle of the night.

Weekend traffic was nothing like it was during the workweek. She was just happy for the daylight, however gray it might be. As her eco-friendly car hummed down the four-lane road, she breathed out and flexed her hands on the wheel, wincing a bit at the cars zooming past her on the other side.

She hummed along with the music, but within seconds was belting out, off-key and with wrong lyrics, her accompaniment as the cold air swirled outside.

Behind her, a dark SUV surged close, giving no indication of slowing down. She eased her foot off the gas, pumped her brake just to make certain to be seen. But the car kept its speed up.

Her stomach clenched. Her hands tightened on the

wheel. Tailgaters were the worst, and her already shaky relationship with driving didn't make things any better.

"Just go around," she said as the music grew louder in her ears. "Go around, go around…"

She took her eyes off the mirror for a moment, checking for other vehicles that might be preventing the driver from moving over. Vivian slowed, debated easing onto the gravel shoulder, but there wasn't one for at least another half mile. The long, iced-over drainage ditches stretched endlessly.

The SUV was so close now she could see the muddied license plate.

"Go around!" she yelled, swerving to the right side. The left lane was clear. It didn't make any sense…

She screamed when the car hit her from behind. That deafening sound of metal against metal, that heartstopping *bang*. Her hands gripped the wheel. She tried to speed up, but her little car wasn't having it. It stuttered a bit, then shot forward, but not before the SUV hit her again.

Every muscle in her body tensed up. She could feel each one of them from her shoulders right down to her toes. Terror tightened her throat and had her swiveling her head back and forth looking for somewhere, anywhere, to go. She could hear horns blaring when he hit again, but the sound didn't quite register before the SUV swerved around her and kept pace with her.

She pulled her foot off the gas. As if anticipating her action, the SUV rammed her from the side, sending her careening off the road before it sped off.

Her tires caught the top of the ditch and pitched the car up and over. She covered her face and, for a moment, felt as if she were almost airborne. The back of the car slammed down with enough force to flip one more time. The front windshield cracked and spider-webbed, the horrific crackling echoing in her ears for what felt like hours.

It landed diagonally across the icy ditch. Water from beneath the frozen top layer seeped in below the door, freezing her boot-covered feet. Around her, brakes screeched and people shouted while a car door slammed and footsteps raced closer. She could only breathe in short, painful bursts. Her fingers seemed frozen around the wheel.

"Ma'am?"

She screamed again when someone pounded on her window. It was a bearded man wearing sunglasses. His red-and-black flannel shirt gleamed in the early morning, cloud-breaking sun.

"Are you okay?" He pointed down, indicating she should lower her window.

She did so. Her hands were shaking so hard she could barely see them.

"Call an ambulance!" the man called over his shoulder as more people raced over. She could hear people asking if anyone had caught a plate number, or if they'd seen the driver. Vivian released her seat belt and tried to stop sobbing. All she wanted was out of the car.

"Get me out." She pulled hard on the handle before realizing the door was locked. She unlocked it and, with the man's help, shoved it open. She grabbed her bag, held it against her chest as she shoved her legs out of the car.

A couple of people grabbed her and pulled her free,

immediately sitting her on the level ground above the ditch.

"Ma'am?"

"I'm okay." She touched a hand to her head, expecting to find blood, but she didn't. "I'm okay." Her memory fogged over as if protecting her from recalling the event.

"An ambulance is on the way," one person called as they raced over.

An older woman, silvery hair knotted on top of her head. "Hon, what's your name? Can you tell me your name?"

"Viv-Vivian," she managed. "Vivian Maylor." She shivered hard enough that someone noticed and draped something warm over her shoulders. In contrast to the malicious driver, she felt concern and gentleness from the growing crowd.

"I called the police," another woman yelled.

"De-Detective Nate Colton," Vivian managed as she drew in a shaky, lung-aching breath. "Boise PD. He's…a friend." Tears burned her throat. She'd gotten snippy. Petulant even. Rejection never brought out the best in anyone, especially herself. She'd wanted to pretend he didn't exist, so she hadn't bothered to say goodbye. Maybe if she had… "I have his card…" She blinked hard to clear her vision as she dug into her purse. When she found it, she held it up to whomever snatched it from her hand. "I'd be grateful if someone could call him for me."

Nate leaned back in his chair, chin resting in his hand, a finger poised over his lips as he stared at his phone. The cell had buzzed a few times in the past couple of hours, but nothing came through of importance. Noth-

ing from Sullivan about Vivian's session with the sketch
artist. Nothing from the hospital about any change in
Wexler's condition.

Just…nothing.

Irritated, he snatched the phone up and called Sullivan himself, only to get blocked by voicemail.

He swore, hung up, tossed his phone back on the desk
and tried to refocus his attention on the file containing a
list of Marty DeBaccian's arrests and his one conviction
for armed robbery. Funny that was the only one, given
his file was more than an inch thick. Since his release,
he'd become as slippery as the lawyers who represented
him. More so even.

He'd gone from being a one-trick pony to having his
hand in everything from illegal gaming to loan shark-
ing to felonious assault and, in at least two instances,
attempted murder. But arrest-worthy proof was a completely different story.

Nate and most of the Boise PD had little to no doubt
DeBaccian had committed far more crimes than he'd
been arrested for, but that was only supposition, and
supposition was not evidence.

At least Nate wasn't alone in thinking DeBaccian
was one seriously bad dude. There wasn't a cop within
a couple hundred miles of Boise who didn't have this
guy in their sights. DeBaccian needed to be locked up,
but even that might not do much to crush his growing
criminal enterprise.

Nate was a realist if nothing else. He was well aware
of the failings of the penal system. Oftentimes, convicts
only became better criminals during their sentences,
even to the point of continuing to run whatever organi-

zations or rackets they had in place. But Nate was still of the belief that chopping off the head of the snake was the best way to kill the business and rid Boise of a good portion of organized crime. DeBaccian had become notoriously solitary. He didn't have a right hand or a number one. He had his favorites, but didn't completely trust anyone, which made the promise of information Wexler might possess all the more important.

Nate's fingers itched to call the hospital, but he'd already spoken to Cooper when the officer had returned to the station after being relieved at the hospital. Nothing out of the ordinary had occurred, no visitors, no strange happenings. As far as Cooper had been able to glean, there had also been no change in Wexler's condition.

Which left Nate standing completely still while the rest of the world kept spinning.

"Screw it." He pocketed his phone, grabbed his blazer off the back of his chair and took the stairs down to the second floor. He scanned the semi-empty bullpen for Sullivan, looking for that shock of red hair that always made the other detective stand out in a crowd.

"Hey, Nate." Stacy Crum headed toward him, bundled up in a bright purple down jacket and matching scarf. "I was just on my way out. If you're looking for Vivian, she left maybe a half hour ago."

"Left? Already?" He glanced at his watch. It was almost noon. Then he remembered she'd mentioned having a meeting with a client. "Where's Sullivan?"

"No idea," Stacy said. "Haven't seen him since he escorted Vivian downstairs. Your girl did great, by the way. Scary accurate, according to Sullivan."

His girl. Hearing that should have annoyed him, if for

no other reason than it confirmed the department gossip mill was running smooth and steady. Instead, the very idea of Vivian being his girl left him feeling oddly... warm. And slightly dim-witted at how he'd left things. "I'm not surprised." Despite finding herself smack in the middle of chaos, near as Nate could tell, Vivian had weathered the shooting pretty well. "Anything come of her description?"

"Sullivan didn't call?" Stacy frowned. "Must have slipped his mind."

"I'm sure it did." Nate didn't believe that for a second. The detective had a rumored habit of putting ambition above all else and he definitely wasn't enthusiastic about Nate's involvement with his case. "Can I see what the two of you and Vivian came up with?" He indicated the large, long-strapped artist satchel Stacy had slung over one shoulder.

Stacy shrugged. "I guess it'd be okay." She looked behind her. "Let's go back in Interview."

He followed, impatience hitting as Stacy took her time extricating her sketch pad from her bag. It took her flipping through a good half dozen pages before she got to the first one.

He let out a low whistle, shook his head. "Now that's some detail." The man's eyes chilled him to his marrow.

"I've never had anyone describe malevolence before," Stacy observed. "He looks real, doesn't he?"

"Yes, he does," Nate murmured.

"Here's the second one."

"The second...?" He flipped the page. "She saw both of them?" The Cyrillic tattoo on this one's neck would make him easier to trace. Chances were that was prison ink. "This clearly?"

"She saw all three of them," Stacy corrected and turned one more page. "She didn't remember until I took her under. Meet bachelor number three." Her smirk was one of pride, but the man looking back at Nate stole the air from his lungs. "Nightmare fodder for sure."

Something icy and slippery slithered up his spine as he looked at the face. And the ring on his hand. "Sullivan saw these?"

"Of course. Why?" Stacy frowned. "Or are you going to go all secretive on me and keep me in the dark? Who is this guy?"

Nate's mind spun. His instinct about Wexler being connected to Boise's latest crime boss was dead-on right. Had to be, otherwise DeBaccian wouldn't have come out to make sure the job was done himself.

"Thanks, Stacy." He turned and ran back up the stairs, beelined for his boss's office. Lieutenant Haig was getting to his feet when Nate's cell phone rang.

He checked the screen. Unfamiliar number, but no spam warning.

"Yeah. Colton." He held up a finger when Haig stood up and came to the door.

"Detective Nate Colton?" An unfamiliar woman's voice echoed. Beyond, he could hear sirens and shouts and rapid conversation. "I'm calling for a Vivian Maylor."

"Vivian?" He turned fear-filled eyes to his boss. "Why? What's happened? Where is she?"

The person gave him a location on the back roads between Conners and Owl Creek. "There was an accident.

She's okay. Pretty shaken up, but a car ran her off the road. Straight into a ditch. The car did this flip thing—"

"Flip?" His lungs turned to ice. "But you said she's all right."

"Near as we can tell. Miracle if you ask me."

His cop brain kicked into gear at the last second. "What about the car that hit her? Did anyone get a good look?"

"Long gone. No question it was deliberate. Road rage, I guess you could say. Hang on." Silence for a moment. "The ambulance just got here. I'm pretty sure they're going to take her in."

"Ambulance?" Nate demanded in a loud enough voice to garner the attention of his fellow detectives.

"Precaution, I'm sure. The car's totaled."

Despite the fear clutching at his heart, he let out a sigh of relief. "Okay. All right. Tell her I'm on my way and that I'll meet her at the hospital." Hopefully, that alone would stave off any argument she might make against yet another ride in an ambulance. "I'm on my way now."

"I'll tell her." The caller disconnected.

"Report," Lieutenant Haig ordered in a way that jerked Nate back to reality.

"Vivian was run off the road on her way home. Sullivan…" Anger surged. "One of Vivian's sketches is of DeBaccian. Right down to that family crest ring he wears." She hadn't missed a single detail, and those details may well have almost gotten her killed. "He was in the car last night when they tried to take out Wexler."

"Ballsy," Haig said in that stern, detached way he had. "If that's true, that's a change in behavior for him."

"Indulgent," Nate said. "Arrogant." And proof DeBaccian had it in for Wexler. His gut had been right. "He's covering his tracks." Which put Vivian straight in the man's crosshairs. "Sullivan knew she'd seen him, and he still sent her home alone." His hand tightened around his cell phone. "I need to get to the hospital." He hurried to explain. "The person who called me said Vivian's car flipped into a ditch. She seems okay, but…" He hesitated. "We need her car in evidence." He was ping-ponging between cop and concerned…whatever he was to Vivian.

"There might be trace evidence we can link back to DeBaccian. Nice shortcut to an arrest, even if it is a Hail Mary pass." Haig nodded. "Okay. Paulson, Renard." He snapped his fingers over his head so loud nearly everyone in the bullpen shot to attention. The two detectives stepped out from behind their desks. "You two head out to the scene, control what you can and make sure every single witness is questioned. We want Ms. Maylor's car impounded, and I want Cassidy Barrett brought in to oversee the evidence collection."

Nate's fellow detectives quickly grabbed their jackets and, after giving Nate a reassuring pat on the shoulder, headed out.

"I need to—"

"Go," Haig said. "Let me know of any developments. And Colton?"

"Sir?" Nate skidded to a stop before reaching his desk.

"Consider Vivian Maylor in protective custody," Haig ordered. "Yours and yours alone. Don't let her out of your sight. She might be the best witness we've ever had against DeBaccian, and he clearly knows about her.

I'm going to order surveillance on DeBaccian's known hangouts while we wait for a warrant."

"What about Detective Sullivan?" Nate demanded.

"Leave Sullivan to me." The chill in Haig's voice left Nate almost feeling sorry for the other detective. "Go. And report in when you can."

"Thank you, sir." He retrieved his gun from his desk drawer, strapped it into his holster. "Will do."

"Are you sure you're all right?" The desperate plea on the other end of the line only added to Vivian's anxiety. She'd gone her entire life without having ridden in an ambulance. Now, within the space of twenty-four hours, she was on trip number two. This was not an item she'd had on her meager and pathetic bucket list. At this rate, she was going to have a reserved bed in the ER.

"Harlow, I'm fine." She grimaced as the aches began to settle in. She was back at Boise General. Back in one of their triage rooms, only this time instead of the midnight glow of the moon, she got full-on sunlight. "I'm just sorry I missed our meeting."

"It wasn't a meeting per se," Harlow said with the teensiest edge of guilt in her voice. "I mean, it wasn't like official business or anything. You've already gone leaps and bounds beyond what I expected from a publicist. You hooked me up with Sandy Flemming, the queen of morning talk! I'm happy where I am at the moment." She paused. "Mostly."

Vivian frowned. "I don't understand." Harlow had been a bit cryptic in their last email exchange, mentioning some impulsive plans she was considering implementing. Vivian had assumed it was in regard to

Harlow's ever-expanding audience for her online relationship advice. Whatever was beyond viral, Harlow
had hit it in the perfect sweet spot. Hence her needing
a PR person to help manage the cascade of offers and
opportunities while trying to grab hold of even bigger
ones. "So our call wasn't business related?" She sighed
as the nurse tightened the blood-pressure cuff around her
arm, forcing Vivian to switch her cell to her other hand.

She might have shot the nurse a look but found her
own irritation mirrored in the older woman's face. Vivian glanced down, noted the woman's name was Helga
and offered a strained, apologetic smile. "Cell phones
really aren't allowed in here," the nurse said without
bothering to try to keep her voice down.

"We're almost done." The familiar drab-blue curtains
hung as limp as Vivian was beginning to feel. Talking
to Harlow was at least helping her set aside the panic
over losing her car and being run off the road by some
reject from a bad *Mad Max* rip-off.

"You should go," Harlow said. "We can talk later."

"It's fine," Vivian lied. "What did you want to talk
about?"

"Well." There was that pause again. "I think I'm going
to come back to Owl Creek for a little while."

"Oh?" Harlow's career in Los Angeles was just beginning to take off into the stratosphere. Seemed an odd
time to take a break. "You sure you want to do that?"

"I think it's time, you know? To finally put my folks'
house on the market and get all that behind me. I was
hoping we could get together in person once I hit town.
I'll be there for a while, so I'm sure we can eke out some
time?"

"Oh." The prospect might have brightened her mood if it hadn't been sitting at rock bottom. "That sounds great. Of course we can get together."

"Great. It'll be nice. Change of scenery, focusing on something other than...work."

There was that hesitancy again, a hesitancy that signaled something deeper was bothering her client-turned-friend. Given the *tsks* Vivian heard emanating from her nurse, now wasn't the time to question Harlow.

"I've got some things to tie up before I head to Idaho," Harlow continued. "But I wanted to touch base with you first."

"I'm glad you did. Seeing you gives me something to look forward to."

"You're sure you're okay?" Harlow asked again. "Car accidents aren't anything to laugh about, and it sounds like yours was a doozey."

"Could have been worse." Vivian blinked back the sudden rush of tears, but she refused to give in. She was alive. That was all that mattered. "But I'm really fine. I'll figure out everything that comes next. I just didn't want you to think I flaked out on our meeting."

"You're incapable of flaking. If you're sure, I'll let you get back to the nurses hassling you. Take care, okay? You need anything, you know where you can find me. Seriously, I'm just a call away."

"Thanks, Harlow." It felt odd, Vivian thought after she hung up and stared down at her cell: she'd spent so much of her life alone. Other than Lizzy Colton, she could count the number of friends she'd had on maybe three fingers. At the rate she was going, she might be all the way to five pretty soon.

"I'll take that." Helga plucked the phone out of Vivian's grasp and plunked it out of reach on the table beside the bed. The satisfied smirk on her face seemed like overkill, but Vivian supposed nurses needed to find a way to make the most of a bad situation. And right now, Vivian was definitely on the precipice of becoming a difficult patient.

She hadn't wanted to come back to the ER. She wanted to go home and bury herself under her covers and sleep away the last couple of days.

"We've got a CT scan scheduled for you within the hour," Helga advised her. "You should rest until then."

"Great." A CT scan was going to take ages. She'd be lucky to get back to her cozy little town house before sunset.

The nurse left, pulling the curtain closed to give Vivian the spare bit of privacy possible in a bustling ER room. One bed over, the patient was dealing with some serious stomach pain that, unfortunately for Vivian's batlike hearing, was indicative of either a seriously infected gall bladder or ruptured appendix.

"All the more reason to be grateful," Vivian mumbled to herself as she scooted down in bed and curled up on her side. "At least you've only got bumps and scrapes." And one seriously aching body. At least she had a different cubicle this time, one with a gorgeous view of the loading dock at the back of the hospital. Still, it felt as if an avalanche of the past had landed on her full force.

She should sleep. She wanted to. But every time she closed her eyes all she saw was that black SUV barreling up behind her in the rearview mirror. She'd spent

most of her life hoping, praying, that history didn't repeat itself and yet...

She turned her head, this way and that, trying to
push aside the haunting, nerve-wracking sound of metal
scraping metal. Hugging her arms around her body, she
curled tighter, hating the tears and fear threatening to
explode if she gave them half a chance.

She covered her eyes, repressed the urge to growl
when she heard the rattle of the curtain being pulled back.
"Please, just leave me alone." She was already shaking
so hard her teeth ached. If she was going to fall apart,
she needed to do so without an audience.

"Vivian."

She dropped her hand and looked over her shoulder. "Nate."

The tears she'd been trying hard to bank flooded instantly. She wanted to ask why he was here. What he
was doing here. She hadn't wanted to believe the kind
woman who had called him when she'd assured Vivian that Nate would meet her at the hospital. And yet...

He closed the curtain and approached the bed. Her
gaze shifted to the chair in the corner, but he walked
right past it to sit beside her on the bed, up close to
where she could grab hold of him. Instead of clinging to
him, she pulled herself up and slipped her arms around
his neck.

She wasn't alone.

A sob lodged in her chest.

That he immediately responded by wrapping his arms
around her and pulling her in so close she could hear his
heart beating over hers had her closing her eyes again,
this time in relief. And comfort.

"I was so scared," she whispered, hating the helplessness she heard in her voice. She knew how to take care of herself, but the last day had definitely left her wondering if leaving the house was worth it. Taking chances clearly wasn't for her. Except...

Except that it had led to where she sat now. In the one place that felt perfect.

"I never should have left you," he murmured against the side of her throat. "When I got that call, I'd never been so scared in my life." He caught her face between his hands, set her away from him.

The fear she saw on his face, in those blue eyes of his, made her feel, at least in this moment, that she mattered to someone.

"You aren't going to ask me what happened?" Her question came out slightly broken, hitched, as if her words couldn't piece themselves together any easier than the rest of her could.

"Not yet." He drew her back against him, cradled her head under his chin, against his chest. "I will. But later. I just need a few minutes first."

"I'm fine." Her fingers felt bruised, as did her forearms. From gripping the steering wheel so tightly she supposed. "They want to put me through a CT scan just to make sure."

"Good." He pressed a kiss to the top of her head, and it was, quite possibly, the most caring gesture she'd ever experienced. "I'm here. I'm not going anywhere."

"That's nice."

"You don't believe me." She could almost hear the smile in his voice.

She shook her head, still unwilling to release her hold on him. "You have a job to do. An important one."

"You're my job now." He shifted before he slid off the edge of the bed. "Lieutenant's orders."

"Oh?" That piqued her curiosity, and she sat back, just enough to look up at him.

"Definitely *oh*." He flinched and doubt rose in his eyes. "The man you ID'd, from the back seat of the car. His name is Marty DeBaccian." He paused. "He's the man I was hoping Dean Wexler could give me information on."

She blinked, processed. She blinked faster. "But...you told me the man you were after was a really bad guy."

"He is." He stroked his thumbs down her cheeks, before sliding one across her lips. "He's a very bad guy. I think that's who came after you this morning. I can't prove it yet, but unless you really ticked someone off while you were driving, I think it's a safe bet."

"I might have." He clearly thought she was joking. "I'm a terrible driver. I go way too slow. It's why I'm always going to the right. It's... I hate it. Driving. I've lost track of the number of tickets I've gotten."

"I don't think—" He nodded as if humoring her.

"My parents died in a car accident when I was nine." She chewed on her bottom lip, considered. "I was with them, but I don't really remember. One minute they were there, and the next..." She wanted to shrug it off as if that event hadn't defined the rest of her life. "I woke up in the hospital alone. All of this, it's just so surreal." And familiar. Far too familiar.

The sympathy on his face was almost too much to bear. "I'm sorry."

"I didn't get my license until I was twenty-two. Every time I climb into a car, I can't help but think it might be the last thing I do. And if I drive past an accident?" Her laugh was harsh. "It sends me spiraling back. I can't explain it any better than that. Nine years old and I was left all alone."

"Alone?" His brow furrowed. "You didn't have any family?"

She shook her head. "My grandparents were all gone by the time I was born, and my parents were only children. We traveled a lot and were spending the summer on a road trip. The crash happened in Boise. I spent the next nine years in and out of foster homes in and around Owl Creek. That's when I met Lizzy. Your sister. When I started school that fall." Tears filled her eyes again. "She made me feel as if life might be okay again."

"Yeah, well." He rested his hands on her shoulders. "We Coltons have a bit of an unofficial code. Family finds family."

She sniffled and nodded. "I really lucked out in that department." She lifted a hand to his face. "Twice maybe, it seems."

He kissed her, gently. Carefully. As if afraid of breaking her. Instead, it brought all the fear and panic back to the surface and gave it someplace to go. When she broke away, she scooted closer and hugged him, hard. For however long he was around, she planned to make the most of their time together.

"What happens now?" she whispered.

"First we're going to make sure you're in the clear medically," Nate said. "That'll give me time to make some plans. But fair warning—" he spoke as if he expected her to protest "—I'm not taking you home. Not for any length of time. Don't worry," he added when she sat back and gaped at him. "We'll figure it out so your life isn't completely upended. Last night, you said you'd trust me. I need you to trust me again, Vivian. And know that this time I won't leave you behind."

"You promise?"

He nodded and pressed his lips to her forehead. "I promise."

It was, Vivian admitted silently when she closed her eyes in relief, the only thing she'd needed to hear.

Chapter 6

Guilt was a funny thing. Oftentimes, Nate thought as he waited in the registration area of the emergency room, guilt was also blinding. It descended with a familiar ferocity that shoved everything, including irrational thought, aside.

This was a roller coaster he'd been riding for as long as he could remember. Growing up with a less than stable influence of a mother—one who, while physically present, didn't come close to being emotionally invested in the children she'd brought into the world—meant growing up fast.

There was no defining the type of pain one carried upon realizing early in life that you aren't remotely close to being the center of anyone's universe.

He'd become an overachiever, a protector, especially where his sister Sarah was concerned. When Robert Colton, his father, had all but disappeared from their lives when Nate was around ten, Nate found himself instantly stepping into the caretaker role. It was a role that brought with it a particular resentment, one that grew with each calculated, cruel step Jessie Colton took away from her family. But with all of that came guilt.

No matter how many years passed or how successful or accomplished he became, Nate could always find a way to feel as if he could have done something, anything, everything, better.

It was too late to reconcile with his father, or even have any kind of confrontation or conversation with Robert Colton. A stroke had ended his life earlier this year before any kind of emotional peace could be sought, for either of them. It didn't quite seem real, that his father was gone. It should have been easy enough to accept. Robert hadn't been around for most of Nate's life. But with all the questions Nate had, not to mention the family dynamics that continued to swirl into the realm of complicated, it also felt as if Robert was still smack dab in the middle of everything.

Even Jessie had seemed—what was the word?—*contrite* about the situation as a whole. Contrite to the point of...

Nate squeezed his eyes shut as if attempting to clear out his brain. His suspicious nature surrounding his mother's actions had no place in his thoughts. As far as he was concerned, Jessie herself had no place in them, but blood was blood. No matter how much he distrusted and disliked his mother, she was still his family. Whether he liked it or not.

Seated in a worn vinyl chair, he rested his elbows on his knees and stared at the linoleum floor. The attempt at festive decor didn't feel quite complete. Some windows were outlined with dollar-store threadbare tinsel garlands, while a pair of one-armed frolicking elves looked more demented than celebratory. Clearly, they'd been dug out of a holiday bin probably stored in the basement. He definitely wasn't feeling the holiday cheer.

He was being too harsh, no doubt. Internalizing what he should have been trying to find a healthy outlet for. But he couldn't help it. Dwelling on the *should haves* and *wished he hads* was pretty much a pattern for him.

He shouldn't have walked away from Vivian the way he had. He shouldn't have pushed her away and into Sullivan's irresponsible, self-centered hands. He'd built up her trust then turned his back when he felt himself getting too close. It would be so easy, too easy, to take that slide he could sense hovering before him and fall. A fall that terrified him far more than any dangers of his job.

He'd felt it the second she'd walked into the restaurant the other night. That pull that had only gotten stronger. That...gravitational force that seemed to have been created just for the two of them. And yet...

He couldn't let himself surrender to it. That attraction that had struck and settled dead center in his heart from the start. It had no place here, between them. Inside him.

Especially now that her life may very well depend on him remaining attentive, on guard, and most of all, ready. He needed to put her safety first. End of story.

If only he didn't know what it felt like to hold her in his arms...

The swinging doors bounced open. Nate shot to his feet as a young female nurse pushed Vivian's wheelchair into the open space. He hadn't noticed the bruises before, or the cuts and scrapes she'd received, no doubt, from the shattered glass. She had her arms wrapped tight around herself, as if cocooning against everything around her. A couple of new bandages had joined the one near her eye where her glasses had cut her during the shooting.

She looked as if she'd gone a good three or four rounds in the ring with a less than sympathetic opponent.

"And here we are!"

Nate couldn't tell whether Vivian was embarrassed or annoyed, but the way she rolled her eyes at her escort's cartoony tone told Nate, more than any clear CT scan could have, that she was just fine.

"I can take her from here," he offered in an effort to spare the nurse any potential reaction. He could only imagine how frayed Vivian's nerves must be by now. She'd been shot at, questioned by the police, spent hours with a sketch artist and been run off the road. All that was beyond Nate's own capabilities of coping. "Really." He reached into his pocket and pulled out his badge. That action earned him another eye roll from Vivian, but he accepted her reaction as another good sign.

"Oh." The nurse straightened and looked a little disappointed. "Sure, of course, Detective. Just make sure you leave the chair in the depository just outside?"

"You've got it." He was well aware how effective a perfectly aimed smile could be for some people.

She settled her bag in her lap as Nate wheeled her outside into the sunny yet frosty day. She shivered.

"We need to get you another jacket."

"I just want to go home." Her grumble made Nate worry she didn't recall what he'd told her just a few hours ago in her cubicle.

"I'm taking you home to pack," Nate said in a way that he hoped left no room for argument. "Then we're headed back out."

"Is that really necessary?" She yelped a bit when he bounced over the metal threshold.

"Sorry. And yes," Nate told her as he steered her over to where he'd parked in the ER lot. "It is. I'm also going to need your phone."

"My…phone?" She made it sound as if he'd asked her to cut off her arm.

"Can't take any chances you're being tracked. Whoever ran you off the road—"

"It could have been an accident." She glanced over her shoulder at him, barely there hope swimming in her hazel eyes. "We shouldn't overreact."

Nate bit the inside of his cheek and remained silent until he had her in the car. Before he left to return the wheelchair, he pulled out his phone and tapped open the photos he'd been sent from Lieutenant Haig. "If you can look at these and still tell me you think it was pure coincidence this happened to you, we can discuss further. I'll be right back." He closed the door and grabbed the chair.

Showing her the photos wasn't something he'd planned to do. Personally, he'd have preferred not to show her the evidence of her own attempted murder, but they both needed to start looking reality in the face. If only to make some smart decisions.

By the time he returned to the car and slid in behind the wheel, he didn't have to ask if he'd made his point. She'd set her phone on the console between the seats. The tension swirling inside the SUV was more than enough evidence of that.

"You okay?" It was, perhaps, the dumbest question he'd ever uttered in his life. But it was the only thing he could think to ask. He quickly turned off her phone, popped out the SIM card and placed both in the glove box.

"Not really, no." She handed his phone over, and he

pocketed it so he could use it again in an emergency. "I guess I'd convinced myself it wasn't as bad as it was." She sighed, sank down in her seat. "My car's totaled."

"Yes, it is." The images had been sent from their evidence station, where Lieutenant Haig had ordered Detective Sullivan to meet him. Nate's superior had wanted Sullivan to see the results of his dismissing a witness without thinking things through. Nate could only hope the conversation made some kind of impact, but he doubted it. Sullivan was a decent cop, but not the best human being. "But you weren't, so let's count that as a win."

"Go me."

Her sense of humor was intact, at least. "We'll worry about your car another time. Right now, let's get you home."

"What about you?" She looked over at him. "If we're leaving town, don't you need your stuff?"

"I keep a go bag in the back." He jerked a thumb toward the rear window. He reorganized the duffel every couple of weeks, just to be safe. He'd only had call to use it a handful of times since becoming a detective, but at least he knew it was reliable. Anything he might have missed they could pick up down the road. "I can live out of that thing for weeks if necessary."

"I still haven't given a statement about the accident." She took hold of the grab bar over the door and the center console when he reversed out of the parking space. "Sorry." Her eyes squeezed shut for a moment. "Getting back on the horse isn't easy. Stupid." She gave her head a hard shake and had him wincing.

"It's natural, not stupid. It'll get better. And I'll try

to go slow." Truth be told, he'd considered having her drive his car to her place. Slapping fear in the face was usually his mode for getting past things. But she wasn't him. Vivian would have to be eased back into the driver's seat. Or at least be strongly motivated. Tiny steps, he told himself. "As far as your statement goes, we'll get that taken care of once we get to where we're going."

"And where is that exactly?" She hadn't released her grip on the grab bar. If anything, she'd tightened her fingers to the point her knuckles had gone white.

Because Nate wasn't entirely sure himself, he shrugged. "Does it matter?"

She went silent for a moment. "I suppose not."

"It's not going to be for long, Vivian. Just until we catch whoever is behind these attacks on you."

"Despite your best efforts to prove otherwise, you aren't a superhero," Vivian said. "You can protect me, or you can work the case. I doubt you can do both."

"Oh, ye of little faith." How she underestimated him. And it would be something akin to a pleasure to prove her wrong. "I'm capable of multitasking all sorts of things. Besides, I've got lots of friends in the Boise PD, and most of them owe me more than one favor. We'll get you home and back to your life soon enough."

She caught her lower lip in her teeth and turned her head to look out the window. The sun still shone, but a light dusting of snow fell from the gray clouds hovering overhead. Days like this felt like doom and gloom with the barest hint of light on the horizon.

"My lieutenant said there were more than a dozen people who stopped to help you." He was grasping at straws to help identify something positive out of all this.

"They all gave statements and a description of the car that hit you. Most of them asked about you."

He couldn't see her reaction. "Do you think…" She stopped, took a deep breath. "When this is all over, do you think I could get their names so I can send them thank-you notes?"

It seemed both a ludicrous idea and so incredibly Vivian. "I think we can make that happen."

She glanced at him. "That's weird, isn't it?"

"Incredibly," Nate said without hesitation. "But more that you thought of it now, when you're still reeling from what happened." Her grimace told him she was doubting her own sanity. "Feel and think what you need to in order to get through."

"I can compartmentalize better than most people." Her voice was low now and carried a familiar sadness Nate could relate to. "Sometimes you have to do that in order to survive."

Like she'd had to when her parents were killed. Like he did when his father had returned to his other family. His *real* family.

"Don't ever apologize for being who you are, Vivian." Because he couldn't resist the urge, he reached over and laid his hand over hers. His heart jumped when she folded her fingers around his and squeezed. "You're you. That's the only thing that matters."

"You missed your calling, Detective," Vivian said softly. "You really should give poetry a try."

He laughed, shook his head, and because she cast nervous eyes at his driving with only one hand on the wheel, he released his hold and put her mind at ease. "My expertise with poetry extends only so far as the naughty limericks one of my school friends used to recite."

"You underestimate yourself," she said in a tone that left no room for argument. "I think you have more talent in the word department than you realize. Can I ask a favor?"

"Sure."

"Before we hit the freeway, can we please, *please* stop for some coffee?"

It felt strange having a man drive her home. Strange in a good way, perhaps, but strange nonetheless. It was as if she'd left her home Friday evening one person and was coming home a different one. Maybe it was the fact that Nate was the man.

She didn't think it was the badge he wore or the job he did or even the last name he possessed, but perhaps it was the combination that made Vivian feel utterly and completely safe and content when he was around. Even while her entire world seemed to be falling off its axis.

For a woman who had spent the majority of her life alone, she wasn't completely pleased with the idea of feeling even the least bit reliant on another person for her emotional well-being but…there it was. Reality. And his name was Nate Colton.

Guided by his onboard GPS, he parked in front of her garden-gated town house and turned off the engine. There was an unexpected relief at seeing her house again. There had been moments before she'd crashed that she had honestly believed she wouldn't ever see it again.

"Can I have your keys, please?" Nate held out his hand.

She frowned, looked down at his empty palm. "Why?"

"Because I'm not taking a chance that they don't know where you live. They spent enough time looking at your license plate. Getting your address wouldn't take much more effort."

"Awesome." She hadn't even considered that. She dug into her purse, wincing at the slight dampness of the leather, to retrieve them. She hoped the bag wasn't ruined by its time in the icy water after the crash. "I suppose you want me to wait in the car while you check things out?"

"I'll only be a couple of minutes."

"More than five and I'm coming in." She was already mentally packing as he headed inside. She was also attempting to come up with some argument, any argument, to change his mind about letting her stay. She finished the last of her extra-large double-shot latte without the usual guilt at the caffeine level. Jittery was better than feeling helpless. At least, that was the idea she'd had when she'd placed her order.

Her home was her fortress, the one place she always felt untouchable and completely herself. What Nate was proposing was leaving all that security behind. As much as she trusted him, she wasn't completely on board with this idea.

Watching him approach her gate gave her an unobstructed rear view of the perfection of the male form. She let out a slow breath, appreciating the way he moved, even as he reached behind him and pulled a gun out of the back of his jeans.

"And there's the reality check." She was really getting sick of them, to be honest. She was not a fan of weapons. She didn't own a gun. Heck, she'd never even fired one!

Now she found herself getting tangled up with someone who carried one for a living. As if a handful of steamy kisses equaled entangled.

The metal fence clanked shut, and he made his way up the short walk to her front door. He took a moment before sliding the key into the lock and disappearing inside.

Vivian's heart pounded hard against her ribs. What if someone was inside? What if Nate found them in there? Could she ever feel safe again after her space had been invaded? Or if he was hurt protecting her?

No sooner had she begun the internal debate than Nate reappeared and returned to the car. He pulled open her door. "Everything looks fine to me." He held out his hand, and for an instant, she had an image of a particular glass-slippered princess being welcomed by her prince charming. She rolled her eyes, shook her head and wondered when her teenage self had been reawakened. Clearly the last couple of days had made a jumble of her thoughts and long-suppressed longings and dreams.

"It shouldn't take me too long to pack a bag." The sensation of his hand against the small of her back felt incredibly intimate. "How long should I plan to be gone for?"

"A week." His answer sounded as if he'd given it some thought. "We'll re-evaluate after that."

"Right." She left her purse on the floor in front of the small entryway table before heading up the stairs. "I'll be back down in a bit."

"Take your time," he called up after her. "I'm not going anywhere."

* * *

Nate closed the front door to Vivian's town house and, out of habit, snapped the lock. He'd only given a cursory glance to her home's contents on his initial entry. He'd been looking for disturbances, signs of someone else's presence. Not a reflection of Vivian's character and personality.

Since he'd found nothing disturbed, he relaxed and took in his surroundings. Not that there was much to take in. The ground floor mostly consisted of a spacious living area, where she had a small sofa, coffee table and rather large television set up in the corner beneath the stairs. There wasn't any art on the walls or knickknacks on the shelves.

Behind the sofa, taking up the entire back wall, was a bookcase crammed with titles of every sort, forced into precarious storage as she clearly read more than her system could contain.

A collection of blankets covered the sofa. One in particular, a black one over the back, near the window, had an indentation in it. He frowned, walked over, touched gentle fingers to the blanket, which was coated with cat hair.

He turned, looked around and spotted a pile of cat supplies in the corner by the front door. A cat perch with a cubby, a scratching post and a paper bag filled to overflowing with toys, food bowls and water dishes.

There were only a small number of framed photographs on display. One showed Vivian cuddling a beautiful, sleek white-and-gray cat with enormous yellow eyes. Another photo gave him a start as it was most definitely of his half-sister, Lizzy Colton. The two of them wore their caps and gowns at high school graduation. They'd been caught mid-laugh, and the sight stole his breath.

The other three were of Vivian as a little girl, being cuddled between two people he assumed were her parents. One during the summer, one at the holidays and a third at what appeared to be one of Vivian's birthdays. The light in her eyes was almost blinding with happiness as she blew out the candles on her cake. Those three pictures were more faded than the others, had folds and creases in them. Five pictures seemed a small and sobering number to represent thirty years of life.

In the corner by the window stood a round table on which a small, not even three-foot fake Christmas tree sat. Without the lights, it looked more than a little sad, with only a handful of ornaments on it, but there was one small, handcrafted paper angel sitting on the top with stringy blond hair. Other than that, there wasn't a hint of the holidays around her home.

"Hey, Nate?" Vivian came down two steps and leaned over. Her wet hair spilled over her shoulders. Heat and the fragrance of flowers wafted off her skin, a result of the shower she must have taken.

Gone were his sister's jeans and T-shirt. The sweater she wore now over faded jeans was a deep turquoise blue that accentuated her beautiful eyes. "We are staying in civilization, right? Electricity and everything? Internet?"

"We are if I have anything to say about it," he confirmed and earned a smile from her.

"Cool." She disappeared back upstairs.

He wandered through to the kitchen and small nook where a table and two chairs stood. Files and papers sat stacked in what he assumed was a system only she understood. Outside, a collection of empty bowls sat alongside the sliding glass door leading out to a small garden that contained nothing resembling plants. Instead, there were tumbles of rocks where grass or pots might have been.

He stepped outside, checked the back gate and noticed the garbage and recycling cans out along the back road where tenants parked. Deciding he might be of some help, he returned inside and rummaged through her refrigerator. He was shoulder deep into a collection of leftovers and takeout boxes when she came up behind him.

"Hungry?"

"Yes, actually." He grinned over his shoulder at her. The warmth of her hand on his shoulder had him once again needing to remind himself that he was actually working. Now wasn't the time for flirtations. "But I thought maybe we should empty this out just in case you're away longer than a week."

"Probably." She sighed. "Shame. There's some good food in there. I found this new Peruvian place that… Where are you going?"

"I've got a collapsible cooler in the back of the car." He shrugged. "Like you said, it's a shame to let it go to waste." Because her smile of gratitude was almost more than he could take, he made a quick exit, taking deep, refocusing breaths as he retrieved the cooler. He'd no sooner slammed the back shut than he found himself coming face-to-face with an elderly man with glasses so thick he looked like a goldfish. "Hello."

"You visiting Ms. Maylor?" The man was a bit stooped and barely reached Nate's chest. He held a small package in one hand, a four-footed cane in the other. His

T-shirt declared him to be a marine veteran, as did the steely, almost suspicious look in his bright blue eyes.

"I, well, yes, I am. Nate Colton." He held out his free hand, refrained from flashing his badge. "I thought I'd take Vivian on a bit of a vacation."

"A vacation?" His eyes went wide. "Well, land's sake. Never expected to hear that. Don't really see her unless she's coming out to get her mail. I'm Edgar Bartholomew. I live next door." He indicated the town house to the right. Potted poinsettia plants lined the walkway, interspersed with solar lights that no doubt cast a festive glow onto the red and white petals. His front window was filled with an enormous lighted tree twinkling bright enough to be seen from the space station. "Folks just call me Eddie though. Vacation. Huh." He frowned again, quirked his head in question. "Really?"

"Really." It shouldn't have surprised him that this news came across as unexpected. Vivian didn't strike him as the impulsive type. "Was there something you needed, Eddie?"

"Me? Oh, no." Eddie shook his head, then shoved the box at Nate. "Delivery came for Vivian yesterday afternoon. It needed to be signed for, and I was out tending to my roses. Even in winter, they need tending to."

"Of course," Nate agreed, noting the line of blankets draped over the pruned bushes.

"I came over and rang last night, but no answer." His smile was quick. "Guess I know why now. Anyway. This is for her."

Nate accepted the box. "I'll make sure she gets it."

"Appreciate it." Eddie started to hobble away, then turned around and nearly toppled over catching his balance. "Nice to see she's found someone to take care of her. She's a lonely one, I think," he observed with a sad shake of his head. "Hate to see it. Put a smile on her face, would you? No one should be all alone. Especially during the holidays."

"I'll do my best," Nate assured him before he headed inside. He returned to the kitchen where he found her sorting containers and setting aside produce that wouldn't last much longer. The bowls that had been outside the back door were in the sink now. "I just met your neighbor, Eddie."

"Oh?"

"He accepted a delivery for you yesterday." He held out the box.

She accepted it with more than a question on her face. "I wonder what…" She read the label, then hugged it to her chest. She sighed and closed her eyes. When she opened them again, they were filled with tears.

"What is it?" Nate asked.

She grabbed a knife and sliced through the packing tape. Once open, she pulled out a small cedar box with *Toby* engraved on the top. "My cat's ashes. I had to put him down last month. Kidney disease." She sighed and touched her fingers to the polished wood. "I had him for over eleven years." Vivian attempted a laugh, swiped at the tears on her cheek. "Boy, when it rains, it pours. I wasn't sure when to expect this, but it makes sense it would come now. The hits just keep coming."

"Vivian." Her name was the only thing he could think to say. The toys and cat things in the corner made sense now. She was giving it all away because her cat had died.

"Thanks." She sighed. "Boy, I'm a piece of work, aren't I? Can't begin to understand why I'm still single."

"I, for one, am glad you are." He took hold of her shoulders and turned her to face him. "I'm sorry about Toby."

"Thanks." Her smile was both sad and sentimental. "He was the best cat. My best friend. My shadow. Never left me alone. Because of him I didn't feel quite so..."

"Alone?" Nate supplied when it seemed she couldn't.

"Yeah." Her voice was thick. "Geez, you don't want me blubbering all over you." She stepped away, bent down and grabbed a bag of cat food out of a cabinet. "I didn't want all this going to waste." She quickly filled four of the bowls to the brim, set them aside then did the same with water in the others. "I've been feeding the neighborhood strays in his honor. He was an indoor kitty," she said as if that explained everything.

"A fitting tribute," Nate agreed. "I've never had a pet."

"No?" She looked shocked.

"My mother had little interest in taking care of us. I didn't dare try to add an animal into the mix." As always, he didn't let that thought carry him very far. "Let me take care of loading up the food. You take care of the cats."

Her eyes were clearer now, and the two of them traded positions. Once she slid the back door closed again, Nate spotted two cats hopping over the fence and diving straight at the food.

"You all ready to go?" he asked, once he added a couple of handfuls of ice and zipped up the soft-sided cooler. She had her still damp purse on the counter, along with a different bag to transfer her things into. He didn't comment when she slipped the box containing Toby's ashes into the bottom.

"Just need to get my laptop and some files together." She did so in record time, and pretty soon he was carrying the cooler, one small suitcase and another smaller bag out to the car. She had her laptop bag over her shoulder when she locked up the house. "I'm going to ask Eddie if he wouldn't mind getting my mail while I'm gone," she said.

"Good plan." Nate stayed near the car while she did just that. That Eddie thought of Vivian as lonely had done something to Nate's heart. It wasn't fair, what life did to some people. The last thing Vivian deserved was to be pitched headfirst into this mess with Dean Wexler and Marty DeBaccian. Then again, if she hadn't gone on that date, then Nate never would have met her, and that, he realized as he pulled out his cell phone and stashed SIM card, would have been a terrible shame.

"Did you get a call?" Vivian asked when she appeared at his side again. "Is there any word on Dean Wexler?"

"No. I was just thinking about a call I need to make." One he didn't want to make in front of her. Mainly because he had no way of knowing how this call was going to go. "Why don't you get on in? I'll be there in a sec."

"Okay." It was obvious she knew why he was asking her to, but she didn't argue.

The now familiar dread that wound its way inside him when his thoughts turned to his siblings did so at extraordinary speed. His time in Owl Creek last month had been cursory and brief, but necessary given the events surrounding his sister Lizzy's kidnapping. He hadn't hesitated when he'd heard about the family dinner, but he'd also had to face a lot of truth by doing so.

Things had ended well, but it wasn't as if they'd all gotten to know each other very well. They were still, for all intents and purposes, walking on eggshells around each other. At least, that was the way Nate and Sarah felt.

Neither Nate nor his sister had summoned up the courage to call any of them to see if that truly was the case.

"Well, you've got a chance now," Nate muttered as he dialed one of the numbers he'd been given. His pulse kicked into overdrive as the phone rang.

"Detective Colton. Speak."

"Fletcher, it's Nate. Colton." He paused. "Your brother." Nate winced. Brilliant. "Sorry. You know that." He pinched the bridge of his nose and squeezed his eyes shut. "I don't know if it's okay that I called—"

"Of course it's okay." Fletcher's no-nonsense tone was, as far as Nate knew, his default and not to be taken personally. "What's going on?"

"I don't think there's a way to summarize." The last twenty-four hours spun in on him, robbing him of words but solidifying the one thing he knew to be true. "But I also don't think there's anyone else I can trust. I need your help, Fletcher." He paused. "More specifically, I think I need Colton help."

Chapter 7

"Are you sure no one is following us?" Not for the first time, Vivian twisted around in the passenger seat to look out the back window. The snowcapped mountain vistas ahead really should have captured all her attention, but she was used to seeing them, having lived in the area most of her life.

How she envied the ease with which Nate—and just about everybody else on the planet—maneuvered the highways and roadways, especially in the wintertime. Snow drifted down and coated the car in a delicate dusting as she scanned the vehicles behind them.

"I'm sure."

"How do you know?"

"Because it's my job."

She gave him points for patience. She was on the verge of annoying herself; she could only imagine how her continued paranoia must be coming across.

"I'm watching for it, Vivian." He took hold of her hand and gave a gentle tug, one she took to mean she should turn back around. "You need to stop worrying."

"Apologies," she muttered. "It's my first time being targeted for death." She glanced over in time to see his jaw tense. "They say your sense of humor is the first thing to go when you're stressed."

"Mine just gets more obnoxious," he said, and when she tried to tug her hand free, he slipped his fingers between hers and squeezed. "You aren't alone in this, Vivian. I don't know what else I can say or do to convince you of that."

"I don't know, either." She stared straight ahead at the sign that said the turnoff for Owl Creek was only a few miles away. "Things like this don't happen to me, Nate."

"Things like this don't happen to most people," he assured her. "How about we get your mind off the possibility of being followed and play a round of twenty questions? Anything you want to know, ask me."

Bold move. Not one she would have made. Or would she? She looked at him for a long moment, pondering how he affected her emotional state. What was it about this man that had her thinking in completely different ways than she normally did? There was such ease with him, such comfort, that her life-long developed fears took an almost back seat to reality. "Anything I ask, you'll tell me the truth?"

"It wouldn't be much of a game if I didn't," he said. "Go ahead. Try me. Question one. Let's have it."

"How old are you?"

"Interesting way to start." His lips twitched. "Twenty-eight."

"Oh." She blinked, not sure whether to laugh or frown.

"For the record, I've always had a thing for older women."

She snort-laughed, covered her mouth in surprise when he chuckled. "I'm not that much older than you."

"Two whole years according to your driver's license."

"Yeah, well, that license also gives me permission to drive, and we both know how that tends to go."

"What did you do for your thirtieth birthday last month?"

She narrowed her eyes. "I didn't realize this game was reciprocal."

"How else am I going to find out more about you?" He tightened his hold on her hand. "Come on. Give. What did you do?"

"Ah." She sighed. "I met Lizzy at The Cellar in Owl Creek for some wine tasting."

"That's it?"

She shrugged. "I'm not big on birthdays." Birthdays always reminded her of her parents, and the fuzzy memories she did have of them faded with each passing year. "That's our happy place. I drove down, and we went there after...well, after she was back home."

"I hope Lizzy gave you a great birthday present, at least."

"She signed me up for multiple dating apps," she deadpanned and earned a gasp from him. "Kidding!" She laughed at getting one over on him. "Actually, she tracked down a rare edition of *Pride and Prejudice* for me. It's my favorite Jane Austen book."

"That explains why you have an entire shelf of copies in your living room."

She didn't know why, but the idea of him noticing things around her home actually warmed her.

"Okay, my turn again." She started to look back again, but he squeezed her hand hard.

"Every time you look back gives me an extra question."

She resisted temptation. This time. "Why aren't you married?"

"Wow. Going straight to it." He shook his head. A strand of hair fell across his forehead, giving him a bit of a rakish appearance with that smile of his. "I could go with the usual, just haven't found the right woman. Which is true. Being married to a cop isn't something most women aspire to." He shrugged as if it didn't much matter. "The truth is probably more in line with the fact that I have no frame of reference for the institution."

"Oh." She instantly regretted the impulsive decision to ask. "I'm sorry. I didn't mean to—"

"You ever notice how much you apologize?" he asked. "Honestly, Vivian. It's a perfectly fine question, and considering where we could have easily ended up last night, you should probably be brought up to speed on my familial situation. Not to mention we're headed right into the heart of Colton country." Nate gestured to the increasing signs identifying Owl Creek. "What all has Lizzy told you about the family?" His eyes were glossy and unreadable when he looked at her. "I'm not asking so I can decide what not to share. I just don't want to rehash what you already know."

"Okay." Vivian's mind raced. She'd always found the Colton family tree a bit...confusing. Overwhelming to be sure. Lizzy came from such a huge extended family while Vivian had well, Lizzy. "You, Sarah, Lizzy and her three brothers share the same mother, Jessie, and she walked away from that family when Lizzy was really young. Like three or four, I think. They were raised by their father, Buck Colton." She smiled. "I like Buck.

He's a nice guy. Loves his kids. You can always tell, you know?"

"I've only met him a few times, but you're right. He seems like a good guy," Nate agreed. "Far more gracious than he has any right to be. What Lizzy and her brothers and cousins recently found out was that Jessie walked away from them to take up with Buck's brother, Robert Colton."

"Robert was married to Jessie's twin sister, Jenny, correct?" She really didn't want to get any of this wrong. It felt…disrespectful somehow.

"Yes. Robert and Jenny have six kids. Chase, Fletcher, Wade, Ruby, Hannah and Frannie."

"Frannie owns a bookstore in Owl Creek." She felt rather proud at remembering that tidbit.

"She does. Book Mark It," Nate said. "Should have figured you'd know that. I'm betting that's how Lizzy got hold of that rare book for you."

"Lizzy mentioned that Robert Colton died earlier this year."

"Yes, he did," Nate confirmed. "Unfortunately, my mother used that opportunity to make a familial comeback." His mouth stretched into a tight smile. "One of my dumber moves, believing she extended an olive branch on our behalf." His jaw tensed as if gnashing his teeth together. "She took his dying as her opportunity to tell the entire family about me and Sarah." He winced. "And no, she didn't give us any warning. And they didn't exactly throw out the welcome mat."

"Eeesh." Vivian cringed.

"Definitely *eeesh*. Personally, I don't think my mother took two breaths before she tried to stake a claim on

Robert's money by presenting me and Sarah as two of his heirs. She literally used us as exhibits A and B."

"Oh." Vivian chewed on the inside of her cheek. "Wow. That's…" She tried to find the words. "I seem to remember Lizzy mentioning some additional unpleasantness about Robert's passing. So, Robert was your dad."

"Father," Nate corrected. "I don't recall him ever being a dad. He was gone a lot when I was younger, then pretty much vanished from our lives when I was ten. I saw him maybe a handful of times after that. The story goes he had a change of heart and went back full-time to Jenny and their kids." He winced. "Couldn't have sat very well with any of them knowing that Sarah and I were born at the same time Hannah and Frannie were."

"I suppose not."

"Sarah and I were teenagers when we found out our parents were never married. Then there was the fact that our father was *the* Robert Colton, who was primarily responsible for putting Owl Creek on the map."

Her heart went out to him. "That must have been a lot for a teenager to process."

"It's been a lot for everyone to process," Nate said with a hint of sadness in his voice. "Maybe more when you're an adult. One of the reasons Sarah and I drove out to Owl Creek a couple months ago, to break the ice and clear the air."

"Did it work?"

Nate shrugged. "Can't be sure. I'd say we're in a bit of a strained time of existence. Sarah wants so much to make a lasting connection with our half siblings. It's like a dream come true for her, the whole big-family thing. But given who our mother is, our newfound family isn't totally trusting. I don't blame them." He hit the turn signal and moved two lanes to the right. "I don't blame them one bit. Jessie is unpredictable at best, malicious and cruel at worst. My mother doesn't have the capacity to care about anyone other than herself, so whatever her motivations regarding exposing our existence, you can bet they're self-serving." He flashed her a look. "Which brings us back to your original question about marriage. My perception of the institution of marriage is all a bit... What's the word?"

"Skewed?" Vivian offered. "Tarnished? Tainted?"

"Those work well enough."

She couldn't quite reconcile why that sounded so sad. "So, between Robert and Jenny's kids and Jessie and Buck's kids, you went from having one sister to having..." She did the math. "Ten brothers and sisters?"

"Yep." He took the turnoff leading into downtown Owl Creek, circling around the off-ramp before veering off to the left. "You out of questions or did I shock you into silence?" He shifted his gaze to the rearview mirror as he'd been doing since they'd started driving.

"I guess I'm wondering what questions are appropriate. New ones have popped to mind since we started."

"Already told you, nothing's off-limits."

"Okay." Time to put that to the test. "So, Robert went back to Jenny. What happened with your mom?"

"Jessie? She spent a good few years playing the victim and the martyr. That takes real talent in case you're wondering. Despite none of us being willing to give her even the time of day."

"Lizzy's never talked about her," Vivian said. "She's only brought her up recently because of what happened after Robert died." Coming face-to-face with the mother who had walked away and never looked back must have been excruciating for her friend. She'd covered, of course, and played it off like it wasn't anything other than ridiculous family drama, but how could it not have hurt?

"Sometimes, I think Lizzy and her brothers got the better end of the deal." Nate made easy work of the traffic. "They had to deal with Jessie being gone. Sarah and I had to deal with her...well, *with* her. I readily admit which road I'd preferred to have walked."

Vivian frowned. There was a kind of detachment in his voice, a tone that belied more than a tinge of resentment where his mother was concerned. It was, Vivian thought sadly, something she had no reference for. The vague memories she had of her mother, of both her parents, were so fragmented she couldn't piece them together. She'd tried to. For years. But they were just... ghosts.

"Hearing all this explains a lot about Lizzy. How she was growing up," Vivian said. Lizzy had always had serious trust issues and more than a suspicious nature when it came to anyone looking to the Coltons for a payout. "You said you were a teenager when you found out about your siblings."

"I was fifteen," Nate said. "I played basketball that year in high school. The team traveled to Owl Creek for a game. It was around the time some new construction project was getting off the ground. We were staying in this fancy—well, fancy to me—hotel in town. I went downstairs to work out and stopped in the lobby. There he was, my father, on the front page of the local

paper. Along with his family. Jenny and all the kids."
He hesitated. "His real family. Funny." Nate shook his
head. "As shocking as that was—and believe me, I read
everything I could about Robert Colton after that—seeing that picture, being in Owl Creek, walking through
the town he was responsible for, everything about my
own life suddenly made a lot more sense. It also made
me a lot more self-conscious. I spent years worried about
what would happen if the truth got out."

Her heart broke for the boy he'd been. How alone he
must have felt in those days following his discovery.
"But you didn't say anything to anyone."

"There was no point. I told Sarah a few weeks later.
Once I'd worked everything out so I could answer her
questions." A flicker of bitterness crossed his face. "I
quit the basketball team first, though. I didn't need or
want any more surprise trips to Owl Creek. We decided
together to keep it to ourselves. We figured if our father
wanted anything to do with us, he'd be the one to reach
out. He'd already messed with the two of us. We didn't
want to be the cause of destroying his other family."

Sympathy swirled through her. No. His mother had
taken care of that, hadn't she? "I don't know that I'd have
been that generous."

"It wasn't generous," Nate said. "It was survival. We
had enough to deal with where Jessie was concerned,
and honestly, if we had done things differently, who
knows what might have happened." He frowned, gaze
pinned to the rearview mirror. "Huh." He pulled his
hand free of hers.

"What?" Forgetting the potential cost of looking, she

turned around, scanned the steady stream of cars. "Do you see something?" Everything seemed to blur together.

"Maybe." He turned right at the next light without signaling. "Let's see what this might be about."

Vivian turned back around, gripped the seat in her hands and squeezed until her fingers went numb.

"Nothing bad's going to happen, Viv." He didn't look at her this time, just kept his eyes straight ahead or on the mirror as he drove. "We're in this together, remember? Do me a favor? Write down this plate number?" He read off the letters and numbers once she took her phone out of the glove box and began typing.

He took a left, bringing them through a residential area coated with a light dusting of snow and varying degrees of holiday cheer. One fence line in particular boasted oversize Santa hats perched atop dividing posts. When she let her gaze drift to the passenger-door mirror, an SUV similar to Nate's turned behind them a distance back.

"That car look familiar?"

"No." She shook her head. "It's not the one that ran me off the road."

"You sure?" He hit the gas, and they sped up. The car still followed, but maintained its same speed, and the distance between them grew.

"That one had a weird decal on the front window." She gasped. Stacy had been right. When her mind relaxed, it seemed to set things free. "I just remembered that. I'm—"

He shot her a look that included an arched and challenging brow.

"Not sorry I didn't tell you before," she corrected herself. He was right. She really did spend a lot of time apologizing for innocuous comments or thoughts.

"You remembered now. That's all that matters. We'll put a call in to my lieutenant when we stop. Bring him up to date. Get that information added to the case file."

"Are we going to stop?" She couldn't have stopped her voice from squeaking if she'd tried.

"Not yet." He took another couple of turns and got them back on the road they were previously on. He tapped on his dashboard screen, scrolled down a list of names. Vivian frowned when he hit Call for Fletcher Colton.

Nerves tangled around themselves in her stomach. As close as she was to Lizzy, she hadn't seen her friend's brothers in years. When it came to the extended members of her family, she must have been ten the last time she was around any of them. "I thought you said you don't talk to your brothers?"

"Not on a regular basis, I don't." Nate said. "Given the situation we're in, couldn't really think of anyone else to ask for help."

"Nate." The deep voice bounced around the car like an echo. "You here yet?"

"We just got into Owl Creek. I've got you on Speaker with me and Vivian," Nate told him. "I'm pretty sure we've picked up a tail."

"Oh?" The alertness that came through on that one word added to Vivian's anxiety. "You close enough for a description?"

Nate rattled off the bare minimum. "And we've got a plate. Viv?"

"Hi, Fletcher." She swallowed the lump of anxiety lodged in her throat. "I'm sure you don't remember me—"

"Lizzy's friend from school," Fletcher said. "Sure. You spent Christmas at the ranch with us one year. You were what, fourteen?"

"Thirteen, actually." A very awkward, silent thirteen. Not that she'd ever needed to say much with Lizzy around. That was one of the reasons they got along so well. Vivian was always happy to let her take the lead. "It's nice of you to remember."

"That was the year Lizzy stuck a fake rattlesnake in my underwear drawer," Fletcher said. "I broke two of dad's favorite lamps trying to kill it."

Vivian's lips twitched. She'd forgotten about that.

"Every Christmas since," Fletcher went on, "someone buys me a lamp. The ugliest lamp they could possibly find. I hope no one shares that story with Kiki."

"Kiki?" Vivian asked before she thought better of it.

"She's a DJ here in Owl Creek. We're...dating."

Vivian shot Nate a look at the same time he gave her his own. They grinned at each other but didn't say anything more until Fletcher asked for the plate number.

Vivian read it back and was answered by silence.

"Well." Fletcher coughed. "Okay, then. How about you come on by the station for a bit? I'll meet you outside, and we'll see what the driver does when he realizes where you've led him."

"Okay." Nate frowned. "Is something going on?" He looked back into the mirror. The car was backing off but still visible.

"Nope. See you in a few." Fletcher disconnected before Nate could push harder.

"Didn't take long to get strange," Nate muttered. "Okay, then. Owl Creek police station it is." He accelerated through a yellow light and sped up again. "And the sooner the better."

Chapter 8

Nate's constant assurances to Vivian that no one would be following them had been uttered in good, solid faith. The chances DeBaccian's men would take another risk by running Vivian off the road twice in one day were, at least to Nate's mind, a million to one. And that wasn't even taking into account Nate's being along for the ride. Going after a cop was something DeBaccian wouldn't be stupid enough to do. Doubt niggled. Or would he?

That idea did not sit well. Still, lying to Vivian, intentionally or otherwise, was not something he ever wanted to do. Faith and trust were difficult enough to establish and build, especially with someone with Vivian's relatively solitary past.

"You're worried," Vivian said. Her voice was as quiet as he expected, as if she was worried about startling or offending him.

"A little." The full day was heading into the evening. Hard to believe things had been almost normal this morning when she'd walked into his kitchen wearing nothing but a T-shirt. What he wouldn't give to go back and take the day in a different direction.

"But going to the station is a good thing, isn't it?" The uncertainty rang loudly in Nate's ears.

"It is." He couldn't shake the idea that Fletcher knew something he didn't. It wasn't brotherly instinct—they didn't know each other well enough for Nate to claim that prerogative. But cop instinct was a completely different story. "You're going to be safe here, Vivian. I promise."

Her smile was almost wide enough to convince him she believed him.

Downtown Owl Creek opened up ahead and welcomed them like an old, festive frenemy. Nate's hands tightened on the steering wheel. He'd spent years limiting his trips here to official business and necessary excursions. Being this close to the Coltons was a lesson in tempting fate, and that was one thing Nate went out of his way to avoid doing.

Driving in like this, with his own trust placed firmly in the hands of a brother who would no doubt be happier not knowing Nate existed felt like a dangerous game to play. Especially where Vivian's life was concerned. But it was Vivian's life he was worried about, and—honestly? He couldn't think of anyone he could trust more when it came to her safety.

It was a bit like driving through a time portal, he noticed, as they made their way through town.

The town had developed into a year-round resort with skiing and other winter-centric activities taking center stage, yet during the warmer summer months, people flocked to the lake and consistent sunshine as a getaway. In February, the winter carnival would kick into high gear and feature incredible bigger-than-life snow sculptures, dog-sled racing and countless other events that would bring in a good deal of cash to the local economy. From the Tap Out Brewery that served local ales and pub grub, to Frannie's Book Mark It, the town had developed into a significant destination both for travelers and those looking for a laid-back, more relaxed way of life. Varying decor highlighted storefronts, walkways and lampposts. With the snowcapped mountains the perfect backdrop, it was like a kind of Christmas village had been plopped into the middle of civilization.

While the drive from Boise to Owl Creek was a good two hours, travel time—at least how Nate drove—from Vivian's town house was just shy of forty-five. Which meant the police station came up fast once they started down the main, business-lined thoroughfare.

"There's a space right in front of the station." Vivian pointed ahead of them. "Doris Day parking."

"What?" Nate glanced at her.

"You know, classic movies? How Doris Day always found a parking space in the front of wherever she was going? Sorry. I think of weird facts when I'm nervous." And with the way she kept looking at the car following them, she was most definitely nervous.

Nate shook his head. He couldn't recall the last time he'd watched a movie that didn't include explosions and car chases.

He pulled into the spot she'd pointed out, his attention partially divided and focused on the man standing with his back against the wall beside the entrance to the Owl Creek PD.

It was entirely possible, Nate thought, that Detective Fletcher Colton had a natural tolerance to the cold. With his worn jeans, thick, snow-friendly work boots and a khaki button-down shirt displaying his police badge, he may as well have been sunning himself in the middle of July.

"You look alike." Vivian's comment startled Nate back to reality.

"Do we?" Of course they did. Most of the male Colton offspring in these parts shared the brown hair and lighter color eyes. None of them could particularly look down on one another; height was another shared family trait. As was a natural propensity for athletic, fit builds and a low tolerance for bull. Yeah. Looking at Fletcher now, he definitely saw the resemblance.

Nate shifted, looked behind them as the car that had been following them pulled to a sudden stop in the middle of the street a few spots back. "Okay, here we go. Stay here."

Nate jumped out of the car, hand going to his back waistband for his weapon. He heard Fletcher yell his name, but it got carried off by the wind as Nate pulled out his gun and lifted it, both hands locked around the hilt, finger pressed against the side of the trigger. He aimed straight at the driver.

"Police!" Nate yelled. "Out of the car, now! Slowly!" He gestured with the gun as the man behind the wheel held up both hands. The sun visor obscured most of his face, but not so much that Nate didn't see the flicker of humor quirk his lips. A quick glimpse to the passenger seat told Nate that at least this guy was alone. Unless there was someone in the back seat...

"Nate—" Fletcher's voice sounded directly behind him now, but Nate wasn't going to take any chances. Not with Vivian's life.

"I said out!" Nate yelled again as he advanced.

Out of the corner of his eye, he saw Vivian push open the door and drop to the ground. She was bundled into the jacket she'd pulled out of the closet on their way out of her town house. Even from a distance, he could see her shivering.

"Nate, put the gun away," Fletcher said calmly.

"Not until he's out of the car." Despite the cold, he didn't shiver. He didn't move. He simply stared.

"Okay." Fletcher stepped around and motioned to the driver. "You heard him!" Fletcher called. "You'd best get out."

Nate stood there, staring as the door opened as he wondered why Fletcher was acting so nonchalant. Until the man stepped out of the car. Nate balked, glared and lowered his gun to his side. "Son of a— Max?" Max Colton, Nate's half brother through Jessie, slid out of the car, arms raised, an unfamiliar smile stretching across his mouth. "Did you skip surveillance-duty training back at the FBI?"

Max's expression came across as it usually did where Nate was concerned: guarded, suspicious and bordering on dark. But also, for the first time, Nate thought he saw impressed. That was a boost he hadn't expected.

"When did you spot me?" Max asked after he exchanged a hearty handshake and quick bro hug with Nate.

"About two seconds after you pulled out of the gas station parking lot just off the freeway." Nate holstered his gun, adrenaline draining. Only then did he begin to feel the December cold seep into his bones.

"We wanted to make sure you two were covered as

soon as you hit town," Fletcher said on a laugh. "This is one for the books. Max Colton, serial-killer hunter, bested by his baby brother."

Nate froze. Baby brother? It took a moment to shake himself clear of all that thought encompassed. He was still a bit foggy when Vivian appeared and touched his arm.

"Everything okay?"

"Yeah." Her question had him nodding absently. "Fine. I might have overreacted." As Max and Fletcher closed the distance, cars crawled around Max's SUV. Out of instinct or protection or perhaps wanting to make a point he'd never anticipated making, Nate slipped his arm around Vivian's shoulders and drew her against his side. He immediately felt warmer. "Vivian Maylor, you probably already know my…" He stopped at the other two men's sharpened gazes. He swore, shook his head. "Well, hell. Fletcher already started it. Might as well start to get past it. Fletcher and Max Colton." He swallowed hard around unexpected emotion. "My brothers."

"Of course." Vivian held out her hand. "Fletcher of the rattlesnake Christmas."

Fletcher grunted and grinned when Max chuckled.

"And Max." She shook both their hands. "It's been a while. Lizzy said you only get back to Owl Creek between cases."

"True enough," Max said, and immediately shoved his hands into the front pockets of his jeans. "I've got some downtime at the moment. Fletcher said you two ran into some trouble back in Boise." He eyed Nate, then Fletcher. "Glad you thought to call. Looking forward to being read in."

It was on the tip of Nate's tongue to admit he was out of options, but there was no need to go burning down a just built bridge. He hadn't known what to expect coming to Owl Creek, but he was planning to make the most of it.

"I'm waiting on a call to make sure the house is ready for you." Fletcher motioned them to the station.

"House?" Vivian blinked. "What house?"

"Max, park that thing somewhere legal, will you? We'll wait on you." Fletcher slapped a hand on the back of his shoulder before he motioned for Nate and Vivian to follow him to the station house. "You two hungry?"

"Not really," Nate said.

"We have food in the car," Vivian explained as if she thought Nate's response bordered on rude. "I cook to relax, and I'm feeling ready for a distraction."

"Understood. And lucky Nate." Fletcher pulled open the door and waved them in ahead of him. "I have a bet with Wade that Nate lives on toaster pastries and root beer."

"Close," Nate said without missing a beat. "Brownies and Mountain Dew. You going to tell me why you thought the escort into town necessary?" Nate asked the second the door closed behind them.

"I am." Fletcher accepted a clipboard offered to him by a khaki-uniformed officer, scribbled his name at the bottom before handing it back. Another officer handed him a manila file folder, and he nodded his thanks. "Had a long talk with your Lieutenant Haig a little while ago. He gave me the rundown. Extra precautions seemed warranted. Our break room doubles as our conference room, so we can talk in there. Monroe?" Fletcher rapped his knuckles on the counter, and another officer, this one looking as if he'd just stepped out of high school, shot to attention. "Send Max back when he gets here, will you?"

"Sure thing, Detective." Monroe's baby face stretched into an eager smile.

Nate sighed. He remembered being that young, but had he ever been so…innocent?

The station house was nicer than Nate expected. Cozier, with its wood paneling and collection of framed photographs, it didn't have quite the harsh, sterile yet aged feel his own station house did. Images of Owl Creek officers over the years were displayed among other ones featuring town events both big and small. Funny—the place had an unexpectedly homier feel than most police stations he'd been in.

"I'm going to make a quick stop in the ladies' room." Vivian pointed to one of the doors they'd passed before disappearing behind it.

"Does Lizzy know what's going on?" Fletcher asked as he grabbed a couple of clean mugs out of an overhead cabinet. "Coffee?"

"Yeah, thanks." At the rate he was going, coffee would soon replace the blood running through his veins. "With Vivian, you mean? Not that I know of." He grimaced. "I suggested Vivian call her, but she refused. Mentioned that Lizzy had enough to cope with at the moment." He paused. "How is Lizzy doing?"

"Okay." Fletcher didn't seem of the mind to elaborate. "She's good at covering, though. She mentioned using Vivian as a sounding board on more than one occasion. That's good since the rest of us have kind of been hovering. Ajay's been good for her."

That bit of information didn't surprise Nate in the least. He'd been impressed with Ajay Wright, a K9 search and rescue agent. No doubt Ajay would view what happened to Lizzy from every angle and help her accordingly.

"How about you?" Fletcher eyed him with more caution than Nate felt comfortable with. "The last few months can't have been easy for you. How've you been doing?"

Nate couldn't tell if Fletcher was being polite, big brotherly or simply curious. "Okay, actually." He shrugged. "I'll be doing better once a psychopath criminal isn't chasing after Vivian."

"I hear that," Fletcher muttered. "We seem to be a magnet for psychopaths these days." He paused as Max strolled into the room. "Found your way back here okay, then?" he teased. "I thought about leaving some breadcrumbs..."

"Ha-ha." Max glowered, but in a way that had Nate laughing on the inside. An unexpected yet sadly familiar pang of envy struck him with pinpoint accuracy. He'd spent years wondering what it would be like to have a relationship with his brothers. The brothers who hadn't known Nate existed. Sure, it would have been easier on everyone if he'd remained an unknown Colton element, but even now he could feel those family ties knitting and forming. "This is where you fill me in."

"Just waiting on Vivian." Fletcher motioned for them to take a seat in one of the chairs around a large, circular table.

"Got anything to eat around here?" Max started yanking open cabinets that had more office supplies inside than munchies.

"Doesn't Della feed you?" Fletcher teased.

Max glowered again but gripped an open bag of nacho tortilla chips in one hand. "Our brother, the wannabe comedian," he said to Nate. "We don't starve," Max said in a way that made Nate wonder if Max ever gave a straight answer. "Fletcher mentioned a guy named Marty De-Baccian."

"Are you familiar with him?" Nate pulled out a chair as Vivian joined them, quietly sitting beside him. Without even asking, Fletcher poured her a mug of coffee and set it in front of her.

"No, not really...we've never crossed paths." Max shook his head, drank some coffee and winced. "Wow." His eyes almost watered. "Congratulations, Fletcher. Takes some major talent to make a brew worse than what I get at headquarters."

"Look at you with the compliments." Fletcher closed the door before joining them at the table. "Eat your chips. CliffsNotes version—" he said, looking to Max "—Nate and his fellow detectives in Boise have been building a case against Marty DeBaccian. Wannabe crime lord with his hands in all kinds of dirty dealings."

"Up until last year, he'd made a name for himself loan-sharking and getting in on the local betting action," Nate added. "He's got a taste for things now. You name it, he's made a play for it. Drugs, extortion, protection rackets, which goes hand in hand with money laundering through local businesses whose owners aren't in a position to say no."

"Garden variety scum bucket, got it," Max said.

Nate glanced at Vivian. She had wrapped both hands around the brown coffee mug, but she'd hunched her shoulders and scrunched down almost into a shell of herself. Nate rested a hand on her knee, gave her a comforting squeeze. He'd needed it, but feeling the tension ease a bit in her body told him she'd needed it as well. She sat up straighter, offered him a quick smile that eased his mind a bit.

"DeBaccian's been building himself up as a kind of overlord of whatever criminal activity is running rampant in the city," Nate said. "I've had my eye on Dean Wexler for a while, trying to link him to a number of burglaries of single women. He's got a record that makes that possible. I thought if I could make the connection, I could use that information to flip him on DeBaccian."

"Apparently DeBaccian doesn't like it when people work outside of his purview," Fletcher added. "He likes to take his cut of the action."

"Which is where I come in," Vivian admitted. "Not the action part." She frowned, as if reconsidering her words. "I met Dean on a dating app. Seems I was his next planned target."

Nate didn't miss the ice flashing in both his brothers' eyes.

"Needless to say, our first date didn't go as expected." Vivian summarized it far more precisely than Nate probably would have. "Now Dean is in an induced coma, and I've become a material witness."

"Against Wexler?" Max's brows shot up.

"Against DeBaccian," Nate said. "He was in the car when Wexler was shot."

"And you saw him." Whatever Max had been thinking, his eyes turned to steel.

"Yes," Vivian said firmly. "I saw him."

"And he knows she did. Someone trying to run her off the road this morning proves that."

"It proves something, and I'm fine," she said at Max's suddenly sharp gaze. "Lucky, but fine. But Nate didn't think it was safe for me to be anywhere familiar or predictable for a while."

"Nate's right," Fletcher said. "And he was right to call. Lizzy would never forgive us if we didn't do everything we could to help."

"I appreciate that." Vivian's mouth curved. "And the trouble you're going to."

"It's no trouble, Vivian," Fletcher said. "If anything, Nate calling gave us all a bit of a kick. We're family. We need to start acting like it. We appreciate the faith, however tenuous."

Nate wasn't entirely sure what to do with that statement. So he did what he always did when emotions started clouding his judgment. He shifted back to the job. "You said you spoke with my lieutenant?" Nate asked.

"Yeah." Fletcher took a deep breath. "No change in Wexler's condition. He's continuing the protective duty you ordered in the hospital. No joy on the burned-out car they've identified from the drive-by."

"Awesome." Not a surprise, but still disappointing. That meant Vivian's description of DeBaccian was the only evidence they had that he was involved.

"There's been a bit more luck with the SUV from this morning." Fletcher leaned back and retrieved the folder he'd been handed at the front desk. "He emailed this over so it was waiting for you." He set it on the table and flipped it open. "The car was found abandoned about ten miles from where they hit Vivian. Same MO as the first car."

"They didn't do such a great job, this time, did they?" So much of the car was still intact. A break for them for sure.

Vivian gasped, pointed at the half-worn decal in the bottom corner of the windshield. "That's what I saw. The sticker. That's what I remember seeing in the mirror."

Nate's hand curled into a fist. He'd known they'd gotten close enough to ram her off the road, but so close that she got a clear look at a sticker? He repressed a shudder.

"Your lieutenant recognized the logo from a strip club in downtown Boise," Fletcher said. "Place called Shake It Loose."

Nate's stomach tightened. "That's one of DeBaccian's properties." He'd spent an unholy number of hours parked across the street while Dean Wexler was inside. "He's either getting careless or desperate."

"Or arrogant," Max said. "Never underestimate the destructive power of ego. It takes a lot more of these criminals down than you think."

"True enough," Fletcher agreed. "Evidence is still working on the SUV, but they've got a couple of sets of prints so far. They're rushing it through the system." Fletcher looked to Max. "Anything you can do about that?"

"Sure." Max shrugged. "But I'd advise you to leave me in reserve." He pulled the file close and scanned the reports, flipping up the pages. "I'd want to do this on the up and up, and if I do that, you⬤⬤deral interest, which could pull this case out of yo⬤⬤rol." He eyed

Nate. "Unless you're looking for someone with FBI contacts to take the lead?"

Nate took his time answering. He wanted to make a good case against DeBaccian. Federal or state, locked up was locked up. His ego required a win. He'd worked this case a long time and had DeBaccian in his sights for months. He didn't like the idea of handing it off, even unofficially, without getting at least some credit.

Beside him, he could feel Vivian shaking. She was holding it together, but the longer this went on, the more anxiety and fear she was going to develop, and he didn't like the idea of being responsible for that—it was even worse than losing credit.

"I want DeBaccian taken down and out. I want Vivian out of the line of fire." He couched his words carefully. "Would I like a hand in that? Absolutely. But I'm more interested in seeing his operations shut down. Boise needs him gone." And so did Vivian. "If that means bringing the FBI in officially, I'm fine with it. Not my call, though." He looked back to Fletcher. "My lieutenant would have to take that up the chain in Boise PD."

Fletcher glanced at Max. "We're in a holding pattern for now on that front. He's got surveillance up and running on a number of DeBaccian's businesses and hangouts and his main residence. When he pops his head up, Haig will let us know." Something akin to admiration flickered in his brothers' eyes when they looked back at him. "In the meantime, it sounds like we're all on the same page."

Max grimaced, leaned to the side and pulled out his wallet. When he slapped twenty bucks into Fletcher's hand, Nate frowned. "What's this about?"

"That's about Fletcher betting you'd put the end re-sult and Vivian's safety before your arrest record," Max said. "I was less...confident."

"Let me guess." Nate didn't have to hear more than that to understand Max's meaning. "Given who our mother is, you were thinking the apple didn't fall too far?"

He started to pull his hand away from Vivian's knee, but she dropped her own hand under the table and covered his. When she curled her fingers under and squeezed, he felt a boost of confidence and understanding surge through his system.

"More like birds of a feather," Max said easily. "But that's neither here nor there at the moment." His gaze slipped over Vivian, as if he didn't want to discuss their family drama in her presence.

"I know about your mother," Vivian said quietly. "I know the generalities of what she did going back to when you all were kids. Lizzy brought me up to date the last time I saw her. And, just so you know, Nate's been perfectly up front about his and Sarah's situation where Jessie Colton is concerned."

"Vivian—" Nate began.

"You all are Texas two-stepping around this, and no offense, but I've got enough to worry about without having to learn to dance," she said in a tone Nate hadn't heard from her before. "Nate's not his mother, Max. No more than you are. From the time this whole nightmare started for me, Nate has been the only consistent thing I could hold on to. Whatever else you might think of him, he's an honorable man who only has the family's best interests at heart."

The doubt in Max's eyes faded, not completely, but

enough that Nate felt grateful to Vivian for knocking down at least one invisible wall between them.

"It's taking us some time to come to terms with a lot of what happened over the past thirty years," Fletcher said slowly. "We got blindsided when Dad died. It's obvious a lot of mistakes were made."

"Yes, they were," Vivian insisted. "But by Robert and Jessie. Not Nate or Sarah. Not that anyone asked me, but I think you're all lucky to have them as siblings. So either talk it all out or set it aside at least until I can go home and get back to my quiet, unassuming life."

Nate couldn't have stopped the wave of affection washing over him if he'd tried. "I was wrong." He squeezed her hand. "You would have made a fantastic cheerleader."

Her cheeks went bright pink, and her hand tightened around his.

"There's something else your lieutenant thought you should know," Fletcher said. "Regarding a Detective Jim Sullivan."

"Let me guess," Nate muttered. "He's complaining about my being involved with the case."

"No one knows what Detective Sullivan's doing," Fletcher said slowly. "He's disappeared."

"He's...what?" Nate frowned. "What does that mean?"

"Would you like the dictionary definition or—"

"Max." Fletcher glared at his cousin and shook his head. "All your lieutenant said was that they've been unable to make contact with Sullivan since he left the station after Vivian's session with the sketch artist. He'll get back to us when he knows more."

"Get back to *us*?" Nate hedged.

Fletcher didn't flinch when he met his confused gaze. "If DeBaccian and his men are looking for Vivian, then they're probably looking for you by now. The less communication you have with anyone back in Boise, the better. For the foreseeable future, what you're told, I'm told." He looked over to Max. "You have what you need?"

"Yeah." Max leaned forward again, reached into his back pocket and pulled out a flip phone. He slid it across the table to Nate. "This is untraceable," he said easily. "A few numbers programmed in. Your lieutenant's. Mine, Fletcher's. And Chase's." He paused. "I didn't include Sarah's. I didn't have it, and I wasn't sure how much she knows."

"Nothing," Nate said instantly. "She knows nothing, and I'd like to keep it that way."

Max nodded. "Understood."

Relief surged through him. His sister was a schoolteacher, for heaven's sake. The last thing he wanted to do was put her in the sights of a career criminal. The further away she was from all this, the better. He scrolled through the solitary page of numbers. "Chase." Chase Colton was CEO of Colton Properties. He didn't have anything to do with law enforcement. "Why Chase?"

"Because it's thanks to him you two have a place to hole up until this is all settled." As if on cue, Fletcher's cell phone vibrated. He looked at the screen, shook his head in mild disbelief. "Speak of the devil. Looks like we're all set." He got to his feet and motioned for them to follow. "Let's get you two settled in."

Chapter 9

"You look like you've been caught in a whirlwind."

Nate's comment had Vivian pulling her attention away from the scenic, winding drive through the outskirts of Owl Creek and back to the reality of her current situation. "I kind of feel like it," she said. "From the outside, the Colton family feels like a force of nature."

"Newsflash," Nate said as he followed Fletcher's marked police SUV. "Doesn't feel much different from that on the inside." Behind them, Max followed, this time keeping a fair distance.

She wanted to smile, wanted to believe he meant that in good humor, but she couldn't be sure. The tension among the three brothers had been palpable. So much needed to be talked about, but she doubted it was ever going to happen where those three men were concerned. Not without a bit of a nudge. Which is what she'd been attempting to do by sticking her nose into something that was most definitely not her business.

"It's a pretty drive." She'd been to Owl Creek plenty of times over the years, mostly to meet up with Lizzy, but during the holidays, not so much. This time of year was always hard for her. It wasn't necessarily the being alone that triggered it, but the reminder that she was. Maybe it was being here with Nate or maybe the anxiety from the past few days, but she found herself feeling far more lighthearted about the season.

She loved how the dusting of snow cast the passing homes into a kind of exhibit in an art gallery. December in Idaho definitely put on a beautiful show. Add to it the festive outdoor lighting, the occasional decorated trees and decked-out front porches, and it was almost like stepping into a painting. The backdrop of snowy mountains conjured a longing for simpler, nature-focused times rather than the technological roller coaster the world found itself on these days. She had to remind herself, frequently, that it wasn't chance that had brought her to Owl Creek, or even that had put her in the vicinity of Nate Colton, but violence and danger that, even now, stalked her.

Surreal didn't come close to describing her current state. But she found herself wanting to push through the fear and embrace what had come to pass. Since walking into that restaurant the other night, she felt as if she were on some kind of self-awareness journey. One that was most definitely aided by the man sitting beside her.

Never in her wildest dreams would she have imagined finding herself traversing snowy mountain roads with someone who, near as she could fathom, might be responsible for reminding her she had a pulse. And a heart.

"Any idea where we're headed?" she asked.

"Not a clue." Nate did not sound happy about that, but she wondered if he realized the trust he'd displayed in the past few hours. He had, for all intents and purposes, placed both their lives in his brothers' hands, and that, she thought as her heart cracked open wide enough for a fraction of the Colton men to spill in, might make this entire situation worth it. "At this point, I wouldn't be surprised if it's a two-room shack with a padlock on the door."

She laughed, happy to pile onto the ridiculous suspicion, only to have every thought tip out of her brain. Fletcher veered off to the right and soon stopped at a guard post situated outside a large, iron-gated community.

"What the—" Nate's mutter only echoed her own disbelief. Eyes wide, she took in the vast area around and in front of them. The intricate welding of the gates offered both protection and elegant decor that stretched in both directions as far as she could see. "Guess the family business is doing pretty well."

The young, uniformed woman leaning out of the security office was pointing beyond the gate that was currently sliding open. She nodded and waved Fletcher through. Nate pulled up and powered down his window.

"Detective Colton." The woman offered a solid, welcoming smile. "Ms. Maylor. I'm Maya Baxter. Welcome to Colton Crossing."

"Nice to meet you, Maya." Because Nate seemed a bit tongue-tied, Vivian leaned across the center console and rested her hand on Nate's arm.

"Chase will give you the rundown for how to contact us here at the security office," Maya told them. "Someone will be here twenty-four seven. We've been made aware of your situation and will be on alert for anything out of the ordinary. If you have any questions or concerns, call the office at any time."

"Appreciate that," Nate said finally before he followed Fletcher's vehicle through the gate. Vivian checked her passenger-side mirror, saw Max stop for his intro then nip through the gate. "Apparently, I missed notice of this place in the family newsletter."

Vivian grabbed hold of his hand and squeezed. "This isn't easy for you, is it?"

"Entering Shangri-la?" His attempt at humor sounded strained.

"I meant dealing with your brothers. Your family." But he had a point. The sprawling homes that made up Colton Crossing ranged in size. Some were smaller, bungalow-type homes while others stood two stories with wide, wraparound porches. The complex was obviously in various stages of construction. She counted a few dozen homes that appeared completed, while other foundations were mapped out, and other cleared-out areas were no doubt going to begin construction once the snow stopped falling.

It was only when she looked past Nate and out beyond the security gate that she noticed all of them offered a stunning view of the mountains along with Owl Creek nestled into the valley below.

"I don't think they're taking us to a shack with a padlock."

"I think you're right." Nate waved at Fletcher, who after parking and climbing out of his car, indicated he should pull into the long driveway just beyond. When he stopped the car, they both leaned forward and gawked up at the house in front of them. "Am I the only one thinking both your place and mine would fit inside this place?"

"You are not." So much for cozy and close quarters.

Disappointment and relief crashed against each other inside her. Something told her she and Nate could go days inside without seeing each other.

"I'll come back for our things." Nate pushed open his door and came around to open hers. "Looks like we aren't in Boise anymore." As if completely normal, he took hold of her hand, and they walked down the driveway side by side.

Fletcher and Max stood at the end of the walkway with another, slightly older man wearing a suit beneath his long wool coat. Vivian couldn't help but think he'd stepped off the cover of a men's quarterly magazine. Slightly lankier than his brothers and cousins, he had a professionalism about him that screamed competence and success.

"Nate." The man pulled one hand out of his coat pocket and extended it. "Good to see you again."

"Chase."

"Welcome to Colton Crossing." Chase's smile came a bit easier than either Fletcher's or Max's had, and she could feel Nate relax a little. "Ms. Maylor."

"Vivian, please."

"Vivian." Chase nodded in approval. "Welcome. I'm afraid the house is a little sparse furnishings-wise. We've got the bare minimum set up since this is going to be our first market model, but it should be enough for the two of you. On the plus side, there's a furnished office, and Nate mentioned you needed a place to work."

She probably looked a bit doe-eyed when she glanced up at Nate.

"Shall we?" Chase turned on his heel and took the lead.

"Like we're going to say no?" Vivian muttered so only Nate could hear.

They followed Chase inside, their footfalls echoing on the large porch landing. Up two steps and through an enormous, heavy wooden door. Inside, the foyer opened up and branched off into multiple hallways and directions.

"You met Maya down at the guard house," Chase said and led them straight ahead and off to the left. "The security company we've hired has been thoroughly vetted by multiple security experts, including SecuritKey and Max here."

"I love running background checks," Max said from where he trailed behind them. "Not that Sloan needed double-checking. I'm curious, Chase. Did you visit Versailles before you came up with the plans to this house or did you just wing it?"

"We call this the Colton-size house," Chase said easily. "Lots of room for a large, ever-expanding family. We've still got some touch-ups to do on the other finished homes, but this one is move-in ready. Permission to enter?" he called.

"Ack! Two seconds!" a female voice called back before a blond head popped around the corner. "Seriously. Just…" She held up a couple of fingers and had them stopping in the hallway.

"Ruby takes this kind of thing rather seriously," Fletcher said as he leaned back against the light yellow wall. "Especially these days."

"What kind of thing, exactly?" Vivian asked.

"Three things, actually," Max said. "Homecomings, the holidays and surprises."

"I'm guessing that makes us the family trifecta," Nate said.

"Okay!" A curvy, dark-haired woman with deep auburn tips and brown eyes jumped into view and waved them in. "Hey, Detective." She waggled her eyebrows at Fletcher, who moved in to catch her around the waist and pull her in for a kiss. "Nice to see you, too," she murmured and looked into his eyes in a way that had Vivian thinking they should all be someplace else. "You must be Nate." She held out her hand. "And Vivian. I'm Kiki Shelton. Ruby and Sloan recruited me to lend a hand."

"A hand for… Oh." Vivian blinked at the sight in front of her.

Not only was there a gourmet kitchen fit for a houseful of kings and queens, but the attached great room boasted a deep, comfy sofa, large-screen television and an enormous seven-foot Christmas tree in the corner. Lights had been strung to the point of setting it aflame with glowing white bulbs and a beautiful gold star sitting atop.

Two large plastic bins sat beside the tree, crammed full with colorful boxes and shiny ornaments.

"Hi. I'm Sloan Presley. We thought you could do with some holiday cheer." The woman stepped under Chase's outstretched arm and gave Vivian and Nate a wave. "There's more in the boxes if you want to play yourselves." She had her thick, curly dark hair pulled back from her round, friendly face. "Seeing as you're going to be stuck here for a little while, might as well pretty the place up."

Vivian was agog. The place was already prettied up near as she could tell. "The tree's a lovely addition. Thank you." The only other time she'd ever seen such a grand tree had been that aforementioned holiday she'd spent at the Colton ranch. "It wasn't necessary to go to so much trouble."

"No trouble at all." Ruby Colton, a familiar face from Vivian's childhood, came over and nudged Nate with her shoulder. If memory served, Lizzy mentioned Ruby recently had a baby boy. Named... Vivian's mind raced. Sawyer. Yes, that was it. And the baby's arrival also explained the new mother glow about Ruby. "We wondered what it might take to get you back to Owl Creek, Nate. Guess we know now, huh?"

"How about I show you around." Sloan stepped away from Chase and set her attention on Vivian. "Don't worry. We'll leave you two alone soon enough so you can get acclimated. Let's start with the best thing about this house." She tugged Vivian by the hand through the kitchen and dining area to the glass double French doors. She pushed them open and flung them wide to give an unobstructed view of the mountain range. "How about that view, huh?"

"Yeah." Vivian looked back over her shoulder to where Nate remained standing amidst his newfound family. He looked both shocked and awed, but also, whether he wanted to admit it or not, exactly where he belonged. Vivian smiled and released at least some of the tension she'd brought with her in the car. "That is most definitely a great view."

Chapter 10

Fletcher gave Nate his own tour well after Vivian's concluded. He'd also waited until well after Ruby, Kiki, Chase and Max had taken off under the guise of giving Vivian and Nate some acclimating time. Nate didn't need acclimating. He could settle in easily wherever he went.

But he had not missed the knowing looks that passed among his brothers. Looks that made the back of his neck prickle to the point of pain.

With the car unloaded and Vivian occupied with storing the cooler contents as well as going through the well-stocked refrigerator, freezer and pantry, Fletcher showed Nate the lay of the land, ending, to Nate's surprise, on the second floor and the balcony outside the massive bedroom suite that could have doubled as a ballroom.

"You worried about Vivian hearing whatever it is you're going to tell me?" Nate challenged.

Fletcher didn't blink. "More like I'm leaving it to you how much you want to tell her. Consider it my gift to you, offering a return of control you're going to be lacking for the next little while."

Nate almost grunted a reply. Seemed his new siblings really had thought of everything.

Outside, as it was coming up on five o'clock, the sun had begun its nightly surrender, and the chill factor dropped. The cold air blasting into the house was blocked by the bedroom door Fletcher had closed behind them.

"I'm guessing you all like your space." Nate twisted off the top of a beer bottle he'd grabbed out of the fridge and pocketed the cap. The house was beyond anything he could have ever imagined vacationing in let alone living in. *Tasteful elegance* was a phrase that came to mind.

"Colton Properties is Chase's baby these days. He's a fan of giving prospective buyers a wealth of choices." Fletcher pushed open a pair of French doors identical to the ones just off the kitchen downstairs and stepped outside. "He's hoping it'll offset some recent business blowback."

It didn't sit well, Nate realized, having this much space between him and Vivian. But Fletcher seemed to have a plan in mind, even if said plan meant turning them both into Popsicles. Good thing he'd noticed a stash of firewood by each of the fireplaces. He couldn't wait to get a fire started.

"Small homes, large homes, long-time residents, vacationers," Fletcher went on. "Chase has developed Colton Crossing for a myriad of income levels."

"It's called hedging one's bets," Nate countered and earned a nod of approval as Fletcher took a pull of his beer. "So, I give. What's with the cone of silence?"

Fletcher leaned back, sat on the edge of the banister and stretched out his legs. "I've been elected to broach a subject that might be considered a bit tricky."

"Elected by whom?" Nate needn't have asked. As

much as he'd been hoping for an uneventful arrival, it was unrealistic to think it wouldn't come with a price.

Fletcher dismissed the question with a smile that didn't come close to reaching his wary eyes. "What do you know about our father's death?"

Whatever Nate had been expecting to hear, it certainly wasn't that. "I read it was a stroke." He braced his feet apart, folded his arms across his chest, beer bottle dangling from two fingers.

"Read?" Fletcher's brow furrowed.

"Yeah, online. In the paper. Saw it on the news ticker." An unease he thought he'd left in Boise re-knotted low in his belly. This didn't have anything to do with Vivian's current situation as a target.

"You didn't hear about his death from Jessie?" Fletcher asked.

Why did everything have to come back to his mother? "Until Robert died, I hadn't seen or spoken to my mother in years. She wasn't thrilled with me becoming a cop, and when I made detective, I became persona non grata, for want of a better term." He didn't add that earning that status had been such a relief he'd privately celebrated. "I'd heard about Robert dying before she came knocking on my door a few days after it hit the press." At the rate he was drinking his beer, he was going to run through his supply pretty darn quick. "I know now she stopped by on her way to Owl Creek. She thought she had me, talking about regrets and how we'd lost the chance to mend family fences." He rolled his eyes, shook his head. "I didn't believe it for a second."

"Why not?"

"Because the only regret my mother is capable of feeling has only to do with her own failures. She tried to offer sympathy to me and then to Sarah. She tried to talk about the good times and bring back memories that, to be honest, I have no recollection of." Sometimes, he was convinced he'd lived a completely different life than the one Jessie recalled. "I remember him being around the first ten years of my life, but not really present, if that makes sense. He traveled a lot. For business, we were told." Business. Hardly. Unless maintaining two completely separate families was a new kind of Colton enterprise. The entire conversation was enough to turn his stomach sour. "I told her I didn't think it was a good idea for her to come here, but that fell on deaf ears. Next thing I know, she's back from having met with all of you here in Owl Creek, as angry as I've ever seen her, ranting and raving over being pushed out of the inheritance." He shook his head again. "As predictable as she is spiteful."

"*Pushed out* meaning you and Sarah?" Fletcher asked.

Nate smirked. "Hardly."

"So you're of the belief Jessie came to us because she expected a payout."

"Expected?" Nate shrugged. "Couldn't say. Wanted? Definitely." He shivered. "Is there a reason we're having this talk outside?"

"Extreme temperatures make it easier to tell when someone's lying."

"Huh." Nate had to give Fletcher points. The reality of being interrogated by his older brother hit him with a bit more force than expected. So much for happy families. He toasted Fletcher with his beer. "Thanks for living up to my very low expectations." Maybe he had made a mistake coming here.

"You and Sarah came out of nowhere, Nate." Fletcher's voice was even and calm. "Of course we were going to be suspicious. You have no idea the pain Jessie's inflicted on the family over the years."

"Fair." He nodded, but it didn't dispel the disappointment he felt. "Just like you don't know what it was like to grow up in her house." Or to find out your father chose one portion of his family over another. "It might be easy for me to say, but don't paint me or Sarah with any brush connected to Jessie."

Fletcher glanced down. "You said it had been years since you saw Jessie. How long exactly?"

"I don't know." Nate frowned. "Three, maybe four years? Sarah sees her more than I do. My sister's a lighter touch when it comes to our mother's financial failings and machinations." Guilt he didn't like to ponder surged. "It hurt Sarah, more than me, to know Robert kept us secret from all of you. That we had this enormous family living only a few hours away. Sarah's always wanted to be part of something bigger than just us. When I found out about you all, I was terrified about what it all would mean. But Sarah? It was all I could do to stop her from jumping on a bus and coming out here to introduce herself as one of the family. Right now, I'm real thankful I won that fight."

If Fletcher took offense, he didn't show it. "Sarah didn't care that our father lied about everything?"

"Sure she did." Nate ducked his head, let out a soft laugh. "She just got over it faster than me. Sarah's far more forgiving. Which explains why she always lets Jessie back into her life. Despite knowing it won't end well."

"Hope's a dangerous thing," Fletcher said.

"Especially in the hands of someone who knows how to wield it," Nate agreed. "So." He took another drink. "What is it you want to ask me that requires a deep-freeze lie detector?"

"I guess I was curious if you thought Dad's death was...suspicious in any way."

"I hadn't seen the man in almost a decade," Nate said carefully. "I'm not in a position to suspect anything about him." He paused, looked his brother in the eye. "Do you think it was?"

The clouds opened up and sent a heavy cascade of snow down upon them. Fletcher motioned him back inside, closed the doors, then led him into an alcove off the main suite that contained two overstuffed cream-colored chairs with matching storage ottomans.

"It's been discussed," Fletcher said as he got comfortable. "That there might be more to Dad's death than originally believed."

Nate tried not to react to the use of the word *Dad* where Robert Colton was concerned. Instead, he focused on putting the pieces of this conversation together. "If you're going to kill someone, especially a man as powerful and well-known as our father, there are better ways than to trigger a stroke."

"Unless someone is already prone to them. Then it would be—"

"Understandable and not wholly unexpected," Nate finished. His cop brain clicked on. "I take it his medical history proves that out?"

"He had a minor stroke a few years ago," Fletcher said. "And, okay, to be completely honest—"

"*Now* we're being honest?"

Fletcher looked at him. Really looked at him this time, then gave a slow nod. "Okay. I had that coming. We all had that coming, I suppose. Look." He let out a sigh. "I don't want you thinking we considered Dad some kind of saint or perfect father. Or a perfect man. He wasn't any of those things."

"Do tell." Nate took his last drink of beer.

"Jessie wasn't his first or his only affair. He had a lot of them," Fletcher said. "After Jessie, he stopped trying so hard to hide them. Near as we can tell, he didn't have any other kids."

Nate smirked again. "Time will tell."

"He was a hard-drinking, heavy-smoking, live-life-to-excess kind of man. His first stroke was a warning he didn't heed." Fletcher sounded both resigned and regretful. "The second one didn't come as a big surprise. Still, he was bigger than life, and it was a shock when he died. But then Jessie turns up. Out of the blue. And tells us all about their life together. Tells us about you and your sister." He rubbed a tired hand across the back of his neck. "Suffice it to say, none of us handled it very well. When we didn't acquiesce to her demands for an equal share of the estate, she talked to anyone who would listen. Papers, reporters, bloggers. She didn't just air out the family closet, she fumigated it."

"Yeah," Nate said. "I am well aware." He and Sarah had both needed to change their phone numbers multiple times to avoid the press's attention. At least the camp-outs on their front lawns hadn't lasted more than a few days. Small blessings, he supposed. Thank heavens for the media's short attention span.

"Chase has had to work nearly 24/7 to keep the scandal from destroying the family company," Fletcher said. "It took a while to stop the financial hemorrhaging, reassure our investors and shareholders. The rest of us just did what we could to wait it all out."

"He seems to have done a pretty good job of things. You all have," Nate added with some reluctance. "None of this answers the question you asked of me, though. About Robert's death. You haven't mentioned anything that argues the ruling of natural causes."

"That's because there isn't an argument. It's more a gut feeling. On the surface, yes, everything points to a stroke. But then there are other things to take into consideration." Fletcher pursed his lips. "You ever hear of the Ever After Church? It's run by a man named Markus Acker."

"Of course," Nate said. "It's hard not to living around here. They have some kind of church compound, don't they? Near Conners? Although calling it a church seems a bit of a stretch."

"Mmm." Fletcher nodded. "You'd be right on that front. It's a cult, pure and simple to anyone on the outside looking in. Acker's a con man, plain and simple. This Ever After Church isn't the first time he's pulled this stunt, but so far it seems to be his most successful. He's got about a thousand followers living with him. Living under his rules, working his land, giving over their life savings in exchange for atonement, forgiveness, who knows what else."

"Free labor in exchange for the promise of redemption?" Nate supplied. "There's dozens of men like Acker working scams like this all over the country."

"True enough," Fletcher agreed. "Acker's especially

insidious, though. He doesn't hide his love of money, or the power he thinks it gives him. He sucks everyone he comes in contact with dry, and once they are, he puts them into situations where they can get him more. And then there's his seduction ratio. He goes after what he wants, especially if he thinks it'll add to his coffers. Or if they're female." He paused, eyes shifting as he decided on his next words. "Jessie's one of his followers, Nate."

Nate blinked. Frowned. Opened his mouth to respond, then closed it. Tried again. "You're sure?" was all that came out.

"We're sure," Fletcher said. "From what we've been able to find out, she has been for years. Maybe even from before Acker hit Idaho four years ago." Another pause. "One thing Acker's followers all do is confess to him. They tell him every detail of their life before they found him, and no doubt he keeps impeccable notes. Jessie wouldn't have been an exception."

Nate could only imagine how a man like Markus Acker would have reacted to hearing one of his devotees had her claws in Robert Colton. "You think she told Acker about Robert and their life together."

"She had to have. And if Acker's as dangerous as we think…"

It took Nate a moment to pull together the threads of their conversation. "You're thinking Acker might have somehow had Robert killed so Jessie could make a claim on his estate."

"That's part of what I'm thinking." Fletcher watched him carefully, as if poised for a fight once Nate caught on to whatever else lurked beneath the surface of accusation.

It was Nate the cop who needed to step up now. The

cop who needed to stop lurking in the shadows and see this situation from the outside, taking into consideration everyone involved in the story. It took a moment to step away and look objectively, but once he did, the answer became more than evident. It became probable. "You're thinking it's possible my mother had a hand in killing Robert." He waited for the doubt or disbelief to land and steal the air from his lungs. But it didn't.

"As much loathing as there is for Jessie, we're struggling with that idea," Fletcher admitted. "We haven't brought the entire family in on this yet. It isn't time, and honestly, this isn't something any of us want to think possible. Right now, it's just you and me talking. Cop to cop." He hesitated. "Brother to brother."

For the first time, hearing that word didn't make Nate flinch.

"I think the timing of Dad's death is beyond coincidental," Fletcher went on. "Acker's rise to prominence, Jessie running out of cash, the companies' success. Given the resulting chaos Jessie's bomb created, it all feels a bit calculated. And cruel."

"My mother's specialties. Okay." His mind was spinning in a dozen different directions, not one of them good. "Okay, I'm not saying you're wrong, but I'm also not ready to say you're right." It should have hurt, far more than it did, to even consider his mother might be capable of murdering Robert Colton. But the truth was his days of predicting Jessie Colton's behavior had long ago passed. Given what he'd seen being a cop for as long as he had been, one thing was true in this life: anyone is capable of anything at any time. "That said, I'll agree this is something we should dig deeper into." He took a deep breath. "I hate to say it, but that should probably fall on me." As Jessie's son, it would be far less suspicious for him to go investigating the last few years of her life and any connection she had to Markus Acker.

Fletcher dropped his head forward as if in relief. When he lifted his chin once more, he had an odd grin on his face. "Max owes me another twenty bucks."

"Does he?" Nate didn't know why it mattered, but it did. Clearly Max Colton was going to take more time to be convinced about where Nate's lack of loyalties lay. "He doesn't have much faith, does he?"

"It's been hard on him, and Greg and Malcolm and Lizzy, knowing that Jessie chose to raise you and Sarah when she walked away from them. He was what, eight when Jessie left? That's a hard age to witness a family breaking apart."

Any age was as far as Nate was concerned. "And like I said before—"

"Yeah, I know," Fletcher agreed. "Living with Jessie wasn't a picnic. And I get it. I really do. But you've known about us for a while, haven't you?"

Half a lifetime, Nate almost admitted. Instead he simply said, "Yes."

"We've had months. Give everyone a bit more time to adjust. We'll get there, Nate. And believe it or not, we might all actually be worth it."

Nate wanted to believe that was true, but Fletcher didn't seem to be taking one thing into consideration. That Nate's mother may very well be responsible for what happened to Robert Colton.

And if that was the case, would Nate and Sarah ever truly be accepted?

* * *

"Good night, Vivian."

Vivian glanced up from her laptop screen, sliding off the barstool at the kitchen counter when Fletcher poked his head in to wave goodbye.

"Oh. Good night, Fletcher." She flashed him her best "not a care in the world" smile and lifted her hand. "Everything okay?"

"I've given Nate a crash course on the security system." He pointed to the keypad by the back door. "He'll fill you in on everything you need to know."

"Okay." It didn't escape her notice he hadn't answered her question, but it wasn't her place to push. Clearly what the brothers had to discuss needed to be addressed in private. Didn't mean she wasn't curious about it, though. "Thank you, again, for everything. I hope…" She moved closer to him. "I hope we won't inconvenience you for long."

Fletcher's cool expression immediately shifted and, for want of a better term, opened. "You're the one being inconvenienced, Vivian. Your life shouldn't have to come to a screeching halt because you accepted a dinner invitation."

"No, it shouldn't, should it?" Easy enough to say, but at the same time, if she hadn't said yes, she might not ever have met Nate. And that, she knew without a doubt, would have been a terrible shame.

"Don't let all this family stuff get to you," Fletcher continued. "It's taking us some time to adjust to everything that's happened these past few months, but you were right back at the station. Nate's family. It's time we started acting like he is."

"I'm glad to hear it." Despite Nate's detached attitude about his place in the Colton family, she couldn't help but think that deep down, in places he didn't even know existed, he really did want to belong. But he also was preparing himself for disappointment. Something she could relate to all too well. "Nate will be glad, too. Especially for Sarah."

"Yeah." Fletcher nodded. "Yeah, I got the message on that. We'll get there. Eventually. I'll check in with you both tomorrow." He walked back down the hall, and a few moments later, the front door shut behind him.

The silence in the house was beyond deafening. Nate hadn't been wrong earlier about the size of this place. It was nearly cavernous and even echoed in places. Despite its beautiful decor and design, it didn't feel remotely homey to her. Or maybe she was just too comfortable with the way her life had been up until now. These last few days—despite the disastrous underpinnings of misadventure—had been a kind of awakening for her. Lizzy had been right all those times she'd worried that Vivian had locked herself away to stay protected from the world. Sure it was dangerous and scary, but it also contained wonders and excitement. Like a particular detective currently occupying the same house.

A detective who had her thinking about all kinds of activities the two of them might do together. Her face went hot, but instead of pushing the fantasies away, she embraced them. And settled them into the back of her mind to dwell on later.

"I smell something delicious." Nate's declaration as he walked into the kitchen startled her out of her reverie. He opened three bottom cabinets before finding the one housing the recycling bucket for his and Fletcher's empty beer bottles.

"Kiki suggested I break the kitchen in," Vivian admitted. It had been almost an hour since Nate had followed Fletcher upstairs, and she was dying to know what they had talked about. "I've got the leftovers sorted, and there's a whacky cake in the oven."

"A what cake?" He wandered around the large center island that housed a farmer's sink and extensive counter space, as if transfixed by the aroma emanating from inside the oven.

"Whacky cake." She flexed her fingers. "It's the first thing I learned to bake, actually. It's a kind of ritual for me. First night in a new house, I make it. My first foster mother gave me the recipe. It's from World War II, when rations limited store supplies. No eggs or butter, just pantry items, you know, like flour and sugar and... Sorry, babbling." She had to stop herself from twisting her hands into knots. "I'm nervous." She slid back onto the stool and tried to refocus on the emails waiting in her inbox. There wasn't anything urgent. Nothing that couldn't wait until tomorrow.

"Nervous about what?"

"Everything." Deflecting, she gave in to temptation. "What were you and Fletcher talking about upstairs?"

He pulled open the fridge, had his hand on a second bottle of beer, then changed his mind and shut the door without taking it out. "Trust me, you do not want to know."

"Oh." She scrunched her mouth. "Okay, sure. I understand." She closed her computer and stood back up, made a beeline for the remote. "How about we find something on TV to watch while we—"

He moved so quickly and quietly she almost yelped when his hand gently wrapped around her wrist. "Vivian."

She squeezed her eyes shut. She didn't want to admit how her name on his lips made everything inside her quiver. She didn't want to get any more attached to this man than she already was. She wasn't the kind of woman men noticed or gravitated toward, and she certainly didn't want to lean into the whole damsel-in-distress modus operandi. It took all her confidence to believe that the attraction she'd felt when she'd first kissed him, that *zing* of excitement that coursed through her whenever he touched her, wasn't one-sided.

"Do I make you nervous, Vivian?" He stepped closer, so close she could feel the heat of his body radiating through both their layers of clothing. He made her shiver, that baritone voice of his, that way he had of making her feel as if she were the only woman in his world.

"You know you do," she whispered. Her thoughts tumbled over one another as if caught in an avalanche of unchecked emotion. "I don't know how to do this, Nate."

"Don't know how to do what?" His thumb moved across the pulse in her wrist, tempting. Teasing. The slightest touch of his skin to hers, and she could feel herself melting.

"You know what. Interacting. I'm terrible at...this." Only now did she turn, if only because she had nowhere to hide. She lifted her chin, forced her gaze up to meet the eyes of the man who had stoked every fire inside her from the moment she'd first seen him at the bar.

"Well, Ms. Maylor." He released her wrist, threaded his fingers between hers and lifted her hand to his lips. "I think this deserves further investigation." He pressed his lips to the back of her knuckles, nudged her a bit closer as his mouth trailed across her hand. "You don't seem so terrible to me." His smile silenced her, emptied her mind of every thought except what it had felt like to be kissed by him. "Shall we see what else you aren't terrible at?" He let go of her hand, smoothed both of his down her sides, until they rested on her hips.

She whimpered behind pressed lips. Desire weakened her knees, and she clung to him, catching his upper arms in her trembling hands and willing herself to remain on her feet. When his lips brushed against hers, she sighed, opened her mouth and let him in.

Kissing him in the car yesterday had been pure impulse. A way to remind herself that she was still alive. But now, being here, in his arms, every cell in her being fired as his tongue swept in and engaged hers in a dance instinct led. He tilted his head, took the kiss deeper, and she rose up on her toes, stretched her body against his.

Her breasts tingled as he drew her in to him. She could feel every part of him pressing into her. He dipped down, wrapped those muscular arms around her waist and lifted her off her feet, his mouth creating a miracle of magic on hers. She could feel her arms move, as if on their own, up and around his neck. Her fingers tangled in the thickness of his hair at his neck. Silky, soft. Sensational. She sighed and sagged into him.

In the distance, she heard a buzzing, a ringing of sorts. Loud enough to break the spell, but not so intrusive that she unwound herself from around him.

"I think," Nate murmured against her throat when she dropped her head back, "your cake is done."

"Mmmmm." It took a moment for her head to clear,

for his words to seep in. "Oh." Her smile came slow this time. "Right. Cake." She'd baked out of habit, and craving, only to find herself not the least bit satiated by the man in her arms. "I should get it out before it burns."

He nodded and the quirky smile that curved his lips felt as if it had been created just for her.

"I'll…just…" She let her arms drop and stumbled back. Her knees hadn't quite got their strength back, but given the self-satisfied expression on Nate's face, she wasn't going to add to his ego boost by falling flat on her fanny. Whatever else she might think, he was here protecting her; he felt responsible for her. And that cold splash of reality was enough to have the self-doubt surging afresh.

"I've got frosting to make." It was, quite possibly, the dumbest thing she'd ever said in her life. Nonetheless, she pushed her way around him and retreated.

She smiled to herself as something unexpected and powerful bloomed inside her.

For now, at least.

Chapter 11

While Boise wasn't sensory overload when it came to noise, the utter midnight silence of Owl Creek pressed in on Nate to the point of insomnia. He could feel the exhaustion creeping through his system, but every time he closed his eyes and tried to sleep, there was a kind of electrical zap that had him staring back at the ceiling.

He groaned, snatched one of the pillows off the bed and shoved it over his face.

How was it possible for a mind to travel multiple roads at lightning speed? It clearly wasn't enough for him to be worried about Vivian being targeted by a narcissistic Godfather wannabe, or what might happen should Dean Wexler, his best and only lead in the case, succumb to his injuries. Nor was his ever-expanding and confusing family dynamic happy to play second fiddle to the first worry. It wasn't even the fact that he had to consider that Fletcher was right and that Jessie, his own mother, could very well be responsible for his wealthy and estranged father's death.

He smushed the pillow harder on his face. Who was he kidding?

None of that was responsible for his inability to sleep.

What was keeping him awake was one beautiful, curvy, slightly timid brunette who could kiss like a dream and made magic cake with a snap of her fingers. It would have been easy, so easy, he supposed, to nudge her gently up the stairs and into that spacious palace of a main suite she currently occupied by herself.

He'd always prided himself on following the rules. He had no doubt where it stemmed from—backlash against his parental examples who both excelled at making the world bend to their will. Rules were in place for a reason. It was inappropriate, unprofessional and irresponsible of him to even be considering getting involved with a witness, especially one connected to a case that could make his career. And yet...

And yet.

Nate tossed the pillow aside and grabbed the ridiculous toy-like flip phone Max had given him in place of his usual one. Two in the morning.

"Hour of the wolf," he muttered before he sat up, wishing, not for the first time, he'd surrendered to the idea of taking the bedroom next door to hers. Instead he'd sequestered himself downstairs. "This is ridiculous." If he wasn't going to sleep, he could work. Or at least stop circling the same mental track over and over.

Barefoot, and wearing only a pair of pajama bottoms, he grabbed the bag containing his laptop and whatever printed files he had on him and quietly padded down to and around the living room toward the kitchen.

He saw the glow of the Christmas tree well before he rounded the corner. Kiki, Ruby and Sloan had put enough lights on that thing for it to act as an airport landing strip. It had been sweet of them to add some holiday cheer, considering everything Vivian was being put through.

With only the tree lights on, the kitchen was cast in shadows. It wasn't until he set his bag on one of the barstools that he noticed Vivian sitting on the sofa, legs curled in under her, her hands cupped around a mug as she looked at the lights.

She turned her head, casting her profile in a shimmery glow that stole the air from his lungs.

"Did I wake you?" Her voice was as soft as the snow falling outside.

"No." All thoughts of work evaporated. "No, I couldn't sleep."

"Yeah." She sighed and returned her gaze to the tree. "Me, either. It's beautiful, isn't it?"

"Stunning." He wasn't certain he'd ever seen anything, anyone, more so.

"I made some hot chocolate. It's on the stove if—"

"I'm fine."

He sat down, purposely keeping some distance between them. He could smell the sweet cocoa steam drifting into the air. He'd been imagining what she might wear to bed. Somehow, the simple turquoise blue tank top and loose-fitting flowered pants hadn't come to mind. His thoughts had included...steamier selections. But with her hair tumbling free down and around her shoulders, her creamy skin gleaming in the dim light, reality won, hands down.

"That first holiday after my parents died," she said quietly, "I was living in a foster home with six other kids. The house was chaos, but in a good way, I suppose. It was...different. Shocking, actually." Memories clouded her eyes. "It was just me and Mom and Dad before that. To be suddenly in the middle of…" She sighed, shrugged. "Something strange is going on."

"Given the last few days, that statement is definitely a multiple-choice selection."

She laughed, just a little, but the sound took the clouds from her gaze. "For so long, I've felt like I'm sleepwalking through someone else's life. Like mine stopped all those years ago, and I'm just…adrift. Lost. Or, at least, I did feel that way." She looked up at the tree. "A tree like this seems like such a luxury. I used to dream about having one just like it. But as I grew older, it didn't seem… practical. As if I somehow wasn't worth the effort."

"Christmas shouldn't have anything to do with practical." Something his sister Sarah had said on occasion, usually when she was elbow deep in ornament boxes and trimmings.

"I didn't see a tree at your place when we were there." It wasn't an accusation, he thought. More of an observation.

"No." He shrugged. "No, I usually take extra shifts during Christmas so the detectives and officers with families can be home."

"Of course you do." She leaned forward, set her mug on the large, square coffee table. It was only then he noticed the small, wooden box sitting there. "It's funny. Before you came in, I was trying to convince myself you aren't as perfect as you seem to be."

He couldn't help it. He laughed. "Allow me to set your mind at ease," he teased. "I am not remotely perfect. There's a reason I cycle through partners the way I do. I'm difficult to deal with."

"Not from where I'm sitting." She uncurled her legs and scooted forward to the edge of the sofa. "I've never felt safer with anyone in my life, Nate. And I'm not referring to my physical safety." He looked for the uncertainty, the apology that had been hovering in her eyes since the moment he'd first seen her. As if she felt the need to apologize for existing. "I'm me with you. I don't have this…this need to put on a show or pretend to be something I'm not. I can't explain it."

"You don't have to explain it," Nate told her as his heart expanded to double its size. "I'll simply take it for the compliment that it is."

"You know what else I was thinking?"

Given that spark he saw in her eye, he had a pretty good idea. His fists clenched. She faced him, inclined her head.

"I was thinking," she went on when he didn't respond, "that I'm tired of living my life in the shadows. I don't want to live—or die—with any regrets." She stood up, smoothed her hands down her hips, took one, two, three steps toward him.

"You aren't going to die, Vivian." He leaned his head back to look up at her. Behind her, the tree's lights set her to glowing. "I'm not going to let you."

"Hmmm." She nodded, moved one foot then the other until she straddled his legs. "Then that means I'm going to live." She lowered herself, lifted her knees until she settled herself on his lap. He went as hard as stone in an instant, his breath hitching in his chest when she rested her hands on his shoulders, kneaded them gently with her fingers. "I don't think I've really lived much of a life, Nate." She leaned forward, placed a soft, nibbling kiss against the side of his throat. "Maybe it's taken almost dying twice in two days for me to see that. Maybe this is an awakening after all."

He squeezed his eyes shut, kept his hands at his sides as the scent of her washed over him, enveloped him. Her hair brushed against his face, his throat, as her lips moved ever so lightly, ever so gently, across his skin.

"Vivian, I don't think—"

"Don't." She sat up, caught his face between her hands and waited until he opened his eyes before continuing. "Don't think. Not now. This is what I want. You. Us. Together. Tonight. For however many nights we might have in this…place. Our place."

He felt himself standing on the edge of a precipice he'd tried so desperately to avoid. "I don't know that I have anything to offer you, Vivian." He couldn't stop himself. His hands finally shifted, skimmed feather-light up her thighs, over her hips, fingers slipping beneath the hem of her shirt to caress her back.

"I don't need anything but you," she told him. "I'm not special, Nate. I'm not made of glass. I'm not…innocent."

His brow arched. "Aren't you?"

"I've had sex before." She inclined her head as if contemplating something he wasn't privy to. "What I haven't had is lo—" she stopped herself but didn't look away. "Intimacy. Sex is one thing." She brushed the backs of her fingers down his cheeks. "Giving myself over, letting go, actually being with someone is another thing entirely."

Love. Despite everything else she said, that was what he'd almost heard. The word shuddered through him and stole what was left of his breath. Was that what this was? Was that what he felt? This all-encompassing desire, the absolute determination to keep her safe, not only from what existed in the outside world, but from himself?

"You don't have to say anything," Vivian whispered. "I don't expect you to. I'm still trying to figure all this out myself. But it's there. It's here." She caught one of his hands, drew it around to her stomach, under her shirt and up to her heart. Her breasts. "I need to know what it feels like to have your hands on me. To feel you inside me."

She kissed him, drawing him forward as she took what she wanted, her core pressing against the hardness of him.

"Don't turn me away, Nate." Her breath was hot against his face, his lips. Her words singeing his heart. She moved his hand over until it cupped her breast, which filled his hand to perfection. "I don't want reason or rational thought or anything other than you. And me. Upstairs. In that big bed I can't bear to be in alone."

He stared up at her, unblinking. Transfixed.

She moved against him, let out a soft moan as his palm slid over her hardening nipple.

Seduced.

"Never let it be said I ignore a lady's request." Reason and restraint fractured. He surged forward, caught her mouth with his and dived in. Her thighs tightened around him as she folded herself around him, matching his kiss with one of her own that left him shaken to his core.

He pulled his hand free, and as if reading his thoughts, she leaned back far enough for him to draw the tank over her head. She moaned when he used both hands this time, cupping, teasing. Nate dipped his head, replaced his palms with his lips and drew one hardened peak into his mouth.

She gasped. Her head fell back as he circled her nipple with his tongue, leaving only to pay the same attention to her other breast. She clasped the back of his head, her hips rocking against him as she held him to her. She rubbed against him, the hot core of her against that which ached to be buried inside her.

"Stop." He gasped, struggled for control, and pulled his mouth free of hers. "Just…" He tried to catch his breath. "We need…" The word. What was the word he… "Protection."

She kissed him again, slowly, tortuously, slid off of him. She stood, slipped her hands beneath the waistband of her pants and slowly lowered them down her legs.

He groaned at the sight of her naked, glistening body against the blinding glare of the tree lights. She held out her hand, took a step back. He followed, rising from the sofa as if caught in a spell. When their fingers entwined, the explosion threatening to undo him built again.

When they reached the stairs, she turned, taking his other hand in hers and drawing him with her.

"It wasn't only the pantry they stocked," she said, her lips curving into a beautiful smile. "I found a nice selection of condoms in the main bath." Her eyes glinted. "Made it very difficult to sleep after that. Thinking how they should be put to use."

Nate wanted to respond. He wanted to spout poetic words of perfection, but any capacity to utter a word had been stolen from him. The last steps to the main suite seemed to take both an eternity and a moment. No sooner had they crossed the threshold than he had her in his arms again.

Beside the bed, the table lamp glowed and the box she'd found sat open and waiting. With the mountains cradling them in their snowy wonder, he lifted her, kissed her. Devoured her. And lost himself.

She wound her bare legs around his hips, gasped into his mouth as he walked them to the bed. Kissing her, tasting her, should have been enough. It might have been enough if he hadn't already known what it was like to touch her. To have her touch him.

He lowered her, gently, until she was lying on the bed. He backed away, only enough to see her writhing on the mattress as she opened herself to him. "Nate, please." Her voice beckoned him with longing, but not yet, he told himself. Not until...

He knelt down, gently grasped her open thighs and drew her forward. Until he could feel the heat of her against his chin. His face. His lips. He licked her, one steady, firm swipe of his tongue before nibbling at that tiny nub of pleasure at the apex of her core.

She whimpered. Her hands grabbed his head, dived into his hair as she lifted her hips against him. Her back arched off the bed. Her breath turning into gasps that created a surge of power inside him. When she came, it was an explosion of unreserved passion that left her limp on the bed.

Even as her arms stretched out for him. For more.

He had never, in his entire life, seen a more beautiful sight than that of this woman laid bare before him, wanting him inside her.

Nate made quick work of discarding his pants. He

had the condom on in record time, doing his best not to meet the teasing gaze of Vivian's oh-so-easily read eyes. Her hands reached for him, eager fingers clutching for him as he placed a knee on the edge of the mattress. She shifted back.

He moved forward, loomed over her, lowered himself and pressed his length against her.

"More," she whispered, bringing one leg up and around his hips, nudging him forward. "More, Nate. All."

He surrendered and sank into her. Her moan echoed in his ears, in his soul, as he moved, slowly at first, wanting her to get the feel of him, even as he held back. When she curled around him, her arms, her legs, he increased his thrusts, determined to set her climbing back toward release. There was no rationalizing what he felt being inside her. There was no way to describe the absolute bliss of joining with her. Her hips pumped in time with his. Their breathing came in gasps, even as he stared into her eyes.

"Come with me," she whispered when he felt the urge overwhelm him. Unable to hold back, unable to deny her, he erupted inside her.

And set her to soaring as well.

"Well." Vivian had never felt so utterly relaxed and fulfilled in her life. "There's only one problem with us having done this."

"Only one?" Nate said on a sleepy laugh. He'd been efficient in the way he'd adjusted them in bed, had them snuggling beneath the comfy, warm down duvet once they could both move.

She lifted her head from the curve of his shoulder,

rested her chin on her hand that was placed over his still rapidly pounding heart. "Well, only one comes to mind at the moment." She cuddled against him and felt her heart zing when he tightened his arm around her as if trying to draw her even closer. "One time isn't going to be nearly enough."

Vivian smiled and laughed at his arched brow. She traced a finger down his nose and allowed it to be caught in his teeth when she reached his lips.

"Did I mention I've always had a thing for older women?"

"You did," Vivian said seriously and moved her leg between his. She felt him stir, anticipated the minutes until they could try to outdo round one. "You're quite… adept for such a young man."

Nate snorted and laughed. "What do you think young men spend most of their time thinking about?"

"I don't have to think." She rose up, kissed him, all but melted into him. "I have firsthand experience." She tucked her head under his chin, closed her eyes against the sensation of his hand smoothing her hair, cupping her cheek. "Can I tell you something?"

"You can tell me anything," he assured her.

"Seriously. I don't want you to laugh."

His hand stilled. He tucked a finger under her cheek and lifted her chin so he could look into her eyes. "I will never laugh at you, Vivian."

"You know the first time I thought about this happening between us?" She hesitated. Exposing her body to him had been one thing. Exposing her heart? Well. She'd been wanting to take more chances with her life, hadn't she? "When I first saw you sitting at the bar."

"Yeah?" He looked inordinately pleased with himself.

"Yeah. It made focusing on dinner quite impossible, I can tell you." She trailed a finger across his chest.

"Tell me about it." He caught her hand and brought it to his lips. *Talented lips*, she thought as she pushed aside any regret or doubt. She was not going to let anything ruin this time she had with him. "You know when I first thought about this happening between us?"

She smiled, entertained at his amusement. "Tell me."

"When you took off your jacket at the restaurant." He blinked, and she searched for the teasing, for the lie. And found none. "It was like being hit by a lightning bolt." His hand sunk into her hair. "And that was before I even saw your face. Or your glasses." He tapped her nose and earned a laugh. "We should get bonus points for resisting temptation for as long as we did."

"Yes, well, you did your best to push me off. Didn't work though." She'd meant what she'd said earlier. Sex was one thing. Making love with Nate Colton had been entirely another. "I do believe almost dying…twice," she added quickly, "might have finally taught me not to be quite so…timid."

He kissed her, long and deep. Until her head spun.

"There is nothing timid about you," he assured her when she reached down and grasped him in her hand. "Not one little bit."

"No," she said as she slithered down his body and lowered her mouth to him. "I don't think there is anymore."

When Vivian opened her eyes, it took her a long moment to remember where she was. She wasn't staring at dull white walls or a mirrored dresser she'd found at a yard sale shortly after moving into her town house. She didn't feel the chill of the straining heating unit doing its best to spit out warmth on a cold December morning.

Instead, she was buried beneath a comfy, cozy down-filled duvet, looking out to the stunning mountain range encircling the town of Owl Creek. An unfamiliar yet welcome weight had settled over her, behind her. Around her.

The smile that spread slowly across her lips had her reaching up and resting her hand on the top of Nate's head. Her fingers sank into the thickness of his hair as she drew her fingers down. He shifted, moved more snuggly against her in a way that both brought a tint of color to her cheeks and a slow boil to her blood.

"Don't start something you might not have the energy to finish." Nate's voice rumbled against the side of her neck. He tightened his hold around her waist, pressed his lips against the pulse at her throat.

"Believe me," she said on a half moan as his hand wandered down her bare stomach. "If we start, I'll make absolutely certain we finish."

Still, she found her gaze drawn back to the mountains as she clung to the memory of this perfect moment. A moment that only months before she couldn't have conceived of.

His stomach rumbled, and she laughed. "Hungry?"

"Starved." He nipped at her neck, and she gasped as he rolled her onto her back. He gazed down upon her as if he were an art aficionado looking upon a classic painting.

"I can cook," she offered, linking her hands behind his neck. "Unless you have someplace to be?"

"I do not." He kissed her. "Have any place." Kissed her again, longer this time. "To be." This kiss had her melting beneath him to the point of becoming utterly putty in his hands as the sun completed its ascent into the sky.

She hadn't lied to him last night, when she'd told him she'd had sex before. But she wouldn't necessarily qualify it as…rewarding. A quick tumble with a boy her first week of college had been the result of curiosity rather than passion. It certainly hadn't been anything that warranted a desire for a repeat performance either on the boy's part or hers. As a result, she'd added sex to the list of things she could live without.

She caught a giggle behind her still vibrating fingers.

She definitely couldn't say that anymore.

"Do I even want to know?" Nate lifted his head from where he'd been dozing against her breast.

"I don't think you do." This time, it was her stomach that rumbled. "Okay, that's embarrassing enough to warrant me heading down to the kitchen. After I take a shower."

"Mmmm." He nuzzled his cheek against her. "Couple more minutes."

She sighed. It was so easy to forget everything, including what had brought them to this place, this moment. And yet the threats hovered, as did the reality of needing to return to her actual life. They both needed to return. Once she was out of danger, he wouldn't be responsible for her safety any longer. His job would be done, and if there was one thing she'd learned about him the past few days, it was that his job always came first. "Nate?"

"Yeah."

"Are you going to tell me what you and Fletcher talked about up here last night?"

She knew asking would break the spell, but one of them had to be practical about things. Fairy tales were all well and good as a diversion, but she knew, better than most, that real life rarely brought a happily-ever-after.

"It doesn't have to do with you." He rolled onto his back but curved an arm around her when she leaned over him, catching the sheet between them. He pinched the bridge of his nose, squeezed his eyes shut.

"So it's none of my business?"

He dropped his hand, looked at her, and she wondered if it was possible to actually fall into the ocean blue of his eyes. "I didn't say that. It's...complicated."

"I'm a smart woman." Funny. It was something she'd always known, of course, but rarely was it anything she said. Out loud, at least. "Maybe I can help?"

"What makes you think I need help with it?"

"This." She traced a finger from his furrowed brow, down his nose, to his swollen lips. "It appears every time you start thinking."

"Then it must be permanently etched on my face." He stopped, sighed. "I don't know that I'd even know where to start."

"Anywhere." She hesitated, then plunged ahead. "If it doesn't have to do with me, does it have to do with your mother?"

"Okay, flag on the play." He sat up and scooted back against the headboard. "Let's not put you and my mother in the same sentence. Or mention her while we're in bed, okay?"

She knew he meant it as a tease, a joke, but there was definite pain behind the thought.

"Tell me." She sat up and crossed her legs, pushed her hair away from her face. "Talk to me, Nate. You've certainly listened to me enough."

He looked a bit lost for a moment, confused, and she caught a glimpse of a younger Nate, struggling with the truth about his complicated family life. When he spoke, it was with a resoluteness that made her heart ache for him.

"Fletcher thinks my mother might have had a hand in our father's death." His smile was quick and cursory. "Surprised you, didn't I?"

"Not...exactly." She frowned, frantically searching for the right words. But she didn't have a chance to say anything else before he went on.

"How about this, then? Apparently, for the past few years, she's been involved with this Ever After Church, and the guy who runs it. Markus Acker. You've probably heard of them."

"I definitely have." She nodded as her blood ran cold. "One of my clients, he runs a Fortune 500 company out of New York. He hired me to do some damage control when his son got caught up with Acker last year. Just press releases and statements to the media. He didn't want it to be full-blown news, but he didn't want his shareholders thinking he was being held hostage by the fact his boy was being used to essentially extort him."

"Did he get out? The kid?" Nate asked, a bit more alert.

Vivian ducked her head. "I don't know how much I'm legally allowed to say since I signed a nondisclosure agreement, but…" She nodded. "Without going into details, I can tell you my client hired a specialized team to get him out."

"Like an off-the-books mercenary kind of group?"

She shrugged, a non-answer. "The last I heard he'd had his son sent to a facility overseas that specializes in… I don't know if this is the right word…*deprogramming*." While she'd been relieved the boy was safe and out of the cult's reach, she hadn't found working that kind of job to be anything other than stressful and gut-wrenching. She much preferred working with authors looking to sell their books and brand, or actors and actresses hoping to up their profile. That particular client had helped her learn to set boundaries and not jump at every professional opportunity just because it might up her profile. "Do you think… Is it possible Fletcher's right about your mom being involved with this group? Does he have any actual evidence?"

As horrific as the stories were about Jessie Colton— and she'd gotten an earful from Lizzy as well as Nate— the idea Jessie may have murdered Robert came across as a little too *Game of Thrones* for her liking.

"Do I think it's possible?" Nate's brows went up. "Yes. As far as evidence? He doesn't have anything concrete. It's a gut feeling on Fletcher's part. Others, too, if I was reading him right. I don't know if he's talked to Max about it or not."

"I would think yes," she said and rested a hand on his thigh. "They might be cousins by birth, but they're brothers by choice. Something like this, if Fletcher truly believes it, enough to talk to you about it, then Max knows." She caught her bottom lip in her teeth. "That could explain why Max has been a harder sell on you."

"I told Fletcher I'd look into it. Later," he added quickly. "Once we're on the other side of this DeBaccian mess, and you're safe."

Once they were back to their real lives. Where neither one of them particularly fit with the other. When his job with her was done. "Then we'd best get to that." She tugged the sheet with her as she scooted off the edge of the bed. "I'm going to jump in the shower, then fix breakfast while you take one."

"Or." He caught her around the waist before she took two steps from the bed. He spun her around and kissed her breathless. "We could conserve water and shower together." The grin he gave her contained none of the hopelessness she'd seen shining in his eyes moments before.

"I do like conservation," she agreed, but her attempt to remain completely serious failed, and she laughed as he scooped her into his arms and carried her into the bathroom.

Chapter 12

Nate quietly stepped into the front downstairs bedroom that had been set up as a home office. It had made sense for Vivian to set up shop in here, where she'd have privacy to conduct whatever work she needed to take care of. When he set the fresh mug of coffee onto the coaster, he earned a thankful smile as she pressed a finger to her ear and the headphones for her online call.

"No, Wanda, this should work out fine. I'll send you my compiled list of agencies I think we should send your press release to, and we'll go from there. Uh-huh. I'm hoping to be back up and running sometime next week."

Nate offered an encouraging nod.

"Great. I'll check in with you then. Okay, bye." She clicked off and sagged back in the leather chair. "I could get used to this. Gorgeous view." She pointed out the front bay window that overlooked the sloping view of Owl Creek below. "Despite the constant run of construction trucks and crews."

Nate grimaced. The banging and buzzing of construction equipment had started right at eight. The fact that winter meant everyone was working on home interiors only made the noise echo louder, near as he could tell.

"Could be worse." They could be dealing with cement trucks and paving equipment.

"I also have coffee at my beck and call."

"Not just coffee." He bent to kiss her, determined to keep it quick, but, as always seemed to happen, the moment he tasted her, he wanted more.

"Stop." She laughed and pushed him away. "I've got one more client to call and a ton of emails to answer." She gestured to her laptop. "Give me an hour, maybe ninety minutes tops, then I'll be all yours."

"Sounds like a plan." He walked backward out of the room. "I'll check in with Fletcher and my lieutenant. See if there have been any developments."

She nodded and spun around in her chair, but not before he saw a flash of sadness in her eyes. Before he could ask, she was clicking into her video system to make another call.

Later, he told himself. He'd ask her what was bothering her when she wasn't as focused on work.

He returned to the kitchen, where he'd set up his own makeshift workstation at the table near the door to the backyard. He was already getting antsy, being stuck in one place, but the view helped. As did the woman who would soon be joining him.

He'd spent the better part of the morning digging through police reports that contained any mention of Marty DeBaccian, going back the last few years. Even if Lieutenant Haig had someone doing this already, it was research that felt like they were making progress. More information was power moving forward. There was little that irritated him more than being bored and useless, so he'd take what he could get.

He was compiling lists of any businesses mentioned, any suspected co-conspirators and even the names of former detectives and officers who had come across him. Leaving no stone unturned was the only way they were going to catch this guy.

No stone... Nate pursed his lips, stared at the screen and the list of detectives he'd been making. "Sullivan." It didn't sit well with him at all that the detective assigned to Vivian's case had done a disappearing act. In his experience, that meant one of two things.

Either Sullivan had gotten too close to something and DeBaccian had reacted or...

"Definitely leaning toward *or*." He hated voicing it, hated the very idea of it, but there was no getting around the fact that Detective Jim Sullivan could very well be on DeBaccian's payroll.

Someone had to be, Nate reasoned. DeBaccian had been staying a good few steps ahead of law enforcement for a while now. Having someone on the inside of the Boise PD could explain that. Accusations like this were never made lightly, however. Even a false accusation of corruption could follow a cop around for the rest of his life, and if Sullivan was clean...

That thought didn't develop beyond that. He couldn't shake the feeling there was more going on, given Sullivan's recent disappearance. The timing couldn't be a coincidence.

Like Fletcher had said yesterday about their father's death: too many coincidences.

"Down the rabbit hole we go, then." He hunched over his laptop and got to work.

When his phone rang a little while later, he had to

remind himself how to use a flip phone to answer. Distracted, he all but growled a greeting.

"Catch you at a bad time, Detective?" Lieutenant Haig's voice sounded surprisingly lighthearted.

"No, sir, sorry." Nate cringed, pushed his laptop back and blinked his eyes wide to clear the blur. "I've been doing some digging." Tapping his pen against one of the notepads on the table, he wondered how best to approach this.

"I just got a call from the hospital," Haig told him. "Wexler's stable enough for surgery. They're taking him in later today."

Finally, Nate thought. *Progress.* "What's his prognosis?"

"Fifty-fifty." Nate could all but hear his commanding officer's shrug. "If he comes through, we should be able to question him in a day or two."

A day or two. He gazed around the house that, because of Vivian, felt more like a home than his own ever had. It would be a shame to leave it. And her. "Sounds good, sir."

"Good to hear it. Now, tell me about your digging."

"Ah." Nate glanced over his shoulder as Vivian came in. Barefoot and with her hair loose and long around her shoulders, she wore silky, flowy pants that hung low on her hips, along with a short-sleeved shirt. The color reminded him of the syringa, Idaho's state flower. She looked like a summer oasis in the middle of a snowy, frigid winter. "I'm not entirely sure you'd approve of where I've been excavating, sir."

Vivian frowned at him, as if trying to decipher his

code. She walked over to sit across from him, pointed to some of his notes as if asking permission. He nodded.

"Then it's a good thing this isn't an official call," Lieutenant Haig said. "Out with it, Colton."

"I've been looking for a connection between DeBaccian and Sullivan." Before giving his boss a chance to push back, he plowed ahead. "It's just a thought, and a rough one, but unless Sullivan's popped back up—"

"He has not. I sent a couple of patrol officers to his place this morning under the guise of a wellness check. His car's gone. No sign of him. We're hoping to locate his wife—"

"Officially separated as of last year," Nate said. "Near as I can tell, neither has filed for divorce. Haven't been able to track where she's gone."

"So he's rudderless," Haig murmured. "Okay, I'll get someone to track her down. Did you find the connection you were hoping for?"

Hoping wasn't exactly the word. Nate couldn't think of any police officer who hoped to find evidence of a dirty cop. "Maybe." He shuffled through his notes as Vivian rested her bare feet on the bottom rung of her chair. "Seven years ago, DeBaccian was arrested as a suspect in a string of electronics store burglaries. Sullivan was one of the investigating detectives."

"Is that it?"

Like Fletcher, Nate trusted his gut. And his gut told him there was something more. "The case was dismissed when one of the key pieces of evidence went missing. Security tape footage." He scrolled through the online evidence-storage database. "The assistant DA prosecuting the case had the evidence brought to her office. A day later, she had it sent back. According to her statement, she placed everything back in the box before it was picked up. When they retrieved it for court, the recordings were gone."

"Whatever it is you don't want to say—"

"Detective Sullivan was responsible for the transport, sir. According to the sign-in sheet, he was the last person to have access to the evidence box."

"All right, then." Haig lowered his voice. "Keep following this where you can. Put it together for me but keep it with you. Right now, there's no place safer for any evidence against DeBaccian than with you in Owl Creek."

"Yes, sir. Anything else, sir?"

"Not at the moment, no. I'll check in once I get word on Wexler's condition."

Nate slapped his phone closed. "You get all that?"

"I did." Vivian nodded as she flipped through his scribbled notes. "Looks like we're both making progress where our jobs are concerned. I've officially moved into the world of new client referrals."

"Yeah?" He wasn't entirely sure what that meant, but she seemed happy about it.

"Oh, yeah. Someone recommended me to this digital content company out of Texas. Their website certainly makes them sound promising." She frowned. "I had to email them and let them know I wasn't available for a consult for a while yet. But if they're really interested, they'll wait."

"Because you're the best at what you do," Nate said.

"Yes." She straightened in her chair, a hint of surprise in her eyes. "Yes, I am."

"Hopefully, we'll have you back to your life sooner

than later. My lieutenant called to let me know Wexler is going in for surgery sometime today. If he wakes up and talks, I'm hoping we won't need your testimony against DeBaccian."

"A girl can dream." She flipped more of the pages of his notepads. "You really think Detective Sullivan is a bad cop?"

"The more I look into him, the more it looks that way." Despite needing to, this wasn't something he felt any pleasure in undertaking. "Personally, I just want him found so we at least know where he is." DeBaccian coming after Vivian was one thing. Like Max said at the station, criminals often let their egos get the better of them.

But having a trained cop hunting her? A person who knew the ins and outs of protecting witnesses, who understood how the police went about their jobs in the most detailed of ways? The very thought made the bitter coffee churn in his stomach. Her face tightened. The tension he'd been hoping would melt away for them surged. "You know what I saw out on the back patio?" He stood up, carried his coffee to the sink and set it to soak. "A hot tub."

Vivian looked out the window, into the graying, threatening sky, then back to him. "In December?"

"You've never been in a hot tub when it's snowing?"

"Ah, no." She laughed, shook her head. "Is that really a thing?"

"Let's find out." He returned to the table, held out his hand.

She didn't look convinced as she grabbed hold and allowed him to pull her up. "Funnily enough, I didn't think to pack a swimsuit."

He grinned and tugged her close, kissed her hard. "Neither did I."

Her brow arched, and she pulled her hands free, slipped them beneath the hem of his dark T-shirt. "Well, in that case..."

When Vivian was little, before her parents died and before discovering the unpredictability of life, one of her favorite games to play had been "house."

She'd recruited her dolls and stuffed animals, lining them up on the bed while she cooked pretend food on the pretend cardboard stove her father had made for her out of an old shipping box. On occasion, she'd snuck into the kitchen, opened the cabinets she could reach and pilfered whatever items her mother had stashed away. A bag of rice. A potato. A dented can of tomatoes. She'd spent hours "feeding" her companions as she talked to them, telling them about all the fun things they were going to do together.

Funny. Vivian sliced through an onion and set to chopping. She'd never imagined playing house again since becoming an adult. But being here, now, with Nate, it felt exactly like that. She wouldn't outgrow it this time, but she would have to leave it behind when everything was resolved and life returned to normal.

Her eyes filled with tears, but she had the perfect excuse. She turned and slid the chopped onions off the cutting board and into the pan that had been heating on the stove.

Post–hot tub—and they'd definitely given it a workout in more ways than one—he'd returned to his computer, losing himself in chasing down the people who meant to do her harm. To prevent her from returning to that normal she'd existed in.

Normal.

The word didn't seem quite so defined any longer.

It hadn't taken her more than waking up in Nate's arms to realize that aching void of loneliness she'd lived with for so long was gone. She pressed her lips together hard, wiped the back of her hand under her eyes as she sorted through the meager selection of dried herbs.

She'd run on a handful of emotions her entire life, and never to extremes. Anxiety had tamped all that down and back to where, most of the time, she didn't have to acknowledge or deal with it. But being with Nate, loving Nate, she couldn't help but feel as if every emotion possible had jumped on board the spinning carousel that was her heart.

Loving Nate. She squeezed her eyes shut. She'd almost said it last night. Before she'd let herself think about it. Before she'd come to terms with it. It was one thing to fall in love with a man. It was quite another to admit it out loud and have him with no way to escape.

"So, what's for dinner?" Nate's domestic-tinged question had her thinking of her long-lost stuffed animals and dolls and how they'd remained silent. And forever perfect in her memory.

"Pasta." She had to assume it was Sloan, Ruby and Kiki who had stocked the kitchen, and they'd done so with an overabundance of attention to carbs. "I'm making my homemade meat sauce."

"Sounds great." He flashed her a smile. The way he looked at her—even as he plowed through the potential criminal activity of a fellow cop—had those unbelievable fairy tales surging to the surface of her thoughts once more.

"I'd have made bread, but I didn't have time." Time to get back to the teasing and playing of the relationship. "Someone distracted me in the hot tub."

"Totally worth it," he said. The humor in his voice sounded forced. His cell phone vibrated to the point of dancing across the table. He flipped it open. "It's my lieutenant."

Vivian turned the flame down on the stove, grabbed a towel and circled the island.

"Sir? Any word on Wexler?"

She stood beside him, tempted to touch him, but also worried it was too familiar a gesture. How was it she could share a bed with this man, make love with this man, and still be afraid? Not of him. But of what he made her feel. Even now, she could see the concern on his face, and she knew it was because of her.

He was a man dedicated to his job, so by extension she was his concern. And maybe, for a little while, a distraction.

"Okay. Great. Thanks for letting me know. Yeah." His gaze met hers, and in those blue depths, she saw a glimmer of hope. "I'm just about done with my report. I'll check in with you tomorrow. Yes, sir. Thank you."

He clicked the phone closed and sagged back in his seat. "Wexler's surgery went well."

"Yeah?"

"They got the bullet, but most importantly, he's stable. Lieutenant Haig thinks we'll be able to talk to him as early as tomorrow."

"That's great news." She let out a sigh she hoped

would be heard as relieved. "That should make your job a little easier."

"We'll see. You know what's even better?" He collected his papers, stacked them up and, after hitting Save, closed his laptop. "I'm calling it a day. Just in time, too, since it's after five."

"Keeping bankers' hours now, are you?" She returned to the kitchen and searched for a cheese grater. She found one, on a shelf under the center island. When she popped back up, he was standing across from her, hands planted on the gold-specked black marble countertop.

"Can I help?"

"I don't know." She eyed him. "How good are you in the kitchen?"

That grin of his reappeared.

She was onto him this time. Even as she laughed, she held up both hands. "Oh, no. Not again. Not now."

"Why not now?" He challenged, stalking around the counter in a very precise and familiar way.

"Because nothing interferes with me making my meat sauce." She turned, tried to dive away, but he caught her around the waist, spun her around and straight into his arms. "Nate—"

Whatever else she was going to say was caught by his mouth. His wonderful, talented, undeniably tempting mouth. Bittersweet tears burned the back of her eyes. She felt so lucky, to be wanted by him. And he wanted her. There was no denying that.

When he lifted his mouth, and she blinked dazedly up at him, he reached out and turned off the stove. "What room would you like to try next?"

* * *

Nate's eyes snapped open.

What was that?

He sat up, dislodging the blanket he'd dragged over them from the back of the sofa. Mind racing, he jumped to his feet, shoved both hands into his hair. "Vivian?" Her name all but echoed through the kitchen and great room.

The tree lights burned yet again. The remnants of the pasta dinner she'd finally found time to make for them still sat on the stove. Food didn't come close to satiating him, not since he'd gotten his first taste of her. But something felt...

Wearing only his jeans, he retrieved his gun from where he'd left it and his holster on the back of a kitchen chair. Something... He turned, scanned the room. Something was different.

He froze, listened. An empty house had an entirely different feel to it. The energy was lower but nonetheless heavier. As if the silence were pressing in on him.

"Vivian?" he called again as he searched the first floor. No sign of her.

He raced to the stairs, skidding to a halt with one hand on the banister. His keys. He'd kept them on the small marble table by the front door. They were gone.

He walked to the door, heart pounding.

It had been left ajar.

He swore, pulled the gun free and tossed the holster to the floor. He carefully placed his bare foot in the opening and pulled open the door.

The cold blast of air hit him like an avalanche. Locking his jaw, he stepped onto the porch, weapon poised at his side, ready to react.

"Vivian?"

He heard it again. A *click*. A *beep*. He swung toward the SUV he'd parked in the driveway. Gun raised, he made quick work of the path, circling down and around to the car, which, only now could he see, had its passenger door open.

Nate almost forgot to breathe until he saw two feet dangling from a pair of white pants. He grabbed the door and yanked it all the way open. "Vivian!"

She yelped, sat up and nearly slipped right off the seat. "Geez, Nate." She glared at him, pressed a hand to her chest. "Who needs a hitman chasing them when I've got you?"

"What. Are you. Doing?" It took every ounce of patience he had to quell his anger. "You aren't supposed to leave the house. Especially not without telling me."

"You wouldn't have heard me, anyway. You were snoring." She snapped the glove box shut and got out of the car.

"I do not snore."

She rolled her eyes. "I wanted to get my phone." She waggled it in front of him. "Okay?"

"Not okay." He snatched it from her hand. "Who were you going to call?"

"I wasn't—" She scrunched her mouth like a petulant toddler. "None of your business. Give it to me."

"No." He held it up over his head, well out of her reach.

"Give me my phone, Nate." She jumped once, twice, then growled and stepped back, slammed the car door so hard his teeth rattled. "I'm well aware of your sensitive areas, *Detective*, so unless you want them to meet my knee—"

"You don't have anyone to call," he reminded her. "Lizzy's out of town, and everyone else is a client. So I ask again." His patience wore thin. "Who were you going to call?"

She straightened, an odd, dim light flashing in her eyes that had him lowering his arm. "I wasn't going to *call* anyone."

With unnerving speed, she snatched the phone out of his grasp and spun on her bare heels. Head down, she turned on her phone. The glare of the screen cut through the darkness of the night.

Feeling ridiculous, he trailed after her. "Vivian, what is this all—"

"Here, okay?" She shoved the screen in his face. The screen that displayed a picture of Toby. Her cat. "I was missing him. I woke up and saw that stupid box with his ashes, and I was missing my cat, and I didn't have..." She stopped, tears glistening in her eyes. "I didn't want to wake you up and ask permission to see his pictures."

"Vivian." He heard it, the sympathy, the pity that had anger erasing the grief he saw on her face.

"There!" She stabbed a finger into his face. "Right there. I didn't want that. Just...forget it." She made it only a few steps before a car, headlights blazing, turned the corner.

His hand tightened around his gun. "Get inside."

"Nate?" He heard the fear, the uncertainty, but she didn't move toward the house. She moved toward him. The car stopped.

Nate shoved her behind him, feet braced apart; he

watched, then gaped and rolled his eyes as he glared at the familiar face beyond the window as it slid down.

"Just checking the neighborhood to make sure all is calm." Max Colton leaned over, his expression, as always, unreadable. "'Tis the season, you know."

"Seriously, Max?"

"Della's working late, so I told Fletcher I'd just drive past." He shrugged. "I'd ask what the two of you are doing out here this late at night, but I'm not entirely sure I want to know."

Nate could feel Vivian shiver behind him. "Go on back inside, Vivian. Please." He could only hope his more solicitous tone would work better than his irritated one had. He didn't like to admit it, but scared was not a mode he operated well in. And finding her gone from the house had definitely scared him. "You want to come in?"

Max's eyes went wide with surprise. "You sure?" He watched Vivian make it up the path. "I've got time before picking Della up, but I don't want to intrude."

"Just park already." Funny how easily they'd fallen into the big-brother/little-brother routine. Nate wasn't entirely sure he was comfortable with that. Nate headed inside before his feet turned to blocks of ice.

"I put the coffee on." Vivian was already headed up the stairs. "I'm going to bed."

"Don't put the card back in your phone. We don't want anyone tra—" The second the words were out of his mouth he wanted to take them back.

"Thank you, yes." She gave him a look that had previously active parts of him withering. "As I have the IQ of a turnip, I was in need of the reminder."

"Wow." Max closed the door behind him as Vivian

went upstairs. "Chilly in here." He detoured straight past him into the kitchen.

"It's December," Nate called as he retrieved his holster and keys and followed. "It's chilly everywhere." But his brother had a point.

Something told him he was about to experience his first-ever deep freeze where Vivian was concerned.

Chapter 13

Vivian prided herself on not dwelling on the dumber things she'd done in her life. Picking a fight with Nate over her phone—and Toby's pictures—would no doubt remain at the top of that list for the foreseeable future. At least that was the thought she woke up to late the next morning.

That she found herself staring at the box containing her cat's ashes rather than debating how to extricate herself from her lover's arms didn't seem an ideal way to start the day. Like most people, she didn't do well with being embarrassed or being caught. Of course, she'd overreacted last night, but honestly, she hadn't expected to take more than a few minutes to retrieve her phone.

Still feeling cranky, she slugged out of bed and took a shower, got dressed and headed downstairs. She found Nate eyes-deep in his laptop, and while it didn't improve her mood, she was grateful for the distraction. And the delay in needing to apologize.

"Sleep okay?" Nate asked as she poured herself some coffee.

"Well enough." She'd slept like crap, but criminals weren't the only ones susceptible to ego. Hers had definitely been dented, but mostly by her own behavior. "I'm sorry I worried you last night."

"I'm sorry I overreacted. When I woke up to an empty house, I got scared. The things that went through my head—"

"Blame your car." She pulled open the fridge despite having no appetite for breakfast. "If the stupid alarm thing would have disconnected on the first try, you never would have known I was gone."

"I'll make a note to share that with the manufacturer."

She squeezed her eyes shut. She did not want to fall further under his charm. They couldn't afford for her to. "Nate—"

He was standing behind the fridge door when she closed it.

"Yes?"

She had so many questions for him. What happens after she isn't in danger any longer? What happens if they don't catch DeBaccian? What happens if Wexler dies and she ends up having to testify in the murder trial?

What was going to happen to them when there wasn't a case pulling them together? Or ripping them apart?

None of those questions made their way out of her mouth. Instead, she retrieved her coffee and moved away. "How long did Max stay last night?"

"Long enough to clean up the kitchen."

"Oh." She frowned, hoisted herself up onto one of the barstools and sipped. "Dishes. Totally slipped my mind."

"Worked out okay," Nate assured her. "I told him he could eat whatever he wanted in exchange. You earned his seal of approval as far as meat sauce goes. And he might have taken a container of it home to share with Della."

"That's fine." There was always more sauce to be made. "I think we need to talk."

"I'm glad you're the one to say it." He leaned his arms on the counter and pinned her with those blue eyes of his. "Or *am* I?"

She frowned, confusion finally taking hold despite her best efforts to avoid it. "What's going to happen when this case is over?"

He hesitated, but didn't pull his gaze from hers. "I'm going to assume you don't mean with DeBaccian and the justice system."

She inclined her head. "I don't... I don't know how to do this, Nate. Getting caught up in all this excitement and danger, it's been a bit of a mind-spinner for me. You have been. And I'm afraid we're becoming blind to the reality of our situations."

"Right." He nodded, then shook his head. "Nope, sorry. Not getting it at all."

"Do we just stop everything now, before it gets too messy?" she asked. "Or do we take it as far as we can go and then worry about it? If I have to testify, the DA probably won't like the fact we slept together—"

"It's none of the DA's business—"

"Nate." She dropped her voice and the shield of protection she'd been unwittingly wielding. "Of course it's his business. You don't want the case corrupted because you were sleeping with your main witness. But that's neither here nor—"

"I don't want to stop." He blurted it out so fast he seemed to have surprised himself. "Seeing you. Sleeping with you. Being with you." He shoved his hand into his hair and sighed. "I had a feeling I was going to botch this up. Okay." Nate took a long, deep breath. "Okay, let me come at this a different way. Once this is all over, however it ends, I would like to continue to see you. Socially." He frowned. "Why does it sound like I just stepped out of a Jane Austen book?"

She tried to catch the laugh behind her lips but didn't quite manage.

"Look." He leaned on the counter again, only this time he reached across to capture her hands in his. "I don't know how to do this, either. You're a new experience for me, Vivian. This...thing between us. It feels special. Like a gift. And I don't want to walk away from it before we find out if it's something serious, we can make a go of."

She wanted to believe him. All her life, she'd wanted to belong to someone, anyone, who was willing to put their heart on the line for her. But thirty years of life can tarnish even the most hopeful of dreams. "You're no Jane Austen hero," she said finally. "Mainly because none of them ever say so much at one time. I..." She'd told him the other night she'd felt as if she'd been awakened, thrown into a life she'd only been a passive participant in up until now. He was giving her a chance to embrace that fully.

What a fool she'd be to walk away from everything being offered to her. Even if it was for a fraction of time.

"I would like to continue to see you, socially, as well. Maybe even carnally," she added in a moment of inspiration. She earned a smile and his raised brows. "And maybe we'll both be more clearheaded about the future once we don't have this whole DeBaccian thing looming over us. Speaking of..." She looked over her shoulder to the kitchen table, which was once again a mess. "Did you finish your report for your lieutenant?"

"I did." He released her and turned back to the fridge. "I worked some things out with Max. He suggested I run it past Fletcher, too."

She wasn't going to discourage him from spending more time with his brother.

"You hungry?" He bent down and pulled a box of frozen waffles out of the freezer.

"Seriously?" She narrowed her eyes.

"Yeah, why?" Nate looked at the bright yellow box. "What's wrong with—"

"You want waffles, I'll fix waffles." She joined him on the other side of the counter, dropped the box back into the freezer, then grabbed his shirt and pulled him toward her for a kiss. It was, to her mind at least, a new start. A reboot, so to speak. Something she planned to use to keep the hope she was determined to cling to alive. "Go clean up the table while I try to remember where I saw a waffle iron."

"Remind me to talk to Chase about the noise level around here," Nate grumbled as he tossed the remote onto the coffee table and gave up on whatever the plot might be of the movie Vivian had chosen. "Those trucks are driving me nuts."

"Just block them out." She sat beside him on the sofa, her bare toes tucked under his thighs as she typed away on her laptop. "I've got a pair of headphones in my bag if you think they might help."

"No. It's fine." He sighed and dropped his head back on the sofa. "Sorry. I'm just…"

"Antsy?"

"Frustrated."

"And bored?"

He rolled his head to the side, expecting to find her looking at him, but instead all her interest was on her screen.

"Go get your cell phone," she said. "You must have some kind of game or something on there you like."

"I don't want to play any games. With my phone," he added and earned a roll of her eyes.

"What time are you supposed to meet with Fletcher in town?"

"I'm not going."

"What?" She had something akin to panic in her eyes when she looked at him. "Why not?"

"Because you're here and I'm charged with protecting you. I'm not leaving you here alone."

"Are you suggesting I come with you?"

"No." They needed to keep her locked up tight until they had DeBaccian in custody, and last he heard, that wasn't remotely close to happening. "No, you need to stay here."

She sighed and closed her laptop. "Nate, go."

"Nope."

"If you don't—" her voice had an almost too sweet quality to it "—Fletcher's going to have another crime scene to worry about. One that involves your murder." Her smile promised much pain. "I've got plenty to work on getting ready to pitch to this next client. Plus, Harlow's got some new interest from a production company.

I know how to operate the security system and the panic button. Plus, there's security down at the guard gate. If anything happens, I'll hit that first and call you second."

"On what?" he countered. "You won't have a cell phone."

"I have one." She opened her computer again. "I'm just not allowed to use it as anything other than a photo album."

He didn't move. But he was thinking.

"The faster you close this case, the sooner we can get started on a real relationship." How she could make perfect sense to him and keep typing away like that was a multitasking miracle. "Go meet with your brother. I'll be fine. I won't leave the house. I won't even use the hot tub if it makes you feel better."

A car door slammed outside, followed by the quick staccato sound of heels against the concrete. He was up and moving even before the doorbell rang. When he pulled it open, he felt both relief and uncertainty.

"Lizzy."

"Hi, Nate." His half sister, with her long, strawberry blond hair draped over her slim shoulders, flashed familiar, worried blue eyes at him. "Ajay and I just got home this morning. I ran into Sloan in town, and she told me…" She peered around him, her gaze frantic. "She told me Vivian's here? Where is she?"

"Lizzy?" Vivian stepped clear of the hall, a surprised smile on her face. "Yes, I'm here. It's okay. I'm right here."

"Oh, my gosh, Vivian!" Lizzy pushed past him and enveloped Vivian in a hug so tight Nate could feel it himself. "You're okay! When Sloan told me… I imagined all sorts of horrible things."

Vivian looked over Lizzy's shoulder at him, and he immediately regretted not pushing Vivian harder to call her friend. His sister.

"What on earth is happening?" Lizzy demanded. "What are you doing here in Owl Creek? In this house? Sloan said you were shot at? That you're some kind of witness to an attempted murder?" She swung on Nate. "Tell me what's going on, please? Why didn't you call me? You should have called me."

"Okay, Lizzy, stop." Vivian surprised Nate by grabbing Lizzy's arms and spinning her back around to face her. "Everything's fine. I will tell you everything, I promise. But all you need to know right now is that Nate's been watching over me, and I'm here and safe because of him. Okay?" She touched a hand to his sister's cheek. "No need to spiral. Everything's fine. It's going to be fine." She looked to Nate again. "I promise."

He understood. She wanted him to know that he was an integral part of making certain her promise was kept.

"Okay." Lizzy sighed and sagged a bit. Nate closed the door and followed them back to the kitchen. "Okay, I'm sorry. I kind of freaked out after talking to Sloan. Sometimes, I swear it's like this switch gets flipped, and I—"

"You've been through a lot lately," Vivian assured her. "Which is why I didn't want to call you just yet. Sit down." Vivian pointed to the kitchen table.

"Should I make coffee?" Nate offered.

"Don't think she needs any caffeine," Vivian muttered under her breath. "How about some tea? We've got plenty of that, so hot water will do. Tell you what, Nate. Since you were worried about leaving me alone, why don't you take off and go see Fletcher, and Lizzy can stay here? Get this whole ball in motion, yeah?"

"You sure?" Nate eyed Lizzy.

"I'm sure," Vivian said as he gathered up his things. "I can handle this. And you need to get out of here before you go stir-crazy."

He both liked and didn't like the fact she recognized that about him. "Lizzy, can you stay with her until I get back?" Nate asked.

"Sure." Lizzy nodded and shrugged. "Sure. I'm not meeting Ajay at The Tides until five."

"Five, okay. Got it." Nate checked his watch. That gave him a few hours. "I'll be back by then for sure. Vivian?" He inclined his head to draw her over. "I've never seen her like this."

"You haven't been kidnapped before," Vivian said quietly. "It comes in waves. Most of the time, I've been around for her to confide in. You Coltons are pretty good at keeping your feelings to yourself." She arched a brow at him. "Never show any weakness, right?"

"Tell me she's getting professional help."

"We've talked about it." Vivian looked back as Lizzy wandered over to look out the back glass doors. "We'll be talking about it again. And hey, we have a few more things in common now. Me with the flying bullets and killer SUVs. Her with… Yeah." She steered him to the door. "It'll all be fine. Just give us some time."

"Some." He was already counting the minutes until he could get back. "But not a lot."

It took two full mugs of tea before Vivian felt as if Lizzy was back on even keel. She'd bet just about every penny in her bank account that Lizzy Colton had kept things together for everyone else. There was an unexpected burst of pride in knowing that Lizzy felt comfortable enough to break down in front of her. But it also waved a red flag. Trauma was tricky and insidious and often snuck up to slap its victims when they least expected it.

A lesson for Lizzy, Vivian wondered. Or herself?

"I'm so embarrassed." Lizzy curled up in the corner of the sofa, a half-full mug clutched between her hands as Vivian dug out one of the many packages of cookies that had been left hidden around the kitchen. "I can only imagine what Nate might think."

"I can tell you exactly what he was thinking." Vivian pulled out four crunchy chocolate chip cookies, set them on a plate, then left those on the counter and brought the entire package over. "He's worried about you. Here." She handed Lizzy the package and plopped down beside her. "Which means congratulations, you're now on his list of people to take care of." She snatched a cookie and bit in. "Welcome to the club."

Lizzy's eyes had stopped spinning more than an hour ago, once Vivian had gone through everything that had transpired since she'd first walked into Madariaga's. She'd felt odd rehashing everything, as if it were some kind of story she'd committed to memory.

"Is that a club I'm happy to belong to?" Lizzy's knowing look had Vivian squirming in her seat. "You and Nate? You're…together, right?"

"We are." Vivian had wondered how her best friend would feel about her getting involved with Nate. Given the strained family dynamic at the moment, there was no way to predict what was coming next. "Do you remember telling me the first time that you met Ajay?"

Lizzy ducked her chin, but not before Vivian saw the healthy pink tint to her cheeks. "I have a vague recollection of that conversation."

Considering the amount of wine that had been poured that evening, Vivian was impressed. "When I was sitting there, listening to you, all I could think at the time was that you were still caught up in the excitement of everything that had happened. That you were, I don't know, too susceptible to his charm. That you'd fallen as much for the romance of the situation as you had for him."

"You think being kidnapped was romantic?"

"No, of course not," Vivian said. She wasn't explaining this very well. "I think the end result has proven itself out though. You seem to have this, I don't know, calmness about you." Despite the anxiety that had sprung up. "As if you've stopped looking for something you were unaware you needed." Vivian sipped her tea, considered her words carefully. "The first time I saw Nate, sitting at that bar, that kind of warning in his eyes, like he was already protecting me, I don't know if I can explain it."

"Like finding your other half?" Lizzy suggested.

"No." She didn't need someone to complete her. "It was like being around him unlocked my other half." Her silent, intimidated half. Even now, the doubt remained. But since her conversation with Nate, her faith was stronger. "I'm not...afraid around him."

"Afraid? Oh, Vivian." Lizzy tilted her head.

"I mean I'm not afraid to be myself. There's no expectations. No show to put on. I don't have to impress him or pretend to be something or someone I'm not. He sees me." The admission lifted her heart. "Who I really am. And he has from the start. Everything I never thought I would have has clicked into place. Which brings me to a question I have for you."

"For me?" Lizzy frowned. "What about?"

"About Nate. And me. Lizzy, you're the best friend I've ever had. The only friend, really." She was already slipping into excuse mode, something she knew Nate would call her on. "But given everything that's going on with your mom and finding out about Nate and Sarah…" She screwed up her courage and just put it out there. "You're okay with me dating him, aren't you? I don't want to complicate things further."

"I could approach this question in a couple of ways." Lizzy ate another cookie, sipped her tea, looked at Vivian over the top of her mug. "But I'm not going to draw this out any longer than necessary. What's going on where Nate and Sarah and the rest of the family is concerned has nothing to do with you. There's only one thing I've ever wanted for you, Vivian. To be happy. And to be honest, until I saw you with him before he left, I don't think I ever have seen that side of him. You care about him, don't you?"

"I love him." The simple statement rocked the foundation of her life. "I haven't told him, of course." She laughed a little. Cried a little. "I haven't lost all my senses." But the time was coming when she would. She had to. If for no other reason than to put her heart out there one more time.

Lizzy's eyes filled. "Then take that ride with him, Vivian. Don't let go. Even when things get difficult or complicated or… I think he's probably worth it. You're right. About the family. Things are weird and frustrating, but everything I know about him—that he stands up for his family, even when he doesn't really know us? That's about as good a guy as you can find." She grinned. "That said, you might want to give him fair warning that he and I are about to become a lot closer because where you go, I go. End of story."

"Okay, then." Another weight she hadn't realized she was carrying lifted off her shoulders. "I'll do just that. And I'll go on that ride." For however long it may last.

Chapter 14

Sitting across from Fletcher in his office at the Owl Creek Police Department, Nate watched his brother read through the report he'd put together on Detective Jim Sullivan and his plausible connection to Marty DeBaccian. The situation reminded Nate of his trips to the principal's office once upon a time.

Either his brother read at the speed of a comatose turtle, or Fletcher was committing every word Nate had written to memory. The only thing that made the waiting tolerable was Max, who, seated on the side cabinet by the door, kept rustling an open bag of chips that he'd found in the break room.

Nate checked his watch. The afternoon was ticking away, but he had plenty of time to get back to Vivian before Lizzy left. Storm clouds had accompanied them on the drive, which meant the snow would be coming in hard and fast. All the more reason to get all of this behind them.

"So, Lizzy," Max said between crunches. "How'd she seem when you saw her?"

Fletcher's gaze didn't flicker from the printed file Nate had run off as soon as he got to the station.

"Stressed." It was, Nate thought, the best word he could think of to describe their sister. "Worried. I think she might need some assistance dealing with what happened to her last month."

Max nodded, dug deeper into the bag. "I thought the same thing before Ajay took her away for some downtime. Good to know we're all on the same page."

"We'll make sure Lizzy gets whatever help she needs." Fletcher sat forward in his squeaky chair. "Vivian's always been a solid support person for her. It's good Lizzy showed up at the house. Means she's getting back on track. I appreciate you running this past me before sending it to your lieutenant."

"Figured it would be safer to send it from here on one of your more secure computers than from the house." Nate pointed to the pages Fletcher had insisted on printing out. "Took some finagling to track down all of Sullivan's logins for the past few years. Seeing the cases he was keeping an eye on tells me that when we get him into custody, we should look beyond DeBaccian. He's worked in a number of departments over the years, which means he's had access to more information than I feel comfortable with at the moment."

"No, I think you're exactly right," Fletcher agreed. "And I think the sooner we shoot this over to Boise PD, the better." He glanced at Max. "You've read this?"

"I have." Max chomped a chip. "Last night. Early this morning," he corrected.

"Thoughts?"

Max wrapped up the bag and set it aside. "I think, once Sullivan's been questioned, he might prove quite beneficial to a number of federal investigations currently on the books. Half the names DeBaccian has been in contact with are being actively investigated. More to the point, if you can flip Sullivan, you get him a deal to turn on DeBaccian and you remove Vivian from the equation altogether, which, let's face it, would be a major win for everyone involved."

"Not going to argue with that." Nate nodded. "I'm anxious to head back to Boise and try to put this whole thing to bed."

"Yeah, well, that isn't happening just yet," Fletcher said in a warning voice. "You're about to bust open what is tantamount to a nationwide organized crime ring. The longer you keep your head down, the better."

"Actually..." Max slapped his hands together before wiping them on his jeans. "I was going to recommend the opposite. Make some noise. Get down there and pull the attention off Vivian."

"Give DeBaccian a bigger target, you mean," Fletcher clarified.

"The second this report of Nate's hits the Boise PD system, all hell is going to break loose," Max went on. "Unless either of you can convince me that the server and anyone with access are locked down one-hundred-percent."

Nate considered it, and he didn't like the implied suggestion. "You're thinking Sullivan isn't the only one we should be worried about."

"Where there's one bad apple..." Max trailed off. "There's something to be said for scaring the crap out of people, even cops. Makes them do stupid things. Careless things."

"It also might push someone into coming forward

with information you can actually use as evidence against Sullivan." Fletcher nodded. "It isn't a horrible idea."

"You do have a way with compliments, Fletch," Max said.

"I don't know." Nate's reluctance had more to do with the idea of leaving Vivian alone even longer than planned.

"I can have one of my deputies sit on the house, if that's what's stopping you," Fletcher said. "Unless Max wants to take on protection detail?"

"Can't." Max slapped his hands together. "I'm going to Boise with our baby brother. Just to make sure he stays out of trouble."

Nate waited for the irritation. Or the embarrassment at his newly acquired nickname. Neither descended. But a smile lurked. A smile that came far more easily since Vivian had entered his life. One thing he'd learned in the past few days was that there was definitely a lot more to life than just work.

Fletcher laughed as his phone rang. He answered with a brusque "Detective Colton."

"Do people get confused, do you think?" Nate asked Max. "With all the Coltons in law enforcement."

"Nah," Max said easily. "We all sound different."

"Hang on, Lieutenant." Fletcher eyed Nate. "Let me put you on Speaker." He tapped a button on his phone, hung up the receiver. "You're on with me, Nate and our brother, Max Colton, who's a special consultant. You want to go through that one more time?"

"What's going on?" Nate asked his boss.

"We found a set of partials in the SUV that ran

Ms. Maylor off the road," Lieutenant Haig reported. "I went with your gut, Nate. I ran them against Sullivan's. They're a match."

Nate swore. So Sullivan had tried to kill Vivian. "He must have followed her from the station house."

"Probably," Haig said. "I've got Renard and Paulson running the security footage from the station to confirm. I've got an arrest warrant in the works."

"What about DeBaccian?" Max asked. "Any sighting of him yet?"

"None." And Lieutenant Haig didn't sound pleased about it. "But I'm not giving up hope. He's out there. We'll find him. In the meantime, Nate, I'm afraid your presence is required."

"In Boise?" He shook his head when Max opened his mouth, no doubt to tell Nate's CO they were already planning to head south. "Why?"

"You have a confidential informant on record who goes by the name Ferret Face?"

"Yeah." Nate frowned. "Real name's Colin Michaels. He's a hacker. Specializes in virus creation. Nasty ones that take down entire computer systems, but usually only for his own amusement. Did he call in with some intel?" Odd. He hadn't heard from Ferret in months.

"Not exactly," Haig said. "Someone tried to kill him a few hours ago."

"Tried?" Nate couldn't quite process. "And failed?"

"He's still alive. A bit crispy around the edges, though," Haig told them. "Said he did a job for someone, only instead of paying, they tried to shoot him. Bullet grazed his head, and he played dead. Then tried to put out the fire they set to take out his network with his bare hands."

"Ouch." Max winced.

"First I've heard of Ferret going commercial," Nate said. "Makes sense, I suppose. He's been putting his younger sister through college, and his mother's had medical expenses."

"Is that information in your CI file?" Fletcher asked.

Nate nodded. "Sure." He liked being able to use specific motivations when approaching one of his sources for information. Ferret might be one of the smartest computer hackers he'd come across, but compared to other criminals Nate had dealt with, the guy was a kitty cat.

"Did he say who hired him, Lieutenant?" Fletcher asked.

"That's the problem," Haig said. "He's not saying anything. He'll only talk to Nate. Either him, or he'll lawyer up. We've got him in an interview room, but he's going to start asking for additional medical attention pretty soon. I'd rather not take him out of the station until we have to."

"Ferret's always been wiggy," Nate told his brothers. "Makes sense he'd get more squirrely after something like this." If someone had tried to kill a rather insignificant hacker like Ferret, he must have taken on a really big job.

"Yeah, well, Mr. Wiggy underestimated our lab techs," Haig said. "They tapped into the security feed at his warehouse hideout." Haig paused. "Did Ferret ever mention Sullivan to you, Nate?"

"No." Nate couldn't make sense of this. "Cops don't poach other cops' CIs." What would Sullivan want with Ferret Face?

"Sullivan's not other cops," Fletcher said. "Lieutenant, I'm sending you the report Nate's put together on

Sullivan. Right..." He turned his attention back to his desktop and clicked a few buttons. "Now. You should have it soon. In the meantime—"

"I'm on my way," Nate told his boss. "I can be there in—"

"*We'll* be there in a little under an hour." Fletcher hung up on Haig and headed for the door, grabbed his jacket off the hook. "Work out who's riding shotgun," he told Nate and Max. "Because we aren't stopping once we hit the siren."

"I should not have drunk so much tea." Lizzy straightened her pale yellow shirt as she came out of the bathroom. "I'm going to be lucky to make the drive before I have to pee again."

Vivian smiled, closed the door to the refrigerator, where she'd been taking mental inventory so she could figure out what to fix Nate for dinner. "Yes, well, I'm sure you'll have a great night with Ajay, nonetheless."

"Oh, I know I will." Lizzy's cheery smile was back in place, a welcome sight compared to how she'd looked when she first arrived. "I'd say we'll have to compare notes in the morning, but seeing as it's my brother you're seeing..." She gave a little shudder. "Yeah, best not to have those images running around my head." Her cell phone rang from deep in her purse. "I bet that's Ajay now, checking in." She dug around, pulled out her phone, looked at the screen. "Huh. Totally wrong on that." She tapped Answer. "Fletcher? What's going on? Oh." Lizzy headed straight over to Vivian. "Sure, Nate. She's right here." She handed her phone over. "Nate needs to talk to you."

"Hey." She tried not to let the butterflies that had fluttered to life in her belly multiply. "Everything okay?"

"Honestly?" He sounded on edge, and the background noise surging through the phone included a siren. "I don't know what's going on. I'm with Fletcher and Max. We're headed into Boise right now. Something about one of my informants being in contact with Detective Sullivan. He's refusing to speak to anyone other than me."

"Oh." She glanced at her watch. Outside, the construction crew's trucks began heading out as a bright white van carrying custom glass drove in. "So you'll be later than you thought. That's okay." If anything, it was brilliant. She could get a jump start on her to-do list for tomorrow.

"You want me to stay?" Lizzy whispered.

Vivian shook her head, waved her off.

"Fletcher sent a patrol car to sit on the house until I get home," Nate said. "It's a Deputy Jeff Bricks. You probably saw him at the station the other day."

She'd seen a lot of people at the station.

"He left when we did," Nate continued. "So he should be there any time now. Even with the storm that's coming in, I should be back soon."

"Okay." As she approached the window, she saw the patrol car pull up and park right in front. "I'll check in with him. I'll be fine, Nate. Do what you need to do. Be careful."

"You sure? Maybe Lizzy—"

"Lizzy is already on her way to meet Ajay for dinner." She wasn't about to ask her friend to change her plans. "We had this conversation before. I know how the security system works, and now there's a cop right outside. Focus on your job, then come home, Nate." She paused. "To me."

"Yeah." She could almost hear the smile in his voice. "Yeah, that sounds like a perfect plan. I've got the deputy's number. If I need to call, I'll reach you that way."

"Got it. Oh, and Nate?" Those butterflies swarmed to life, but this time she embraced it. "I've got something to tell you when you get here. Something…important."

Lizzy tilted her head, pressed a hand to her heart.

"Even better. Stay safe." He clicked off.

"You two are just so cute," Lizzy said. "Are you sure you don't want me to—"

"I'm sure." Vivian handed her back her phone and walked her to the door. "He won't be gone that long, and it's starting to snow. Go. Have a good evening with Ajay."

"Always do," Lizzy confirmed.

Vivian followed her outside, waved her off in her car before she headed to the patrol car. "Hi." She smiled as the young deputy powered down his window. "Nate called and said you were coming. Vivian Maylor." She held out her hand.

"Jeff Bricks." With his dark hair and boyish smile, he reminded her a little of what she imagined Nate had looked like shortly after becoming a cop. "I checked with the guard at the gate. Updated them on what's going on."

"I'm sure we're in for a quiet evening. I'll be working. You want anything? Coffee? Snacks?"

"I'm good." He patted the green thermos sitting in one of the oversize cup holders. "Hopefully, you won't have any need to see me again."

"Okay, then." She stood up, gave him another smile.

"Thanks for doing this. You change your mind about wanting something to eat, just ring the bell."

"Lord love a duck, Ferret looks like he spent this morning in an air fryer." On the other side of the two-way mirror, Nate stood bookended between his brothers and his lieutenant.

"We had him sign a waiver stating he'd postponed medical attention," Lieutenant Haig said, hands shoved into the front pockets of his slacks, gray-haired head shifting against the fluorescent recessed lighting. "EMTs did the best they could."

"He's got to be in pain." Even Max flinched.

"Which means whatever it is he has to tell me is worth postponing treatment." Nate shook his head. "Guess I'd best get in there and find out what it is."

A knock sounded on the observation room door. The four of them turned as it popped open. Detective Julia Renard poked her head in. "Sorry. Lieutenant, patrol just radioed in. They've got movement at Shake It Loose."

"Is it DeBaccian?" Nate demanded. There were only two things he wanted right now: DeBaccian and Sullivan in custody, and to be back home with Vivian.

"Unconfirmed," Detective Renard said. "Our guys are too far away for a positive ID."

"I'm going to send two more cars out there for backup," Lieutenant Haig said. "Detective, get in there, and let's get to the bottom of this."

"Yes, sir." He looked to his brothers.

"You've got this," Fletcher told him. "But we're here if you need us."

"Thanks." Nate nodded. "Appreciate that." He didn't

give himself much time to think. Thinking might lead to mistakes. He needed to be impulsive, even as he reminded himself how to deal with Ferret Face. He tended to be cagey, hyper and, more often than not, smarter than he looked.

He didn't knock, just walked right into the interview room. "Colin." Using his hacker name wasn't something he tended to do. He needed to talk to the man behind the moniker. "What's going on, man? I hear you need to talk to me." He couldn't stop his wince of sympathy at the sight of the burns on Ferret's face, neck and arms. A stark white bandage had been taped to his right temple, and his hands, both of them, were thickly bandaged and wrapped up. "Just looking at you, I can see you're in over your head."

Beady brown eyes, usually magnified behind thick glasses, widened as Nate took a seat across from him. "You're here. Nate, dude, I need your help."

"That's why I'm here." Hands folded on the table, he did his best to keep calm and maintain his patience. "You been working with Detective Sullivan behind my back, Colin? I thought you and I had a deal."

"We did, man, we did." Ferret leaned forward. "I didn't want anything to do with this guy, right? I told him, I only work for you. Detective Nate Colton. Because you have my back. You always have."

"You'd best come out with it, then, just to make sure our relationship stays intact."

"But that's just it. I can talk now. Because you're here." The relief shining in Ferret's eyes seemed out of place. "This was part of the deal I made with him."

"Deal you made with who?" Something slimy and uncertain slithered in Nate's gut. "Detective Jim Sullivan?"

"So you know already?" Ferret squeaked. "Ah, man, does that mean Laura's okay? You've got her?"

"Your sister?" Nate glanced at the mirror, hoped Fletcher and Max got the message. "Sure, yeah, we've got her, Colin." Now wasn't the time to tell the truth.

Colin sobbed and lowered his head, banged his red, raw skin against the table. "Okay. Okay, I knew you'd get her. I knew you wouldn't let me down. He said he knew where she lived, that he could get to her anytime if I didn't do what he wanted."

"Detective Sullivan?" Nate had to be careful how he asked. It could just as easily be one of DeBaccian's henchmen, or even DeBaccian himself. "Colin? Look at me. Stop banging your head and come clean, okay? I can't keep helping you if you don't. Was it Detective Jim Sullivan? Describe him for me."

"Yeah, yeah, that's the name he gave me. Red hair, mean eyes. He shows up at my place a couple of nights ago, says he's heard about this new program I've created. Might have gotten too chatty at the Down and Dirty a few weeks ago in that poker game—"

"Colin," Nate warned. "Focus. What's this new program?"

"It's a virus that doubles as a tracker. Send an email with a virus, not as an attachment, but embedded in a link. Like in a sig line. It's mad brilliant, man. They click on it and *bam!* We can trace whatever device they use."

Nate nodded as if he understood completely. "So you did what he wanted, yeah?"

"Yeah, I sent the email that night. Told him I wasn't

sure it would work. I'm still, like, beta testing it and everything, but he promised me ten K if I took the job. That's like a semester and a half for Laura's school. And sure, yeah, he threatened her if I didn't take the job, but ten thou!"

"I get it, Colin." Nate resisted flinching. "She's family. You do what you have to do for family. That's all he had you do? Send the email?"

"Yes. Well, no." His eyes shifted, and he sank back in his chair. "He came back last night. Man, I'm sorry. I didn't want to do it, but it was the only way he said he wouldn't kill me. The only way he wouldn't go after Laura. And my mom. He threatened my family!"

"You told the officers who brought you in that this guy tried to kill you." Nate pointed to the bandage on his head.

"I had to tell them something!" Ferret cried. "It was the only way they'd call you, and I needed to get you back here, to Boise!"

"Get me back…" The pieces fell into place as if in slow motion. "He didn't really try to kill you, did he, Colin? Colin? Ferret!" Nate slammed his hand hard on the table. Ferret jumped. Guilt swam in his watery eyes. "Was all this a setup? Did you set fire to your own place?"

"It was the only way, man! I'm sorry! I didn't want… You've always been—"

Nate looked up when the door swung open. Fletcher and his lieutenant stood in the doorway, looming. Brooding.

"What?" Nate demanded.

"DeBaccian's club, Shake It Loose?" Fletcher said.

"What about it?" Nate asked.

"We just got a 911 call," Lieutenant Haig said. "It's on fire."

"Unbelievable," Max muttered from where he stood beside Nate, across the street from the now smoldering building that housed Shake It Loose. The parking lot contained a handful of cars, two fire engines and one ambulance. The fact the strip club had been closed for the past two weeks had probably saved lives. DeBaccian knew how to run a successful—if sleazy—business. "They should rename this city Coincidence Central."

Lieutenant Haig had accepted Fletcher's offer to be a second pair of eyes and ears when speaking with the fire chief leading the charge to douse the remaining embers of the fire. The fire had been out for a good half hour, but the smoke continued to billow as water dripped into frozen rivers and streamed into the street.

"Patrol units at each corner around this place, and none of them saw who was inside?" Max said. "How does that even happen?"

"Nate!" Detective Kevin Paulson, Renard's partner, hurried over from where he'd been speaking with two of the uniformed officers. "Patrol officer in the third car on scene hit Record on her body cam. Not sure if she caught anything, but it's worth a shot. We've got the footage coming through anytime."

It was something, at least. He'd feel a heck of a lot better if he could speak to Vivian, but between spotty cell service and the frenetic activity, there hadn't been a chance. "Any updates on who was inside?" Nate had never prayed so hard for a dead body in his life. If De-

Baccian was dead, that would kill any case the feds might be able to build against his associates, but it would put Vivian in the clear.

"Firefighters found three bodies in the back office." Fletcher joined them, his voice low and intense. "Just finished talking with the chief. Fire was started near the front, so it didn't get to them."

"Cause of death?"

"They were shot," Fletcher confirmed. "Close range."

Nate held his breath. "Tell me one is—"

"Chief's got a picture." Fletcher signaled the chief over, and she approached, still loaded down with equipment. She flipped up her face shield. "Chief Gibbs?"

"Detective Fletcher and Lieutenant Haig filled me in." The shorter, stockier woman handed over her cell phone. "Goes against protocol, but I took this. Hope it helps."

"There, bottom left corner." Fletcher pointed to the image. "Zoom in."

Nate took the phone and did just that. The familiar family crest glinted. "That's DeBaccian's ring."

"Looks like he didn't make it out of town after all," Max muttered before he swore and turned away.

"So he's dead." Nate couldn't quite let himself believe it.

"We've got the medical examiner's office sending out a team now," Lieutenant Haig said. "You should get back and finish with Ferret Face, Nate."

"Evidence tech is working with him at the moment," Nate said. "Ferret said he could access his cloud storage to retrieve the virus information."

"Probably go a lot faster if the guy could type quicker with those bandages," Max said.

Lieutenant Haig's cell rang. "Yeah." He turned away as he answered.

"So, that's it?" Nate looked at Max. "After all this, it's just over?"

"Sometimes that's the way a case breaks." Max shrugged.

"And all these coincidences?" Nate challenged. "They don't bother you?"

"Didn't say that." Max waited a beat. "They bother you?"

Yes, but his gut wasn't capable of overriding actual evidence.

Lieutenant Haig rejoined them. "Security at Boise Airport just stopped someone using Jim Sullivan's ID to board a flight to Mexico."

Fletcher, Max and Nate simply stared at him.

"Yeah." Lieutenant Haig smirked and ducked his head. "I'm not buying it, either. He'd know we'd have locked down the airports, train stations and bus terminals in the city. No way he's that careless. I asked the officers to send me a photo..." His phone chimed. "And there it is." He turned the phone around. "Definitely not Jim Sullivan."

"Misdirect," Fletcher said. "A stupid one."

"None of this explains Sullivan going to Ferret Face," Nate said, more to himself than anyone else. "What good would a tracking virus be...?"

"Was Sullivan tracking someone for himself or for DeBaccian?" Fletcher asked.

"Only person that we know of that DeBaccian would want found is Vivian," Max said. "Do we have a copy of the email he sent yet?"

"Still working on it," Lieutenant Haig said. "Apparently there are seven levels of security that need to be traversed in order to gain access to Ferret Face's cloud storage."

"No one's more paranoid than a hacker," Nate growled. Smoke continued to plume into the air from inside Shake It Loose. "Only three bodies inside. No one else?"

"As far as surveillance reported," Lieutenant Haig said. "No one else went in or came out the front or back in the past eight hours."

"What about the alley?" Nate asked.

Lieutenant Haig blinked. "What alley?"

"There's a narrow one between the club and the abandoned building next door. I read about it in one of the initial surveillance reports from a few months ago. It's not wide enough for a vehicle, but DeBaccian used it as a private entrance. And he had at least two security cameras working twenty-four seven."

Lieutenant Haig shook his head. "I just reread all those reports this morning. No mention of the alley or the cameras."

"That list of databases Sullivan accessed that you came up with," Fletcher said to Nate. "One of them was the official records files, right?"

"He could have deleted the mention from the report," Nate said. "I couldn't go deeper than a cursory examination without raising an alarm." He looked back to the club. "We need to get in there. There might be security footage. Proof of Sullivan getting away." Maybe even proof he was guilty of murdering DeBaccian.

"Chief!" Lieutenant Haig called to Chief Gibbs.

"We're going to need your help. And a couple of helmets. We need to get inside."

With the television on for background noise—she preferred old Hollywood musicals to keep her mood elevated—Vivian made slow and steady progress on her always growing to-do list. Cyber-handholding had become her specialty. Selfishly, she preferred clients who liked communicating via email rather than spending countless hours on video or phone calls.

With the Christmas tree providing ambient lighting and the dim glow from over the stove, the house felt even cozier than before. Instead of tea—she'd definitely had her fill for a while—she had opened one of the bottles of wine she found in the dedicated wine refrigerator. Nothing rounded out the day quite like a bold Bordeaux. Sipping, she sighed and resisted the urge to check her watch for the hundredth time.

As the sun set and the night crept in, she couldn't help but feel anxious for Nate to return. Not just because she didn't relish being alone in this big house. Because she missed him.

Needing to stretch, she set her laptop on the coffee table and stood up, twisting and reaching her arms over her head to work out the kinks. She took a short walk down the hall to the front of the house. The patrol car hadn't moved. The now familiar shadow of Deputy Jeff Bricks shifted in the darkness. She waved, whether he could see her or not, and headed back into the kitchen.

She caught the oven timer before it started beeping and retrieved a pair of potholders to pull out the pork roast she'd set to cooking earlier. She tented it with foil, telling herself she could reheat it should Nate be much later.

With Bing Crosby and Danny Kaye singing on the television, she settled back onto the sofa and picked up her laptop again.

The second she started typing, the power cut out. The house went dark.

"Good thing the fire inspector won't be here until to-morrow morning," Chief Gibbs grumbled at their backs as Nate and Lieutenant Haig made their way through the burned-out strip club. It had taken some convincing, letting any of them inside, but she'd eventually given in, probably just to get the lieutenant off her overburdened back.

They'd donned evidence booties—those lovely blue cloth shoe coverings that would prevent them from dragging any trace evidence of their own onto the scene. Nate was relieved she hadn't put them in hazmat suits.

The alley door had been left ajar. Ash and soot had spread outside the club. Fletcher and Max remained outside, acting as a point of communication should they need it.

It wasn't Nate's first fire scene. The charred, wet wood gave off its own particular aroma, and the smoke settled into his lungs like an unwanted resident. He'd be smelling this place for weeks, no doubt. Maybe the hazmat suit would have been okay. He could hear the *drip, drip, drip* of the hose water used to knock back the flames.

"At first glance, I'd say whoever started it hedged their bets. I've got traces in the front and back entrances," Chief Gibbs called over her shoulder, a hand keeping her bright yellow helmet steady on her head. "Be careful where you step, please. I really don't want to fill out a report about you two being in here."

"Consider yourself having earned multiple favors from the police department," Lieutenant Haig told her.

She stopped outside a barely holding together door frame. "I'll remember that." She stepped back. "Your bodies are back there, near the desk. What's left of the desk," she corrected. "I'm going to take another walk-through, make sure we didn't miss anyone. Ten minutes," she told them. "That's it."

"That's all we'll need," Nate assured her. Unable to choke down any more smoke, he pulled the collar of his T-shirt up over his nose, stepped carefully through the debris and burned carpet and flooring. "Well, I see three." He didn't know what he expected other than what had already been reported.

He crouched down, carefully lifted one of the three bright yellow tarps covering the bodies. The flames hadn't done enough damage to obscure the markings on both men's skin.

"These two match the description Vivian gave of the shooters." He flipped the tarps back up, stood up, turned and took four steps the right. The exposed hand, stretched out as if for help, displayed the now familiar ring that had, for years, represented DeBaccian's growing power. He'd wielded it like a weapon, frequently shifting it to his right hand in order to leave a lasting mark.

"Nothing surprising." Lieutenant Haig nodded to the large safe across the room. "That's been emptied out."

"Guns, no doubt. And cash," Nate said, shaking his head. "Chief Gibbs was right. This was a waste of time."

"I heard that!" Chief Gibbs called from outside the room.

Nate almost laughed. He pushed to his feet, slipped his foot free of the corner of the tarp that caught against his shoe. The tarp fluttered and settled, exposing part of the victim's face.

Shock cut through him like a knife. Nate dropped back down, ripped the tarp back and stared at the body, with its dead wide eyes. "Lieutenant? You seeing what I'm seeing?" He pointed to the red hair gleaming in the dim light of their helmet lights.

"It's Jim Sullivan," his lieutenant confirmed.

"Nate!"

Nate pivoted as Fletcher dived into sight.

"Hey!" Chief Gibbs stalked toward him, hands up. "I told you to wait—"

"Nate, we've got the email Ferret sent." Fletcher plowed right past her. "It was an inquiry addressed to PR Perfection."

"PR…" Nate's heart skipped a beat. "That's Vivian's company. Ferret was hired to track Vivian's laptop." He stared blankly at his boss, then turned to look down at the body. "Sullivan's dead," he murmured. "Which means DeBaccian isn't." Fear wrapped its talons around his heart and squeezed. "He's going after her."

"We have to get back to Owl Creek," Fletcher commanded. "Now!"

Chapter 15

Vivian groaned and dropped her head back. The marvels of living in snow country. At home, she had a generator that would kick in when the power went out. But up here? She used her laptop as a light and untangled herself yet again from the sofa.

She heard a car door slam and quickly hurried to the window. The handful of street lamps that had been installed had gone dark as well. The only things casting any light were the moon and the interior of the deputy's car.

Deputy Bricks headed up the walkway, zipping up his jacket.

She set her laptop on the floor, hurried to the door and pulled it open. "What's going on?" she asked.

"No idea," the deputy said. "I'm going to take a walk around. There might be some crews working late... Maybe they tripped something." He offered a smile. "You okay in there?"

"Everything's fine." She shrugged.

"Let me take a quick look, just to be safe."

She shrugged and stepped back. "Okay. I think I saw some candles in the pantry."

"Great." He closed the door behind him and headed down one hall while Vivian retrieved her laptop.

"Oh!" She snapped her fingers, remembering her cell. It might be useless for calls, but it made a better flashlight than her computer. She headed upstairs to the bedroom, grabbed it from where she'd set it last night when she'd spent almost a half hour looking at pictures of Toby. She left her laptop on the bed, turned on the flashlight.

A soft thud echoed from downstairs.

She froze. "Deputy Bricks?" Taking slow steps, she moved into the hall, walked to the landing of the stairs. "Deputy?" The light wavered as her hand shook. "Hello?"

She cast the light around, eyes adjusting to the harsh light against the shadows.

"Deputy?" She yelled this time and winced against the echo that shot back at her.

Footsteps sounded. Dull, heavy.

Growing closer.

She shivered against a sudden chill and only now realized she could hear the wind blowing. Her mind raced. Everything she'd been told about the house seemed to tumble in her head. Alarm. Guard house. Panels.

She raced back into the bedroom, forced herself to be quiet when closing the door.

The keypad on the wall seemed to mock her as she flipped open the panel and hit the emergency button.

Nothing happened.

She pounded a fist against the console.

Frustrated tears burned the back of her throat. Blurred her eyes.

The footsteps were coming up the stairs. Slowly. Closer.

Her bare toes scrunched into the hardwood flooring.

She spun around, looking for something, anything, with which to defend herself. Moonlight shimmered against the glass door.

Swallowing her panic, she ran forward, threw open the doors, raced to the balcony railing, then forced herself to slow down, turn and return to the bedroom, placing her feet in the same prints she'd made in the snow.

She left the doors open, ran quietly tos the closet and ducked inside, pulling the door closed behind her as the bedroom doorknob rattled.

She killed the flashlight, hugged her phone against her chest. Moonlight streamed across the slats of the closet door.

She stepped back into the corner, into the darkness, as a large, shadowy figure stepped into the room.

"I'm not getting any response from Bricks," Fletcher said from the back seat. Max had reached the driver's side first and had them speeding out of Boise, siren blaring. "I'm calling the station now."

"We'll get there," Max said. "I promise, Nate, we'll get there in time."

"You know as well as I do that's an impossible promise to make." He was a cop. He'd been a cop for almost a decade. He was well aware of the realities of the job. "I shouldn't have left her."

"Don't go down that road," Fletcher ordered. "It doesn't lead anywhere good. If we can't get to her, I'll get someone who can. Yeah," he yelled into the phone. "Monroe, I want all hands on deck and up at Colton Crossing. We've got a wanted suspect on-site." He recited the address of the house. "Be on the lookout for

Vivian Maylor..." He rattled off Vivian's description. "I'm about— Max! Watch it!"

Nate gripped the passenger seat with both hands as Max weaved his way in and around slowing traffic.

"We need to get there alive to help her," Nate ground out between gritted teeth.

"Doing my best," Max said as he pressed his foot even harder on the gas. "Don't worry. I'm motivated. Lizzy will never forgive us if anything happens to Vivian."

"*I'll* never forgive us." Nate stared into the snowy night and did something he hadn't done in a very, very long time.

He prayed.

Terror, Vivian thought as she watched the figure pass, worked as a surprisingly effective mental reboot.

She knew what she didn't have at her disposal—the alarm and warning system she'd been told about time and again. No communication because her cell phone was little more than a door weight. She was currently a sitting duck. But hopefully a silent one.

Vivian stepped forward, angling her head to peer through the closet slats.

The man was following her footprints, stepping outside the bedroom. Onto the balcony. One step from the door. Two...three...

She pushed open the closet door and squeezed out. She couldn't risk closing it again for fear he'd hear. Moving as quietly as she could, she hurried out of the bedroom door toward the stairs.

She was three steps down when she heard him. No. She *felt* him. An energy of rage that pulsed through the house and nearly knocked her off her feet. She lost her grip on her phone, heard it skid away after it hit the floor.

Panic had her scrambling, tripping, nearly tumbling to the landing, but she stayed on her feet, using the banister to propel herself to the front door.

He'd locked it. Bolted it. She tugged on the handle, tried to flip the lock, but he was coming down the stairs. Too close.

Too, too close.

Her feet slipped and slid as she scrambled toward the kitchen. There had to be something—anything— she could use...

"There's nowhere to run." His voice didn't echo through the house. It settled inside her mind like a dark mantra of warning. "No one to help. I'll make it quick. And painless."

She sobbed, feeling her way down the wall and imagining the path she'd taken countless times in the past few days. Vivian cried out when she ran straight into the corner of the kitchen island. She could already feel a bruise forming as she grappled her way around the stove, knocked over the salt and pepper shakers. Biting back a sob, her hands flailed almost desperately until she finally felt the curved neck of the oil bottle.

His presence pressed in on her. Moonlight shone through the doors, and her eyes adjusted enough for her to grab the bottle and douse the top of the stove.

He stood only a few feet away now, his height making her tilt her head back to see the top of him. He flexed his hands, the leather of his gloves creaking in the silence.

Braced with her back against the stove, she reached behind her and twisted the knob. *Click, click, click, hisssss...*

Vivian dropped to the ground as the gas burner flamed to life.

The flames exploded up, straight into his face. The man screamed, held up both hands to protect himself, stumbled back and crashed down onto the coffee table.

The fire alarm blared, the horrific screech cutting through her head like a hot knife.

Vivian didn't stop to evaluate her actions. Or the damage she may have done to the kitchen.

She raced around the island, down the hall, wrenched open the locks. She flung open the door and ran out into the stormy, snowy night.

"What on earth did they teach you at the FBI academy?" Nate demanded as Max took the off-ramp that would lead to Colton Crossing at nearly twice the legal speed limit. "Holy... Is that black ice?"

"Maybe." Max plowed over it anyway, leading Nate to believe, without a doubt, the tires of Fletcher's SUV weren't even touching the ground.

"My officers are four minutes out," Fletcher yelled over the noise of the engine, the storm and Nate's frayed nerves. "We had a multicar accident in town. They couldn't get away until that was settled."

Nate clenched his jaw tighter. Four minutes. A lot could happen in four minutes.

Max rounded the first corner on two wheels. The siren continued to blare. Nate had no doubt he'd be hearing it in his head for years to come. He should have let her have the stupid cell phone. He needed to talk to her again. Needed to hear her voice again. Needed to tell her...

"Almost there." Max raced down the road as the snow

continued to fall. Another left turn and he zoomed up the final hill.

"There! I can see the guard house!" Fletcher pointed between their seats.

Behind them, more sirens screeched through the night. Nate looked back. Down, in the distance, he could see three patrol cars making their way up the mountain.

Max screeched the SUV to a stop in front of the guard gate.

"Where's the officer?" Nate yelled as he jumped out of the car. He all but leaped at the door that swung open by the hand of a middle-aged man with a full, dark beard. "Open the gate!"

"Power's out!" the guard, whose badge identified him as Angelo, yelled back. "I've been trying to reset the generator, but it's not connecting. Must be the storm!"

"It's not the storm." Nate shoved his way inside, Fletcher right at his heels. "How do I…" He started flipping switches, anything that might trigger the eight-foot wrought iron gate to open.

A red light started blinking, and an alarm sounded.

"What's that? What did I do?" Nate demanded.

"That's a fire alarm," Angelo said. "There's only one house that's occupied."

"Vivian." Nate slammed out of the guard house and went for the fence, looking for a way to squeeze through the slats or pull open the lock.

"Get back!" Max yelled before he ducked back behind the wheel. He screeched the car back, set the tires to spinning and hit the gas full throttle. Nate dived out of the way seconds before Max ran the car straight into the gate.

It didn't open. But the crash jarred it enough to break

the connection on the lock. Nate wedged his hands into the fractured opening, pushed with everything he had. His forearms burned with the exertion, but all he could think was that Vivian was on the other side of this gate. He had to get through. There wasn't any other option.

"Let me help!" Fletcher appeared, and sliding in behind Nate, he got his own hold on the frame. Together they shoved, crying out as the gate finally began to shift down the track.

Nate didn't wait to be sure he'd fit before he shoved his head through, then squeezed through the rest of his body. He tripped on the way out to the other side.

"Go!" Fletcher yelled when Nate looked over his shoulder. "We'll be right behind you! Max!"

Nate didn't have to be told twice. He turned and ran.

Vivian stopped out in the street, the house she'd escaped well behind her. She spun in a dazed circle. The thin fabric of her clothing gave even less protection than she would have imagined. Her feet had gone numb. The rest of her body was quickly following.

Above the gentle roar of the snow, she swore she heard sirens. But it could also be the alarm still blaring from the house. Which way to go? One way would take her to the guard house. The other...to the partially completed construction site. But which was which? She could barely see the sidewalks. But there...in the distance, whether her imagination or not, she saw lights.

She saw hope.

She only had one choice. Trust herself.

Ducking her head, she tightened her arms and, moving as fast as she could, headed into the snow.

* * *

The distance from the guarded gate to the house was a lot longer on foot than it was by car. Nate didn't have the luxury to stop and reevaluate his route. He went by memory, hoping, praying he was headed in the right direction. He ran full out, lungs expanding to the point of catching fire. His legs had long ago gone numb, his feet hurting with each strike on the ground. He was having trouble seeing as the snow flurries whipped around.

He skidded to a stop. There. He squinted, tried to peer closer. He saw something. A flash of shimmering white amidst the white. Like a sharp slice through the night.

"Vivian." He knew it was her even before he saw the whip of dark hair. She was moving slowly, but in the right direction. "Vivian!"

He heard his name on the wind, a sob of relief, of desperation. He couldn't be certain which. Nate raced forward, only to feel his heart leap into his throat at the sound of her scream.

"Nate!"

He kept moving, his line of sight clearing just in time to see the dark shadow of Marty DeBaccian. He had one arm locked around Vivian's throat. And with his free hand, he held a gun to her head.

Nate reached back, pulled out his gun and held it up. He shook his head, tried to see through the falling snow. He couldn't get a lock. He aimed up, then down, to the side, shook his head. He couldn't get a lock.

"There's nowhere to go, DeBaccian!" Nate yelled as he did the only thing he could. He stepped closer. "You've got the Owl Creek cops and an FBI agent coming behind me. You're not getting away."

"There's more than one way out of here!" DeBaccian yelled back.

Nate was close enough now. Close enough to see the abject terror in Vivian's eyes as she struggled to breathe. As she clawed her hands at his arm to dislodge his hold.

"She comes with me!"

Vivian gasped as he lifted her higher, to where her bare feet dangled inches above the snow.

He felt rather than heard his brothers behind him. That charge in the atmosphere could only be one thing: backup. The sound of car engines, the reflection of spinning lights exploding against the falling snow released some of the fear coursing through him.

"She's coming with me!" DeBaccian yelled again, desperation in his voice now.

Nate released the safety on his gun. "She is not."

One more step and he was close enough to fire. He was poised to hit DeBaccian at point-blank range. One shot and it was all over. His finger tightened on the trigger.

Vivian shifted and blocked his shot. He pulled his finger away as she twisted and kicked until she could open her mouth. She kicked back hard, caught DeBaccian on the knee and sank her teeth into his arm.

DeBaccian howled with rage more than pain. He dropped her. Vivian hit the ground on all fours, but before DeBaccian reclaimed his hold, he aimed at Nate's head.

"Freeze! Police!" The voice wasn't familiar. Not to Nate.

DeBaccian spun, looked behind him, gun raised.

A shot rang out. Then another. And a third. Vivian remained crouched on the ground, shivering hard.

DeBaccian dropped to his knees, pitched forward. Landed face down in the snow.

"Vivian." Nate ran to her, had her up and off the ground and in his arms in seconds. He swore, he cursed, he held her as tightly as he could as she shivered so hard she practically vibrated out of his hold.

"Okay?" Fletcher came over with a spare coat and boots from his vehicle for Vivian, then dropped a hand on Nate's shoulder as Max passed right by.

"Yeah," Nate whispered as Vivian nodded against his throat. "You're okay, right, Viv?" He pressed his lips to the top of her head, gratitude and relief flooding through him when she offered a choking whimper. "Is he dead?" Nate yelled at Max as his brother nudged a booted foot under DeBaccian's shoulder and shoved him onto his back.

DeBaccian groaned.

"Not nearly." Max bent down, ripped open DeBaccian's jacket. "He was wearing a vest. Fletcher, your deputy." He pointed to the staggering Jeff Bricks, who had a hand clutched against the back of his head as he made his way toward them.

"Son of a… He clocked me from behind." Bricks spat out the words as Fletcher grabbed him by the shoulders to keep him on his feet. "When I woke up, I swear I thought he was on fire."

"He was," Vivian murmured against Nate's neck. "I put oil on the stove and lit it in his face."

Nate couldn't stop himself. He laughed even as he held her tighter. "Watching all those murder mysteries finally paid off. It's over, Viv." Nate didn't think he could hold her any tighter. "It's all over."

"No," she said as he bent down and slipped an arm under her knees, swept her high into his arms. "It's just beginning." She pressed her lips to his. "I love you, Nate. I needed to tell you that, you know, in case something else happens."

"Nothing else is going to happen." He started walking back to the house. "I'm not going to let anything else happen to you. Ever. You hear me?"

"I hear you. Did you hear me?"

"Yes." For now, he left the fear, the anger and the cleanup behind with his brothers. "I love you, too." He'd always thought when he uttered the words they would come with a question, or with doubt. Or, at the very least, uncertainty. Instead he knew, without any hesitancy, that this thing with Vivian was one-hundred-percent right. "I want to take you out on a date. To celebrate everything," he told her. "How does that sound?"

"Madariaga's?" she asked as he rounded the walkway up to the porch.

"Where we first met?"

She looked up at him, a smile spreading across her lush, perfect lips. "Where else?"

Chapter 16

Nate pulled open the door to Madariaga's just as a gust of wind and snow blew in ahead of him. He took a moment to stomp his feet and shake his head free of the weather.

"You're late."

"Yeah, I know." Nate offered Seb a quick smile as the bartender took the box containing Vivian's Christmas present off his hands. "She been here long?"

"Long enough you'll be glad you got her a gift."

"Awesome." Nate removed his coat, hung it up and slid a finger under his suddenly too tight collar. The flurry of activity that had taken place in the days following Marty DeBaccian's apprehension put the recent snowstorms to shame. But finally, the last piece had been placed, and he was officially on vacation.

"You want your usual?"

"Club soda?" Nate laughed. "Nah. Tonight we're celebrating. Scotch, on the rocks, please, Seb."

The bartender nodded. "You've got it."

"You weren't worried, were you?" Nate said as he slipped up behind a seated Vivian and brushed his lips against her cheek.

"Me? Worry?" She covered the hand he rested on her shoulder and squeezed. "I figured you'd call if you couldn't make it." She didn't look worried. But she did look nervous. Beautiful in an embroidered blue-and-white dress that made her look like a Grecian princess. "You look…" Her smile radiated the warmth of the dining room. "Wow, Detective. You need to wear a suit more often. Everything okay?"

"I'm going to give you the short version." He sat, smoothed his tie down his chest. "Because I don't want to spend tonight debriefing you."

She reached over, slipped her fingers through his. "Well, that's too bad." Her smile lit up her eyes. "I was kind of hoping to be debriefed."

That comment went straight to his groin. "Noted. DeBaccian cut a deal."

Her brow furrowed. "What kind of deal?"

"The kind that guarantees he'll be in prison for life. He turned state's evidence on multiple organized crime figures. In exchange, he gets a new identity and a private cell in a federal prison in Colorado."

"Well, good for him. And us." She lifted her glass of red wine as his drink arrived. They clinked in a toast. "How'd your Colton conference this afternoon go?"

"Colton conference," Nate mused. "I was thinking it was more of a summit, but yeah." He nodded. "It went well, I think. Chase said to thank you for putting their security system through the paces. He and Sloan are going to be making some changes after what happened with the power outage."

"You ever figure out how DeBaccian did that?" Vivian asked.

"He stole a glass repair van and got in with the construction crew. Early enough he gained access to the office and all the information he needed. He already knew what house you were in, thanks to that tracking email."

"Your ferret friend owes me a new computer," she grumbled. "But after the holidays is fine."

He wasn't the only one taking some time off. She'd put her clients on notice and said she'd be back in touch after the New Year. As for Nate, after the holidays, he planned to do a deep dive into his mother's reported connection to Markus Acker and his so-called church. He was not going to let Jessie ruin another holiday for him. "I'll get it taken care of," he told her. "So, about that summit, er, conference—"

"Before I forget." She held up a finger. "I stopped at the hospital today to visit Dean Wexler."

"Did you?"

"I did. He's going to be okay." She looked at him, narrowed her eyes. "You already knew."

"Lizzy told me this afternoon. Did Wexler tell you he's going to plead guilty to the robberies?"

"He did. And he apologized for putting me in danger." She ran her index finger around the rim of her wine glass. "I think he's had a change of heart when it comes to a criminal lifestyle."

"One can hope." But Nate wouldn't bet money on it. "So." He cleared his throat. "I have some, well, family news."

"Okay." She leaned her arms on the table and looked into his eyes.

"We've been invited to Christmas Eve dinner at the ranch in Owl Creek."

"We?" she teased.

"Well, Sarah and I have. And you have, too, but hopefully you'll be coming with me. As my date." He tightened his fingers on hers. "Does that sound like something you'd like to do? I know the holidays aren't the easiest thing for you."

"One thing almost dying does for you is help release the past." Her black hair glinted in the candlelight of the votive flickering on their table. "One of my happiest childhood memories is that Christmas I spent with Lizzy on the ranch. It only seems fitting our first Christmas together happen there as well. That's my long way of saying yes." Her smile was full and generous. "I would love to go with you."

He had no words. But he did have a gift. He looked over to the bar, caught Seb's eye and signaled to him. "Then we should seal this plan with a gift."

"Not a kiss?" She pouted. "You're really striking out tonight, Detective."

Maybe he was. But not for long.

"What's this?" Vivian asked as Seb appeared with the rather messily wrapped package topped with a big red bow. She accepted it with both hands, shot him a look. "Nate, what did you do?"

"It's why I was late. Ruby called at the last minute. I hadn't planned to do this until Christmas Day, then the whole invitation to the ranch happened and... I'm babbling."

"Happens to the best of us. Can I?"

"If you don't, we won't have anyplace to eat." The box took up a good part of the table.

"Okay." She smiled at the box, tears glistening in her

eyes. "Other than from Lizzy, I haven't gotten a present for Christmas in a really long time." She rested her hands on the top of the box. "Thank you, Nate. Oh!" She started when the lid jumped. "What on earth…?" She popped open the lid, peered inside. "Oh. Oh, Nate." She reached in and pulled out the little black kitten. "Oh, he's— He?" Nate nodded. "He's beautiful."

Nate put the box on the floor as she cuddled the kitten against her chest. The tiny gold bell around his neck tinkled as the cat gave Vivian a good sniff, then licked her chin. "Ruby picked him out for you. He was the last in a litter and the only black one. She said they don't get adopted as often and are often lost." He inclined his head, reveling in the joy on her face. Tears streamed down her cheeks. "I thought you might appreciate that."

She shook her head, leaned out of her chair enough to brush a kiss across his lips. "You are the best thing I could have ever hoped for."

"Yeah?" He reached out, tapped the kitten on the top of his head. "You think?"

"I don't think," she murmured. "I know."

Epilogue

"You ready?"

Nate looked down at Vivian's hand, clasped around his. He'd needed a moment, after the drive to the Colton ranch, to get his bearings. It was one thing to have met most of his brothers and sisters in town or in Boise. It was another to be stepping foot on their land, into their home.

But it was time. He reached out and took hold of Sarah's hand. He could feel his own nerves in his sister's grasp, heard her nervous breathing as he tugged her close. He met her eyes and, for a moment, was transported back to that night he'd told her the truth about their father. Their family. Their brothers and sisters.

Back then, this day hadn't seemed possible. All the fresh pine garlands decorated with gold bells and bright red bows. The various trees decorated with lights and ornaments and the wrapping around the water vessels for the wildlife and ranch animals to drink out of. The snowcapped fences stretched to and fro, framing the picture-perfect setting in an image he didn't think he'd ever forget.

"We're ready, yeah?" he asked his sister. Sarah nodded. The three of them walked up the path, hand in hand.

The closer they got, the louder the laughter and celebration sounded on the other side of the door.

Taking the stairs up, Nate's heart pounded.

He nearly stepped back when the front door burst open.

"Finally!" Lizzy leaped out and caught him in a huge hug. "We were wondering when you'd get here."

"I like to be on time," he said, glancing at his watch. "You said—"

"Yeah, yeah. Did you bring Jinx?"

"We left the kitten well tended to at Eddie's," Nate said.

"My neighbor," Vivian said. "He's declared himself an honorary grandfather."

"Fabulous." Lizzy beamed at Vivian, then turned her smile on Sarah, who, for the first time since getting out of the car, looked as if she might be changing her mind about coming. "Sarah. It's nice to see you again. I'm Lizzy."

"Yes, I remember. Oh." She found herself on the receiving end of another hug. "Thank you for inviting us."

"Of course. You're family, after all. No place else you should be. Come in." She stepped back inside and waved them in.

"They're here!" Lizzy yelled into the house as Ajay stepped out from where he stood with Chase and Wade.

"Forgive her," Ajay said as he closed the door behind them. "She started the eggnog at breakfast."

"Did not!" Lizzy called over her shoulder.

"Vivian." Buck Colton, standing slightly shorter than Nate, approached, held out his arms to her. "I feel like you should still be a little girl. Welcome back to the ranch."

"Thank you." Vivian shifted uneasy eyes to Nate. "Thank you for including us."

"Of course," Buck said easily. "You're family." He turned his attention to Nate and Sarah. "You're always welcome here."

It was on the tip of Nate's tongue to ask if Buck was sure, but he could see, with the lively humor and good intentions shining in Buck's green eyes, that he meant what he said.

"Jenny, Nate and Sarah are here." Buck stepped back, held out his hand. "I'm not sure you were properly introduced the first time we met."

Nate, still holding his sister's hand, felt it tighten around his. He knew immediately what she was thinking because he was, too. She was their mother's twin, but whatever resemblance they might have borne to one another no longer existed. Where Jessie was all harsh angles and anger, Jenny Colton radiated a warmth and maternal generosity that reached out and enveloped them.

This was, Nate realized, the moment he'd been most dreading. "I'm—" He was what? Sorry for actions he'd had no part in? Sorry for existing? Sorry for causing her and Buck pain he couldn't begin to fathom. Vivian leaned against him, wrapped her arms around his and gave him a gentle nudge. "Merry Christmas," he said instead.

Jenny lifted a hand to his cheek, then to Sarah's. She smiled. "Merry Christmas."

"Does this mean we can finally eat?" Max hollered and earned a combination of cheers and jeers. He hoisted four-year-old Justin, Greg and Briony's adopted little boy, over his head as Lucy Colton, only a year older, jumped up and down as she clung to her mother Hannah's hand.

"Let's get you something to drink, yeah?" Jenny pulled them farther into the room just as Frannie walked up a couple of stairs, turned and clinked her spoon against her wine glass. Her beaded white dress flared around her knees, and her blond hair had been sharpened into its usual bob.

"Before everyone goes nose down in the turkey…" She looked down, held out her hand and drew a man up beside her. "Dante and I have a bit of a surprise for all of you."

"No more surprises, please!" Lizzy called over the din. "We've had enough for the year."

"Well, then," Frannie said, then waited for quiet. "This should bring this year to a perfect close. Since we weren't sure when we could get the entire family together again, we figured we might as well make this day, a day when we're *all* here—" she toasted Nate and Sarah "—even more special. So…"

"We're getting married," Dante said, as if tired of waiting for her to get to the point. "Today." He glanced at his watch. "Right now, as a matter of fact."

It was impossible not to get caught up in the joyous cheers that erupted through the room.

"No one saw this coming?" Nate asked Vivian, who shrugged.

"And thank you to Hannah," Frannie yelled to get the family quieted down again. "We couldn't have pulled this off without her, especially since we had to have a cake!"

Hannah did a little curtsey, which her daughter copied. "Always happy to help with a wedding that isn't mine."

That earned another round of laughter.

"What do you say, Reverend Bostick?" Dante called to a middle-aged man wearing an ugly Rudolph sweater. "You ready to do this?"

"Me? Now?" Reverend Bostick seemed to choke on his eggnog as his eyes went wide.

"We're ready if you are," Frannie confirmed.

"Well, all right, then." The reverend patted his chest for his glasses. "I think I can wing this. Merry Christmas, indeed."

Ruby and Lizzy came over to draw Sarah away while Nate and Vivian made their way to a pair of chairs scooted together. Nate ran his hand down his tie, and when he looked at Vivian, he saw her beaming at him. She rested her hand over his.

"You know what this is, don't you?" she whispered.

"What?" He pressed a kiss to her lips.

"The best Christmas ever."

He pulled her close, tucked her head under his chin and watched his family swarm and settle and sigh. "I think you're right," he agreed. "You're absolutely right."

* * * * *

Don't miss the stories in this mini series!

THE COLTONS OF OWL CREEK

MILLS & BOON

Last Mission
Lisa Childs

MILLS & BOON

New York Times and *USA TODAY* bestselling, award-winning author **Lisa Childs** has written more than eighty-five novels. Published in twenty countries, she's also appeared on the *Publishers Weekly*, Barnes & Noble and Nielsen Top 100 bestseller lists. Lisa writes contemporary romance, romantic suspense, and paranormal and women's fiction. She's a wife, mum, bonus mum, avid reader and less avid runner. Readers can reach her through Facebook or her website, lisachilds.com.

Visit the Author Profile page
at millsandboon.com.au for more titles.

Dear Reader,

It is with mixed feelings that I bring you *Last Mission*, which is an appropriate title since it's the last installment in my Hotshot Heroes series with Harlequin Romantic Suspense. While I've loved writing these books, I'll hate leaving Northern Lakes, Michigan, and all the heroes and heroines I've developed over the course of twelve books. The first four were Harlequin Blaze books and the last eight Harlequin Romantic Suspense titles.

I have so enjoyed these characters, and the two main ones in this book are some of my favorites of the whole series. State trooper Wynona Wells has been trying to find out who's been going after the town's hotshot heroes, but they've been reluctant to share information with her. When Mack McRooney takes an open spot on the team of elite firefighters, he isn't there just to put out fires. He's starting a few—with the passion that burns between him and Wynona and with the saboteur who is determined to take out Mack and Wynona before they can figure out who he or she is. If you haven't read the other books in the series, don't worry; you'll still know what's happening, and I hope you enjoy the exciting conclusion. It really goes out with a bang!

Happy reading!

Lisa Childs

DEDICATION

For my hotshot hero and amazing husband who inspires all my heroes: Andrew Ahearne

Prologue

Sixteen months ago...

The flames consuming Charlie Tillerman's corner tavern lit up the whole town of Northern Lakes, Michigan. The fire cast a sunrise-like glow over Main Street. The arsonist had struck again, setting the bar on fire where it was well-known that the Huron Hotshots, a team of elite firefighters, hung out. That son of a bitch had been coming after them for the past six months.

But some damn firebug wasn't going to beat them. They got out while making sure the other customers got safely out as well. Except for one...

Nobody could find the superintendent of the hotshot team. Not that *everyone* was trying to find him. Someone would be damn happy if Braden Zimmer was never found.

The hotshots were out on the street now, hooking up the hoses, working together to put out the flames before they spread to the other buildings on the block. The noise of the engines was loud, so loud that this particular person didn't immediately hear the shouts. Then they turned and saw hotshot Ethan Sommerly barreling out of the smoke, carrying a small blonde woman over his shoulder. Owen

James, the paramedic on the team, rushed forward to help, pressing an oxygen mask over the woman's face.

"Braden's in the alley!" Ethan yelled.

The woman, the arson investigator, pulled down her mask and shouted, "Get in there! Please, save him!"

She wasn't the only one yelling, though. Another hotshot, Michaela Momber, emerged from the front of the building. She was dragging the bar owner, Charlie Tillerman, out with her. "Clear!" she yelled. "The building is about to collapse!"

Just as she said it, the structure shuddered and imploded on itself, sending out flames and a thick cloud of acrid smoke.

This was it.

An eerie silence fell like the building just did. Everybody had to know. There was no way that even the great Braden Zimmer could have survived a building collapsing on him.

But then someone gasped and pointed to the alley between the burning remains of the Filling Station Bar and Grill and the building next to it that had flames licking at its roof and walls. From that narrow space and all that thick smoke, a man emerged. Like Michaela had carried Charlie, Braden was carrying someone, too. The body of Matthew Harrison, that damn kid who'd wanted so badly to be a hotshot, too. He was the arsonist. He had to be the person who'd targeted their team and Braden specifically for not hiring him for the last open position on the Huron Hotshots.

Owen and Ethan and the others rushed forward to help Braden and the kid. While the paramedics treated them, the other hotshots stepped back and cheered and applauded. Tears rolled down soot-streaked faces, tears of relief that their fearless leader was okay.

Everybody was so happy—everyone but one person.

While the others were happy about Braden, they were probably also relieved that the arsonist targeting the Huron Hotshots team of elite firefighters was going to jail. The team should have been safe and might have been if the arsonist was the only one after the team, the only one trying to hurt them.

But there was someone else. And while the arsonist was going to spend a lot of his life behind bars, this person had no intention of ever winding up there and had no intention of ever stopping either.

They weren't going to rest until the Huron Hotshots team was destroyed, even if they destroyed themselves in the process…

Chapter 1

Sixteen months later...

What the hell am I doing?

Mack McRooney tried to focus on the meeting his brother-in-law, Braden Zimmer, had called in the conference room on the third floor of the Northern Lakes fire station. But while he stood behind the dark-haired man, that question—*what the hell am I doing here*—kept running around Mack's mind like his younger brother Trick used to run around the house when he had too much sugar.

Even though Mack was only thirty-seven, he was supposed to be retiring from all of this. From danger. From any more missions. He'd turned in his *official* paperwork. He'd gone home six months ago, not to Northern Lakes since he had never lived here. He'd gone home to the house where he'd grown up on the Pacific coast, in Washington.

But what was that damn saying?

You can't come home again...

He'd spent a few months in the Pacific Northwest, in the national forest in Washington where his dad had raised Mack and his siblings pretty much on his own while training smoke jumpers and hotshots to fight wildfires. While it had taken a couple of months for his dad to train Mack how to be a hotshot and a smoke jumper, it hadn't taken Mack long to realize that place wasn't home anymore and hadn't been since he'd left.

Hell, it hadn't been *home* since his mom had left, abandoning her husband and kids in order to find herself. But Mack was really the last person who could judge her for that since instead of staying to help his dad out with his younger siblings, he'd taken off, too. He'd left right after high school graduation because he'd already enlisted in the army. Instead of finding himself, though, he got lost somewhere… maybe even before he left home.

He sure as hell wasn't here, in Northern Lakes, Michigan, looking for himself, though. He was looking for a saboteur. For the person who'd been messing with his brother-in-law's hotshot team. The equipment, rigged to malfunction, might have been a prank, but with a job as dangerous as a hotshot, pranks like that could kill. Then there had been some blatant attacks on the team members. The threats and the violence had escalated to the point where someone was definitely going to die.

That was why Mack was here. So that the person who died wasn't someone he cared about, like his younger brother Trick, who already had some close calls thanks to the saboteur and also an obsessed stalker. But the stalker, Colleen Conrad, their sister Sam's former college roommate, was behind bars now.

Trick wasn't the only one Mack was worried about. He liked his brother-in-law, too, and he knew how devastated his sister would be if she lost him. Sam had finally found happiness, and she was due any day now to give birth to her and Braden Zimmer's son. Sam didn't need the stress of worrying about her family.

And neither did Mack.

"So let's all welcome the newest member of our team, Mack McRooney," Braden said, and he stepped back to pat Mack's shoulder. Then the hotshot superintendent clapped his hands together to lead the applause.

There was a slight hesitation before the other firefighters on the twenty-member hotshot team joined in. Instead of being offended, Mack grinned. They had to suspect why he was really here. It wasn't to just fill the spot Michaela Momber had opened up on the team when her pregnancy compelled her to go on medical leave.

His hire wasn't even nepotism, which was probably what the other hotshots thought when Braden hired Trick—Patrick McRooney—onto the team months ago. Trick was younger than Mack and looked like a younger version of their dad before the old man had shaved off what was left of his red hair. Trick's hair was thick and long and more auburn than red. Mack didn't look anything like his dad or his brother except for size. He was probably even a little taller and broader than them. He didn't resemble their sister either, who had their mother's petite build and blonde hair. Mack's hair was black, buzzed short like he was still in the military, and his eyes were dark.

Sometimes, he wondered about his actual paternity. But that was something he'd rather not know because it didn't matter. The man who'd raised him was his dad and after their mom took off, Mack Senior had been their mother as well.

And what actually mattered was catching this saboteur.

When Trick came onboard eight months ago, the other hotshots hadn't realized then that there was a potential saboteur among them. Braden had begun to suspect, though, and a mysterious note he'd received had made him even more suspicious. So he'd brought in Trick to be objective and investigate the other members of the team to find out who wasn't, as the note claimed, whom Braden thought they were. Well, one of them might have known why Trick had been hired if the saboteur was actually a member of the team.

Mack wasn't sure about that, though. He wasn't sure about anything yet except for the same thing everyone was well aware of by now: they were in danger.

Some of them had nearly died because of the sabotage and those outright attacks. Fortunately, the ones who'd been attacked, like Ethan Sommerly with an exploding stove, and Rory VanDam, with an axe handle to the back of the head, had survived. Unfortunately, they hadn't seen who had attacked them.

They were applauding along with Braden nearly as hard as he was. Probably because they had no secrets to hide anymore since their true identities had come out. And they wanted another identity revealed—that of the saboteur.

Rory, or Corwin Douglas, as Mack had known Rory VanDam, was well aware of the work Mack had done in the special forces and other branches of the military and homeland security. While Mack's family didn't know as much about what he'd been doing all these years, they were aware that he'd participated in top secret missions.

This mission was no secret though. Someone had to catch this saboteur. Nobody was any closer, after all these months, to figuring out who that was. So if the team suspected Mack was here to investigate, they all should have been happy, not just Braden, Ethan and Rory. If Rory had shared what he knew about Mack, how he'd successfully completed every mission, then they had to know that he was damn well going to figure out who'd been terrorizing the team. And in order to do that, he was going to have to uncover every secret any of them had left.

After the meeting concluded, only a few of the other team members, besides Rory and Ethan, approached him. Trent Miles, Carl Kozak and Ed Ward joined him, Rory and Ethan near the table of coffee, bagels and fruit.

Trent was a big guy, like Ethan, and was that kind of movie-firefighter-good-looking that a lot of people expected real-life firefighters to look like. But there was no expression on his handsome face. "So you're the one who saved Rory's life?"

Mack shrugged, surprised that word had spread like it had. He'd tried to stay under the radar five months ago when he'd dipped into town to check on Rory. He hadn't known for certain then how he was going to help Braden, from a distance or like he was now, up close and maybe a little too personally. Although he'd been able to save Rory while watching from afar, it hadn't brought him any closer to learning the identity of the saboteur.

"I don't know whether I should thank you or not," Trent continued.

Instead of being offended, Rory laughed. "He's just pissed that his little sister has fallen for me."

Trent held out his hand to Mack who shook it. "I do appreciate that you saved *her* life that day, too. And because, for some reason she has fallen for this loser, I am glad that you saved Rory's ass."

Rory laughed again.

"So, you're what?" Ed Ward asked. The guy was in his mid-thirties, the kind of guy that was average in every way. Height. Build. Coloring. He probably blended into every crowd, but in this one, he stood out more for being nondescript in comparison to all the other larger-than-life people. "Retired military or something?"

"Something," Mack said. "I've always gone where I was needed."

"We need you here," Rory said, and he slapped his back. Rory was thinner than the other guys, with pale blond hair and a cleanly shaved face, but while he didn't look quite as strong as the more muscular guys, Mack knew very well how tough the guy was. "We need you to figure out who the hell is messing with us."

"Yeah, before my sister tries to investigate any more and gets herself killed," Trent added.

Rory flinched as if just the thought brought him pain.

Mack was surprised that a guy like Rory, who'd lived like Mack had, under different identities for different agencies, had let himself get attached to anyone, let alone fallen for her. Mack couldn't imagine ever doing the same. But his aversion to relationships had less to do with his career choice and more to do with his childhood, with how his mom had so easily abandoned their dad and them. He knew how shallow and selfish people could be, so it would be hard to trust anyone with his heart.

And maybe it would be even harder to let anyone trust him with theirs. He had already hurt his family when he'd taken off like he had. He didn't want to hurt anyone else, especially when he had no idea what he was doing after this mission. His last one. And it wasn't just to find that saboteur, it was to make up to his family for taking off, by making sure they stayed safe.

"Is that why you're here? To investigate?" Carl Kozak asked. Most of the team called the older guy Mr. Clean because of his shaved head and muscular body. "I heard you were retiring from all that."

Mack wondered how he heard. Had Rory told him? Or maybe Trick or Braden? They were all too trusting of their team members, but that was why they needed him. He could be objective.

"I am retiring," Mack confirmed. "I turned in my papers months ago." Against the wishes of his superiors, who'd begged him just to take some time off instead since he rarely had. But he'd been able to stack up that vacation and personal time in order to retire early. That hadn't been his reason for not using it, though. He'd worried that if he went home more often, it would have been too hard for him to leave again. Or maybe too easy...

And then he would have that confirmation that he was just like his mother.

"Shh," Carl said. "Don't let my wife hear you say that word. She's been harping on me to retire. Now that the kids are all grown up and out of the house, she wants to travel, go on cruises." He shuddered. "But I figure you have to be old to retire."

"You are old, Mr. Clean," one of the younger guys joked as he walked up to join them. Bruce Abbott or Howie Lane. They were the youngest guys on the team, hired just before Cody Mallehan had filled the last open spot. Until the death of hotshot Dirk Brown had opened up another seven or eight months ago. Trick had filled his spot.

Most of the other hotshots gradually stepped forward and welcomed him except for Trick. Mack's younger brother held back, talking quietly to Braden near the podium of the conference room. Maybe they were just talking about the next assignment, like these guys were talking about the job they were heading to after this meeting.

Another fire had recently threatened the town, so the team had to make a few more breaks in order to protect it.

Because of that fire, Braden had taken them out of the wild-fire rotation for a while. They were going to stay local instead of heading off to wherever they were needed or back to the day jobs most of them had in addition to being hotshots.

Mack was the one who had actually asked Braden to make sure they all stayed in Northern Lakes. That way he could fully investigate every member of the team at the same time that he investigated every person in town who could possibly be the saboteur.

If anybody on this team—hell, if anyone in this town—had any secrets, Mack was going to find them out. And he was going to find the saboteur. But this, one way or another, was going to be his last damn mission.

Wynona Wells had a secret. A big one.

One that could potentially affect her career if anyone found out. But the state trooper didn't know what to do. People already suspected her of being complicit in the sabotage happening to the hotshot team that operated out of their headquarters in Northern Lakes. And if they knew what else she'd done…

They wouldn't believe she wasn't involved, that she wasn't as corrupt as her training officer who was now in jail. The only way to prove her innocence in all of this was to find the real saboteur.

She parked her police SUV at the curb near the fire station and stared up at the three-story concrete block building. Was he or she in there right now, thinking that they were going to get away with it?

With everything they'd done?

She had to make certain that didn't happen, and that she was the one who finally brought the perpetrator to justice. Her career depended on it.

And maybe even her life…

Because lately she had a strange feeling, like she was being watched. As she stepped out of her vehicle and walked around the front of it toward the fire station, she felt it again, and the skin between her shoulder blades tingled as if a chill was racing down her spine despite the warmth of the June day.

Someone was watching her.

From where?

She peered around, but the people walking on the sidewalk across the street from the firehouse seemed uninterested in her. They were engaged in conversation either with each other or with someone or something on their cell phones.

So where was the watcher?

In one of the buildings across the street? In an alley? She looked around, and then with that sensation intensifying to the point that her chill became a bead of sweat rolling down between her shoulder blades beneath her dark blue uniform, she looked up.

On the third story of the firehouse, in the conference room where the team meetings were held, stood a dark shadow behind the glass. Big, broad, imposing. Quite a few members of the hotshot team were big and broad. But nobody else was quite that imposing…at least not to Wynona.

He was back.

She'd only seen him once, five months ago, coming out of her boss's office after the shooting at this very firehouse. He'd barely glanced at her then, as if she was insignificant to him, and maybe she was. So why would he be staring at her now? Or watching her over the past few days when she had that strange feeling?

A couple of days ago, she'd been standing outside the

house she owned on the biggest lake in the Northern Lakes area, and she had noticed a glint in the distance, like sunlight reflecting off glass. At first, she'd suspected someone was watching her with binoculars, but there was just one glint, like a scope. Like the one on the long-range rifle that had been used to kill an FBI agent five months ago, that *he* had used. And ever since that day, he'd been on her mind entirely too much. Something about him had frightened her then. And so, once she'd thought a scope might have been trained on her, fear had raced through her, and she'd ducked down, expecting a bullet to come toward her.

But if someone had fired at her, it had been silent and had missed. After, she hadn't been able to find any bullet near her or any casings where she'd seen that glint, and she concluded that it must have been something else. Maybe even a camera lens. Because she knew if this man had fired at her, he wouldn't have missed. If he hadn't hit that FBI agent all those months ago, a few other people would have died that day: Rory VanDam, Brittney Townsend and the kid who helped out around the firehouse, Stanley.

Probably even his dog would have died. That massive bull mastiff-sheepdog mix now bounded out of the open overhead door of one of the firehouse garage bays. Annie rushed toward her as if they were old friends and jumped on her, knocking off the trooper's hat as she tried to lick Wynona's face. Instead of being annoyed like some of the other troopers were with Annie whenever they had a call at the firehouse—which had been all too often over the past almost year and a half—Wynona was charmed.

Once Annie had warmed up to her, and it had taken a little while for her to get used to both the gun and the uniform, they had become fast friends, probably because Wynona always brought her a little treat. She pulled the doggy dental chew from her pocket.

"Here, girl," she said as she pushed it between Annie's drooling jowls. "We can all use a little fresher breath." The only kisses Wynona had gotten recently had been from this dog. She had officially sworn off dating and had no intention of changing her mind.

Annie dropped back down to all fours as she gobbled up the treat. Then she sniffed Wynona's pocket for another. Wynona chuckled. "You are so spoiled."

And the dog knew her well enough to assume that she wouldn't have brought just one treat.

"Hey, Trooper Wells," Stanley said as he bounded out of the open garage door with nearly as much energy as the dog. The teenager was tall with a mop of blond curls and a big smile. That smile quickly slipped away as he peered fearfully around them. "Did something else happen? Is that why you're here?"

She assured him, "Nothing's happened." At least not to a hotshot. But she was pretty convinced that someone had been following her lately. Not here though. But now she knew why. The person following her was probably already here, on the third floor of the firehouse.

She continued, "I'm here to make sure that nothing else bad does happen." Not to anyone else and not to her either.

That was her plan anyway, to find out just who was responsible for the bad things that had happened to hotshots— that had nothing to do with the people already in jail or dead. And she knew there were other incidents but the hotshots had been reluctant to share any of those details with her. They were either determined to handle everything on their own, or they didn't trust her to handle anything at all.

Sometimes she suspected her own co-workers felt that way about her, like she couldn't handle the job.

The teenager nodded, tousling his curls. "That would be good. That's why Braden hired Trick's brother Mack. He's going to make all the bad things stop."

"Mack..." So *he* was definitely back. Her stomach lurched with the confirmation.

Stanley gave another vigorous nod, knocking some of those curls into his blue eyes. "Yeah, you know. He's the guy who saved me and Rory and Brittney."

"Yeah, I know." Or she would have known if he'd agreed to talk to her, but he'd disappeared from the scene before she could take his report. Then he'd shown up at the state police post where he'd talked to her superior instead. Was that because he didn't trust her, like the hotshots, or because he didn't respect a woman in law enforcement?

Stanley bent down, picked up her hat from the ground and handed it to her. "Sorry Annie knocked it off," he said. "She sure loves you now."

Wynona pulled back the long red hair that had escaped the pins she used to keep it in place and shoved it all under the hat she settled back on her head. Then she reached into her pocket and gave Annie another dental chew. "I've been bribing her."

"So you do know something about bribes." That deep voice didn't belong to Stanley. And while she hadn't heard it before because he'd refused to answer any of *her* questions, Wynona instantly knew to whom it belonged: *him*.

Mack McRooney. Her boss had told her his name after he'd passed her in the hall that day. He was some kind of military hero with special security clearances that apparently made him exempt from answering her questions or explaining any of his actions.

While she appreciated his service, she didn't appreciate him using it to ignore her. But she shouldn't have been surprised that he would since most of the hotshots did. They didn't trust her. Did they actually think she was taking bribes?

At least *he* seemed to be implying that she'd sold out. If he only knew...

But she wasn't sure if the truth would make people feel less suspicious of her or more. Especially if they knew the other secret she wanted to keep.

But she wasn't sure that she would be able to keep that truth hidden much longer, not with him here watching her. He definitely wasn't ignoring her now.

She looked up from the dog and stared into eyes that were nearly as big and deep as Annie's. There wasn't any affection in this gaze for her like there was in the dog's. There was just suspicion.

What did he know?

Had he already discovered her secret?

A member of your team isn't who you think they are...

Several months ago, Braden Zimmer had found that note folded up on his desk where he sat now in his windowless office in the firehouse. He still had no idea who the writer had been talking about, but there were many possibilities. So many of his team weren't the people he'd once thought they were.

Ethan Sommerly was really Jonathan Michael Canterbury IV, heir to a vast fortune and a family curse. Rory VanDam was really a former undercover DEA agent. And those were just the two whose names were different from what Braden had first known them as.

But there were other ways that people could be someone

he didn't think they were. Like if one of the team was actually the saboteur who had hurt and betrayed the others.

Just a few days before calling the meeting this morning with the rest of the hotshots, Braden had turned over that note to Mack along with all the video footage from the cameras he had installed after Rory was attacked just outside the bunkroom. Braden had also given his brother-in-law a detailed report of all the things the saboteur was probably responsible for and the list of people that he and Trick had already ruled out as possible suspects.

While Mack had thanked him for turning everything over, he'd also been succinct. "Nobody is ruled out as a suspect until I rule them out."

Mack was the fresh eyes and objectivity this investigation needed. Braden knew that, but he couldn't help being a little uneasy about his team. Not everybody had secrets that anyone else needed to know about, like Michaela with her unexpected pregnancy, and Luke Garrison and his wife's former marital issues.

But the person Braden was most worried about was Mack, especially as the new hotshot was heading out with the others today to cut back some trees for fire breaks. The first time Trick had gone out with the team to do that, something had happened to the lift truck's bucket while Trick was in it. If not for the safety cable he'd been wearing and Henrietta's quick thinking, Trick might have fallen to his death with a chain saw landing on top of him. That malfunction of the bucket coming loose from the truck was like so many other things that had happened over the past several months: sabotage.

Messing with the bucket had been the saboteur's initiation for Trick joining the team. What was Mack's going to be? Because Braden had no doubt that the saboteur knew why

Mack was here, and that he or she had something planned for him. While Mack had survived some dangerous missions in the military, Braden was worried that this might be Mack's most dangerous mission yet.

Chapter 2

While Mack had avoided the state trooper the last time he'd been in Northern Lakes, this time he wanted to talk to her. Hell, he wanted just to look at her. She was beautiful with her deep green eyes and pale skin and all that red hair that kept slipping out from beneath her hat.

She was staring back at him, too. No. She was glaring at him, obviously offended about his bribe comment. She wasn't hotly denying it or defending herself either, but that made her look more innocent to Mack than if she'd dramatically reacted to his comment.

"Mack!" Trick shouted at him from the pickup truck he pulled up in front of her police SUV. The passenger window was down, and he was leaning across the console, so he didn't need to yell. He probably just wanted to. "We have to get going," Trick said, his voice sharp with irritation.

"You're leaving again already?" she asked.

Mack grinned. "Why, Trooper Wells, you sound disappointed."

"I didn't get a chance to talk to you yet," she said. "I have questions I'd like answered."

He did, too. He reached out and touched the tendril of hair that had slipped out to slide down her cheek. It was just as silky as it looked. He pushed it back behind her ear.

"Don't worry," he told her. "I'm not going anywhere this time. I'm sticking around Northern Lakes." And, since she was one of the people from town who had come up as a suspect, he intended to stick close to her until he ruled her out as the saboteur.

"Mack!" Trick yelled again. "C'mon!"

He hesitated one moment, as much to annoy his younger brother as that he didn't want to leave her. Not yet. There was something intriguing about Trooper Wynona Wells, and it wasn't just how suspicious everyone else was of the woman. She was as mysterious as she was beautiful, like she was trying hard to act tough. Like she'd been hurt and was determined not to let that happen again.

He understood that all too well.

"We will talk later," he promised her. Then he crossed the sidewalk and pulled open the passenger's door of his brother's truck and hopped inside with him. "What's the rush?" he asked Trick.

"Everybody else is going to be at the site we're supposed to clear for that fire break," Trick said as he sped off. "And if someone on the team actually is the saboteur, we're giving them time to mess with the damn equipment again."

Mack swiveled around in his seat for one last look at the beautiful trooper. His gaze met hers, and his pulse quickened. With excitement, with anticipation even though he had no idea exactly what he was anticipating with her.

"I thought Trooper Wells was your chief suspect," Mack said.

"Michaela's," Trick said. "And Henrietta's too. While I agree there's something not quite right about the trooper, I don't see how she could have done everything that's happened to the hotshots."

"Sounds a little sexist of you," Mack chastised him.

Trick chuckled. "My fiancée and our sister would kill me if I was at all chauvinistic. I meant that I don't know how Wells could have gotten to the equipment so easily and had such free access to the firehouse, too."

"I've heard that Stanley doesn't keep the doors locked." But was that just an accident? The kid had been hanging around the trooper looking as besotted as that dog of his was with the woman. Not that he'd left the doors open for her—unless he was helping her with the sabotage.

But why? What reason could either of them have for going after the team?

Trick sighed. "Love that kid but he can be a little scattered. He's really sweet, though."

Or was that just an act?

Mack knew that at one point Sam had thought the kid could be the arsonist that had terrorized the hotshots and Northern Lakes over a year ago. While he hadn't been, he had been friends with Matt Hamilton who actually was the arsonist. Of course, that friendship had nearly gotten him killed, but still Mack wasn't entirely convinced of Stanley's innocence. He wasn't entirely convinced of anyone's innocence yet.

Trick glanced over the console at him. "Stanley is not the saboteur."

"How do you know?"

"I just… I know…he's not capable of purposely hurting anyone."

"You'd be surprised what people are capable of doing," Mack muttered. Worried that some old images would flash through his mind, he resisted closing his eyes. But when he had to blink, the image he saw was *her face*.

"I heard what you told Braden," Trick said. "That you're

going over everything we did, everyone we eliminated, like we don't know what we're doing."

Mack could have chosen to be diplomatic, but with the attitude his younger brother had been giving him since his arrival in Northern Lakes, he decided to goad him instead. So he asked, "Did you catch the saboteur yet?"

Trick cursed and braked abruptly.

Mack didn't know if his brother had done that because they arrived so suddenly at the site, where other trucks and equipment were already parked alongside the road, or if Trick was just pissed at him. He suspected he was just pissed.

Trick drew in a deep breath and turned to him. "You know I'm not that little kid anymore that you left behind when you took off all those years ago."

"I didn't take off…" Not like their mother had, but Mack wasn't sure his brother saw the difference. "I graduated and started my career."

Trick shrugged. "Whatever. You left. And while you were gone, I grew up. Like I said, I'm not a naïve little kid anymore, Mack. Sure, I didn't catch the saboteur, but it wasn't for lack of trying."

"I know." Mack reached across the console to pat his brother's shoulder, but Trick threw open the driver's door and stepped out before Mack's hand touched him, as if he was avoiding it.

Then he turned back. "And while I know I'm not much of an investigator, I am a damn good hotshot. I know what I'm doing. So out here, you need to listen to me and do what I tell you to do."

"Why? You don't think I know what I'm doing?" Mack was getting annoyed now.

"You haven't been doing this work all these years," Trick

said. "You're new to it, and you're going to get hurt if you're not careful."

"You don't know what I've been doing all these years," Mack pointed out. "But if I hadn't been careful, I wouldn't be here now." He wouldn't even be alive. He was not about to get killed doing the hotshot job that was in his DNA. And he was going to catch the saboteur before he or she could hurt anyone else.

Wynona hated that her skin tingled where Mack McRooney had touched her. She hated that she'd let him touch her when she should have, instead, dropped him with a knee to the groin. But she hadn't wanted him to think that he affected her at all.

She didn't want him to affect her at all. She wasn't even sure why he had.

Sure. He was the epitome of tall, dark and handsome with a whole lot of mysterious, too. And it was that mysteriousness of his that she wanted nothing to do with. No. It was any attraction at all, any *distraction* at all, that she wanted nothing to do with. She didn't have time for things like that, for a personal life. Especially after that disastrous experience the last time she'd tried to date...

She kept a note on her fridge from that *mistake* to remind herself that her judgment was off. And because of that, she couldn't risk having a personal life. She needed to focus on her career and close some cases.

She had a couple of outstanding ones, like who had attacked Rory VanDam and put him in a coma. And who had rigged the stove to explode on Ethan Sommerly? And who had thrown the Molotov cocktail in the parking lot that had sent Michaela Momber and Charlie Tillerman to the hospital?

She was sure there were plenty of other instances that she knew nothing about because the hotshots hadn't reported them. For some reason they figured they could handle this on their own, or they just didn't trust the police anymore.

She stood over Braden Zimmer's desk now, trying to stare him down like she had tried with Mack. But damn...

She let Mack McRooney get to her. And she wasn't happy about that. She hadn't been happy in a long time, though. She'd counted on her new career and moving to Northern Lakes to change that, but it had just made things worse for her. She felt even more alone now than she had when she lost her parents a few years ago.

She drew in a deep breath and willed away the tears that threatened whenever she thought of them. Instead, she focused on her job and on the hotshot superintendent.

"I don't know why you're thwarting my investigation," Wynona said. "It seems like you, more than anyone, would want to know who's been hurting members of your hotshot team."

"I do want to know, *more than anyone*, who has been doing that," Zimmer agreed.

"Stanley said that's why you brought in your other brother-in-law. The older one." *The sexy as hell one.* Wynona bit her lip at the thought, as if she was worried that she might actually let it spill out.

Braden sighed. "Stanley talks too much."

"Stanley knows that I'm trying to help," Wynona said. "Why won't the rest of you believe that?" They'd frozen her out of every investigation just as Mack McRooney had frozen her out that day he'd killed the FBI agent. But, with just that touch on her cheek as he pushed back her hair, he'd thawed her. Maybe a little too much...

"You know what your sergeant, Marty Gingrich, did to us," Zimmer said.

"He was my training officer," she said. "Not my friend. And I had no idea what he'd done until…"

"Until he nearly killed Luke and Willow Garrison," Braden finished for her. "You worked that closely with him and had no idea what he was capable of?"

Unfortunately, Martin Gingrich wasn't the only person whose evilness Wynona had been unaware of since she'd moved to Northern Lakes. And there was someone else out there yet. The saboteur.

"Did you have any idea?" she challenged the superintendent. "You were the one who knew Martin Gingrich the longest, since you were kids in school together."

"And he'd always been a jerk," Braden said. "He was a bully back then. And as he got older, he got more bitter and resentful."

"But still," she said. "You wouldn't have suspected that he would actually try to kill someone." Martin Gingrich wasn't the only one who'd done that recently, though. There were a lot of would-be killers in Northern Lakes. And now that Mack McRooney was in town…

She didn't believe that the corrupt FBI agent was the only person McRooney had killed. Was that what he'd done in the military or special forces or the CIA or whatever he'd been?

Braden sighed again then shook his head. "I didn't know how deranged Marty is."

"And what about this person hurting members of your team?" she asked. "Don't you think that has to be someone close to you?"

He stared at her the way that his brother-in-law just had, with such suspicion.

"Why would any of you think it was me?" she asked. "What the hell would my motive be for messing with the hotshots? For messing with anyone? I barely know anyone in this town." And after her poor judgment regarding the couple of people she had gotten to know, she wasn't willing to risk getting any closer to anyone.

Braden just shrugged.

"I want to catch and stop this person," Wynona said. "Before anyone else gets hurt. So I need everything you have. Every incident report you filed with the US Forest Department. Every bit of surveillance video you've taken. Everything."

Braden shook his head. "*I* don't have any of that stuff."

"You should have reported all those incidents to your superiors at least, and I've seen the cameras you installed after Rory was hurt." Then she realized what he meant. "You already turned it all over to Mack McRooney, didn't you?"

He didn't answer her, but he didn't have to. She knew. "He is not an officer," Wynona said. "He has no jurisdiction here in Northern Lakes."

"He's now an official member of the Huron Hotshots," Zimmer said. "He took Michaela Momber's spot on the team."

"Of course he did." No wonder he'd said he was sticking around. Michaela had months and months of medical and maternity leave coming.

"And as a member," Braden continued, "he can look at the incident reports, video footage, and he can check up on other members of the team."

Wynona had a feeling it wasn't just the other hotshots that Mack was checking up on, but on anyone he considered a suspect. He had to be the one who'd been following her, so he was already investigating her.

What had he found out?

* * *

The buzz of chain saws echoed throughout the woods like a swarm of killer bees. The air vibrated with the noise, and the ground shook as trees fell for the new fire break that would protect the town.

They'd already made some breaks earlier in the spring, but after the last fire, Braden had decided to add more. His efforts to protect anyone were useless, though.

Because there were people in town who would not be protected. Like Wynona Wells. The saboteur had started to worry about Trooper Wells. She'd been getting more persistent, more determined to catch him.

Not that she could.

Not that she was a real threat. But her hanging around the firehouse would become a complication eventually. And complications needed to be eliminated.

But whatever concerns he had about Wells were nothing now. Mack McRooney was a much bigger complication. A much bigger threat…

And the saboteur could not wait to eliminate him. This McRooney had to go as soon as possible. Through the same scope that had been used to watch the trooper, McRooney was being watched now. If only the saboteur had attached the scope to a gun…

But he couldn't risk any bullet or casing getting traced back to one of his registered weapons.

So he was just using the night vision scope to watch his next victims…like he was watching McRooney now.

And when the new hotshot, brandishing a chain saw, finally stepped into the perfect position, the saboteur put down the scope and picked up a chain saw, too. The enormous oak tree had been cut earlier, even before the meeting this morning. Its wide trunk was nearly severed in two.

Just enough of the trunk was left to hold it into place so no one would notice.

This tree hadn't been marked like the other ones, with blue paint. It wasn't supposed to be cut, so no one had come near it but the saboteur.

No one knew what he'd planned.

When this enormous tree fell, it was going to land on something—on *someone*—before it hit the ground. It was going to land on Mack McRooney.

And from the height and breadth of the mighty oak, there was no place that the brand-new hotshot would be able to go to escape from being struck with the limbs or that massive trunk. There was no way for Mack McRooney to survive.

Chapter 3

Mack had spent most of his adult life in the wrong place at the wrong time. Mostly because that had been the assignment. Sometimes he'd survived because of his skill and sometimes because of pure dumb luck.

Like now. Because he didn't hear anything, not with the earmuffs on, but he caught sight of the tree and of its branches moving toward him. He was looking around because he had a feeling someone was watching him...

And when those tree branches began to rustle, he shut off his chain saw and jumped toward the shallow ravine he'd noticed earlier, like his career had taught him to scope out every place for somewhere to hide if necessary. Or to escape...

He dove for that shallow ravine, jumping into it and lying low. And that tree fell, striking the ground so hard that it shuddered like an earthquake. Branches covered him, scratching his skin, sticking through his clothes, and the leaves were so thick he could barely breathe. Or maybe that was because of how close a call he'd just had.

A couple of hours later, he still couldn't believe how close it had been. And how it was sheer dumb luck that he was alive now. Because if he hadn't jumped into that shallow ravine when he had...

He would have been crushed for certain. The tree that had come toward him had been massive. Once it had fallen, the other hotshots had rushed around him, all well aware of how close it had come to killing him. But nobody had admitted to cutting it down or even seeing who had cut it down. Not that it could have been done while they'd been out in the woods. It had been too big. Someone would have had to precut it enough that it wouldn't take much more to send it toppling down toward him.

A few other ones had been cut like that, too, around the perimeter of where they'd been supposed to make that break. They hadn't been cut enough to fall but just enough that it wouldn't take much to topple one over, probably when Mack had been in front of it.

And while he hadn't seen who did it, Mack knew who had: the saboteur.

He couldn't see anything for a moment as he stepped inside the corner bar. Coming from the bright sunlight of the early June afternoon into the dim lighting made everything so dark that he had to wait until his eyes adjusted. And until his legs steadied a bit after he just relived those moments in the woods.

He'd had closer calls before, but this one unsettled him more because he hadn't expected it to happen here. Sure, he knew what had been going on, but Northern Lakes just seemed like such a safe place. But he, better than anyone, knew no place was safe.

And Trick had warned him.

A warning he should have heeded. Just because the saboteur hadn't killed before didn't mean that he or she wouldn't. Obviously, they'd tried to kill before or Rory, as tough as he was, wouldn't have spent so many days in a coma. He was lucky to be alive at all.

And so was Mack after what had happened.

His eyes adjusted enough that he could scope out everybody who was in the bar. That corner booth in the back of the dining room area was filled with hotshots.

Once the tree fell where it shouldn't have, the operation had been shut down. While one of the assistant superintendents had remained at the scene, the other one, Dawson Hess, had already flown out that morning to be with his wife in New York City. Braden and Trick had already cleared him, but Mack had made certain Dawson's alibi was valid for when the other things had happened to hotshots. And he'd been far from the scene then, usually on camera at some red-carpet event with his wife.

The other assistant superintendent, Wyatt Andrews, was back in the woods with Cody Mallehan, probably trying to figure out who the hell had cut down that tree that wasn't marked to be cut.

Mack knew they weren't going to find anything out there that he hadn't already found, like those other trees that had been precut. And he was pretty certain that the saboteur was here, probably in that corner booth. He could have walked over to join them, but he knew that groups like this were a lot like high school. You had to be invited to "sit at the table" with the cool kids.

So he headed toward the bar instead and settled onto a stool. An older guy sat at one end of the bar, a fishing hat on his head, and a defeated sag to his shoulders. He'd obviously not been any more successful than the saboteur had been that morning.

The bartender, who was also the mayor, chuckled as he put a cup of coffee in front of the older guy. "Retirement not all you thought it would be, Les?" Charlie Tillerman said. "Thinking about taking back your mayor job?"

"Nope, it's all yours."

But instead of serving as mayor, Charlie was serving drinks. Mack had considered him a suspect, like the other hotshots had, but the bar owner, along with Michaela Momber, had been victims of the saboteur.

A big hand smacked Mack's shoulder. "After that near miss you had, McRooney, you're probably thinking the same thing about retirement, eh?" Carl Kozak asked. "Not all you thought it was cracked up to be?"

The man standing next to Carl, Donovan Cunningham, shot a cold glare at Mack. But when he saw the bartender staring at him, his face flushed and he hurried off. Carl didn't wait for Mack's reply before ambling off behind Cunningham toward that corner booth that neither of them had invited Mack to join.

Tillerman stared after Cunningham for a long moment. Then he turned his attention back to Mack. "Retirement? Didn't you just start a job? You're the one taking Michaela's spot on the team, right?"

Mack nodded.

"Good thing he did," a husky female voice remarked, and he found Henrietta "Hank" Rowlins standing on one side of him while his brother stood on the other. They were recently engaged, but Mack hadn't had much of an opportunity to get to know the woman who would be his sister-in-law. She was tall and attractive with her long dark hair bound in a thick braid.

Like Henrietta, Wynona Wells was pretty tall, too, with that gorgeous red hair of hers. Mack used to tease Trick about his red hair, but the female trooper was beautiful with it and her pale skin and delicate features. Damn, he had to stop thinking about her.

"What do you mean?" Charlie asked Hank.

"He had a close call just a little while ago with a very big tree," Hank said. "If that had been Michaela…" She shuddered. She must have been close to the only other female hotshot.

Charlie Tillerman, who was definitely close to the former hotshot, shuddered, too. "What can I get you?" he asked Mack. "It's on the house."

While he probably could have used a drink after the morning he had, he ordered an iced tea instead. He was going to need the caffeine to keep him focused. And after that attempt, he definitely needed to stay focused.

The younger guys, Bruce and Howie, called out to Hank from the booth. She clearly had the respect of the rest of the team. She glanced uneasily between her fiancé and Mack. Trick nodded at her to join the others. She offered Mack a small smile of encouragement before she walked off in the direction of the corner booth.

From the look on Trick's face, he clearly wasn't inviting Mack to join them. "What the hell are you doing here?" Trick asked.

"I'm getting a drink," Mack said. And he really wished he had gone for that alcoholic beverage now.

"Why didn't you stay at the scene?" Trick asked. "You took off right after some of the others did."

"The saboteur isn't back in the woods," Mack said.

"How the hell do you know?" Trick asked.

Mack shrugged. "I just do." He was pretty certain that the saboteur was here. At that corner booth or at least back in town somewhere if it hadn't been a hotshot who'd cut down that tree.

While he'd ruled out Charlie Tillerman as a suspect, he wasn't convinced that Stanley was as innocent as everyone thought he was. And then there was *her*.

The outside door opened, letting in a spotlight beam of sunshine. Out of that beam stepped Wynona Wells. And Mack wasn't the only one staring at her. But before he could acknowledge her, his brother drew his attention back to him.

"You think you know everything," Trick said. "But you're underestimating the danger that the saboteur poses. You could have gotten killed out there." His gruff voice cracked, and he shook his head as if disgusted with Mack— or maybe he was disgusted with himself for caring.

"Why are you so damn mad at me?" Mack asked. Was his younger brother angry with him for leaving all those years ago? Or was he angry with him for coming back now?

Trick just shook his head again and walked away, over to join his fiancée in that booth full of suspects. Mack had already ruled out some of them, the same ones that Braden and Trick had ruled out: Trick's fiancée, Henrietta Rowlins. She'd been with Trick when that bucket had come loose and she'd saved his life. The multi-hyphenate hotshot Owen James, who was also a paramedic as well as a veteran, had had his own brushes with the saboteur. Luke Garrison and Trent Miles, like Ethan and Rory, were also crossed off Mack's list of suspects because of the saboteur piling on them with the hell they'd gone through with their own enemies.

But too many of the others were still on his list and in that booth. The younger guys, Howie Lane and Bruce Abbott. And the older ones, Donovan Cunningham, Ed Ward and Carl Kozak. Ben Higgins and a couple of others didn't have alibis during all the acts of sabotage or at least alibis that Mack had been able to verify yet.

Mack had narrowed his list of potential suspects down to include eight of the hotshots in that booth with Trick. So

it was damn ironic that he'd warned Mack not to underestimate the saboteur when he could possibly be sitting right
next to him. And Trick was much more vulnerable than
Mack was because he trusted them. Mack trusted no one.

He felt a twinge of concern for his brother's life. And he
felt another twinge of concern for their relationship. He'd
already realized he couldn't go home again.

Home wasn't just a place, though, it was people. Family.

And apparently, he'd neglected them for far too long.
He'd come back to try to make that up to them, though.
He'd had so many close calls over the years that had warned
him that time was running out for him to do that, and so
he'd retired except for this last mission which was twofold:
to find the saboteur and to make amends with his family.

The two men were both McRooneys, both Braden Zimmer's brothers-in-law, so that meant they were brothers.
While they were both big and muscular, they didn't look
much alike beyond their intimidating size. And the tension
between them had been palpable the moment Wynona had
walked into the bar. That tension was there between her and
Mack McRooney, too. It had been there earlier this morning, and it was there when he'd looked up as she'd walked
into the bar. But that was a different kind of tension entirely.

Mack was staring so intently after his brother that she
wasn't sure if he was even aware that she'd settled onto the
stool next to him at the bar.

"Are you okay?" she was compelled to ask.

He jerked his head around to her then, his dark eyes
wide. "How did you hear?"

"Hear what?" she asked, and now dread tightened her
stomach. "What happened?" Because something obviously had.

He shrugged. "Nothing. Just…nothing…"

She wasn't as good an investigator as she wanted to be, obviously, or she would have known that her training officer was more than an obnoxious jerk. She would have known he was a criminal. Unfortunately, he wasn't the only one she'd misjudged, though. So she probably shouldn't rush to judgment on Mack McRooney. But she couldn't help but let one word slip out. "Liar."

His lips twitched as if he was trying not to grin. "What did you call me?"

"Something happened," she said. It had to have happened after he'd left with his brother earlier. "And you're trying to keep it from me just like your whole damn team tries to keep everything from me."

"My team? Yeah, right…" he muttered, his voice thick with sarcasm, and he glanced toward that corner booth again where his brother was sitting with the other hotshots.

"You're not joining them?" she asked.

"I haven't been invited," he remarked.

"Your brother-in-law said you took Michaela Momber's spot," she said. "He actually admitted to me that you're not just working as a hotshot. Apparently, you're moonlighting as an investigator."

He grinned. "Ah, that's what you're talking about." Then he glanced toward that booth again, and his grin slid away from his handsome face.

"Oh," she said. "You're talking about *their*…" She held up two fingers on each hand to make air quotes, "…booth. Your own brother didn't invite you to join them?"

He chuckled. "It really is like high school, isn't it?"

She sighed. "I wish it was. I was popular in high school."

"You're definitely not popular in Northern Lakes," he said. "Apparently you've been hanging with the wrong crowd..." He arched a dark brow as he teased her, but it was more than that.

And she knew it, dread settling heavily in the pit of her stomach. He *knew*.

"But then I guess Gingrich was your boss," he said, "so you didn't have much choice about hanging with him."

Not about Gingrich.

"I had no idea what he was doing," she insisted.

"That's not exactly a ringing endorsement of your investigation skills," he remarked.

Heat rushed to her face with a wave of embarrassment. "I just didn't think the man training me to be a police officer would be breaking the law." She drew in a deep breath. "But just because I missed what he was doing doesn't mean that I don't know what I'm doing now. I am a better investigator than any of the hotshots."

"Apparently not better than Luke Garrison," Mack said. "He and his wife figured out how dangerous your former boss was pretty quickly."

He hadn't been living in or even visiting Northern Lakes then, but he obviously knew everything that had happened in town over the past several months.

That heat was burning up her skin now, but she drew in another deep breath to force down the embarrassment. She didn't have to answer to this man. He had to answer to her.

"Can I get you anything, Trooper?" Charlie Tillerman asked her, albeit reluctantly.

She shook her head. "No, thank you. I was just looking for Mr. McRooney here."

Tillerman walked away then.

"You got about the same reception from him as Donovan Cunningham did," Mack remarked.

He was observant. She bristled though at the comparison between her and the hotshot. "I'm surprised he would serve the guy at all after his kids broke in here a couple of weeks ago."

Mack didn't look particularly surprised to hear that. "What's going to happen to those kids?"

"That's for the judge to decide," she said.

"This break-in all they did?" he asked.

She shrugged. "I don't know. If you're thinking they're responsible for some of the other stuff, I don't think they could have pulled it off. They could have slashed the tires in the parking lot and lobbed that Molotov cocktail at Michaela and Tillerman. They probably could have even struck Rory over the head. But I don't think they could have rigged the stove to explode like it did on Ethan Sommerly."

"Or for the bucket to come loose on my brother," he murmured. "But their dad probably could have…"

She sucked in a breath with the confirmation that things had happened that they hadn't reported to her, like that incident with his brother. "What? When did the bucket come loose?"

He shrugged. "I don't know…"

"Bullshit," she muttered as irritation chafed what was left of her nerves. "Braden gave you all those incident reports and evidence. No matter what he thinks, you're not an investigator. You need to turn all that stuff over to me."

"What evidence?" he asked.

"Are you calling your brother-in-law a liar?"

He shook his head. "No. I don't call people liars until I have evidence. And right now, I don't have any *evidence*—" he made air quotes with his fingers now "—of anything. If I did…"

"If you did, what?" she asked. "You better not be considering acting like a vigilante." But that was basically what he was if he really had retired from his previous career and was investigating on his own.

"If I had any evidence, I would turn it over to you so that you could make your arrest, Trooper Wells," he said, but he sounded more like he was humoring her than being honest with her.

She narrowed her eyes and studied his face. "Somehow I don't believe you."

He grinned. "So you're calling me a liar again?"

"I've learned that some people find it easier to lie than to tell the truth," she said.

"Some people? Not just Sergeant Gingrich?"

Damn. He probably was as good an investigator as his brother-in-law must think he was since Braden had turned everything over to him. Mack McRooney was already getting more information out of her than she'd intended to give up while she'd gotten nothing out of him. Yet.

"I'm in law enforcement," she said. "A lot of people lie to me."

"Why?" he asked.

She sighed. "Because they don't want to get in trouble or don't want to get someone else in trouble."

He leaned closer to her and lowered his voice. "Are you going to get me in trouble, Trooper Wells?" he asked, his breath warm against the skin of her cheek. Then he leaned in even closer, until his lips almost touched her face. "Or are you trouble?" he asked in a deep whisper.

She resisted the urge to jerk away from him, to show him how much he was affecting her, how aware she was of him and of that attraction she felt for him. Instead, she just smiled. "Not me. I'm not trouble." But he was. Ever since he'd shown up in town, he'd been trouble at least for her, with how he'd unsettled and upset her.

And if he was actually going to stick around Northern Lakes for a while, he was going to prove to be even more trouble for her to deal with and to resist.

Despite the beer he'd just guzzled, Trick couldn't stop shaking. That had been such a damn close call for Mack. If he hadn't moved when he had...

He would have died for certain. There was no way even the indomitable Mack McRooney could have survived that tree falling on him.

But Trick really had no idea what his brother had already survived. He had no idea about his older brother at all. And that infuriated and frustrated him.

"Are you okay?" Henrietta asked, leaning close to whisper it in his ear.

He shook his head. "No. That was so damn close..."

Under the table she covered his hand with hers. "He's fine," she said. "He didn't get hurt."

"This time."

But he knew that there would be a next time. With the saboteur, there was always a next time. Mack wouldn't necessarily be the target again. But someone else Trick cared about would probably be.

And Mack...

Trick was going to lose his older brother one way or another. If the saboteur didn't take him out, Mack was going to leave again just like he'd left before, like their mother had left.

Like Trick used to leave, going from team to team as a temp, before he'd fallen in love...with Northern Lakes, the Huron Hotshot team and most deeply in love with Henrietta Rowlins.

Now he didn't want to go anywhere.

And he didn't want his brother going anywhere either after all these years of being away from the family. But Trick couldn't get over the feeling that he was going to lose Mack again.

And maybe this time, it would be forever...

Chapter 4

Someone was following him. Mack knew it even before he glanced into his rearview mirror to see the dust rising up from the vehicle that had turned onto the same dirt road as him. That vehicle had been behind him since he'd left the Filling Station a short time ago. Staying a safe distance back but close and steady enough that he knew it was the same one, the same driver trying not to lose sight of his truck.

He could have lost them. If he'd wanted to.

But he wanted to see who it was. If they got a little closer, he would be able to identify the vehicle and the driver. Even though its automatic headlights had come on, it wasn't dark out. Just overcast, as if a storm was brewing this afternoon.

Mack felt it. He'd felt it in the woods with the ground shuddering beneath him as trees fell. He'd felt the darkness coming, threatening to suck him in like it had before. And maybe that was what had made him move at just the right time.

He hadn't just stepped aside, he'd jumped over the edge of that shallow ravine which had served as his protection, like a foxhole during an air raid. And maybe because he'd jumped into so many foxholes in the past that was why he'd already scoped out the ravine, why he'd already known where to take cover if he needed to.

While he'd done that this morning in the woods, he didn't want to do that now. He wanted to see the danger coming, and he wanted to face it head-on. His hands gripped the steering wheel of the truck, as the temptation to spin it nagged at him. He could have turned around, could have pursued his pursuer.

But then the person would run like they had earlier. While Mack had jumped into the ravine, the person who'd sawed down that tree had slipped away. They had either blended in with the rest of the hotshots who'd gathered around him with concern. Or they'd taken off toward town.

Was this person following Mack to finish what they'd started earlier in the woods? Were they going to try to finish *him* off now?

He chuckled. Whoever the hell this saboteur was had never dealt with someone like him before. He continued on, turning off the dirt road onto a dirt driveway that led to the cabin in the woods that he'd rented. Sam and Braden had offered to let him stay with them. But he'd known this might happen, that he might become the saboteur's next target, and he hadn't wanted to put them or anyone else in danger.

So it was better that he was out here, away from town, away from everyone. Except whoever was following him...

That vehicle behind him slowed down when he turned. It wasn't going to pass. It was waiting. And he had no doubt that it would turn onto the driveway behind him, just as it had turned onto the dirt road from the main one. Or maybe it would park on the road and the driver would head through the woods to his cabin.

And when they did, Mack would be ready. He reached under the seat and pulled out his weapon. And he really hoped that was the saboteur following him.

He really hoped he could end this now.

* * *

Where the hell had he gone?

One minute he was there, turning his truck onto the driveway off the dirt road, and the next...

It was like his truck had vanished. Was there a garage behind the cabin? Was this even his place? But if it wasn't, where had the truck gone? Because the road seemed to stop at the cabin, and the trees were pretty thick on either side of that driveway. How could he have driven off between them?

No. He had to be here. Somewhere.

Wynona had no idea where, but she intended to find out. She intended to find Mack McRooney and find whatever Braden Zimmer had handed off to his brother-in-law instead of turning it over to the police like he should have done.

Like he would have if he'd trusted them or her...

After how Gingrich had targeted him and his hotshot team, he had every reason to be a little distrustful. She would like to think she hadn't done anything to earn that distrust. But she hadn't figured out what the sergeant had been doing, and they'd been working together. How had she missed it? And not just what he'd been doing, but what someone else had been up to as well...

Maybe she should be happy that the other hotshots considered her complicit and crooked like Gingrich instead of what she'd really been: inept.

She had to prove herself now. Not to the hotshots. But to *herself*. That was why she didn't call in to dispatch and share her location, why she didn't report what she was about to do...

Break and enter.

But as she approached the door to that cabin, she found it ajar. It wasn't locked. It wasn't even closed tightly.

"Ma—" Even though she thought of him that way, she couldn't call him that, by his first name or nickname or whatever *Mack* was. "Mr. McRooney?"

Nobody answered her. There wasn't even a bird chirping outside. The forest around the cabin had gone as silent as it sounded inside the small building with its board-and-batten siding and metal roof.

She reached out and pushed the door inward a bit and peered through the wider crack. "Hello?"

Nobody answered her. But she noticed something just a short distance inside the door. A big whiteboard on wheels like the detectives used, more so on TV than on any actual case she'd helped with. Not that she'd helped much...

She had to do more than just help now, though. She had to solve this, or she wasn't only in danger of losing her job. She was going to lose all of her self-respect, too.

She stepped through the door then and glanced around to see if anyone else was inside before she moved closer to inspect that board. The cabin was small. A kitchenette against one wall. A bathroom was probably behind the two walls partitioning off a corner of the open area. And a king-sized bed was behind that board, sticking out on both sides.

She moved closer to the whiteboard to inspect the pictures and names written on it in bold handwriting, like someone had pushed the marker hard against the surface. All the hotshots' names were written on it, some with lines already through them. And Stanley was there, too. And Charlie Tillerman. And...

She heard a gun cock and turned back toward the door and to the man who'd stepped out from behind it, a gun in his hand. Pointed at her.

She could have pulled her weapon from the holster strapped to her belt and would have if she'd considered

Mack McRooney a physical threat to her. But she was pretty sure that he wasn't going to shoot her.

"Where did you park your truck?" she asked Mack.

He didn't lower his weapon. "There's a gap in the trees midway between here and the road. I'm surprised you missed it with as close as you were following me."

"I wasn't following you that closely," she said. "Or I would have seen it. And you have some nerve complaining about that when you've been following me."

He snorted and finally holstered his weapon.

"I should ask to see your permit for that," she muttered more to herself than to him. He'd been wearing it that day he came into the police post, and he wouldn't have been allowed inside with it on him if he hadn't shown his permit at the front desk. She hadn't noticed him wearing it earlier today, though.

"I'd be happy to show it to you," he said. And he actually pulled out his wallet and flipped it open to a laminated card on one side.

On the other side was another type of card. Something with an official looking shield and his picture, but before she could read the details, he flipped his wallet shut again.

"Who are you?" she asked.

"You just saw my ID," he said.

"I saw your name," she said. It was Mackenzie McRooney. "But what are you? That wasn't a driver's license." It had probably been something indicating his level of security clearance. Was he a CIA agent? Special forces? Homeland security?

"I'm a hotshot," he said.

"What were you before you were a hotshot?"

"Retired," he said, and his mouth curved into a slight but still infuriating grin.

"Retired from what?"

"I'm not applying for a job," he said. "So why are you checking my résumé?"

She wished he would give her his résumé. She turned back and pointed at that board. "Apparently you have applied for a job. And it's not as a hotshot."

"Are you afraid I'm going to take your job, Trooper Wells?" he asked, and that infuriating grin widened.

But she couldn't deny that was a fear of hers. *She* needed to be the one to solve the open cases in Northern Lakes. But she needed that more for herself than for anyone else. She needed to prove to herself that she wasn't the fool she felt like she'd been. And she needed to prove that she could take care of herself as well.

"Is that why you've been following me?" she asked. "You are after my job?" A lot of the officers at her local post were retired from some branch or another of the military. Maybe that was what she should have done before going into law enforcement. Maybe then she would have been better at her job.

But it was really the first one she'd had despite being thirty-one years old. When her parents were alive, she didn't have to work. After they died a few years ago, she had even less reason to work. It wasn't as if she needed money. But she needed a purpose.

So she'd gone back to school, once again, and instead of another degree in philosophy or art or French cuisine, she'd gone into criminal justice. Nursing or medical school would have taken longer, and she'd wanted to help others as soon as possible. While she did that with writing checks, she'd wanted a more active role—she wanted to personally protect and serve others. Once she'd completed the police academy, she'd applied for jobs in remote areas where no one would know her so that she could start over fresh. And she'd wound up in Northern Lakes.

"Why do you keep thinking *I've* been following you?" he asked.

For one, his crack about the bribes...

She'd been very careful to make sure that nobody knew exactly where she lived because they would probably think she was supplementing her public servant salary somehow in order to be able to afford the lake house she owned. She hadn't become a police officer to get rich, she'd done it to help people that needed help, to make a difference.

But she hadn't made much of one. Yet. People were still getting hurt in Northern Lakes, they were still in danger.

"Wynona," he said. And he reached out like he had earlier that day and pushed back a lock of her unruly hair. "Why do you think I've been following you?"

She stepped back and pointed toward his board. "Because I'm on your suspect list."

"A lot of people are on my suspect list," he said. "I'm not following any of them."

The photo he had of her was a copy of her driver's license picture. He hadn't gotten that from Braden Zimmer. So he probably had access, with that security clearance, to personal records.

"What makes you think you're being followed, Wynona?" he asked, and he stepped closer to her again as if he was concerned.

But he didn't even know her. Nobody really did. The couple of people she'd spent the most time with after she'd moved here, Sergeant Gingrich and another man, had wound up being such horrible men that she hadn't risked getting close to anyone else.

"I just…have this feeling that I'm being followed, watched…"

He moved closer and touched her shoulders, turning her to stare up at him instead of at that board where he'd crossed off names and circled some other ones. "Has anyone tried to hurt you? Or made any threats?"

She shook her head then shrugged, and his hands fell away, but it was as if she could still feel them on her, lightly holding her. "I really don't know. If they did, obviously they failed."

"Not the last time they failed…"

"What?" she asked. "What happened earlier today that you thought I heard about?"

"Another miss," he said with a sigh.

Alarm jolted her. "Did someone shoot at you?" And nobody had reported it. What the hell was wrong with his team?

He shook his head. "Nobody shot at me unless you consider a tree a bullet."

"What are you talking about?" she asked. "Tell me what happened."

He sighed again. "When we were cutting that firebreak, a tree nearly hit me. It might not have been intentional, though. I might have just been in the wrong place at the wrong time."

"Bullshit," she said because she could tell that he was downplaying the incident. "You know it was no accident. This saboteur, or whatever you guys are calling him, is more dangerous than you thought he was."

"Him or her," Mack said. "Don't be sexist."

She laughed. It just kind of slipped out of her at the irony of him saying that. A big man like him usually considered women like her too weak and emotional to handle the job. At least that was the way Gingrich and some of her co-workers and superiors treated her. Michaela Momber had recently been treated the same way by one of her co-workers, so it was no wonder she'd gone on medical leave. She couldn't trust her fellow hotshots to have her back any more than Wynona could probably trust hers.

"What's so funny about me saying that?" he asked as if he was offended now.

"The saboteur could be a woman," she acknowledged. "But it's not Michaela Momber." The saboteur had gone after Michaela and Charlie Tillerman. But she noticed he'd already crossed out the former hotshot's name and Henrietta Rowlins's name as well. That left Wynona as his only female suspect. She grimaced. "You really can't believe that I would go after the hotshots."

"I don't know," he said, and that grin was back. "You followed *me* home."

"Not to hurt you," she said.

"So I don't have to watch out for falling trees?" he asked, and that grin was back.

She didn't know how he could laugh about what had happened, what could have happened. While she'd purposely chosen a career that was dangerous, she certainly would never be able to joke about the danger. "You're lucky you didn't get hurt. Someone was obviously trying to hurt you."

"Or they just cut down the wrong tree in the wrong area," he said.

"So it wasn't marked to be removed like they do, and it nearly fell on you?" she asked for clarification. When he nodded, she continued, "That wasn't an accident, Mack." She pointed back to the board, to the names he'd circled. "Two of these guys, Bruce Abbott and Howie Lane, work as arborists."

His brow furrowed. "Arborists?"

"They take care of trees, cutting them down mostly. That's their day job."

"So they would have known how to precut that tree at some earlier time so that it wouldn't have taken much to make it topple over on me," he mused.

She nodded. "Yes, but with all the tree removals the hot-shots do to make breaks, probably everyone on the team knows how to do that."

"So you haven't narrowed it down any more than I have," he said, and he was grinning again, like he wasn't affected or concerned at all over what could have happened to him earlier today.

"Someone tried to kill you," she said, spelling it out since he seemed to not be understanding what had happened and what could have happened to him.

He shrugged. "Not the first time someone's tried," he said. "I'm harder to kill than you think."

"And cocky and arrogant and condescending, too," she added. And infuriating and attractive and so intriguing, but she kept those adjectives to herself.

He chuckled. "So you and my brother have something in common. Your opinion of me."

She'd felt the tension between them. And no wonder Trick had been upset with him for not taking that attempt on his life seriously. But if Mack was special forces or any of those other departments that would have high security clearances, he probably wasn't exaggerating the number of times someone had tried to kill him.

"Don't you care about your life?" she asked. "Do you have some kind of death wish? Is that why you went into whatever career you retired from?"

"You went into law enforcement," he pointed out. "Don't you care about your life?"

"I care," she said. "I know that life is precious." And she knew how good she'd had it growing up with loving and supportive parents who she missed every day. But because of them, she felt like she had to give back somehow and not just by writing a check. She wanted to be more involved in helping others while being more independent and self-reliant, too. She had to put herself out there even if it put her in danger.

"I retired from that...career," he said.

"And then you became a hotshot," she said. "That's not a whole lot safer. Even if whatever happened with that tree today had been an accident, and I think we both know that's not damn likely, you still would have died if it had hit you." At least that was the impression he'd given her, and from his brother's frustration with him, she was probably right.

He shrugged. "The world is a dangerous place, Wynona. Bad things happen everywhere and for no reason at all."

Tears rushed to her eyes then as she thought of her parents. She had to close them so he wouldn't see.

But then his hands were on her face again, tipping it up toward his. "What's wrong? What did I say?"

She willed the tears away and opened her eyes. "Nothing... I just...lost someone like that..."

"Who, Wynona?"

She shook her head. If she talked about her parents, she would start sobbing for sure. She'd only told one person in Northern Lakes about them, and that had been a mistake. "I'm not here to talk about that," she said. "I followed you here to get back the stuff Braden gave you, the stuff that should have gone into evidence."

"And like I told you, there is no evidence," Mack replied. "Not yet. I just have all these names written down, and I've eliminated some because there was no way they could be both the victim of the saboteur and the saboteur. But if you want to work together…"

She narrowed her eyes, surprised at the offer. "What are you suggesting?"

"That you tell me whatever you're holding back," he said, "because I can't work with people I don't trust."

"Me neither," she said. "Not anymore…" Then she stepped around him and headed toward the door since it was obvious he wasn't really willing to work with her. And even if he agreed, he wasn't a police officer. He was a hotshot, and as one, his job was to put out fires, not to investigate crimes.

The saboteur wasn't sure why the trooper had followed Mack McRooney home. They'd been talking at the bar earlier. Had he invited her home with him?

If that was the case, though, she probably would have followed more closely. It was almost as if she hadn't wanted him to see her, which was how the saboteur had followed the trooper, far enough back that she hadn't seen his vehicle. Trooper Wells had been followed twice. Because the saboteur already knew where she lived and had a picture to prove it.

A picture and a plan were in place for her, in case she started to pose a problem. And since she was pushing her investigation, she was a problem.

Just like Mack McRooney was going to be a problem. How the hell had the tree missed him?

How had he guessed that it was about to fall?

It was as if he possessed that sixth sense his brother-in-law was legendary for having. Braden Zimmer was supposedly able to predict when a fire was about to happen. That was why Wells's former training officer had been so convinced that Braden had been the arsonist. Even Braden's wife, when she'd first come to town to investigate those fires, had suspected him.

Then she'd fallen for him.

Because that was how things worked out for Braden. He always got everything he wanted. Or maybe he was just lucky like his older brother-in-law, but that luck was about to run out for both of them.

And for Trooper Wells, too.

She and McRooney had no idea that the person they were looking for was standing right outside that cabin that was conveniently remote. And in these woods, there was nobody else around that might see him. That might be able to identify him later.

And now the saboteur had a gun, one taken from a pickup parked in the firehouse parking lot. A weapon that couldn't be traced back to him if any bullets or casings were recovered. So, this time, the saboteur was ready to take them out.

Chapter 5

Wynona Wells had secrets she obviously wasn't willing to share with him. And that made Mack all the more determined to find out what those secrets were.

But she was already heading toward the door he'd left partially ajar in order to lure her inside when she'd driven up earlier. Now he wanted to entice her to stay. But just to learn her secrets.

He couldn't deny that he was attracted to her. She was beautiful, but what drew him even more than her beauty was her determination and her guts. She truly seemed intent on catching and stopping the saboteur. So he doubted that she was the saboteur. But he wasn't ready quite yet to cross out her name on the suspect list.

"I thought you wanted this stuff," he said, gesturing back at the board she'd found.

"You won't give it to me."

"If you leave now," he said, "you'll only be able to come back if you have a warrant, Trooper Wells." He'd already called her Wynona, but at the moment, she seemed determined to keep up her walls, to act all official, in order to keep her distance from him. And maybe she was the smarter one of them to do that because he shouldn't be drawn to her as anything more than a suspect.

But the way she'd looked just moments ago, the tears that had sparkled in her eyes...

She'd lost someone she loved. Mack had lost some people who mattered to him, too, and that had hurt a hell of a lot. But he suspected whoever she lost had mattered even more to her.

"Don't think I won't get one," she said.

"How? I'm the one person in Northern Lakes who absolutely can't be the saboteur," he pointed out. "I wasn't even in the country when most of this stuff happened."

"Yet you have a knack for turning up when you're needed, like when you shot that FBI agent."

"He was corrupt," Mack said. "And my dad reached out to me when that reporter started asking questions about Rory and I got worried." He'd been right to worry about his old military friend. The minute the FBI agent had learned the former DEA agent was still alive, Rory had been marked for death.

"And you showed up just in the nick of time," she said. But she didn't make it sound like a compliment.

"Like you said, I turn up when I'm needed," he said. But that was just because he was trying to make up for taking off when he'd been needed, just like his mom had taken off on their family. While his dad and Sam might forgive him, he doubted that Trick was ready to any time soon, if ever at all. But catching the saboteur and making sure that Trick and his fiancée and Sam and Braden were safe mattered even more than their forgiveness. He had to eliminate the threat to their safety. And once he did...he had no idea what he would do in his *retirement*. "And, Trooper Wells, you just might find that you need me, too."

She snorted now. "I don't need anyone."

He'd thought that once, too, himself, when he'd been so

bitter and angry about his mom deserting them. Then he'd taken off so that he wouldn't get attached to anyone else. But he knew now that everybody needed *someone*. That being alone was too damn lonely.

He needed his family. Friends.

He'd lost so many friends already.

Wynona didn't seem to have many in this town, either. If he thought he could trust her, he might have asked if she wanted to be friends and work together. But he couldn't trust her. And he couldn't trust himself to keep their relationship just as friendship. Not when he was so attracted to her. And trying to have a romantic relationship seemed much more dangerous than trying to find the saboteur.

Before he had the chance to say anything else to her, she stepped through the door. And the minute she did, shots rang out.

Panic struck him, thinking that she was hit and that he hadn't lost a friend, but someone who might have come to mean even more to him...

One minute Wynona was standing, the next she was facedown on the ground. It wasn't a bullet that had knocked her flat, though, but a big, muscular body.

"Are you okay?" A deep voice rumbled in her ear as those shots echoed all around them.

With the wind knocked out of her, she couldn't draw a breath. She couldn't answer him. Then he arched up to roll her over beneath him.

"Where are you hurt?" he asked, his voice gruff with concern.

She shook her head. "I'm not—"

But another shot rang out, this one striking the doorjamb near his head. She pulled him down on top of her. "Are you okay?" she asked now, fear making her heart beat so fast and hard.

"No," he said.

She reached up to check his head, to make sure he wasn't bleeding. His short hair was soft against her palm, but she felt no blood, no wound.

"I'm not hurt," he said. "I'm pissed." He scooted back through that open door, sliding her over the threshold with him. Once they were inside the house, he slammed the door shut. And just as he did, another bullet struck it, splintering the wood on its way through to that board with all the names and photographs taped to it.

Wynona started to lift her head up as she reached for her holster. But Mack was still hovering over her, as if trying to cover her body with his like he had outside the door. His body was so big and muscular and close. But it wouldn't stop a bullet.

"You have to stay down," he whispered as another shot rang out. And finally he moved, rolling off her.

Wynona pulled her weapon from the holster on her belt. "I've got this," she said. Then she drew in a deep breath to brace herself to go back out there.

Mack had drawn his weapon, too. Instead of heading toward the front, though, he was walking, crouched low, toward the back.

"Stop, you can't go back out there," she said, her pulse quickening even more with the fear and adrenaline rushing through her. He seemed so unfazed compared to her. But he'd probably been shot at more times than she had.

"I've got this," he said, throwing her words back at her along with a crooked grin.

He was so damn cocky. Too cocky.

And too sexy.

"You're not a cop," she said. "You need to stay inside and let me handle this."

"You take the front," he said as if he was in charge. "But give me ten seconds."

"Mack—"

The sound of the back door opening and closing cut off her protest. And then the gunfire rang out again.

Fear gripped Wynona. Was he the one shooting or the one getting shot?

She had to get out there, had to try to protect him before he got killed. She cracked open the front door, and gun drawn, started out. She just hoped that she wouldn't be too late to save Mack.

Or even the shooter because she had a feeling that Mack would shoot to kill just like he had with that FBI agent. Her whole reason for going into law enforcement was to save as many lives as she could while not losing her own. Because she hadn't been able to save the people she'd loved the most.

Braden usually couldn't wait to get home when his wife was here in Northern Lakes instead of off investigating an arson somewhere like she usually was. She'd gone on maternity leave a few weeks ago in anticipation of her due date that had passed the week before.

With her so very pregnant, he would have been even more eager to get home if today hadn't gone like it had. If it hadn't happened again...

He'd just closed the door behind himself when she called out the question he'd been dreading, "So how was my big brother's first official day on the job?"

Braden's stomach muscles tightened, but he forced a smile for his wife as he walked into the kitchen where she was standing at the island cutting up something. "Sam, you're supposed to be taking it easy and staying off your feet as much as possible. I was going to make dinner."

She smiled at him. "I know you prefer your cooking to mine, but it was getting late."

"You didn't have to wait for me to eat," he said. He crossed the kitchen to where she stood and wrapped his arms around her. He just wanted to hang onto her. Forever.

She chuckled. "I didn't. I've been eating all day. I shouldn't even be hungry right now."

He moved his hands down, sliding them over her protruding belly. "You're eating for two," he said.

"It better be just me and him," she said. "But I'm beginning to have some doubts about that from the size of me. I think he could have a friend in there..."

Braden chuckled now. "I love you so much."

She turned then and wrapped her arms around him. "If you do, stop trying to distract me and answer my question, my darling husband."

"Question?" he asked, but he was smiling as he feigned ignorance.

She lightly jabbed his chest. "Hey, buddy, answer me. How'd Mack do?"

"Mack did great." Or he wouldn't be alive if the situation had been as serious as Trick and the others had made it sound. Mack hadn't talked to him about it at all, as if it was no big deal that someone had probably tried to kill him.

Sam narrowed her pretty blue eyes and studied his face. "Out with it."

"With what?"

"I can tell you're holding back," she said, and she poked his chest again. This time a little harder than she had before.

He flinched. While she was petite, she was strong. "Hey, there..."

"I'm already frustrated with this kid," she said, and she poked her belly now but gently. "If he doesn't get out of there soon, I'm going to drag him out just like I'm going to drag whatever you're keeping from me out of you."

He chuckled. She was so tough. But with her dad and her brothers, she had to be. And knowing that, he knew she could handle what he told her. "There was an incident with Mack. A tree got cut down and would have hit him if he hadn't moved when he did…"

She sucked in a breath and then nodded. "Of course the saboteur would try for him just like they did for Trick when he first came on the team. They know why he's here."

"To catch them," Braden said. "It's so damn overdue…"

"Just like me," Sam said with a heavy sigh.

Braden steered her away from the counter and toward the couch. "Sit down. I'll finish dinner."

"I'd rather finish this pregnancy," she said. "I've heard that sex sometimes induces labor."

He chuckled. "I'm more than willing to test that theory," he said.

"Good," she said. "But I'm going to call Mack first… while you finish dinner." She grabbed her cell phone from a table beside the couch. She punched in a number. Then she grimaced.

"What? Are you okay?" he asked with alarm. "Did you have a contraction?"

"No. Damn it," she muttered. "His phone went directly to voice mail."

Braden shrugged. "You know Mack has always been hard to reach."

"Yeah, because he was off on some top-secret mission or another," Sam said.

"He's retired from all that," Braden reminded her.

"Yeah, sort of, but he's still on a mission."

"For me," Braden said with regret. This was his team. He should have been able to stop the threat against them without involving anyone else.

"For us," Sam said. And she patted her belly. "For all of us."

Braden couldn't wait to become a father. He wanted to be able to focus on that, on his wife and child, and not on the threat against his team. He didn't want to lose anyone else like he'd already lost one of the members.

The saboteur hadn't killed Dirk Brown, the man's wife had. But the saboteur had nearly killed Rory VanDam and could have killed so many of the others with the dangerous stunts they'd pulled.

Like that one today that had put Mack in danger.

Sam must have hit redial because she cursed. "Went to voice mail again."

Why wasn't Mack answering his phone?

Braden felt that uneasiness again, that concern that of all the dangerous missions Mack had probably been on, this might prove the most dangerous of all of them.

Chapter 6

Mack squeezed his trigger, firing off a couple of shots, trying to draw the attention to the back of the house because he had no doubt that Wynona was going out the front. Just as she had moments ago.

Maybe this time she wouldn't be as lucky as she'd been the first time. Maybe this time she would get shot. Mack shouldn't have left her. He should have stuck with her until backup arrived.

But she hadn't called for it. Sure, there hadn't been much time. But still...

Mack wondered. He rounded the corner of the house, firing a few more shots in the direction where the shooter had to be. Somewhere in the trees between the cabin and the road. But there was no return fire.

"Put your gun down."

He recognized that voice, her sexy, uptight tone. "I'm not a threat, Trooper Wells."

She snorted. "Yeah, right." She gestured at the cell in her hand. "I'm calling it in. Backup will be here soon."

"A little late," Mack said, wondering again why she'd waited to make that call. "The shooter is gone." Tires squealed in the distance, probably as the shooter's vehicle left the gravel side road and hit the asphalt of the main road that led back to the heart of Northern Lakes.

"Then we'll bring in techs to go over everything, get bullets and slugs and see if there's any evidence that will lead us to the shooter," she said.

He didn't know if she was talking to him or to whoever she had on her cell phone.

He shrugged. "Why bother? It was probably just a hunter," he said, trying to downplay it. The hotshots hadn't trusted her to investigate the saboteur probably because some of them suspected she was the saboteur. He knew that wasn't the case now, but even though he'd teased her about working together, he wasn't sure that he really wanted her or anyone else interfering in his investigation, especially if she didn't even trust her co-workers enough to call for backup before now.

For Mack, the best part of retiring was that the only orders he had to carry out now were his own. Except for Braden's—he respected his brother-in-law as the hotshot superintendent.

She snorted again. "The only thing that person was hunting was us."

"Us?" He'd thought he was the target, but he realized now that she was the one who'd been shot at first. And there was no way anyone could mistake her for him.

She glanced back at the splintered doorjamb and shuddered. It had been close, she could have been hit.

So could he, but that had been only when he'd knocked her down, when he'd tried to protect her. Now he was wondering how badly she needed protection. So he didn't protest anymore. He was glad now that she called for backup to go over the scene and to make sure she was safe, too.

He was also glad that they wouldn't be alone much longer because he had a feeling if he spent much more one-on-one time with her, he might be the one needing protection.

Not just because she was getting angry with him, but also because of how he reacted to her.

Sirens wailed in the distance. Maybe her backup had been closer than he realized. But when they arrived, he wasn't that impressed with how they talked to her. Or rather talked down to her like she was inferior to them.

He tensed with irritation. Some of the best operatives he'd worked with over the years had been female. And like his sister, they'd been smart and strong. He suspected Wynona was just as smart and strong. But he seemed more aware of that than her fellow officers.

"What are you doing here, Wells?" a man asked.

Mack recognized the sergeant he'd talked to after the shooting at the firehouse. "Hughes," he said. "Trooper Wells was here at my request."

Hughes was probably in his fifties with graying hair and lines around his eyes and mouth—frown lines. He'd been in the service, too. So he had respect for Mack. When he heard him, he stood up a little straighter. But he was smart enough to look a little skeptical too. "You called dispatch?"

"No. I saw her earlier today at the firehouse," Mack said. "And I wanted to talk with her about the things I heard had been happening to the hotshots."

"Your brother-in-law didn't fill you in on all of that?" Hughes asked.

"I've heard they've been having a hell of a run of bad luck," Mack said. "So, of course, I wanted to know if there was an official investigation going on."

The sergeant glanced at Wells, and that frown was back on his face, as if he wasn't happy with his subordinate. "Trooper Wells has been insisting that we investigate further, but she forgets that every time something has happened, arrests have been made."

"Even one of your own, I've heard," Mack said.

And the sergeant's face flushed. "Gingrich was a little too obsessed with the hotshots." Now the man looked from Wells to Mack. "Sometimes I wonder if Trooper Wells is getting a little too obsessed as well…"

"I'm not, sir," she said. "I'm just not certain that everything that has happened to the hotshots can be blamed on whoever is in custody."

"Or dead," the sergeant said. "Like Jason Cruise. He was responsible for a lot of things, and then he took his own life before we could determine everything that he'd done."

Wells sucked in a sharp breath, and her face flushed. And Mack wondered…

Who the hell was Jason Cruise? The guy who'd gone after Charlie Tillerman and Michaela? He'd also gone after the mayor, too, if Mack had the story straight. He clearly hadn't been the saboteur, though, so Mack hadn't paid as much attention to the story about him as he probably should have.

Wells lifted her chin and stood up straighter, her pride obviously smarting right now with the way her sergeant was talking to her and about her to Mack. "And if the person responsible for everything that happened was already in jail or dead, who took those shots at us?" she asked.

The sergeant glanced back at Mack, and he just shrugged and replied, "I have no idea what happened." That much was true. "I don't know if that person was firing at me or Trooper Wells or maybe some prey they were hunting…"

Because he had no idea which of them had been the prey this time, and he needed to make sure that what happened had only to do with the saboteur and that nobody from his past had found him. Though he highly doubted that since nobody involved in his previous missions had had a clue who he really was.

"You told me that someone tried to drop a tree on you earlier today," Wells reminded him. "That had to be the saboteur."

He shrugged again, and he could see the fury rising in her along with the flush in her pale skin. "Nah, that was probably just a mistake." The mistake had been his assuming it was the saboteur. If it wasn't, and someone from his past had tracked him down like that corrupt FBI agent had tracked down Rory, Mack didn't want her involved. He didn't want her getting hurt like she nearly had been earlier.

Wynona sucked in another breath. She obviously knew he was lying, and she wasn't happy about it. He couldn't help but think again that she was holding something back, too, keeping some damn secret that he was even more determined to discover now. Now that they both could have died. But first he had to make sure that wasn't because of him. That he wasn't the one who'd put her in danger.

Wynona was furious. As usual, her concerns had been dismissed by her boss. She should have been used to that. Sergeant Hughes had been resisting her efforts to fully investigate everything that had happened to the hotshots. He would rather blame the people who had already been arrested or had died for everything and just close those cases. That would help improve the closing rate for this post as well as make Northern Lakes seem safer.

But it wasn't safe. She could have died today. That bullet had come so damn close. Even Hughes must have realized that because he'd told her to go home early and he'd called techs to go over the scene and collect the bullets and casings.

When she stepped out of her car onto her driveway, her knees shook so much that she nearly dropped to the ground like she had dropped at Mack's house. No. Mack had dropped her. And because he'd knocked her down, out of the line of fire, he had probably saved her life.

But shortly after that, he had lied to her boss. And he'd disappeared before they'd even wrapped up at his house. Or at least before the sergeant had dismissed her, too, but at least Hughes had promised to make sure the techs processed the scene. Even though he acted like she'd overreacted, he saw the holes in the door, he knew how close she'd come to getting shot. Not that he seemed to care all that much.

And that was why she hadn't immediately called for backup. She wasn't sure who she could trust.

Even though Mack McRooney couldn't possibly have fired those shots at them, she didn't trust him, especially after how he'd downplayed everything despite knowing damn well that someone had tried to kill them.

And yet he acted like it was nothing and then he'd taken off. What? To return to the bar? Throw back some drinks and pretend nothing happened?

Like he'd acted earlier. Maybe it wasn't a big deal to him. Maybe he was used to people trying to kill him. Maybe that was who'd fired those shots, someone after him...

But why was she the one the bullets had come the closest to hitting? And would she ever get used to someone shooting at her, to the danger? She hoped not.

But she did intend to open a bottle of wine for herself and to cuddle with her kitty. Though if Harry smelled Annie on her, Wynona wasn't sure that the snooty Siamese would let her get close. But when Wynona neared the side door of her house, she found it like she'd found his earlier...unlocked and slightly open.

She reached for the holster on her belt, drawing her

weapon. She could have called for backup, but she didn't for the same reason she hadn't called earlier today. She didn't trust her backup any more than the hotshots trusted her. She needed to prove herself. First, to herself.

As she drew closer to the opening to peer inside her house, a deep voice called out, "The door's open. Come on in."

She'd been irritated earlier, now she was furious. So she didn't holster her gun before she stepped inside her own damn house at his invitation. She didn't point the gun at him, though, and she was glad she hadn't when she saw that her cat was curled up on his lap where he sat on her couch. Harry, Harriet her Siamese cat, did not like strangers and usually hid from them, like she would hide from Wynona if she smelled Annie on her uniform. But the little traitor seemed quite taken with this stranger.

And Wynona was irritated that she understood all too well the fascination with this intriguing but infuriating man. She focused on him instead of her traitorous feline now. "What the hell are you doing here?" she demanded to know.

He gestured, with a wineglass in one hand, toward the bottle of red on the table in front of her white leather sectional. "I opened a bottle of wine. Figured you could use a glass."

It was like he'd read her mind. And she was so tempted to join him. To join them…

Harry peered at her through slitted eyes as she purred from his lap. The cat rarely sat on Wynona's lap let alone a stranger's. She usually avoided strangers. And pretty much everyone was a stranger now that Wynona's parents were gone.

"What the hell are you doing in my house?" she asked. How had he even known where she lived?

Unless…

"You said you weren't following me," she said. And she'd stupidly believed him, just as she had stupidly believed Martin Gingrich and…someone else she shouldn't have.

"I wasn't. I already knew where you lived," he said. "It's easy to search property records."

She narrowed her eyes with suspicion. "This property is not deeded in my name." It was in a trust.

"You're listed as a trustee of that trust," he said.

He was right. But he would have had to do some work to discover that—or maybe, with his security clearances, he just had access to more databases than the average person. Either way, he unsettled her. He unsettled her in a lot of ways.

"That doesn't answer how the hell you got inside," she pointed out. She had a good security system. An alarm should have gone off and alerted her to anyone breaking inside, and if she didn't respond with a code, then a call would go out to the local emergency number.

"The door was open," he said.

She gazed around the room. Nothing looked out of place in the big living room. The wide-screen TV was still mounted over the fireplace. All of the artwork was still hanging on the walls. And through the French doors to her office, she could see the big monitors for her computer. Nothing had been touched. But that bottle of wine…

And the cat was lying on his lap instead of out prowling as she was prone to do whenever she managed to slip outside, which she would have been able to do if a door had been left open. Despite her pampered upbringing, Harry still thought she was a badass. The cat was a lot like Wynona. But until now, Wynona was the only one who'd been aware of that, of how pampered she'd been growing up.

Did Mack McRooney know now? Had he figured out everything she'd wanted nobody else to know? She had enough problems trying to get people to take her seriously, so she wasn't about to divulge how wealthy her family had been.

Because of how she'd been raised, they'd always had good security systems and safety practices. She always locked her doors and windows and activated the alarm.

"The door wasn't open," she insisted.

He sighed as if he was getting tired of this conversation. "So you're calling me a liar again?"

"Yes," she said. "You're lying now just like you did when you told my boss that you thought the gunfire could have been coming from a hunter."

He arched a brow over one of his dark eyes. "You don't think that's who it was?"

"I think it was someone trying to kill us," she said. "And you damn well think the same thing I do, especially after someone just tried to drop a tree on you. You have to know someone is after us."

The brow arched higher. "I do?"

The urge to scream nearly overwhelmed her. But instead of giving in to it, she holstered her gun and reached for the bottle of wine instead.

"There's a glass there," he said, gesturing toward it. "I'd pour for you, but I don't want to disturb the cat. She's so comfy."

Wynona glared at him, ignored the glass, and lifted the bottle to her lips, chugging some back.

"Classy," he said.

He had no idea. Or maybe he did. If so, he was the only one who knew about her past. The only one who was still alive…

The wine slid smoothly down her throat. He'd picked a

really good bottle of Cabernet Sauvignon from her collection. Somehow he knew about wines just like he presumably knew about her.

"Why are you here?" she asked. She dropped down onto the couch next to him and Harry who barely spared her a glance as she continued purring on his lap.

"You stopped by my place earlier," he said as he continued to stroke Harry's fur. "So I figured it was only fair that I stopped by your place. You know, return your hospitality."

"You were not very damn hospitable at your house," she said. "Instead, I got shot at and then you lied about it so that nobody would take me seriously."

"I didn't lie," he said. "I really have no idea who it was. Could have been a hunter."

"You know it wasn't a hunter," she said. "And now you know that I have nothing to do with everything that's been happening with the hotshots."

"That doesn't necessarily mean that," he said. "You could have someone else after you like Rory did and Ethan."

She shook her head. "I have no corrupt FBI agent out to kill me or a greedy brother-in-law." She had no family left now. "It's more likely that you had someone from your former career coming after you..." But he wasn't the one those bullets had nearly struck.

"Even though I'm pretty sure there is no way that is possible, I checked all my sources," he admitted. "There's been no rumblings, no chatter. Nobody from my former career knows where I am. And not even that many people in Northern Lakes know but my fellow hotshots and *you*..."

"Well, you know I didn't fire those shots at myself," she pointed out. "So you should be crossing my name off that suspect list."

He just smiled. "We'll see."

"Is that why you broke into my place?" she asked. "You're looking for something incriminating?"

"I wanted to make sure your place was safe," he said.

Something shifted in her chest. No one had cared about her for a very long time. Not that she believed he really cared. She wouldn't make that mistake again.

"And clearly it is. *Someone* would have to be very smart and have a lot of experience bypassing high-tech security systems in order to bypass yours." His lips curved into a slight grin or a smirk.

"Someone? Yeah, right." Had he done it just to test her system and her safety? Or… "What are you really up to?" she asked.

"You were the one who wanted us to work together," he said.

"No," she said. "I want to work the case on my own. But I want everything that Braden gave you." While the white-board had still been inside his place when the techs started going over it, she hadn't found any of the incident reports.

"Your boss doesn't think there is a case," Mack said. "He thinks everybody who was responsible for the things happening to the hotshots is behind bars or dead."

"And you know that's not true," she said. "You damn well know that someone purposely tried to hurt you with that tree and then purposely shot at us. So why did you lie?"

She waited, but she wasn't about to hold her breath for him to finally answer her.

They could have died. Both of them. Trooper Wells and Mack McRooney. It wasn't so much that the saboteur had missed but that it probably wasn't time yet.

Maybe it would be more fun to play with them. Because

now they knew that he knew where they lived, where they worked, and the saboteur could find them, could get to them, whenever he wanted.

And soon he would want them dead.

Chapter 7

Wynona waited, but Mack wasn't any more forthcoming than he'd ever been since she'd met him months ago. Or actually hadn't met him. He just kept sitting there on her couch with her cat, refusing to answer her question.

"Why did you lie?" she asked again. "About the shooter and about what happened with you and the hotshots?"

He shrugged. "I don't know what you're talking about…"

She cursed him then and said, "I should arrest you for breaking and entering." But instead she took another swig of the wine. It had been a hell of a day.

After the sergeant had told her to clock out early, she just wanted to come home and curl up on the couch with her cat. She never would have imagined Mack McRooney here with them, opening her wine, petting her cat…

Was she dreaming this?

Because it didn't seem real.

But Mack hadn't seemed real since the first time she'd heard about him, swooping in to save his friend and Brittney Townsend and Stanley and Annie. He'd saved her earlier tonight, too. That was why she wouldn't arrest him. That reason and that her boss probably wouldn't believe her that the hotshot had broken into her home. He would accept Mack's lie that she'd left the door unlocked.

"You have a very good security system," he said.

She snorted. "Not good enough."

"Not good enough to keep me out," he said with a grin. "But it'll keep most people out."

"Most people don't know where I live," she said.

"Somebody followed you to my place," he said. "I'm sure somebody could have followed you here. Or looked up your address the same way I did."

She'd felt that here, that strange sensation of being watched. So he probably wasn't wrong.

"But why?" she asked. "I'm not a hotshot. And I really don't have any enemies. So why would anyone want to follow me or come after me?"

He stared at her for a long moment as if considering her question. Then he shrugged those broad shoulders of his. "I don't know. Why would they?"

"Maybe they think I have some idea who they are." If only that were true...

"Or maybe they're worried that you'll figure it out," he said.

She nearly laughed. It had taken her too long to figure out so many things. She was lucky that people hadn't died. At least because of the saboteur. People had died because of other people, like Mack killing that FBI agent. And Jason killing himself.

She was lucky *she* hadn't died earlier today at Mack's cabin.

"Thank you," she said.

"For what?" he asked. "Opening the wine?"

She took another swig from the bottle. It had been a hell of a day. It had been a hell of a year since she'd moved to Northern Lakes, since she'd started working as a state trooper. It had been hell longer than that, though, ever since she'd lost her parents who'd been the only family she'd had and had also been her closest friends. That was why she'd wanted to start over somewhere new. She'd been hopeful when she'd started her new career and found her new home that she could find happiness again.

She'd been so wrong.

"What are you thanking me for?" Mack prodded her as if he really wanted to know, as if he was interested in her as more than a suspect.

And surely, he could no longer suspect her of being the saboteur, not after she'd nearly been shot dead in front of him.

"Thank you for saving my life earlier tonight," she said. If he hadn't knocked her down when he had...

He shuddered, and Harry let out a soft hiss of protest at his movement. "I was scared. The shots rang out just as you stepped outside."

She shuddered, too, and she wasn't sure if it was because of how close a call she had or because she had that strange sensation again. Like someone was watching her...

Mack was. His dark gaze was intent on her face, as if he was trying to see inside her head, to see what she was thinking. Maybe that was why someone else was watching her, to figure out if she considered them a suspect.

She glanced at the big windows of the living room that looked out over the lake. She loved to watch the sunset over the water, but she'd missed it tonight. Mack probably hadn't showed up in time to see it either.

While it wasn't that late, probably just nine thirty or ten, it was too dark for Wynona to see if anyone was standing out there looking in, watching not just her now but the two of them: her and Mack.

Mack looked from her to those windows, too. "You feel like someone's watching you..."

She shrugged. "Maybe I'm just paranoid."

"After what happened earlier, after those shots fired at you, you're not paranoid," he said. "But you need to be careful."

"So you admit those shots weren't fired by some random hunter?" she asked.

"I don't know who was shooting at you, but I do intend to find out." And he glanced out that window again like he felt it, too. Felt that they were being watched...

"Why not have the police help?" she asked.

"Your techs are processing the scene," he said. "They're going to find whatever evidence the shooter might have left behind."

"And obviously you don't think they're going to find anything?"

He shrugged. "Maybe they'll find some slugs and casings. But somehow, I doubt that will lead us back to the shooter."

"Not us," she said. "Just me."

"Happened at my house," he said. "I'm entitled to know who was shooting on my property."

"Then why weren't you straight with the sergeant?" she asked. "Why not tell the truth about everything and share with us the information that Braden Zimmer gave you?"

"Martin Gingrich couldn't be trusted," he reminded her.

"That doesn't mean that I can't be," she said. She was sick of being judged by her professional association with another man. And since she'd been judged for that professional one, she was certain to be judged for the personal one she'd had with someone else, even as short-lived as it had been.

"What about the rest of your co-workers?" he asked. "How do you know they can be trusted?" He studied her face intently now, his dark eyes narrowed. "You don't. That's why you didn't call for backup when you came to my place or even when those shots were first fired. You don't trust them either."

"I don't trust anyone anymore," she said. Not after everything that had happened. The only people she'd truly been able to trust were gone: her mom and dad.

He grinned. "Not even me?"

"You least of all," she said, but she couldn't help but smile back at him. And she couldn't help that her pulse quickened. He was as good-looking as he was infuriating. Maybe being so attracted to him was why he infuriated Wynona so much.

"Then I better leave," he said, and he moved Harry from his lap. The Siamese let out a soft hiss in protest at being moved. Harry always had to be the rejector, not the rejected.

Mack stood up and grinned. "I need to leave before I'm tempted to do something that proves you can't trust me."

She stood up then, too, just to walk him to the door. That was all. To make sure that he really left...

And that the door was locked and the security system was engaged. But she found herself asking, "What are you tempted to do?"

He stepped a little closer to her and stared down at her face, his focus seemingly on her lips. Then, his voice gruff, he replied, "Kiss you."

Her heart started beating as fast and furiously as it had when those shots had been fired at her. "Kiss me?"

Then, as if she'd made a request instead of just parroting his words back to him, he lowered his head and covered her mouth with his. And Wynona suddenly felt as if she had a lot more than a few sips of wine as her world tilted, and she had to clutch his shoulders to hang on while she and her emotions spun out of her control.

Mack should have come here first before going to her place. But he'd wanted to make sure that Trooper Wells would be safe, that she had a security system, because someone had taken those shots at her. And he believed her, too, that someone was watching her. He'd felt that way as well back at her house.

And when he walked into the bar, he felt it again as everyone looked up at his entrance. Northern Lakes was that kind of town where everyone knew everyone else, and the tourists and strangers stuck out like he stuck out. But he wasn't going anywhere, not until he caught the saboteur, so they were going to have to get used to him.

There were only a few of the hotshots left in that corner booth. Maybe they'd gone home for the night or back to the firehouse. Or maybe they were sitting outside Wynona's house like they'd been sitting outside his earlier.

With the security system she had, she was safe. Even her windows were special tempered glass. The builder had probably used them because they could withstand birds flying into them. Hopefully they would withstand bullets, too.

While she was safe in her house, it hadn't been safe for Mack to be there. Kissing her had been a mistake. She'd probably just been repeating his words, but he'd taken them as an order. One he hadn't wanted to refuse. But when his lips touched hers, a current had passed through him, making him so damn aware of every feeling, of the silkiness of her lips, the heat and sweetness of her breath…the scent of her like a fresh rainfall.

God, he was an idiot.

"Hey," he called to the bartender. "Have I missed last call?" Didn't bars close early during the work week in towns like this? Or maybe, since the tourism season finally started given that it was June, they would stay open later.

"We have a couple of hours yet before last call," Charlie Tillerman replied. "Do you want another iced tea? Or can I get you a drink or something to eat now? It's still on the house for taking Michaela's place on the team."

"That's not necessary," Mack said.

"It is," Charlie said. "I hate thinking about what happened to you today and how that could have been her instead. I appreciate what you're doing here. I know you're not just taking her place."

"No, that's not the only reason I'm here," Mack admitted.

Charlie grimaced. "There's that person after them, pulling the dangerous stunts. You need to be careful. Extra careful. They all need to be."

Charlie had cause to worry. Mack was concerned too, but not just about the hotshots. He was worried about Wynona Wells for more than one reason, though. He was concerned about her safety, and he was especially worried about how dangerous she was to him. Because he knew more about her than just how sweet her mouth was, how silky her lips...

He knew something that made him trust her even less than he had before.

"I heard about what happened to you and Michaela in the firehouse parking lot with the Molotov cocktail getting tossed at the two of you," he told Charlie.

Fortunately, they had not been hurt too badly. But Mack knew all too well how badly that could have gone, how badly they could have been burned.

Charlie shivered. "Yeah, that was awful."

"The local police sergeant, Hughes, thinks Jason Cruise was responsible for that, too."

Charlie snorted. "I doubt that. That seems petty even for him."

"Do you think it was the kids who broke in here?" Mack asked. "Donovan Cunningham's kids?"

"Or Donovan Cunningham," Charlie said.

"You're not a fan either?" he asked. He'd picked up on Wynona's low opinion of the guy.

Charlie shook his head and glanced over to that corner booth again. But Cunningham wasn't there now.

Was he outside Wynona's house, watching her?

Charlie shrugged. "I don't know now. Cunningham was there for us during that big fire, and he's been really apologetic to Michaela since he said some horrible things to her. I should forgive him."

"But you can't forget," Mack said. Maybe that was the problem between him and Trick. His younger brother couldn't forget that Mack had left just like their mother had.

"I'd rather believe that Jason Cruise was behind everything," Charlie admitted. "He did keep trying to kill me and Michaela using methods that the saboteur or other people after the hotshots had used in the past. Maybe whatever happened to you today with that tree was just an accident, and Cruise really was the saboteur."

Mack knew that wasn't the case. What had happened with that tree had not been an accident. It had either been meant as a warning or to kill him, and those gunshots could have killed Wynona. A dead man hadn't done those things.

But Mack pulled out a magnet he'd found on Wynona's refrigerator when he'd been looking for that bottle of wine. It had been holding something else to the side of her stainless-steel fridge, something he left in his pocket. He put that magnet with Jason Cruise's smiling face on the counter. "Tell me about him."

"He was smart and determined and greedy," Charlie said. "He was trying to get rich off Northern Lakes. His plan was to increase the property values of places he already owned by rezoning it to commercial and then he was going to bring in developers."

"What developers?" Could one of them be going after Wynona now? But Wynona hadn't been the one who'd killed Jason Cruise. When the Realtor realized his plan had failed, he'd killed himself.

Charlie shrugged. "I don't know. They all backed off after he died."

"How do you think he knew about all those things the saboteur did?" Mack asked.

"You don't think he was the saboteur then?" Charlie asked, and he groaned as if in pain. "I was hoping it was him…"

"So that it would all be over," Mack finished for him. But it wasn't over. For Mack, it was just beginning. Like whatever he'd started with Wynona. But the minute he'd made that mistake, that he'd kissed her, he'd pulled away and rushed off. He wasn't one to mess around with relationships. He knew relationships were riskier than any mission he'd ever undertaken.

"He knew so many of the things that had happened," Charlie continued as if trying to convince Mack.

And Mack had a feeling he knew how Jason had known about those things. Because of the card that the magnet had been holding up…

The card had probably come with a bouquet of flowers, since it had been from a florist, and the words on it had read: *Welcome to Northern Lakes, beautiful. I think our personal relationship has even more promise than our professional one.*

Wynona had been professionally and personally involved with the would-be killer. Mack wasn't just suspicious of her now, he was also jealous...of a dead man.

Charlie left the Filling Station in the capable hands of the bar manager and bartender and headed upstairs to his apartment and to the woman he loved, the woman pregnant with their baby girl. He'd never been as happy as he was now or as hopeful for the future.

But the conversation he just had with Mack McRooney had unsettled him.

"What's wrong?" Michaela asked the minute he stepped inside the door. She was in the kitchen scooping cookies and cream ice cream into a bowl. Fortunately, her months of nausea were gone and she was eating more now for her sake and their baby's.

He grinned at her. "Nothing unless you add some pickles to that, then I'm going to be nauseous."

She grimaced. "No weird cravings here. And you're not distracting me from what's bothering you. What's wrong?"

He stepped closer and kissed her. "Distracted yet?" he teased when he lifted his head from hers.

She smiled. "Nope. You're going to have to do better than that."

But when he reached for her, she stepped back and held up her bowl of ice cream between them. "Spill it, Mayor Tillerman."

He sighed. "It's nothing. Just Mack McRooney asking some questions."

She groaned. "He doesn't think you're the saboteur now, does he?"

He shook his head. "I don't think so. He didn't ask any questions about me beyond what happened to us, about the break-in and Donovan and his sons."

"The hoodlums," Michaela remarked. And she was probably referring to Donovan as well. Like Mack had said, it was harder to forget even if you were able to forgive.

"He was most interested in what Jason Cruise did to us," Charlie said. "I think he suspects that he could have been the saboteur."

She sighed. "No. He doesn't. Hank told me that the saboteur went after Mack today. If he hadn't gotten out of the way, a tree would have crushed him."

"That could have just been an accident," Charlie said. He hoped. He really wanted this to be over, for his town to be safe and especially for his soon-to-be wife and baby to be safe.

Michaela shook her head, and her blonde hair brushed across her cheek. "Nope. The tree wasn't marked to get cut down and nobody would admit to even being in that area when it happened."

"So you think someone tried to kill Mack?"

Michaela nodded.

"He didn't seem really shook up about it," Charlie said. "He seemed more focused on asking about Cruise, about how he tried to kill us using the same methods that had already been used against other hotshots."

Michaela's brow furrowed. "I suspected that Jason wasn't working alone," she said. "Maybe Mack suspects the same thing."

"He asked about the developers."

Michaela snorted. "It wasn't the developers. They wouldn't have known about those things. But I know one person who would have…"

"The saboteur," Charlie said.

"And Trooper Wynona Wells," Michaela said. "Or maybe they're one and the same."

Charlie shrugged. "I don't think *we* have to worry about any of that anymore," he said. "Mack McRooney is determined to get to the bottom of it all."

"Probably even more determined after someone tried to drop that tree on him," Michaela agreed. "I just hope that he manages to escape next time."

"Next time?"

"You know there will be a next time until the saboteur is finally stopped."

Hopefully Mack McRooney would catch them soon before anyone else got hurt. Charlie had taken on the role of mayor to make sure the town was safe, but now, with his daughter coming into the world in a few months, he was even more determined to make sure there were no dangers around her.

The saboteur had to be stopped. Soon.

Chapter 8

Wynona hadn't slept well the night before and not because of someone taking shots at her, but because of that damn kiss. She probably should have slapped Mack McRooney for doing that, but she could see where he might have misconstrued her "kiss me" as an order rather than the question she'd intended it to be. Actually, if she was honest with herself, and she always was, she hadn't intended it as a question at all because she really had wanted him to kiss her.

And once he'd kissed her, she hadn't wanted him to stop. His lips had been so firm, and he tasted like dark chocolate and red wine. There had been this sizzle between them that had had her senses reeling, her skin tingling. She'd wanted that kiss to go on and on, but he'd pulled away. And then he'd walked away, leaving her wanting more.

And more…

But not kisses.

She wanted justice. That was why she'd forced herself to get out of bed after just tossing and turning in it the night before. And she'd gotten ready and rushed to work with one purpose.

She wanted to find out who the hell had taken those shots at her, who'd been going after the hotshots and who'd been watching her. And she wanted to put them behind bars with her old training sergeant.

But first she had to convince her *current* sergeant to let her investigate. Since he'd sent her home from the scene of the shooting the night before, she didn't have much hope that he would agree. But before she could even knock on the door to his office, it opened, and a man stepped out and nearly ran into her. His muscular chest just about touched her face.

She stumbled back a step, and his hands reached out and grasped her shoulders. Last night those big hands had cupped her face when he'd leaned down and kissed her. Her skin tingled and heat streaked through her at just the thought of his mouth moving over hers. She took another step back, so that his hands fell away.

"Why are you here?" she asked.

"Just following up with the sergeant," Mack said. "Letting him know that I might have misread that situation yesterday. I could have been mistaken about the hunter and the hunted, especially given the things that keep happening around Northern Lakes."

A sudden chill washed away the heat she'd felt moments ago. And the little hope she had that Hughes might agree to let her lead the investigation dissipated.

Had he told her boss she was being hunted?

Was she?

And who was doing the hunting? The saboteur or Mack McRooney?

She'd initially suspected he was the one following her, but getting shot at while she was with him had proven her wrong about him. There was no way that he was the one who'd tried to hurt her physically.

But she still didn't feel safe with him, especially after that kiss. And she felt just as hunted by him as by whoever was watching her.

She also couldn't be certain about what she was going to lose. Her job or her life?

Or maybe even her heart…?

Before Mack could say anything else to Wynona, her sergeant called her into his office. As she passed Mack in the doorway, she shot him a look full of indignation and maybe a little hurt. She must have thought he'd betrayed her.

But he hadn't told Sergeant Hughes everything he knew about her. He really hadn't told him anything at all about her except that she was right. Somebody dangerous was out there yet, and the more people looking for them the better.

Once the door closed behind them, Mack headed off to the next sergeant he intended to speak to, but this one was behind bars at the local jail, which was in the same building as the state police post. This was where the sergeant was being held while awaiting trial. At the moment, he was behind Plexiglass, his pudgy body stretching the snaps on his orange jumpsuit.

Mack picked up the phone, and the guy waited a moment before he picked up the receiver on the other side.

"I don't know you," Sergeant Martin Gingrich said. "I thought you were Trick McRooney."

"Trick is my younger brother," Mack acknowledged even though Trick didn't seem too proud that they were related right now.

The guy grimaced, then his sigh rattled the receiver. "You're another one of Zimmer's brothers-in-law."

Mack nodded. "Yeah, I am."

"Why did he send you here?" Marty asked. "Is he afraid to face me himself?"

"Braden is a little busy right now," Mack said.

The balding guy smirked. "Yeah, with that traitor on his team."

"You think the saboteur is on the team then? That he's one of the hotshots?" Mack asked.

The guy shrugged, but then nodded a little eagerly. "Probably. Nobody was that happy when that suck-up Braden got the job."

"What do you mean?" Mack asked. All of the team seemed to respect Braden. And they were all loyal to him. That was why they'd tried to keep the problems quiet, so that Braden wouldn't lose his job.

He shrugged again. "Let's say a lot of us had to work a lot harder than Braden Zimmer has ever had to work in his life." He made woo-woo noises. "His legendary sixth sense about fires is why he got promoted. Not because he put in the time or the work. He had the same luck with school and sports. He always got what he wanted."

And apparently what Gingrich had wanted too, which was undoubtedly why the guy was so bitter and jealous of his old high school rival.

"What about Wynona?" Mack asked. That was whom he really wanted to talk about, probably because he couldn't stop thinking about her and hadn't been able to even before that kiss. After that…he'd thought about her even in his sleep, dreaming about her.

The guy's face was blank like the expression in his beady dark eyes. "Who?"

"Trooper Wells."

"Oh, Wells…" He snorted. "Yeah, stuff probably comes easy for her, too. Money. Looks."

The deed to her house being in a trust had tipped Mack off, even before he saw the house, that she had some money. Once he saw the ultra-modern house on an extra-large lot on the biggest of the lakes in Northern Lakes, he'd realized that she had some *serious* money.

Mack tried to sound casual as he asked, "Anything else I should know about her?"

"What? Are you looking for me to give a recommendation for her?" Gingrich snorted again. "I don't really know her. I don't think I was in her league. She dated that Realtor for a while, the one who bought up half the town."

"Not anymore," Mack murmured.

"Did he sell out?"

"Something like that," Mack said. "He's dead. You didn't hear about that? Don't get a lot of visitors?"

The guy's face flushed a deep red.

Nope. He didn't. So it was unlikely anyone from the local police post was carrying out the vendetta he obviously still had against Braden Zimmer. But was Gingrich the only one with a grudge against the hotshot superintendent? Or did other people resent Braden Zimmer's rapid rise to his leadership position with the Huron Hotshots?

"Is Wells still a trooper?" Gingrich asked the question now.

Nobody was keeping the former sergeant apprised of anything anymore. So it wasn't likely that he was a factor in any of the incidents that had happened since his arrest. And Wynona obviously wasn't in cahoots with her former training officer either since he didn't even know if she was still working in law enforcement. But still…this wasn't an entire waste of Mack's time.

He nodded.

And those beady eyes widened in reaction.

"That surprises you that she's still on the job?" Mack asked. Had Gingrich thought his successor would fire her? Or that she would quit?

Gingrich nodded. "She doesn't have the instincts for police work."

Mack wanted to argue with him, but since she hadn't picked up on how evil this man was, he couldn't. And Jason Cruise...

How long had she been involved with him? And how deeply? Deep enough to help him hurt Charlie Tillerman and Michaela Momber?

"What about sabotage?" Mack asked.

Gingrich snorted again. "What?"

"Could she be the one sabotaging the hotshot team?"

Gingrich laughed. "You think she would get her hands dirty? She's too soft. Too pampered."

"To be the saboteur?"

The former sergeant nodded. "And to be a cop. She's going to get hurt or worse."

God, Mack hoped Gingrich was both right and wrong about Wynona. He didn't want to suspect that she was the saboteur, and after last night, after she'd been shot at, he really didn't think she was. So the former sergeant was right about that, but Mack didn't want him to be right about anything else. He really didn't want her getting hurt or worse.

Usually, Braden sensed when a fire was about to happen, but he had no forewarning about the fire he'd just taken a call about. Maybe that was because it wasn't that big. Because he usually only got the forewarning about the big ones, like the one Jason Cruise had set recently.

And all the fires that arsonist, Matt Hamilton, had set. His premonitions seemed to come about the dangerous fires...

But as long as that saboteur was on the loose, every fire was dangerous. Hell, everything was dangerous. Mack could have been killed yesterday when they'd been cutting that break to protect the town from another fire like the one Jason Cruise had set and they'd barely been able to get under control.

Braden couldn't help but worry that this fire was going to give the saboteur the chance to make another attempt on Mack's life. Maybe it had even been set for that purpose and that was why Braden had had no premonition about it, because it had been set on the spur of the moment.

But Mack hadn't showed up at the firehouse yet. And Braden was kind of hoping that he wouldn't show up. But that thought had no more entered his head than he heard the squeal of tires as Mack's truck turned abruptly into the parking lot next to the firehouse.

When Mack had agreed to help Braden find the saboteur, he'd insisted on being one of the team in every way. He wanted to work the fires, and he'd even gone through hotshot training with his dad before he'd joined the team.

Braden had trained under the older Mack McRooney himself, and so had several other members of the team. Mack Senior was the best, so Braden had no doubt that Mack junior was prepared to do the job.

Despite how badly Braden wanted the saboteur caught, he wouldn't have hired either of his brothers-in-law if they weren't damn good at what they did.

The best of the best.

But no matter how good they were, the job was still dangerous for a lot of reasons. The saboteur was only one of them.

There was always danger with a fire because they were so unpredictable. They could turn without warning. And they could fight back at the firefighters trying to extinguish them. Braden had no doubt that Mack was a fighter, or he probably wouldn't be alive.

But eventually the man was going to come up against something or someone even stronger than he was. A fire or the saboteur...

Chapter 9

A billboard-sized real estate sign was nailed to the side of the burning building. And on that sign was Jason Cruise's smiling face just like it had been on the magnet Mack had taken off Wynona's fridge with the card from a flower store. Wynona had kept that card.

That was probably what bothered Mack most, that this man, this would-be killer, had meant something to Wynona. Was he the reason she'd gotten teary-eyed when they'd talked about losing someone?

Was Jason Cruise the one she missed so much that it still affected her? And why did that bother Mack so damn much? The man was dead. He was no longer a threat to anyone.

The fire was a threat, though, because of the possible exposure and risk. While the burning building was an abandoned warehouse, it was close enough to other structures that it could spread to inhabited businesses and buildings. There was also the threat of backdrafts in a building like this, and it was possibly a Class D fire if there were any chemicals or metals left in that warehouse.

Knowing all those things, because of his training and because Braden had warned them before sending them out, Mack knew he had to stay focused. He couldn't keep thinking about her now. Or even about the saboteur.

He had to focus on the fire only.

Because of the risks with this fire, Braden had chosen only hotshots to respond to it and not any of the volunteers. And despite the risks, it was a fire that the hotshots should have easily been able to handle if there wasn't also the concern that it was a trap.

Mack had that concern, too, but he still wanted to go inside that building. In all the cities where he'd lived and even in some of the remote rural areas, no vacant building was ever truly vacant. Somebody had usually taken up residence inside it, or teenagers might use it for a hang-out. And that could have been how the fire started. Maybe it hadn't been deliberately set.

"It has to be checked," he insisted to Braden. "You know it."

"I'll go in with the rescue company to check it," Braden said.

Mack shook his head. "You're the boss. You don't run the rescue company."

Dawson Hess ran that because he was also a paramedic like Owen James. Dawson was gone, though, on a trip to New York where his reporter wife lived. Since Dawson had long ago been eliminated as a suspect because the saboteur had also gone after him, his leaving Northern Lakes wasn't an issue.

Owen was in charge. And Mack, with his medical training and evacuation training, had been assigned to the rescue company as well. Owen, standing near the back doors of the building, gestured for Mack to come and join him, Luke Garrison and Ben Higgins, who were also assigned to the company.

Braden hesitated for a moment as if reluctant to send Mack, then he nodded. And Mack rushed off toward that burning building. Knowing that it was probably a trap, he would be careful of his safety and the safety of the rest of the rescue company.

While he'd gone through his intense hotshot training with his dad, the older Mack had told a lot of stories of the rescue companies who'd needed rescuing. Mack didn't want that to be the case here. But he couldn't help but think this was a trap. Just before he followed Owen inside the building, he glanced back toward the staging area in the parking lot.

And he saw *her*.

Wynona was here. And if this was a trap, she might be in as much danger as he was. He had to make it out to make sure that nothing happened to her.

Then he adjusted his mask to make sure he had oxygen and he headed inside, letting the door slam closed behind him.

Wynona stood in the glow and the heat of the burning building, but a chill rushed over her. When that door closed behind Mack, her heart sank with dread. Would she see him again? Would he make it back out of the fire?

She rushed up to Braden and tapped his shoulder. "What are you doing?"

He glanced at her, his brow furrowing. "What? We got called out here."

"Why would you let Mack go in there?" she asked, her pulse racing with the urgency gripping her.

"Because it's his job."

"No, no, it's not," she said. "You brought him onto the team to investigate those acts of sabotage, to find out who's after you. He's not a firefighter."

Braden smiled slightly, as if it was all he could manage.

"Don't let him hear you say that. Every McRooney has the firefighter gene, and thanks to their dad, they have the best training, too."

That pressure on her chest eased a bit, letting her draw a deeper breath. But then she coughed and sputtered as smoke burned her lungs. The air was thick with it, making the sky look dark already like night had come before noon.

"You need to get back," Braden said. "And please establish a perimeter with police barricades to keep people away."

"I already have some other troopers blocking off the streets around here," she said. But this fire was even more dangerous than she'd been worrying that it was. "Do you suspect there are chemicals in that building?"

"I don't know," Braden said. "The rescue company goes in first. They'll establish if there are any dangerous chemicals inside when they make sure that there are no people in the building."

There were people in that building. Mack and three other firefighters had gone through that door. They were going into the main level, but the whole structure was burning, flames consuming it and that billboard that hung on the side of it. Jason's face melted, fading into black with flames shooting through where the eyes might have been and his mouth like he was some demon coming back from the dead to destroy them.

But Jason was gone. Even the magnet and that note she had on the side of her fridge, to remind herself not to be sweet-talked and fooled again, was gone. Harry had probably knocked it down between the fridge and the cabinet next to it. But while Jason was gone, the threat was still out there. Or maybe the saboteur was in that building with Mack, waiting for an opportunity to try to kill him again.

"Trooper!" Braden shouted at her. "I need your help."

She nodded, and despite all the smoke, she tried to clear her head, tried to think. She had to secure the scene, had to protect as many people as she could. That was why she'd gone into this career.

After being helpless to save her parents when that virus had ravaged their bodies, she'd vowed then to help as many other people as she could. But she had this horrible feeling that she wouldn't be able to help the person who probably needed it the most.

Mack.

He was already in the fire. And she couldn't get him out of there. He and his team would have to find their own way through the flames.

But then the ground and the building shuddered and fire blasted out the side of the structure, spraying bricks and debris into the parking lot, some of it landing dangerously close to where she and Braden stood. She felt the heat, but more than that, she felt the fear that overwhelmed her.

Not for herself but for Mack.

Because she had an answer to the questions she'd asked Braden. There must have been chemicals inside that had caused that explosion. There had also been firefighters inside that building.

Had they survived?

Had Mack?

Trick was late to the scene. Since Michaela had taken medical leave, he'd taken her "day job" at the St. Paul fire department. By doing that, he was able to work with Henrietta and live with her in the apartment over the firehouse. But that meant that if the hotshots were called up to report to a fire, he and Henrietta would have to drive nearly an hour south to Northern Lakes. That meant that he was an hour late for the fire and the explosion that they'd heard when they'd still been miles from town.

Maybe he was too late to save his brother. Because he doubted that building had exploded on its own. The saboteur was at it again and was getting more and more dangerous the longer he or she eluded justice.

Debris from the building had expanded the cordoned-off area, so Trick had to park more than two blocks away from the scene. He threw open the driver's door and ran toward the old warehouse. Henrietta, as always, was right beside him with her hand in his.

"He's going to be okay," she said.

And he was surprised that she would make that claim, that she would lie to him when she had no way of knowing. He wanted it to be the truth. He wanted Mack to be okay, or Trick would never forgive himself for how he'd treated his older brother. How he hadn't been able to bring himself to forgive him for leaving.

And now Mack might be gone forever...

Chapter 10

The blast rocked Mack, knocking him down, knocking off his helmet. He scrambled around in the smoke, fumbling around the ground for the helmet and the mask. That smoke filled his lungs, and a cough racked him as he gasped for breath. Through his thick gloves, he found the helmet and mask and shoved them on his head again.

"Hello?" he called into the mike built into his helmet. "Hello?" Not even static emanated from the speaker. Were the others unable to speak? Even those outside the building? It looked like more debris and bricks had blown out that side instead of flying around inside...

But where were the others?

"Hello? Hello?" he called into the mike, but there was no reply.

From the rest of the rescue company and from Braden. Were they all hurt? Braden and Wynona were in the parking lot. Had the debris extended that far? Had she or his brother-in-law been struck by anything or by the heat and the flames?

The fire burned brighter now. Hotter. Even with all his gear, Mack could feel the heat. He had to get the hell out of here, but not without the rest of the rescue company. Luke and his wife had just had a baby. He had to be okay.

"Hello? Hello?" he called out again, but the only thing he heard was the roar of the flames and the rush of water from hoses. The others were still out there, pumping water from the outside. And then there was the loud buzz as a plane overhead dipped low and dropped a deluge of fire retardant onto the site, beating down the flames, killing the fire.

Like someone had probably intended to kill him. But had someone else died instead?

As the smoke dissipated, the others emerged. Ben Higgins. Owen. Luke. They made hand gestures, so their radios weren't working either. But they worked, as a team, to avoid the fallen beams and bricks. And finally they made it to an exit. Before the explosion, they'd determined that they were the only humans inside. The rest of what they'd found had been boxes and containers of leftover material of whatever had once been stored or manufactured in the warehouse. Apparently something highly combustible.

While they all had suspected it might have been a trap, they had had to make sure that there hadn't been any other innocent people in that building. Braden hadn't known about the chemicals, though, but Mack had a feeling that someone else had been well aware of how combustible the warehouse was: the saboteur.

That was why they'd chosen it for their next stunt, their next attempt on either his life or the lives of any hotshot. But Mack and his company escaped unscathed, their masks and gear protecting them.

That didn't mean that there hadn't been other casualties, though. Outside...

Once Mack was out of the building, he peered through all the smoke billowing around outside and he tried to find her. Where the hell was Wynona?

Two guys, in gear, ran up and grabbed him. Despite the

masks they were wearing to protect them from the possible fumes, he recognized his brother and brother-in-law.

Trick and Braden led him and the others farther away from the building, farther away from the heat and the smoke. And Rory made another pass over the building, dousing it with something other than water, with the special retardant that would extinguish chemical fires. Smoke and heat rolled out of the structure which was collapsing in on itself and disintegrating into a pile of broken bricks and scorched metal.

Braden and Trick led them farther into the parking lot. Mack peered around them now, trying to catch a glimpse of her. She'd been here earlier. He knew that had been her, in her uniform, standing near Braden just as Mack had walked into the warehouse.

But unlike Braden, Wynona hadn't been wearing any protective gear. Just her uniform, her badge and her gun. He removed his mask to ask about her but a cough racked him for a second as the oxygen he'd been inhaling was replaced with the smoke.

"Are you all right?" Braden asked. He wasn't looking at just Mack but at the entire company.

The others nodded, but Mack coughed again when he tried to speak. Despite the intensive training he had recently done with his dad, he wasn't quite as ready to jump into fires as he thought he was. And in that blast, he'd lost his damn helmet and mask for a minute.

Trick had been right—being a hotshot was much more dangerous than he'd realized and not just because of the saboteur. He needed to tell his brother that. He needed to make whatever this tension was between them go away... because they were both in danger now.

But when he opened his mouth, he sucked in more smoke and coughed again.

"You need an EMT," Trick said, his voice gruff either from the smoke or the concern Mack could see in his eyes.

What Mack needed was Wynona, to make sure that she was all right. But he still couldn't see her. When he tried looking around the parking lot, his eyes teared and his vision blurred for a moment.

"We'll get you to the ER," Trick said.

Mack shook his head and reached out and clasped Owen's shoulder. Owen was a former Marine and tough as hell as well as a damn good paramedic. He'd probably saved Rory's life more than Mack had since Rory had still gotten shot that day in the firehouse garage, the day that Mack had shot the crooked FBI agent.

"My EMT's right here," Mack told his brother. "And he'll tell you we're all fine." Or at least Mack would be once he found her. But with Braden and Trick and the rest of the rescue company standing around him, he couldn't see much beyond them. He couldn't see through the smoke to the rest of the parking lot.

And then she was there, shoving her way between his hotshot team members. Then she shoved him back with her hands on his chest. "What the hell were you thinking to go in there? You know you're in danger!"

Then, right after she finished shouting at him, she coughed and wheezed slightly. While she didn't seem to be hurt, she might have inhaled too much of the fumes already. And with the chemicals that were in them, those fumes could be especially toxic.

Lethal even.

Mack stepped forward and reached for her, intending to pick her up and carry her toward one of the rigs. She was the one who needed to get to the hospital as soon as possible. Because she might have once again become the one that the saboteur nearly killed.

Or depending on the toxicity of those fumes, the saboteur could still succeed this time.

Wynona had been so scared that she hadn't been able to control her reaction to seeing Mack. Or to stay away from the building despite Braden's warning for her to get back as well. When the explosion had blasted that huge hole through the side of the building, she had been so worried about him, so terrified that he had died. And when she saw him acting as if nothing was wrong, emotions overwhelmed her. Her relief got swept up in anger that he was being so blasé again, and she lost her temper.

Shoving him wasn't smart, though. But now he was reaching for her, trying to pick her up right in front of the other hotshots. She shoved him back again. "What are you doing? Have you lost your mind?"

Just moments ago she'd been so damn worried that he'd lost his life. Didn't danger affect him at all? How could he seem more concerned about her than about himself?

"You need to get to the ER," he said.

"I wasn't in that burning building," she said, but she coughed again as the smoke overwhelmed her. Other troopers were holding back onlookers, keeping a wide perimeter around the fire. She hoped it was wide enough.

"The smoke could be toxic," Mack said, and now he coughed, too. "And you don't have a mask." He'd taken his down to talk to her.

"You need to get back, Trooper Wells," Owen James told her. "He's right. We need to check air quality levels before anyone should be inhaling this without masks." After he said it, he pulled his up again.

Mack reached for her again, but instead of trying to lift her up, he just guided her farther from the fire. From the fumes. "You need to be careful, too," he told her. "I'm not the only one the saboteur has targeted."

She wanted to deny that it was true, but she couldn't, not after those shots had been fired at her the night before. That hadn't been a hunter.

And now...

She could feel that gaze on her, the one that made a chill race down her spine despite the heat. The saboteur was out there somewhere, watching them...

From the shadows outside the perimeter of the fire?

Or from closer? Was the saboteur one of the hotshots fighting the fire, the fire that he or she had undoubtedly set to try again to kill Mack McRooney?

The saboteur might have known that she would show up, too, since Northern Lakes was her primary coverage area and a fire this big would need a police presence to secure the scene. And while she was securing the scene, she was putting herself in danger, too.

"Maybe you're right," she agreed with Mack. "Maybe we both need to get out of here."

Because what if the saboteur started shooting again? They might not because there would be witnesses now, but if they didn't care about that, then those witnesses could become casualties of whatever war the saboteur had decided to wage against her and Mack.

The explosion should have finished off Mack McRooney. The saboteur had known that the new hotshot was part of the rescue company. McRooney would have to go in first.

But he wouldn't be going in alone. Others could have died with him.

But now…

With as long as this had gone on, with as deep as the saboteur was in, he just didn't see a way out that didn't include casualties.

But the first ones who had to die were Mack McRooney and that damn state trooper. While the fire and the explosion hadn't taken out either of them, the saboteur, as always, had a backup plan.

Chapter 11

Standing under a spray of water in the firehouse locker bathroom, Mack wanted to shower off the stench of the fire and the chemicals that had burned up in it. Hell, he wanted to shower off the whole damn day that had finally ended after spending hours at the scene. And after showering off the stench, he wanted to start over again.

Hell, he wanted to do last night over, at least that kiss. And this time he didn't want to stop kissing Wynona. This time he didn't want to leave her.

If he'd had any idea that this could have possibly been his last day alive, he would have wanted to spend that last night with her.

But that hadn't been his last night, and Mack knew all too well that he couldn't undo the past. That he couldn't stay after he'd already left...which Trick's resentment had proven to him all too well.

So instead of getting rid of his whole day, he would have to make do with just getting rid of the soot and the grime. For now. But once he figured out who the hell the saboteur was, he would get rid of him or her, too. And the son of a bitch would be lucky if they just wound up behind bars with Martin Gingrich or...

They wound up in hell.

Mack reached out and turned the tap to cool off the water rushing over him. He had the showers to himself. Everyone else had come back to the firehouse before him, cleaned up and left. He'd stuck around the scene to make sure that the fire was out and to make sure that Wynona didn't get hurt stubbornly trying to investigate it. That was a job for an arson investigator like Mack's sister Sam. But with Sam being as pregnant as she was, she had no business investigating this fire.

Not that it would take much to determine it had been deliberately set. There had been no sign of anyone living in or even hanging out in that abandoned warehouse. So it wasn't as if someone had accidentally started the fire with a discarded cigarette or something.

And there'd been flash marks from where an accelerant had caught fire. Someone had wanted the fire to keep burning until those containers exploded.

And probably until some people exploded along with them and the building.

Mack wanted to explode with anger like Wynona had vented at the scene. But she'd been angry with him, not the saboteur. She'd been upset that he'd taken chances even knowing that he was in danger.

But that was the story of his life. That was what he'd done for years, and even though he'd retired from that life, apparently he hadn't retired from danger.

Wynona was also a threat to him and not just because of how angry she'd been with him. He kind of liked that she'd been upset with him because that seemed to indicate that she cared. But he liked that, and her, a little too much for his peace of mind.

He needed to focus on catching this saboteur. Not on her and what she made him feel. She was focused on catch-

ing the saboteur too. After she'd insisted she was fine and
kept working the scene with the other troopers, he hadn't
had a chance to talk to her again. And by the time he and
Braden had left, she was already gone.

Where had she gone?

Back to the police post? Or home?

Once he was done with the shower, he would swing by
her place just to make sure that she was all right. That was
the only reason why. And maybe to ask her questions about
Jason Cruise, like why she'd kept that card on her fridge,
and this time, he would make sure that he got answers.

Those were his intentions.

Not to kiss her again.

He chuckled. She was right. He was a liar, and now he
was even lying to himself.

The lights went off, plunging the showers into darkness,
but the water kept running.

And then he heard it...

The snap and the crackle of electricity.

Specifically of a bare wire snapping with it. Sparks appeared in the darkness, and he knew that current was racing toward where he stood in the water on the wet floor,
and if he didn't think of something fast, he was about to get
electrocuted.

Wynona was off duty now. Her shift was over, but she
couldn't stop working because she could not stop worrying.

After going back to the police post, she'd gone home
and showered off the soot and smoke from the fire. She'd
also filled up Harry's automatic feeder and water fountain
because she knew she had to go out again and she wasn't
sure how long she would be gone.

After what had been happening recently, she wasn't even

sure she would be able to make it back home. But she was absolutely sure that she wouldn't be able to rest until she checked on Mack again. She was clearly not the only one in danger now—he was too.

She'd driven past the warehouse, or what was left of it, but the fire was out, and crime scene tape and cones blocked off the area. Nobody was there anymore.

Maybe, since the techs had finished processing his house and the area around it last night, he'd gone home. But she thought of swinging by the firehouse first before making the drive out to his place. She was just pulling up to the firehouse when the lights went out, momentarily plunging the entire area into darkness.

Then the lights flickered and came back on, but she was still uneasy. There was no storm. No reason for the lights to have gone off and come back on unless someone was messing with them like the night the saboteur had slashed the tires of the trucks in the lot and thrown that Molotov cocktail. He or she had messed with the lights then. But the only truck Wynona saw in the lot was the one she'd followed home the night before.

Mack's. He was here. But was he alone?

She parked at the curb and rushed out of her car, leaving it running while she ran up to the side door of the firehouse. She pounded on the steel surface. "Hello? It's Trooper Wells. Let me in."

There was no sound inside, but she picked up on a strange sensation from that metal, like a vibration or a current. She pounded again then tried the knob. As the others had said, it was often left unlocked.

Thanks to Stanley. Or at least everybody blamed it on the kid. But if the saboteur was a hotshot, then he or she had keys to the firehouse anyway. Maybe they were the person leaving the doors unlocked and blaming Stanley in order to cover up that the saboteur was a hotshot.

The knob turned easily, and the door creaked open. "Thanks, Stanley..." she murmured, although she was beginning to doubt that the teenager was the one leaving the door unlocked, especially tonight. Someone else might have deliberately left that door unlocked. Maybe to lure her inside, too.

She almost reached for her collar and for the radio that was usually clipped to it. Unlike last night, she would have used it this time, because she wasn't the only one in danger now, Mack was too. But after showering, she'd changed out of her uniform into jeans and a sweater, so she didn't even have a collar. But she had her weapon, and she drew that out of the holster on her belt loop.

Holding it in both hands, she pushed the door open farther. As she stepped inside, she called out, "Hello?"

But nobody answered her. The fire trucks filled the bays. They were all back. But where were the firefighters? Where was Mack?

That had to have been his truck. It had a Washington state plate instead of a Michigan one. It was the one he'd driven here from where his dad lived on the West Coast. Mack had a place here now, so he wouldn't have to sleep in the bunkroom like some of the other hotshots, the ones who had day jobs in other areas of the state or the country even. Those hotshots had other places to stay now, or they'd found other places. After that attack on Rory in the firehouse, hotshots rarely spent the night in the bunkroom anymore.

But maybe, after his long day, Mack had been too tired to drive home. Maybe he was asleep in that bunkroom on the second floor. But he had to know about what had happened to Rory there, so he shouldn't have taken the risk of staying here, especially since the saboteur was clearly targeting him now.

She crossed the garage to the stairwell of concrete steps that led up to the second and third stories of the three-story cement block building. The lights were dim in the stairwell, as if they were emergency lights only or maybe working off a generator instead of an electrical source.

But she had this strange feeling, almost as if there was electricity in the air. There was a crackle to it and her hair was starting to stand up, but maybe that was with fear.

When she reached the second-story landing, she heard the crackle and the sounds of running water and she saw the sparks coming out of a door that had been jammed open with a trash can. "Hello? Mack?" she called out again.

"Wynona?" a gruff voice called back.

And she started toward that open door.

But now he shouted at her, "Get out! Get out of the building!"

Was it rigged to blow like the warehouse might have been?

Her heart pumped fast and hard with fear. "What is it? What's going on?"

"There's a live wire in the shower room," he said. "You gotta get out of here."

She wasn't going anywhere, but she was reaching for her cell. She had to phone for help because she had no freaking idea how to deal with this.

And how the hell had he not been electrocuted if there was a live wire in the shower with him? Mindful of the water starting to trickle out the open door, Wynona kept the rubber soles of her boots out of the water, and she peered inside the room.

She couldn't see much in that dim emergency lighting. Just the water coming out of the showerheads, and then she saw the man clinging to the top of a ceramic privacy wall that didn't reach all the way to the ceiling, but it was high and his body was clearly wet, water dripping off his broad shoulders and his bulging arms.

How long was he going to be able to hang on without slipping off the ceramic onto the floor where sparks danced from the end of the stripped-out wire that was lying there?

"You have to get out of here," Mack said again.

"Don't worry about your modesty," she said, trying to keep the panic from her voice. She didn't want him to panic and slip. And she didn't want to panic and slip either. "I'm going to figure this out..."

"You're going to get electrocuted too or maybe even shot," Mack said. "Whoever rigged this could still be around here somewhere."

She sucked in a breath at the thought and peered around the shower area again. But she didn't see anyone but him. While the person could still be hiding somewhere in the building, she wasn't as concerned about the saboteur or her own safety as she was about Mack.

"Get out of here!" Mack shouted again. He clearly didn't want her help.

Or he didn't think she could give it without getting hurt herself. She didn't care about her safety right now. But she backed out of the shower area. Once she was in the hall, she reached for her cell.

But instead of calling emergency dispatch, she called someone else. Someone who knew this building better than she did. Someone who might have a clue how to save his brother-in-law because she wasn't certain how to do it without getting them both killed. All she knew was that she needed to find the breaker box where the electrical current came into the building. But there was a good chance that whoever had set all this up was there, making sure that the breaker didn't go off and break that flow of electricity.

So while she talked to Braden, she tightly grasped the weapon she held in her right hand, and she headed back down the stairs to the main level where Braden was telling her that the box was.

"I'm on my way," he said.

But if the saboteur was waiting for her in the utility room, the hotshot superintendent wasn't going to get here in time to help either her or Mack. Because if the saboteur was waiting for her, Wynona might not be able to shut off that breaker. She might not be able to save Mack.

Trick heard the call come out over the hotshot radio frequency. SOS at the firehouse. At the cottage Henrietta had inherited from her grandfather, she was in the shower, washing off the soot and smoke from the fire.

"What the hell happened now?" he wondered aloud. But he didn't need to ask to whom it had happened.

It had to be Mack.

Why hadn't he hugged his big brother when Mack and the rest of the rescue company had come out of that warehouse earlier today? He hadn't, though. He'd just stood there with Braden, letting his brother-in-law do all the talking.

Why hadn't he told Mack how sorry he was for being such a dick to him since he'd come back?

Trick had to let the anger and resentment go, he knew that now. But he didn't want to let his brother go.

He was afraid that he might not have a choice.

Chapter 12

Mack might have been embarrassed that he was hanging, bare-assed naked, from a shower wall, when Wynona had stepped into the shower room. But he was too worried about her to care about modesty or anything else. Even himself right now.

What if this was a trap? And that son of a bitch was somewhere inside the building yet, waiting to get Wynona alone. Minutes ago he'd yelled at her to leave, but now he wanted to call her back.

But those damn sparks kept bouncing up from the end of that wire. If he stepped down onto the tile floor, into the water, he was going to get electrocuted for certain.

While Wynona had a chance to save herself...

And maybe even him...

But then the lights flickered and shut off again, leaving him in darkness. Complete darkness.

Maybe that live wire had finally blown a breaker. Or Wynona had found and shut off the main switch. He didn't hear anything now but the water running, spraying out of the faucet and onto his back and onto the floor.

His arms started to shake from the exertion of holding up his body weight for so long. And he found himself starting to slide down from that half wall. As his foot touched the wet tile, he cringed in anticipation of the shock of electricity.

But nothing happened...until the lights flashed on again. And he let out a curse as he waited for that wire to spring back to life again.

But it lay limply in the puddle on the floor, like a dead snake. The lights that had flickered on were just the security lights, which would have been on a different circuit than the one that someone had rigged that wire to, so he breathed a sigh of relief.

Until he heard the squishing sound of shoe soles against the wet tile. He glanced up from that wire to confront whoever had walked in, but it was her.

"You're okay?" he asked Wynona.

She held her gun yet, as if she was worried that they weren't alone. He could hear other voices now. Other people were in the building, and in the distance, he could hear sirens.

She nodded, but she wouldn't meet his gaze. Her attention seemed to be elsewhere...

On his body. His naked body. He hadn't grabbed a towel yet. And right now, he wanted to grab her instead, especially with the way she was staring at him, making him even more aware of her than he'd already been, more aware of the attraction that sizzled between them. But he felt more than attraction for her now, he felt gratitude.

"You saved me..." he murmured. He wasn't used to that, to being the one who needed saving.

"Don't sound so surprised," she said, her lips curving into a slight grin. "I *am* capable..." But she sounded a little surprised herself.

"Mack!" Braden called out from below.

"Are you capable of handing me a towel?" Mack asked. The one he'd brought into the shower with him had dropped off the half wall he'd been hanging onto just a short while ago. And it was as wet as he was. But he wasn't cold, not with the way she was staring at him.

And if he hadn't heard other people inside the building, he definitely wouldn't have minded being naked with her.

Her smile widened even as her face flushed. She picked a towel off one of the hooks near the door that had been propped open to the hall. But she held it just a bit out of his reach.

Like she was just a bit out of his reach…

He couldn't quite figure her out. And he didn't have the chance because before he could take that towel from her, Braden was in the showers, too. And he wasn't alone. Owen was with him. And the young guys, Abbott and Lane. Cunningham and Kozak were there, too.

"If this is your SOS, you need more help than us," Kozak said.

"Stand back!" she said, holding up her hand, with that towel, to direct them all back into the hall. "This is a crime scene."

"What's the crime?" Abbott asked. "Indecent exposure?"

"You going to cuff him, Trooper Wells?" Lane asked.

"I'm kind of wondering why she's here at all…" Cunningham murmured.

So was Mack, but he was damn glad she'd showed up when she had.

"Someone tried to electrocute McRooney," she said.

And they probably would have succeeded if not for her showing up when she had.

Trick, who'd just showed up, gasped. "Mack?" he called out to him over Braden's shoulder. "Are you all right?"

"I'm fine," Mack said with a nod. "Or I will be once you all get out of here and let me get dressed." He wasn't sure about that, though. He wasn't sure that he was fine, and it wasn't just because someone had tried to kill him yet again. It was because of her and how much she unsettled him.

Wynona turned back toward him then, and her gaze dipped down once, over his body, before she handed him the towel. And just under her breath, so that he barely heard her, she muttered something that sounded a lot like, "You are fine…"

And now his face flushed. His hands shook a bit as he wrapped that towel around his waist. But that was just from the exertion, not because she affected him so much. And now he was lying even to himself.

The police joined the others out in the hall. "What's going on? What happened?" Sergeant Hughes asked.

He wanted the son of a bitch caught who'd done this, so Mack quickly shared what little he knew. He'd thought he was alone in the firehouse, in the showers, when the power had gone out only to come back on moments later with that damn live wire sparking across the water toward him.

"I want everybody out of here," Hughes said with a hard glance at Wynona.

"Sir, I was—"

"Wynona saved my life," Mack said, though he wasn't sure exactly how she'd managed that.

"Braden directed me on where to find the breaker box," Wynona said. "It had been jammed to keep that breaker on…" She gestured toward the one into which that wire had been plugged. "I had to pry it out with a crowbar. I'm afraid I might have damaged evidence."

"You shouldn't have done anything until on-duty officers arrived," Hughes admonished her.

"If she'd done that, I would probably be dead," Mack pointed out. "Unless that's what you wanted, Sergeant."

Hughes's face flushed. "I don't want anyone to die," he said.

"Then let Trooper Wells do her job," Mack suggested.

She drew in a deep breath that seemed to make her grow a couple of inches taller, and she nodded. "Yes," she said, but she was looking at the hotshots who'd been backed into the hall. "Let me do my job."

While they were all talking, Mack slipped through a side door into the locker room. But he wasn't alone in there—the other hotshots gathered around him. The younger guys catcalled a bit, razzing him. And Trick...

His brother looked like he wanted to say something, but before he could, the sergeant stepped inside the room. "I want all of you out of this building," he said. "Not just the shower rooms. Out. Now."

With varying sighs and muttered comments, the other hotshots filed out. And Mack couldn't help but wonder if the sergeant hadn't just let the saboteur go. But then the crime scene techs arrived, and the sergeant turned his attention to directing them.

Where had Wynona gone? Wasn't she supposed to be doing her job? Or had she, like the saboteur, slipped away?

Mack dressed quickly and headed downstairs to Braden's office. That was where the security footage would be, but when he approached the open door, he overheard the conversation between Braden and Wynona and her sergeant.

"The cameras were taken offline somehow," Braden said, his voice gruff with frustration. "There's nothing on here..."

"Not even Wells saving McRooney," Hughes remarked, as if he doubted that she had.

"The power had already gone out before I walked in," Wynona said.

"Through an unlocked door?"

"Yes," she replied.

And Braden groaned.

"You don't know that Stanley left it unlocked," she said, defending the kid.

And making Mack smile that she did. But he wasn't sure Stanley deserved it. He needed to check out the kid a bit more, make sure that he was as sweet as he seemed.

"If he left it unlocked, I'm damn glad that he did," Mack said.

Braden and Hughes turned toward where he was standing in that open doorway. But Wynona didn't look away from the blank screen on Braden's computer, as if she didn't want to face him. And her face was flushed.

Even though she was ignoring him, he continued, "I probably wouldn't have been able to hang on much longer." He had in fact slipped off the wall, but thankfully only after Wynona had gotten the breaker to the wire shut off. With as strong as that current was, it easily would have killed him if it had still been on.

"We'll have our techs go over the footage," Wynona said to Braden, not to him. "See if there's anything they can recover."

"It'll be hard to recover what isn't there," Hughes chimed in. "If the cameras weren't running, they weren't recording."

Mack hated to admit it, but the guy was right. The saboteur was smart and knew the firehouse and even the security system pretty well, which made him think of the hotshots who'd just showed up. Braden had probably called Owen since he was a paramedic. But why had Carl Kozak and Donovan Cunningham and those younger guys showed up? And Trick?

Had they just been responding to the call? Or had one

of them been around the firehouse, waiting to see if this act of sabotage had caused a casualty? Instead of banishing them from the scene, Hughes should have been questioning all of them about their whereabouts earlier so he could check their alibis.

The sergeant should have taken Mack's advice to let Wynona do her job, but it was clear now that he intended to run the investigation. He glanced at Mack with more annoyance than anything else, though.

"You've given your statement," he said. "You need to leave now. Let us finish processing the scene."

The radio on his collar sputtered something at him, not about the case but apparently about his wife. The man's face flushed, and he pushed past Mack to step out of the office. He continued down the hall, though, before taking out his cell phone, probably to call his wife.

He definitely should have left the investigation to Wynona. But maybe it was a good thing that he hadn't because she was in danger, too.

While Mack was glad that the techs were here, he didn't think they would find anything that would lead to the saboteur. This person was too damn smart. Smarter than Hughes.

But maybe not Wynona. She'd known Mack was still in danger and had showed up in time to rescue him. But she wouldn't even look at him.

Braden was studying his face though, and there was concern in his dark eyes. "You should go home, Mack. It's been a hell of a long day for you. I'm going to stick around here until the techs are done—"

"Me, too," Wynona said with a glance past Mack, as if she expected her boss to overhear and insist on taking her off the case.

She had saved Mack, and if she hadn't been careful, she

could have died doing that. She was the one he could trust the most right now.

"What about me?" he asked.

"You should leave, like the sergeant said. There is no reason for you to stick around," she replied as if letting him off the hook. Obviously she didn't have to stick around either since she was not in her uniform now. She must have clocked out some time ago. And her boss was here to supervise those techs.

"You're just going to let me drive off on my own?" he asked. "You're not providing police protection?"

"I'm actually off duty," she said, gesturing toward her black sweater and jeans.

But that hadn't stopped her from saving him. And why had she stopped by anyway since she was off duty?

Her lips curved into a slight smile. "And you actually want police protection?" She made a soft sound, like a snort. "I already intended to have a trooper follow you home, one who is currently on duty."

"I want a trooper I can trust," he said. "I want you." He had a feeling from the way her face was so flushed and that she kept looking away, that she wanted him, too.

Blood was rushing through Wynona's entire body now, not just in her face like when she hadn't been able to stop blushing over the image of Mack she would never get out of her mind. Naked. He was so damn big and muscular and also so strong and fearless.

So why had he wanted a police escort home?

He hadn't seemed fazed at all over nearly getting electrocuted. He hadn't even seemed as angry as she was that someone kept putting his life and other lives in danger. She was furious that this saboteur cared so little for human life. Cared so little about everyone but...

What was the saboteur's motive?

She could almost understand him or her going after Mack since it was pretty obvious that Braden had hired him for the sole purpose of finding and stopping the saboteur. Not that he couldn't fight a fire because he had handled himself well at the warehouse, too.

He'd survived that explosion. But the saboteur had obviously not been happy about that and had tried again almost immediately after the warehouse fire failed to kill Mack. Obviously he or she wasn't going to stop trying until Mack McRooney was dead.

So it was smart that she followed him home. She pulled her SUV up behind his truck and hopped out quickly, her gun drawn to protect him should the shooting start again. This was why she'd become a cop, to protect people. She'd figured out that there was no protecting someone from an illness, like the one that had claimed her parents' lives, but she could protect people from other threats.

He held up his hands. "Don't shoot," he said, but there was the rumble of laughter in his deep voice. He obviously didn't consider her a threat. "I'm not armed."

She rushed him toward the door. "Hurry," she urged him, "get inside." She covered him while he unlocked the door. But then when he pushed it open, she stepped in front of him. It took her only moments to clear the small cabin. "It's safe," she said. The crime scene techs had collected and cleared the house just hours after the shooting. She holstered her weapon. "And why the hell would I have gone to the trouble of saving your life if I intended to shoot you?"

"I was just joking," he said. "Guess not everyone gets my gallows humor."

She enjoyed gallows humor. Usually. But she was so damn on edge. He could have died too many times over the past couple of days, and that bothered her probably way more than it bothered him. Probably way more than it should bother her. He would only be as blasé as he was about danger if he'd been in it many times before.

And while he claimed he was retiring, she wondered if he would be able to stay away from it. Or if that life, and living on the edge like that, had become an addiction to him. Knowing that he wasn't going to stick around was a good reason for her to not get attached or addicted to him. But there was something about him that had fascinated her even before she'd seen him naked. Now that she had…he was all she could see when she closed her eyes.

"You did save my life," he said. "Thank you."

She shrugged. "Just doing my job."

"Is that why you came back to the firehouse?" he asked. And that look was back on his face, the same expression she'd seen on so many other people's faces in Northern Lakes since her training sergeant's arrest.

She groaned now. "Oh, my God, I can't believe you're still suspicious of me like the rest of your hotshot team. You were here when someone shot at me."

She pointed at the door he'd closed and locked behind them. There was duct tape over the hole the bullet had come through on its way to the board of suspects. She walked over to it now, and her unflattering driver's license picture was still hanging there. The techs had probably gotten a good laugh at seeing her as a suspect.

"And if you're still so suspicious of me, why did you ask for me to specifically be your police protection?" Especially when it was clear he could take care of himself. At least as long as there was no live wire in the shower with him.

"I don't think you tried to hurt me," he said. "But I do have some suspicions about you that I wouldn't if you were more forthcoming."

She felt a little frisson of unease that he already knew her secret. But she forced herself to laugh. "That's interesting coming from you. You won't even tell me who you used to work for."

"The government."

"Which department?"

"Military affairs," he said, but he was grinning slightly now. He knew he was being vague.

"And you're sure nobody from your past could be here in Northern Lakes, coming after you?" she asked. From the scars she'd seen on his muscular body when he'd stood naked in front of her, she knew that he'd had some close scrapes before. That someone else had hurt him. And she suspected that might not have been just physically with the way he seemed to hold himself aloof from the team and even from his brother Trick.

She understood that. Her co-workers probably thought she was aloof, too. But after what could have been the fatal mistakes in her judgment regarding Gingrich and Jason Cruise, she hadn't known whom to trust, and had decided that it was easier to trust no one.

"I checked," he said, then sighed. "And double-checked. Nobody's looking for me." But his jaw clenched as if he was gritting his teeth when he said it.

"Really?"

"Nobody who wants to kill me," he said.

"An old lover?"

He snorted. "No. I didn't even think my bosses liked me much. But…"

"They want you back on the job," she presumed.

And his jaw seemed to clench tighter, so tightly that a muscle twitched in his cheek.

"Will you go back?" she asked.

He hesitated a moment. A long moment. Then he shook his head.

And her stomach muscles tightened. She suspected that he would go back. If he was able...

First, he had to survive his job here in Northern Lakes, which was as much about catching the saboteur as it was about fighting fires.

"I answered your questions," he said. "Now you answer mine."

She swallowed a groan. She wasn't sure if answering his questions would get her name crossed off his suspect board or if it would get it circled. Right now, the only names he'd circled belonged to hotshots, an interesting collection of the older and the younger ones. She turned her attention to the board to see if he'd crossed off or circled any more names, but Mack's big hands cupped her shoulders.

He turned her toward him and asked, "Will you answer my questions?"

Maybe it was time for it all to come out...

She drew in a breath to brace herself and nodded.

"Did you want me to kiss you last night?"

That was not the question she'd expected, so her mouth dropped open.

"I'm really sorry—"

"Don't apologize," she said. She didn't want him to regret it when she didn't. She didn't want to admit to wanting it, to wanting him, either, but she didn't want him thinking he'd crossed a line. "You would have known if I hadn't wanted you to kiss me. I would have dropped you."

His lips curved into a sexy grin. "And instead, you kissed me back…"

She groaned as heat rushed to her face. "I know. That was unprofessional and stupid." And yet she still didn't regret it. The only thing she really regretted was that it had ended with just the kiss. After what they'd been through, how close they'd both come lately to dying, she hated that she might have denied herself pleasure she'd gone a long time without feeling.

He groaned, too, then sighed. "I don't understand this… attraction…myself."

She flinched. "Ouch."

He chuckled. "You know you're gorgeous," he said so matter-of-factly.

She felt like she used to be pretty, but with her unflattering uniform and all the stress of her job, she hadn't felt as if she'd looked well, let alone pretty, for a while. So his comment affected her, had something that felt suspiciously like butterflies somersaulting in her stomach.

He continued, "But usually I don't notice stuff like that…" He brushed one of his hands over his short dark hair, and it almost looked like there was a slight tremor in his fingers. But after how close he'd come to getting electrocuted, it was understandable.

She was shaky, too, but it had nothing to do with that and everything to do with him.

"You're just…you're impossible to ignore," he said. "There's just something about you…something that draws me closer to you…"

She knew that feeling. She felt the same way about him, like something was pulling her closer to him. And closer… every time they were in the same vicinity.

"Something that fascinates and mystifies me," he said.

Then he shook his head. "God, I sound like an idiot. It's just…been a while since I've been involved with anyone."

If she was as jaded as she should have been, she might have thought that he was just putting on an act to get to her, to get her into bed. But she actually believed that he was sincere, and she was touched.

And she was so damn attracted to him, too.

"It's been a while for me, too," she said. "Not that we're involved, we're just trying to find this person…" She gestured behind her at the board. "And not get killed." But they could have been, both of them, too many times. "It looks like you've come closer in your past than you have here…"

His brow furrowed. "What do you mean?"

She pointed at his chest. And his shoulder. And even though he was wearing a shirt now, she could see the ridges of the scars marring the sleek skin that had stretched taut over all those sculpted muscles. "You have so many scars…"

He shrugged. "I've had some close calls in the past," he said. "A helicopter crash. An explosion…"

She shuddered at the thought of how close he'd come to dying. She might never have met him. Even if she hadn't, she had a feeling she would have felt a loss, like the one she felt at the thought of him dying now or leaving again.

He would probably leave again, if those old bosses of his convinced him to come back.

And then she would be alone again. But she wasn't alone now. And she didn't want to be alone tonight.

He stepped a little closer to her, as if he was as drawn as he'd told her he was. "So, when you didn't hand that towel over when I asked, you were just checking out my scars?" he asked, and his lips were curving into that sexy grin again.

She felt a twitch in her lips with the urge to grin back at him. But that wasn't all she wanted to do with him. "Yes, I found your scars very interesting," she said. And she'd wanted to trace each of them with her fingertips and her lips...

And the desire to do that, the desire for him, intensified now to the point she was almost in pain. A pain she knew that he could relieve...

So she reached out, wrapping her hands around his neck to pull his head down to hers. And she kissed him.

The kiss went from a light brush of lips across lips to something much deeper, much more intimate, and passion overwhelmed her. She couldn't remember ever wanting anyone this much.

Maybe it was because of the danger they'd been in and the adrenaline that her feelings were so much more intense than anything she'd ever felt before.

When his tongue slipped inside her mouth, she moaned. He tasted so good, so dark and rich and dangerous. She found herself tugging at his shirt, pulling it up, so that she could see what she had in the showers. His sleek skin marred with an old scar here and there that had healed over long ago, his muscles so hard and well-defined, like he worked out all the time. Or used them all the time.

"You really have been through hell, haven't you?" she murmured, wondering how he had survived everything that had obviously happened to him, all those explosions and crashes.

"That wasn't even the worst of it," he muttered.

"What was?" she asked, wanting to know him more, to know him deeply.

He shrugged and shook his head. "Something that happened a long time ago..."

"What?" Because she knew that was what had hurt him the most.

"You probably heard the story...how my mom took off, left my dad to raise me and my siblings on his own..."

She instinctively knew that was the biggest scar he carried with him. The emotional one. She carried one of those herself.

As if he was embarrassed by the admission he'd just made, he picked her up, using all those muscles of his, and carried her over to that big bed in one corner of the open cabin. As he laid her down onto it, he followed her, his mouth still fused to hers.

Finally, he pulled back, panting for breath, and asked, "What are we doing?"

"I don't know," she admitted. After the fiasco with Jason, she'd vowed to focus only on her professional life and give up trying to have a personal life. But she'd nearly lost her life the day before in the gunfire.

And today he had nearly lost his.

Twice.

"No, *tell* me," he said, his voice gruff with desire, "tell me to stop if you want to stop."

She shook her head. "I don't want to stop. I want you." And she did, more than she could ever remember wanting anyone. The desire was overwhelming, probably because the man was so overwhelming.

He stepped back then and pulled off the shirt she'd only managed to pull up a bit. Then he unbuckled his belt.

She was so eager to be skin to skin with him that she shucked off her jeans, being careful of the holster strapped to the belt. And then she pulled off her sweater, too, leaving her wearing only her underwear, which she had chosen for comfort. She hadn't considered that anyone else might see her in it. It had been so long since she'd even had a date for coffee or dinner let alone a night in. So she wore a sports bra and granny panties rather than some of the sexy stuff she owned, but with the way he looked at her, she felt sexy. His gaze skimmed over her body like a caress. Then his fingers were there, trailing across her skin.

"You are so silky," he said. "So beautiful…" And his voice was even gruffer with the passion burning in his dark eyes.

He was the beautiful one. The one with the perfect body, the chiseled facial features. Even his head, with his dark hair clipped so short, was perfectly shaped. She trailed her fingers along his jaw, down his neck to his chest. When she pressed her palm to his chest, she could feel how hard his heart was beating, how hard he was breathing. He wanted her as badly as she wanted him.

She wound her arms around him and pulled him down onto the bed with her. But he braced himself, putting his weight on one arm rather than on her. And in that arm, the impressive bicep bulged.

"I'm going to crush you," he said.

"I'm stronger than I look," she said. She hoped that was true, and that she could resist letting this attraction between them become anything more. Because she doubted he was going to stick around after he caught the saboteur. So she would be a fool, again, to get attached to him. To fall for him…

But at the moment she wasn't strong enough to resist the desire she felt for him, the need for him that burned inside her. She arched up and kissed him, his lips, his jaw, and then she slid her mouth down his neck.

He shivered despite the heat of his skin, of his body, and then he kissed her back. First he kissed her lips then he moved his mouth down her throat, and as he did, he pushed up her sports bra and freed her breasts.

She arched up to pull it over her head and toss it down beside the bed. Then she wriggled out of her panties. And there was nothing between them but his boxers. He got rid of them, too.

She sucked in a breath of appreciation and anticipation. The man was big everywhere. She reached for him, but he drew back.

"I'll go right away," he warned her, and he was already gritting his teeth and clenching his jaw as if he was struggling for control.

"I'm ready," she said. "I want you."

But it was as if he didn't believe her because he pushed her back onto the bed. Then he moved his mouth down her body, over her breasts, licking and tugging at her nipples before he moved lower.

He barely touched her, and she felt a rush and quivering of her inner muscles as pleasure streaked through her. The orgasm was intense but still it wasn't enough. She needed him inside her.

She reached for him again, sliding her hand around his pulsating erection.

"Wynona..." He fumbled in the table beside the bed and pulled a condom out of the drawer. The packet tore and then he moved her hand aside to sheathe himself.

She pushed him onto his back, and he chuckled, his chest rumbling so much that the bed vibrated. Then she swung her leg over him, and guided him inside her, taking him deep. A moan slipped through her lips at the intensity, the pleasure...

He felt so damn good. He was exactly what she hadn't

known she needed. This was exactly what she hadn't known she needed.

He clutched her hips, helping her find a rhythm as she rocked back and forth and slid up and down. And he thrusted against her. Sweat beaded on his upper lip, as he continued his battle to hold on to control.

But that was a battle she wanted him to lose. She leaned down and kissed his lips, his chin.

His hands moved up to cup her breasts. He flicked his thumbs, rough from hard work, across her nipples. Tension wound from them to her core until it finally snapped, until she finally snapped. She rode him in a fury, screaming his name as this orgasm overwhelmed her.

He clutched her hips again, thrusting deep, and groaned as he pulsed inside her, joining her in that mind-blowing release he'd given her.

She collapsed onto his chest, embarrassed to look at him after how totally she'd lost it. But still she had no second thoughts. No regrets. Because she'd never felt passion like that before…

It had been late when Mack and Wells left the firehouse. It was even later when Braden got home after waiting for the techs to finish up and then for an emergency electrician to fix the damaged breaker box. The Northern Lakes firehouse was the only one within an hour, so it couldn't be shut down for any reason. They had to be able to keep working out of it. But they had to survive the saboteur to be able to keep working.

Braden was surprised he'd survived the night himself, just from exhaustion. But even with as late as it was, when he opened his door, he found Sam on the couch, waiting for him. "You were supposed to go back to bed," he told her.

"I hear Trooper Wells telling you that someone is trying to electrocute my brother and you expect me to go back to sleep?" she asked, her voice a little sharp.

Braden had expected his wife to try to go with him. But Sam was as protective of their baby as she was her family. And she had also heard that Wells was handling the situation, that she'd gotten the breaker out of the box to stop the current of electricity.

"Before I even left, you knew that Wells had everything under control," Braden said. "She made sure he wasn't in any danger."

Wells had saved Mack's life, so it probably shouldn't have surprised him that Mack had wanted her to follow him home. But still...

"What is it?" she asked. "You said he was okay!"

Braden had called his wife and verified that her brother was fine the minute he'd gotten to the firehouse. "Yes, he is," he said. "He even has police protection for tonight."

Sam narrowed her eyes. "Don't tell me Trooper Wells..."

He nodded.

"Why did he let that happen?" Sam asked. "I know she saved him tonight, but that doesn't mean that she couldn't have been the one who set it up, too. She could still be the saboteur and was just trying to prove her innocence. I don't trust her, and I didn't think Mack did either."

"He was the one who asked her to go home with him."

Sam sucked in a breath. "What?"

Braden shrugged. "She did save his life."

Braden was beginning to wonder if his older brother-in-law was a cat because he certainly seemed to have more than one life. He'd used at least two of them in one night. Braden hoped he wouldn't have to use any more of them. But that hope was dim, because the saboteur seemed fixated on Mack now, on making sure the former special forces operative couldn't catch them.

And they probably knew what Braden had come to realize about his brother-in-law. The only way to stop Mack McRooney was to kill him.

Chapter 13

Sunshine warmed Mack's bare skin and burned like an orange flame behind his closed lids. He opened his eyes to the brightness of the new day, surprised that he'd actually survived the night and not just because of those attacks.

But because of Wynona...

He hadn't been able to get enough of her, and she had seemed just as insatiable as he'd suddenly become. Maybe it was that he'd denied himself a personal life for so long that he hadn't been able to stop reaching for her, kissing her, filling her, and she had done the same, waking him up a couple of times with her lips on his skin.

Just thinking about it had his body tensing up all over again. Hell, he was surprised he'd slept at all and not just because of having sex, but because he usually couldn't sleep around other people. He couldn't let himself be that vulnerable, not in the situations he'd been in during his past missions. But he'd found himself in that situation again here in Northern Lakes.

Danger.

But that threat wasn't just from the saboteur anymore. It was because of *her*. She was standing by the board, studying the pictures he'd tacked to it. She was wearing one of his button-down shirts over her bra and panties. Her red hair was tousled around her shoulders, and she had a cup of coffee in her hand. The scent of fresh ground beans was strong, and he turned his head to find a cup sitting on the table beside the bed.

"You're still here," he mused as he reached for the cup.

"You wanted police protection," she reminded him with a small smile.

"We both know that's not what I wanted." He'd wanted her, and he'd thought that once he had her, maybe he would be able to control his attraction to her. But now it was even more intense, his body even more aware of hers. She was so damn sexy.

And he hoped she was as strong as she'd claimed as well because he had a feeling that they were both going to get hurt one way or another. He didn't want to hurt her like his mom had hurt his dad, like she'd hurt all of them. He didn't want to be like her, but Trick wasn't the only one afraid that Mack was. Mack was afraid, too.

"Thanks for the coffee," he said, and he took a long sip. "Hmm...really thanks."

She chuckled. "You're really welcome."

"And really thanks for coming back here last night," he said.

She grinned, and her green eyes twinkled. "Were you afraid to be alone?"

He sighed. "I think I'm more afraid to not be alone." Which was why he couldn't believe he'd fallen asleep with her in his house, in his bed. On some level he had to trust her, and he wasn't sure why.

Her smile slid away then. "So you're not going to stick around once the saboteur is caught." It wasn't a question—it was as if she knew something he wasn't certain of himself. Because he really had no idea what he was going to do after the saboteur was caught. He had no plan for retirement beyond making sure that his family was safe by making it up to them for leaving like their mom had.

He shrugged. "I don't know what I'm going to do," he admitted. "I've never let myself really think about the future before..." He'd always just focused on the current mission.

"The saboteur seems to want to make sure that you don't have one," she said. She pointed at all the circled names. "You have some really good suspects here. The arborists especially, given that first attempt on your life. And I think one of them has a dad who's an electrician..."

He did need to catch this bastard. So he had to focus on the mission instead of how damn sexy she was. "I know. I need to figure out who this son of a bitch is." She'd brought up an interesting point about the arborists. Either Bruce or Howie could have cut that tree to fall on him. And they'd been at the warehouse fire and at the firehouse right after the attempt to electrocute him.

"Are you going to cross my name off the suspect list now?" she asked. "Like you have so many of the others?"

"I want to," he said with a yearning that surprised him. But he didn't want to make the same mistake that his dad had, trusting a woman he shouldn't any more than he wanted to be like the woman his dad shouldn't have trusted.

"What's it going to take?" Wynona asked. She could have flirted when she asked it. After last night, after what they'd done to each other, she could have used that to her advantage, to distract him, to persuade him.

He was that susceptible to her. And that scared him nearly as much as that live wire in the shower had...because he wasn't just susceptible—he was vulnerable in a way he'd never been before.

So he drew in a deep breath, bracing himself, then replied, "Honesty."

All the color drained from her face. And his stomach sank with dread and the realization that he'd been right to have doubts about her. She definitely had something to hide.

Mack had thrown that word at her like a challenge. And Wynona didn't shy away from a challenge. Or she wouldn't have gone back to college, got her criminal justice degree and entered the police academy. But she had.

And she knew she had to answer this challenge, too. She just took a moment to compose herself and to get dressed. And when she came out of the bathroom, she told him what she suspected he already knew. "I was seeing Jason Cruise."

"When he was trying to kill Charlie Tillerman?" Mack asked.

Clearly he knew everything since he didn't seem a bit surprised—just cautious and maybe disappointed with a slight bowing to his broad shoulders. He'd pulled on his jeans while she'd showered, but he wasn't wearing a shirt, which just wasn't fair. He made it harder for her to focus.

She shook her head. "No. I only went out with him a few times after he helped me find my house. He was probably only interested in me because of that…" Because of her money. Too many men and so-called friends had been only interested in that when she was growing up, so she'd trusted few people as friends and especially as potential partners. "And I realized quickly that he was a narcissist. But before I did, when he was trying so hard to woo me, I know I told him too much about my job, about things that had been happening on my job."

"The things that had happened to the hotshots?"

She nodded. "I know it was unprofessional and stupid. And I know Michaela Momber already thinks I was taking bribes or something from him. If they saw my house and knew that I'd been going out with him..."

"Most people don't know you were personally involved with him," Mack said. But clearly he had. "Most people question how close you were to Martin Gingrich."

She grimaced. "That makes me sick to think anyone believes I could have been personally involved with him. He was assigned as my training officer. I had no control over that. Just as I have no control over people thinking whatever they will about me." She drew in a deep breath and let it out in a sigh. "And I guess I shouldn't care what these people think of me. I should just want to do my job."

But she cared. Ever since her parents had died she felt so alone, and she'd wanted to make connections here in the town she'd chosen for herself. She'd wanted to make a life here, not just professionally but personally as well.

"I talked to Martin Gingrich," he said. "I visited him in jail."

Gingrich was still awaiting trial, still trying to push it off as long as he could. Wynona almost felt sorry for him. "Did he know about Jason?" Was that who had told Mack?

"Not that he was dead, but he knew you were going out with him," he said. "But I already knew before I talked to ole Marty." He pulled out a magnet and a card.

"He sent me a lot of flowers," she said. "I think love bombing is what that's called." But after last night, after that warehouse exploded, bombing had a whole different connotation for her. Both types were dangerous, though. Thankfully she hadn't been so lonely that she'd fallen for Jason Cruise's phony charm or for him.

Now Mack McRooney...

He wasn't trying to love bomb her unless he considered an interrogation a version of that.

"I kept one of those notes to remind myself of how I shouldn't trust anyone," she explained. "Something I should have learned when I was a kid and people just wanted to get close to me because of my money. That's probably all that Cruise was after, too. My money and the information I stupidly shared with him."

His gaze was intent on her face, as if he was trying to figure out if she was telling the truth now. Or maybe if she actually cared about Jason...

"I didn't have any idea how dangerous he was," she said. "Just like with my former training officer. Is that why you talked to Gingrich about me? You asked him about Jason Cruise? I wasn't even sure he knew that I was seeing the guy. It was just a few dates." She sighed again. "A few too many..."

"I talked to him about you because you're on the suspect board," he said.

"And you didn't find any reason to cross my name off yet?" she asked, and she turned back to the board. Instead of focusing on the crossed-off names, she focused on the others. "Why are Ed Ward, Bruce Abbott, Howie Lane and Carl Kozak on the board with Donovan Cunningham?"

He cocked his head. "That was an unusual way to say that."

"What?"

"Like you're not surprised Donovan isn't crossed off, just the others."

"Donovan Cunningham is a jerk," she said. "And he's raising his hellions to be as misogynistic and entitled as he is. Michaela Momber may not respect me, but I respect her. Her former co-worker did not."

"And you know how that feels," he said. "Thanks to Marty."

She flinched again at the mention of Gingrich. "He's an entitled, misogynistic jerk, too."

"I agree with the entitled," Mack said. "I just don't know about the rest..."

"You don't think he's a jerk?"

"Oh, he is, but he's so bitter and hateful and jealous of Braden, like the guy's still stuck back in high school and can't get over Braden being more popular than he is."

"Well, Gingrich is in jail," she reminded him. She pointed at the board. "And I assume it's because of that that he didn't even make your list?" But he'd talked to the man anyway to check her out. "But yet, here I am...did you think I was working with him? For him?"

"No. If that was the case, he would still be on there," Mack said.

"So he was on it, but you took him off?"

"I checked his visitor logs. Nobody is going to see him, not even his wife," Mack said.

"He cheated on her during their entire marriage, so that's understandable," she said. "And I sure as hell haven't gone to see him either."

"Neither has anyone else from the post," Mack said. "But if they did, maybe they don't sign into the visitor logs if they're on duty. Although the guards claimed that they would have made them." He didn't seem to trust them any more about that than he trusted her, though. "But Gingrich didn't seem to know a lot about what has been happening since he's been incarcerated, so maybe no one has been visiting him. But I don't know for sure, especially when it comes to your new sergeant."

She nodded. "I don't know for sure about him either," she admitted, especially with how reluctant he was to pursue an investigation into the saboteur. "Just like you don't

know for sure if you can trust me…" Yet he had no problem sleeping with her, not that they'd done much sleeping.
She felt like a fool though for getting so involved with him
when they still knew so little about each other.

"Where did your money come from?" he asked.

The coffee she'd drunk churned in her otherwise empty
stomach. "I told you just a minute ago that I grew up with
that money." Because it had affected every relationship she
ever had, tainting it. "But you probably think I took bribes."

"No, I wasn't sure what to think about you," he said.
"And I'm very curious. You fascinate me."

Maybe she should have been pleased. Even though they'd
slept together, he wasn't bored. That must not have been all
he wanted from her: a one-night stand. But then he hadn't
known about the money. From seeing the house, he knew
she had some. But some people were house poor with huge
mortgages. She didn't have a mortgage, and the house had
not hurt the balance in her bank accounts. Usually, people
tried to latch onto her because of her money, like Jason
Cruise had tried.

"That money is the reason that *I* can't trust a lot of people," she admitted.

He grinned then. "You think I'm a gold digger?"

She looked down at his hands. "Where's your shovel?"

"I don't have any interest in your money, Wynona."

"Then why ask about it?"

He sighed. "I don't want it, but I do want to know how
you got it."

"Not through bribes," she said. "And I would give up the
money in a minute if I could have back what I had to lose to
get it." Tears rushed to her eyes, but she furiously blinked
them back.

"What—who did you lose?" he asked.

"My parents," she replied. "They were world travelers and picked up some illness that they couldn't beat. They were older when they had me and had underlying health issues. So it hit them hard. They were out of the country when it happened, and I couldn't get to the hospital in time. But the nurses told me they died holding hands." She'd always longed for a love like theirs. But she'd never been able to trust anyone to love her for her and not for that damn money.

And now she had even more.

"Wynona," he said, his dark eyes warming with sympathy. As he started toward her, her cell rang.

She was grateful that it had because if he had hugged her, she probably would have lost it. As it was, she was barely holding back her tears. She drew in a shaky breath and answered, "Trooper Wells…"

"I know you're not on duty yet," Sergeant Hughes said. "But somebody said that they might have seen a vehicle down in a ravine near where you live. I wondered if you could check it out on your way into the post."

"I'll check it out," she said.

She'd already worked last night after clocking out, but she didn't need the money or the overtime. She just needed to make a difference. And right now, she just needed to get the hell away from Mack McRooney before she started falling for him.

Trying to kill them together had not worked. One rescued the other instead of dying with him or her. So the saboteur had had to come up with another plan.

A way to separate them.

And since Trooper Wells seemed like the weaker of the two, she would have to die first. Hopefully there were no recordings of the non-emergency police post number. But if there was, he had disguised his voice, hopefully enough that it couldn't be matched. That nobody would figure out *he* was the one who had spotted what might have been a car deep down in that steep, rocky ravine.

He peered down over the edge now, and as he did, a pebble slipped over the top, struck off the shale side that was as hard as granite, tumbled down and broke apart on the big, jagged rocks at the bottom of the ravine.

If a car had gone down there, the occupants wouldn't have survived. The car would have crumpled and broken apart just like he intended for the trooper's body to crumple and break apart when he tossed her over the edge. It would be easier than shooting her, especially since he'd already returned that gun he'd *borrowed*. He wanted his patsy to have it on him in case it was traced back to him. He hadn't wanted him to be able to claim it was stolen, even though it had been.

The patsy hadn't even noticed it was gone. And as far as he knew, it hadn't been traced back yet. Maybe the crime lab was slower than what they showed on TV.

But the saboteur couldn't be slow. He had to get rid of Wells and McRooney before they could figure it out, before they could figure out who he was: the saboteur.

When Wells showed up at this possible accident site, she was definitely going to have an accident of her own.

A fatal one.

And this time, nobody would be able to save her.

She was going to die. Then once she was dead, he would go after Mack McRooney next. And once the hotshot ex-military man was out of his way, he would take down everyone else he'd been wanting to take down, everyone else who deserved to die.

Chapter 14

Mack hated how quickly and easily Wynona had left him. Obviously, she hadn't wanted to answer any more of his questions. And he couldn't blame her.

He'd pried and pushed even though he knew in his gut she had nothing to do with the sabotage. He didn't have his brother-in-law's rumored sixth sense about things, but Mack had learned over the years and through the dangerous missions that he'd had to trust his gut.

But in this case, Mack had more than that to go on. Wynona had proved last night and the night before that she couldn't be the saboteur. Otherwise, she wouldn't have rescued him, and she wouldn't have been in danger herself. Those instances proved she was innocent, but still he wanted some reason not to trust her.

Some reason to keep his distance from her. But when he'd learned more about her, he wanted to get closer. He wanted to console her, to comfort her…but that brought him little comfort. He didn't want to get attached to her because he always tried to stay unattached.

So that he didn't let people down who loved him like their mother had let them down. And like he'd already let down his family.

It was almost easier to deal with Trick's resentment than it was to deal with Sam. She looked so much like their mother that he felt better keeping his distance from her. But her last text had left him no choice, so he crossed the small front porch and knocked on the door to her and Braden's house.

"If that's you, you better damn well not be knocking," she called out, her voice sharp and grumpy sounding.

He breathed deep through his nostrils, in and out, calming himself so that he wouldn't react as he always did to seeing Sam. Then he turned the knob and pushed open the door. "I'm assuming I'm *you*, or did you summon someone else here?" he asked.

She didn't get up from where she was lying on the couch, a bunch of pillows stacked all around her. She should have been able to see out the front windows and watched him walking up, unless she'd been napping.

Alarm shot through him. "Are you okay?"

"No," she fairly growled. "I'm pissed at you, and I'm pissed at this nephew of yours."

"What did he do?" he asked. "He's not even out yet."

"That's why he's pissing me off," she said. "He was supposed to be out over a week ago."

"What does your doctor say?"

"That maybe the dates were off, that maybe we should just wait another week..." She tried to shift on the couch, but her belly looked like it was holding her down.

"I should have called your bluff," he said. "You wouldn't have been able to come to me if I hadn't come to you."

She smiled then. "Sucker. If I could move around, I would be out at the warehouse, checking for signs of arson."

"It was arson," he said. He doubted there was any other explanation.

"Then it was definitely a trap," she said. "And the live wire in the shower was, too."

He nearly shuddered but resisted the urge. He didn't want to upset her, especially now. That was why he'd shown up even though seeing her took him back into the past when he was a kid. When their mom had been pregnant with either Sam or Trick, she'd looked exactly like Sam did now. He'd loved her so much, but she'd had no problem just walking away from all of them.

He'd done the same thing, though, and he still loved his siblings and his dad. He wasn't always sure the feelings were reciprocated anymore. At least not with Trick.

Sam still loved him. And he loved her. While she looked so much like their mother, she was nothing like her. She was probably the most like their father of any of them. Smart. Strong. Good.

If only he could be confident that he was the same...

But sometimes he wasn't even confident he was Mack McRooney's real kid. And having all that doubt just fed into his doubts about himself.

It was safer for him to focus on his career, no matter how dangerous it was, than to focus on his personal life. Maybe he shouldn't have retired. And he might not have...

If he hadn't known that his sister and his brother had been in danger.

"You should not be worrying about any of this," he admonished her. He'd retired so that she wouldn't have to worry or put herself in danger. He would do it instead. "You're supposed to be resting, getting ready for that baby."

"He's determined to never come out," Sam said with a ragged sigh.

"He has no idea how good he's going to have it out here," Mack said. "How much he's going to be spoiled."

"I won't spoil him."

"I was talking about Braden," he said.

She smiled with such love for her husband that Mack felt a twinge in his chest. Not of envy like other people seemed to feel for Braden, if Gingrich was telling the truth that he wasn't the only one. No, Mack was worried about his sister, worried that she would be heartbroken if something happened to her husband.

And Mack's gut was beginning to tell him that this saboteur was after more than him and Wynona. This saboteur was maybe after Braden or his job or his downfall or something.

But if someone really wanted to hurt Braden, they would go after the people he loved more than anyone else in the world. His wife and unborn baby.

"Uh oh, you have that look," Sam said then sighed.

"What look?"

"The look you get just before you head off to something dangerous."

"You think I looked scared?" he asked. Because he had a feeling that was why he'd taken off all those years ago, because he'd been scared of disappointing the people he loved, like their mother had. But he'd probably disappointed them more by leaving than he would have done had he tried to stay.

Could he stay anywhere? Wynona had asked him what he was going to do once the saboteur was caught, and he really had no idea. But the thought of staying anywhere unsettled him.

Sam stared up at him, her head cocked and hair brushing across her cheek. She reminded him of Wynona studying the board so intently, trying to figure out who the saboteur was. Sam's blue eyes widened. "Now you look scared."

Wynona scared the crap out of him. No. The way he felt about Wynona scared the crap out of him. But he wasn't about to talk to his sister about *her*.

"I'm worried about you," he admitted. "Are you being careful?"

She sighed a long-suffering sigh. "Yes, I'm staying off my swollen feet as much as possible. I'm sleeping just about all the time…unless fear for my idiot brothers keeps me up."

"I'm sorry about that," he said sincerely. "I did not mean to worry you."

"I should be used to it." She sighed again but softer now. "I've been worrying about you since you left home all those years ago, Mack. I was scared I would never see you again. And then you came here to help me and I'm even more worried that I'm going to lose you. And I'm sorry about that, about talking you into this. You're supposed to be retired."

He snorted. "I retired from that career." From danger he'd thought, but he realized that wasn't truly possible. There was danger everywhere, no matter what career one had. There was danger just sitting home alone like Sam. "I wasn't going to spend the rest of my days fishing and drinking beer."

"Were you going to spend it fighting fires?" she asked.

He hadn't chosen to go into the family business like everyone else had. In fact, Mack had left to escape from that because as a kid, he'd blamed it for driving their mother away. But he knew now it hadn't had anything to do with the hotshots.

He shrugged. "I don't mind putting out fires," he said. Or starting one like he had with Wynona Wells. That fire was probably going to burn him more than any physical one could. He'd never experienced that intense passion or pleasure before.

"I want to get over to the warehouse and check it out," she said.

"You need to take it easy," he reiterated. "And you need to be *careful*, Sam."

She smiled. "Now you sound like Braden and Trick. They're worried about me over more than the pregnancy. And like I told both of them, it doesn't matter how pregnant I am, I can still take care of myself." She lifted one of the pillows propped around her and showed him the holstered gun she'd stashed beneath it.

He chuckled as pride for her suffused him. "You are a badass, little sister."

"I hope you didn't think you were the only one in the family," she said.

"Nope. Dad's the OG," he said. He'd had to be to do what he'd done, raising his kids alone while training so many hot-shots. Most of the ones that Mack was working with now had been trained by Mack Senior. That was why Braden's team was so good. So hopefully one of them wasn't the saboteur, but that didn't leave many other options on his ever-narrowing list of suspects.

Stanley and Wynona.

And he felt like Wynona was in more danger than she posed to anyone. Like even now, he had a strange feeling about the call she'd taken that morning to check on something on her way to work.

Had that been as innocent as it sounded?

Or was it a trap?

The blow knocked Braden back as he was struck walking inside his own house.

"Sorry," Mack said after colliding with him in the doorway. "I was just on my way out." And true to his word, he rushed across the porch, down the steps and out to the truck parked at the curb.

Braden stared after him for a second before walking in to greet his wife. "Was it something you said?" he teased her.

She shrugged. "I don't know why he suddenly had to leave in such a hurry." She narrowed her eyes as she stared up at him. "Or why you've come back in such a hurry..."

"I can't stay away from you," he said. Because he was so damn scared of losing her, of something happening to her like what kept happening to the hotshots.

"Like I just had to tell my big brother, I can take care of myself." She tapped the pillow under which she kept her gun.

So Braden wasn't the only one worried about Sam being in danger. Mack was too. Mack's investigation was probably leading him to the same conclusion that Braden was drawing, that no matter who the saboteur went after, the person was ultimately trying to destroy Braden.

Wynona knew the area where the caller had reported seeing a vehicle. Not only did she pass it every day on her way from her house to the state police post, but it was also where Stanley had been found after the arsonist tried to kill him over a year ago. She'd been new to the job then, acting more as a ride-along than even as a trainee.

That was the only time she'd actually stopped and studied the area, while they'd been looking for evidence to lead them to the arsonist. But she remembered how dangerous the ravine was, how steep the sides.

After leaving Mack, she'd headed straight there, parked along the road, and was once again studying that ravine. It was even more dangerous than she remembered. After another winter and more rains, there was no slope down, just a sheer drop off, and the side of the ravine by the road was shale and rock, not just dirt. And there were big boulders poking out of the grass and underbrush at the bottom of the pit.

She wasn't sure what had formed the ravine. Had there once been a river flowing through it, or given how much rock was in it, had the area been mined for something? For iron or copper or granite? The side of the ravine and the rocks at the bottom looked that hard, like granite.

Like Mack McRooney's body. Heat rushed through her as memories from last night played through her mind, like they had played with each other in that big bed of his.

She had never before experienced anything like that. She'd never felt as much pleasure as he'd given her. But she knew that it hadn't been smart. They were in danger and couldn't afford any distractions.

And knowing that he was unlikely to stick around Northern Lakes once the saboteur was caught, falling for him would cause her as much pain as if she fell into this ravine.

But she wouldn't let herself worry about that.

Right now, she had to find this vehicle. But from the road, she couldn't see anything down below except those rocks and trees and brush at the bottom. There was no glint of the sun off glass or metal.

No tire marks going off the road and over the edge.

If someone had been driving past here, as she did nearly every day, how had they even seen into the ravine? She hadn't been able to see anything from her vehicle. She hadn't been able to see anything until she'd parked and walked to the edge.

And even standing at the very end of the solid ground before it dropped away, she couldn't see anything like the caller had described to dispatch. There was absolutely no sign of a car accident in this area.

Maybe dispatch had gotten the area wrong?

Or her sergeant had when he called her?

She reached for her collar and realized that her radio wasn't there. She was still in the sweater and jeans she'd worn to Mack's last night but that she hadn't worn for long once she'd gotten there.

She still didn't know if being with him had been a mistake, or if it would have been more of a mistake if she hadn't given in to her desire for him. He could have died twice last night. First at the warehouse and then in the firehouse showers. She could have died, too, had he not called out and warned her about the live wire. And maybe all those brushes with death had just been too much.

She'd either lost her mind, or she'd been caught up in the rush of adrenaline and attraction. He was too much. And he made her feel too much. She wasn't ready to fall for anyone.

To risk her heart.

She knew all too well how it felt to love someone and lose them. She'd lost her parents much too soon.

And with the life he led, and the scars he carried from that life, Mack was too big a risk. Whoever fell for him would probably lose him one day, either because he took off like his mother had or because he came out of retirement to return to his dangerous life. A life that he wouldn't be able to survive forever.

And she still had so much to figure out in her life, with her career, with trying to find this saboteur before *anyone* died.

Now was not the time for her to be seeing *anyone*. But especially not *him*.

Because once again, he'd distracted her even though he wasn't here. She couldn't stop thinking about him, but she had to focus.

She drew in a shaky breath and reached into her pocket

for her cell. She needed to call dispatch and verify the location where the caller claimed they'd seen the wreckage.

But when she pulled the phone from her pocket, hands pressed against her back, shoving her. First the cell flew out of her grasp, flying over the edge and down onto those rocks below where it broke apart into pieces.

Then her feet skidded and slipped across that loose gravel at the top of the ravine and suddenly Wynona was the one going over the edge.

And like her cell phone, would she be broken on the rocks below?

Chapter 15

Mack's call to Wynona's sergeant hadn't relieved that horrible feeling he had. In fact, it had only confirmed to him that he'd been right to worry about her.

She hadn't shown up at the police post or even checked in yet from the site of the supposed accident that had been reported. If she'd found something, she would have called in for help.

If she'd been able to make that call...

Maybe Mack should have requested that the sergeant send a police unit to the scene where he'd sent Wynona. But he couldn't help but think that the sergeant was the only reason Wynona had gone out there at all. And it was only his word that an actual report had come in...

Mack wasn't entirely sure if he should trust Hughes or anyone else who worked for him with Wynona. She was in a worse situation with her job than he was with his. At least he had a few people he could trust on his team—Rory and Ethan and maybe Trick depending on how pissed his little brother was at him. And he could definitely trust his boss, Braden.

Because Mack couldn't trust Wynona's boss, he wasn't sure if the sergeant had even told him the right road and location for him to find her. He figured he'd driven past where he was supposed to be when he caught a glimpse of a vehicle out of his side mirror.

It wasn't in the ravine, though. It was parked alongside the other side of the road where there was more than just the gravel shoulder. There was some grass on which she'd parked her vehicle. Hers was the only one there, so the pressure on his chest eased some.

But then he noticed something glinting farther out in the trees beyond that grass. Like metal or...

Was someone out there with a gun? Or was that where the vehicle was that the caller had seen?

But the ravine was on the other side of the road...

Still feeling uneasy, Mack reached down and pulled out his weapon from beneath the driver's seat. He had to be careful. Had to make sure that, if this was a trap, he didn't fall into it, too.

But if it was a trap, it might already be too late for Wynona.

After those hands on her back had propelled Wynona over the edge, she'd reached out and grasped at whatever she could on the side of that rocky wall of the ravine. Her fingers were scraped and bleeding, but she'd found the roots of something that had been strong enough to break through the shale. Hopefully the roots would be strong enough to hold her weight. While she dangled, she shifted her feet around, trying to find a toehold as well to ease the stress on her aching shoulders and her scratched up hands.

Blood oozed from the scratches and soaked into those roots she grasped. Hopefully the blood didn't loosen them, didn't make them weaker or her weaker.

But she wasn't bleeding much.

Yet.

If she fell...

She glanced down below her, and now she saw a glint, the sun reflecting off the broken pieces of her cell phone. She didn't want to wind up like that. But she couldn't call anyone for help now.

Not that she knew who she would call...

She couldn't trust anyone at her work or any hotshot either. And Mack...

She could trust Mack. Probably. With her life, just not with her heart.

But without her phone, she couldn't call him. She couldn't reach out for help. She was even afraid to yell because whoever had pushed her might be up there yet. And if whoever shoved her was the same person who'd shot at her, she knew that they had a gun.

And shooting her now would be like shooting fish in a barrel. There was no way that they could miss.

Even when she heard an engine on the road above her, she didn't call out. She hadn't seen a vehicle earlier when she'd been looking for the one in the ravine. So whoever had pushed her had parked somewhere out of sight.

And maybe now, after retrieving their vehicle, they were coming back to make sure she'd fallen all the way down. And when they saw that she hadn't...

She had no doubt that they would make sure she fell. Either by shooting her or reaching out to push her off the tree roots. She could probably be reached from the top yet if someone had long arms.

She could be rescued if whoever was up there with the idling vehicle was not the person who'd deliberately lured her here with that false report to the police. She had no doubt now that this had been a trap.

Like the burning warehouse and the shower had been traps for Mack.

At least he hadn't come with her. Because she had no doubt that if they were both here, the saboteur would start shooting for sure.

And now, along with the hum of that idling engine, she heard something else. Like the soft cock of a gun...

Then the crunch of gravel as someone started across the shoulder of the road toward the ravine.

She held her breath, holding back a scream of frustration. She was so helpless, and she hated it. If she reached for her weapon now, she'd have to let go of the root with one hand...

And she was afraid that one hand wouldn't be enough to hold up her weight. But as those footsteps got louder and closer, she knew she had to be able to defend herself. So she tightened her grasp with her left hand, shoved the toes of her boots hard against the shale wall of the ravine, and took one hand loose to reach for her holster.

But the movement had her left hand slipping down the root.

A scream tore free of her throat with the horrifying certainty that she was about to fall. That the person coming toward her wasn't even going to have to shoot her to kill her.

The saboteur quietly cursed. He should have made damn certain that she'd fallen all the way into the ravine. But he hadn't wanted Wells to see his face just in case she survived the fall.

Hell, he should have shot her and dumped her body down there, but after stashing the patsy's weapon back in their truck, he hadn't dared to use one of his own. But if he couldn't kill the trooper and McRooney any other way, he might not have a choice.

But she had to have died. There was no way that she

could survive a fall into that ravine. He hadn't actually killed anyone yet despite having made some attempts lately on her life and on Mack McRooney's life.

He knew that he would have to kill, but maybe just hurting her would have been good enough to get her out of his way. And then he could kill the person that he knew he needed to kill. The one who was going to mess up his whole plan if McRooney wasn't stopped.

Mack McRooney might have been a military hero if the gossip about him was true. And according to Rory Van-Dam, it was. But he was no hotshot.

At least his brother Trick had been trained and was working as one before his nepotism hire onto the team to replace Dirk Brown.

Using Dirk's death to his advantage was just one more thing Braden had done that proved he had never deserved to be superintendent. He didn't care about the team at all, or he would have stepped down months ago.

He would have been able to figure out that was all it would have taken for this to end. His resignation.

But now it was going to take a life.

His brother-in-law's.

Through the trees where he'd parked well off the road, he could see Mack's truck where it sat with its engine idling while the new hotshot started across the road toward the ravine.

Of course McRooney was here to rush to Trooper Wells's rescue just as he had the other night. But instead of rescuing her, he was going to die with her.

Chapter 16

Mack approached the ravine with caution, his gun drawn, as his stomach clenched with dread. Where the hell was she?

She wasn't on the road anywhere that he could see her. She wasn't walking along the edge, looking into the ravine for the wreckage her sergeant claimed someone had seen down there. Had a vehicle struck her and hit her so hard that she'd fallen over the edge?

He glanced back over his shoulder. Or was she in the woods where he'd seen that reflection bounce off something metallic?

Maybe she'd had seen that, too, and had gone to investigate. He probably should check that out as well. But something compelled him closer to the edge of the ravine. He wanted to at least look inside the deep gorge and investigate if that wrecked car someone had reported was actually there. When he looked down, he caught another reflection like he had in the woods. But it was small, just something glinting among the boulders and the brush.

Then he heard the scream, and he looked at the side and saw her dangling there from one hand. "Oh, my God, Wynona!" Her hand was slipping down whatever she was clutching on the side of the rock.

Her other hand must have already slipped off it because she was wriggling now, trying to reach the branch or roots that she was clutching, that was about the only thing keeping her from plummeting to the bottom.

He holstered his weapon and dropped down to his stomach along the top. His legs were probably out in the road, but he didn't care. He didn't care about anything except for saving her.

But her fingers kept slipping, and he was about to lose her, maybe forever if she hit those rocks below. He leaned far over the edge, stretching as much as he could without sliding off. He reached down and clasped her wrist just as her fingers lost their grip.

His shoulder jerked with her weight as her body swung against the side of the ravine. She grimaced as she hit the rocky edge. But then she was reaching again, trying to catch those roots.

He tightened his hold on her wrist, locking his fingers around it. "Oh, my God," he muttered again. "What the hell happened?"

And how was he going to get her up?

He was strong, and she wasn't that heavy, but the way she was dangling like dead weight pulled at his muscles, pulled at his body. He started sliding across the gravel at the top, leaning out dangerously far.

So far that he might slip and fall headfirst down into that gorge. And if he did, he would take her with him, sending them both down onto those rocks.

"I got pushed," she said between pants. "Did you see anyone?"

He thought of that glint between the trees but shook his head. "I've got to get you back up here. Can you get a foothold? Anything?"

"I… I had some roots…"

From the sweat beading on her forehead and dampening

her hair, he could tell she'd been hanging on for a while.
And when she reached her free hand up, trying to clasp
those roots again, her arm was shaking.

Her muscles were obviously cramping. And he was afraid
that his would soon, too, if he didn't hoist her up and over
the edge. His legs slipped a bit more, the gravel grinding
and biting through his jeans.

He flinched now. "Let me try to get your other hand," he
said. Because he was so damn afraid that he was about to
lose his grasp on her wrist.

Like her face, his hand was starting to sweat or maybe
her wrist was sweating, her skin getting so slippery that
he wasn't sure he could hold onto her much longer. He had
to do something. He couldn't lose her.

Wynona hadn't felt this helpless since she had lost her
parents. She hadn't been able to do anything to save them
or to even ease their suffering. Because of how far away
they'd traveled and how remote the hospital was, she hadn't
even been notified of their illnesses until they were too sick.
She'd made it to the hospital before they died, but because
of the contagiousness of their disease, she hadn't been allowed to see them. She hadn't been able to say goodbye to
them or tell them that she loved them. At least they'd had
each other, and according to the nurses, they'd been holding
hands when they passed away within minutes of each other.

She wanted a love like that one day, a love like her parents had had. But Mack wasn't holding onto her out of love.
He was holding onto her because he was a hero, and that
was what heroes did: rescued people.

That was why she'd wanted to become a cop—to be the
hero for others that she hadn't been able to be for the ones
she'd loved the most.

But she was afraid that she was about to be the reason Mack got hurt, too. He was leaning so far over the edge that eventually he was going to fall off. And then neither of them would be able to rescue anyone else ever again.

She'd already slipped too far down to reach the roots anymore. And the side of the ravine she kept slamming against was rock hard and slippery now. It must have been granite or something mined here that made it difficult for her to get a toehold on anything.

She didn't want to give up, but she didn't know how to get out of the ravine. Maybe going down was the only way to make her way out somewhere where it wasn't as steep as it was here. She would just have to figure out a way to slow her descent.

Her hands were already bleeding, and her jeans were torn. Hopefully the rock wall wouldn't tear her up anymore and hopefully she wouldn't hit one of those boulders like her phone had.

But she'd rather take her chances sliding down into the ravine than risk pulling Mack into it with her. He would go down headfirst and get hurt far worse than she would.

"You have to let me go," she said, "or you're going to fall."

"I'm not letting you go," Mack said, his jaw clenched so hard that there was a muscle twitching in his cheek. And a vein was popping out on his forehead, too, and another one zigzagged along his temple. "Come on, give me your other hand…" He held out his other hand toward her. "If I have both of them, I can try to hoist you up."

He was too far over the side already. If she grabbed his other hand, she was afraid that she would just be pulling him down with her. But if she tried to wriggle her wrist free of his grasp, she was afraid that would send him toppling over with her, too.

"If you let me go, I'll just slide down," she said. "I'll be fine." She hoped. "But if you fall headfirst down…" He would free fall right into one of those boulders, and his head would break like her cell.

"You're already bleeding," he said. "You're already hurt. Now give me your damn hand!"

He must have slipped out even farther because it was as if a shadow fell across her. She looked up with alarm, and she saw that the shadow had fallen across him, too.

Whoever had pushed her over the edge had returned, probably to make sure she was dead. And now they would have an opportunity to get rid of him, too.

"Mack!" she yelled. "You're in danger! Someone's behind you."

"I'm not letting go," he growled.

Then she would have to protect him if it was the last thing she did. With her free hand she reached again for her holster, and this time she drew her weapon and pointed it right over the edge at whoever the hell was sneaking up on Mack.

While he was trying to save her, she intended to save him. And if she could hit the saboteur, she would be protecting Mack and the rest of Northern Lakes from any more of the saboteur's dangerous games.

Trick's cell rang, and he grimaced as he saw who was calling. Maybe it was good news, though. Maybe Sam had gone into labor and his new nephew was here. "Hey, Braden," he answered.

"Hey," Braden said, and his voice was low as if he was whispering.

Maybe Sam was sleeping. Or Braden didn't want her to hear him.

And the dread that he'd felt when his phone had initially

lit up with his brother-in-law's contact came back. "What is it?" he asked. "A fire?"

The warehouse fire had been a monster. And that explosion...

And then the stunt with the stripped wire in the shower that...

Mack had survived the explosion though. And then, of all people, Trooper Wells had rescued him at the firehouse, saving him from electrocution.

He shuddered and Henrietta, sitting next to him in that corner booth at the Filling Station, grabbed his free hand, already offering him comfort. Like him, she must have figured he would need it.

"No, no, no fire, at least I don't think so," Braden said. "It might be nothing..."

Might be.

Probably wasn't.

Trick didn't think Braden's sixth sense was just for fires anymore. Sometimes the superintendent just seemed to know when one of the team was in danger whether it had to do with a fire or not.

"What is it?" Trick asked, bracing himself.

"Have you seen your brother?"

Trick's heart pounded faster with fear. He'd known that call was about Mack. He cleared his throat to reply, "No, I haven't."

But he should have. After Mack had two near misses the day before, Trick should have talked to him. But those near misses were like getting all his childhood fears confirmed, that everyone he cared about was going to leave him.

As if she read his mind, Henrietta's grasp on his hand tightened. She wasn't leaving him.

"Yeah, of course, you wouldn't have seen him," Braden muttered. "You're in St. Paul with Hank—"

"No, Henrietta and I didn't go back to St. Paul last night after the warehouse fire and not after the call went out about the showers." He'd wanted to be close in case his brother needed him. In case something happened again. And it sounded like maybe it had. "We stayed at her cottage last night. We're at the Filling Station now."

"So Mack's not there?"

"Nobody is," Trick said. But it was late for breakfast and early for lunch. That was probably why the bar was so dead even though they served three meals in addition to drinks. "Why are you looking for Mack?" he asked over the pounding of his heart. "What happened?"

"Probably nothing," Braden said. "I just…he was leaving here when I brought Sam breakfast this morning. And he was in a really big hurry when he left, and now he won't pick up his phone."

Trick cursed. Not that it was out of character for Mack to ghost them. He'd ghosted them most of his adult life, just like their mother had. That was why he was so angry with Mack, not because he'd left but because he hadn't come back.

Until now…

Until he was in as much danger here as he'd been wherever he'd been all those years he'd been gone. So Trick understood Braden's concern because this time, Mack failing to pick up his cell felt different to him, too.

This felt like the saboteur again.

Had Mack found him or her?

Or had the saboteur found him? And had they managed this time to get rid of him for good?

Chapter 17

"What the hell!" Mack exclaimed.

When she pulled that gun, he nearly lost his grasp on her wrist and just managed to catch it with his other hand before he lost her completely. But as he grabbed for her, he slipped farther over the side, sending gravel toppling down with him, onto her.

She flinched and cursed. "Let go of me!" she shouted. "You have to!"

But he kept sliding over that edge until someone grabbed him. That was why Wynona had drawn her weapon. Someone had come up behind him, and he'd been so focused on her that he hadn't heard them until she'd called out. But if he wanted to defend himself, he had to let her go. And he couldn't bring himself to do that.

Then a deep, familiar voice rumbled, "What the hell are you doing? I nearly ran you over!"

"Ethan!" Mack exclaimed.

"Rory's here, too. He saw your legs or you'd be under my truck tires right now," Ethan said.

"Hang onto him," Rory said as he plopped down on his stomach beside Mack. "What the hell is going on with you two? Is she trying to jump?"

"Someone pushed me!" Wynona said.

"Maybe because you were trying to shoot them," Rory remarked.

"I… I just pulled this…" And now it was as if she didn't know what to do with it.

"You don't need it," Mack said.

"I'm not dropping it," she said. "I slid the safety off…"

Rory groaned. "Great. Two people hanging off the edge and a loaded gun about to go off, too." He jumped up, and Mack thought for a moment that his old military buddy was deserting him.

Ethan must have thought the same thing because he said, "Uh, I could use a little help here. He weighs more than I do. Where the hell are you—"

But then Rory was back with some ropes and a harness. And between the four of them, they managed to get Wynona up from the edge without them or the gun going off.

But once they were lying in the road, Mack could see the scrapes and bruises on her, some from his hand where he'd gripped her wrist so tightly. She rubbed at it, almost absentmindedly, smearing blood across her skin.

"Let me call Owen," Rory said, "and get him in the rig over here to check you guys out."

"We should just take them to the hospital," Ethan said as he studied them both, his face tight with concern.

"I'm fine," Mack said, and he barely had a scratch on him. "But Wynona should get checked out."

"Wynona?" Rory muttered the question as if he hadn't known her first name, or maybe he was just surprised that Mack had used it.

She shook her head. "No…" She released a shaky breath and shook her head again.

Mack was worried that she might have gone into shock. "We definitely need to get you to the hospital," he said.

"No, I have to call this in, report what happened here—"

"You can call it in on the way to the hospital," Mack suggested.

"I just have some scrapes and bruises," she said, dismissing her injuries. "Nothing serious."

"Your wrist could be sprained," Ethan said. "I don't think Mack here knows his own strength." Sommerly was a big guy, too, like Mack. He would know how easy it was for them to hurt someone without meaning to.

"I don't care if he broke it," Wynona said. "He saved my life." She smiled at the other hotshots, her green eyes sparkling a bit with tears of emotion. "And so did you two. Thank you."

Warmth spread through Mack's chest. Maybe it was just relief that she was all right. Or maybe it was appreciation for her gratitude. Or maybe it was because she was so beautiful. And while he hadn't gone over that edge, he still felt a bit like he was falling. But he couldn't let himself do that for so many reasons.

He turned toward the other two hotshots. "What were you doing out here? Does Braden have you following me?"

Rory shook his head. "Yeah, like that would work, like anyone could follow you without you noticing. No. We were out on this road because we were heading to Donovan Cunningham's place to talk to him."

Wynona perked up then. "About what?"

"Just going to ask him some questions," the former DEA agent remarked.

Mack shouldn't have been surprised that Rory was looking for the saboteur, and Wynona didn't seem to be either. But after the person had nearly killed him, Rory had to want justice and answers.

She asked, "So he's your suspect for the saboteur?"

"That's who she suspects, too," Mack said, and she shot him a look.

He shrugged. "Like they don't know what I'm doing here? Or that they don't know what you want to do?"

"I want to catch the saboteur," she said.

"Is that who pushed you?" Rory asked. "Did you see him?"

Her face flushed a bright pink and she shook her head again. "No. I was told there was a car down in the ravine and I was looking for it when someone pushed me from behind."

Ethan sucked in a breath.

Rory nodded. "Well, at least we can eliminate you as a suspect now, Trooper Wells."

She laughed instead of being offended like she'd seemed when she'd seen her picture among his other suspects. Then she turned toward Mack. "Going to take my mugshot off your board now?"

"Board?" Ethan asked.

"Mugshot?" Rory repeated.

"Her DMV photo," Mack said. "The trooper has no record and no reason to go after the hotshots." He'd believed that even before someone had tried to push her into the ravine. He'd believed it before he slept with her. He must have somehow instinctively known that she was a good person, or he wouldn't have been able to fall asleep with her in his house, in his bed. "So yeah, I will be taking your photo down from the board and crossing out your name."

"What is this board?" Ethan asked. He was obviously stuck on it. "Is this like a murder board the detectives use on TV?"

She nodded. "Yes, Mack thinks he's a detective instead of a hotshot."

"With the saboteur after us, every hotshot has become a detective," Ethan said.

"Or you could let the police handle it," Wynona suggested, but with a teasing smile. "Not that I'm not damn happy that you guys were doing some investigating on your own today."

Mack chuckled. He liked seeing her like this, especially with guys he considered friends. She was relaxed and friendly instead of the uptight trooper they'd previously thought she was. He'd somehow always known that was who she really was. Just like he wasn't as unemotional and unattached as he pretended to be.

"So who's your prime suspect?" Rory asked him.

"Well, there's me," Wynona answered before he could. "But you two can rest assured your names were crossed out right away. You didn't get circled."

Rory chuckled. "I would hope not after all we've been through." He extended his hand down to help Mack up from the ground.

Ethan reached out to help Wynona up. She flinched when he touched her, and given how good-looking the guy was, it wasn't because she was repulsed. She was hurt.

"If you won't go to the hospital, at least let us find Owen," Mack said. He was counting on the paramedic telling her she needed an X-ray to make sure that he hadn't broken anything when he'd held her so tightly. Not that he wanted to know—he would feel horrible if he had hurt her however inadvertently.

"Owen's out here somewhere checking out Bruce and Howie," Rory said. "He should be close. They were supposed to be doing an arborist job around here cutting down trees around someone's cabin."

"So they were in the area," Wynona mused, totally focused on the investigation instead of herself. "And I assume Owen is checking them out because he figures that stunt with Mack and the tree could have been one of them?"

Rory nodded as he pulled out his cell to call the paramedic. "Yeah, Bruce's dad is an electrician, so he could have been responsible for the thing in the showers, too."

"He was certainly amused by it," Mack said. "But let's put the investigation on hold now and get Owen to check out Wynona's arm."

"I need to call this latest incident in to the police post, too," Wynona said. "But I need to use someone's phone. Mine fell…"

When she'd fallen…

While Rory made the call to Owen, Mack checked his cell and found a bunch of missed calls from Braden and Trick. Instead of calling them back, he shot them a text. I'm good. Talk later.

But he wasn't good, not after yet another close call, one where he could have lost Wynona. Where she could have slipped right through his fingers…

He handed his cell over to her to call the police, and then he stepped closer to the edge and looked over to where the pieces of metal and glass reflected back light from down below. That was probably what was left of her cell. She could have fallen there on those rocks.

She'd wanted him to let her go, and he knew why. She'd been trying to protect him. To save him…

She really was an incredible person, determined and generous and self-sacrificing. And so damn beautiful that his chest ached just looking at her when moments ago she'd been talking and joking with his friends.

And even though they were on solid ground now, he still felt like he was falling. Maybe not into a ravine, but maybe he was falling for her.

* * *

Wynona was grateful that Mack and his fellow hotshots had saved her. But she was also irritated that Mack and Owen had talked her into the trip to the ER because now her left wrist was in a brace, and she had to go on desk duty for the next three to six weeks while the sprain healed.

It could have been worse, though. Much worse. It could have been broken or she could have been dead. Even if she hadn't been injured, though, Sergeant Hughes would have sidelined her. He'd told her that it was too dangerous for her to be investigating anymore, after this latest attempt on her life. He promised he would lead the investigation, check and see if the call had been recorded that had lured her out to that ravine. But she still wasn't sure he could be trusted any more than his predecessor should have been.

"Thank you," she said again as she and Mack walked into her house. He'd driven her vehicle home for her, even though she could have driven, and Rory and Ethan had brought his truck. So both vehicles were parked in her driveway.

And the hotshots would all know about her house now. Not that Ethan Sommerly could judge her for having money. His real name was Jonathan Michael Canterbury the IV and he was heir to a fortune a lot bigger than what her parents had left her.

They'd also already told her that she was off his and Rory's suspect list now, after being pushed into that ravine. If she hadn't caught herself…

But she shouldn't have been put in that situation. She shouldn't have let herself be lured there like that. But she had to check out the report because it could have been legit. There could have been a car down there with crash victims inside needing help.

Like she'd needed help…

That was another reason she'd become a cop, so that she would be stronger. More independent so that she wouldn't need anyone to help her like her parents always had. She hadn't realized how reliant she'd been on them until they were gone, leaving a gaping hole in her heart and her life.

"You didn't have to give me a hotshot escort home, though," she said to Mack, who was walking through her house with the cat winding around his ankles like she was starving for affection and food.

When Wynona had come home to shower after the fire the night before, she'd given Harry lots of love and had filled the feline's automatic feeder and water fountain. But Harry had clearly forgotten who took care of her. Or maybe she just felt that same draw to Mack that Wynona felt, that even now, scraped and bruised, she felt to him. She wanted to be close to him, too. As close as she could get…

"I wanted to make sure that you were safe," Mack said, his voice a bit gruff.

"You told me that my security system is good," she reminded him. "That it would keep out everyone but you." She expected him to smile, but he turned toward her with his face nearly as tense as it had been when he was holding her wrist on the side of the ravine.

"I shouldn't have let you go off to that call alone," he said.

"I'm a cop," she said. And in a rural area, she always rode alone. She didn't have a partner like they showed on TV. The only time she'd ridden with anyone else had been Sergeant Gingrich during her training. She'd been uncomfortable with him, but she'd thought it was just because he was misogynistic, not that the man was actually dangerous. But now she knew anything and anyone could be dangerous.

Even Mack McRooney...

Maybe most of all Mack because of how he made her feel, how much he made her want him, and she was afraid that she would come to rely on him too much. And he hadn't promised to stick around. He hadn't promised anything except to find the saboteur and stop him.

"You can't go to work with me," she said. Then she lifted her arm with the brace. "And even if you could, I don't think you would want to ride a desk with me for the next six weeks."

He grimaced at the mention of desk duty.

"So much for you retiring," she murmured with a smile. But it was forced because she suspected there was no way he would be able to stay away from the danger of his old career, no way that he would be able to stay retired. With the very real probability of him leaving again, she had to protect her heart from him. She had to make sure that she didn't get hurt as emotionally as she'd nearly been physically. "You're not going to be able to give up your old life."

"I already have. And there are days that I wouldn't mind a desk job," he said.

She would. She wouldn't be able to help as many people as she wanted to from a desk. So maybe she shouldn't begrudge him his old career. She was certain he'd helped a lot of people like he'd helped her.

"Then what's wrong?" she asked because she could see that he was troubled, his strong jaw tense as if he was gritting his teeth.

"I'm just..." He drew in a deep breath. "I'm really sorry about your wrist."

"You saved my life," she said.

"You told me to let you go and that you would be fine," he reminded her.

She shrugged. "Might have been…" But she doubted it. Her phone certainly hadn't survived. With giving her statement to Sergeant Hughes and being seen in the hospital, she hadn't had time to even think about replacing it yet.

"I… I…" he trailed off, his voice even gruffer. Then he wrapped his arms around her and pulled her against his chest. His heart was beating fast and hard like they were still dangling over that ravine.

Hers started beating just as fast and hard because of him. All that adrenaline came rushing back, not over what had happened on the side of that wall of rock, but over the night before. And she wanted him again.

She *needed* him. Despite how badly she hadn't wanted to need anyone anymore, she couldn't deny herself this. Couldn't deny herself *him*. "Mack…"

She barely whispered his name before he kissed her, and she kissed him back. And then she fumbled with her brace as she tried to take off his clothes.

He chuckled and pulled back. Then he picked her up. "Let me take care of you…"

With as determined as she was to be self-sufficient now, she shouldn't want that. But somehow, because he was the one making this offer, she did. So she pointed him toward the bedroom.

He nearly tripped over the cat, and they both laughed while Harry hissed and ran off. The feline knew that Wynona had stolen his attention, at least for the moment.

But after all the horrible things that had happened to them, Wynona wasn't going to allow herself to think beyond the moment. Now was all that mattered.

He was all that mattered.

Instead of laying her on her bed, he carried her through the open door into the en suite bathroom. He lowered her to a bench that sat next to the enormous bathtub which was probably the whole reason she'd bought the house. And then he drew her a bath.

"What are you doing?" she asked with a smile. She wanted him, not a bath.

"You're all scraped up and…"

She glanced down at the torn and dirty clothes she was wearing. "I'm a mess," she agreed. But that wasn't just on the outside. On the inside, she was shaky and unsettled and not just because of having yet another brush with death.

It was him. And how important he was already becoming to her. After losing the last people who'd been important to her, she didn't know if she could risk her heart again, especially on someone who was probably leaving as soon as the saboteur was caught.

But the past few days had been nice, having someone take care of her, drink wine with her, play with her cat. All of that had made her all too aware that she didn't want to be alone anymore. Yet she couldn't count on him to stay.

But with the way he was looking at her, his face so tense but his eyes so warm, she couldn't resist him or the feelings flooding her heart.

He gently removed the brace from her wrist. And when he saw the bruises, he flinched as if the sight of them physically hurt him. He ran his lips gently over the swollen skin, and her fingers tingled and not because of the sprain. Then he removed the rest of her clothes and lowered her into the tub.

"This is big enough for the both of us," she said.

"Just relax for a moment," he told her. And then he stepped out of the bathroom.

She closed her eyes and sank down to her chin in the warm water he'd scented with her bath salts. Moments later, he was back with a tray of cheese and grapes and an open bottle of wine. And he was naked.

Gloriously naked.

She moaned at just the sight of him.

"Hungry?" he asked as he held a big purple grape to her lips.

"You know what I'm hungry for," she said. Him. But he fed her the grape and then a nibble of gouda cheese before he poured her a glass of another Cabernet Sauvignon. They definitely had the same taste in wine. Or maybe he had just figured out what hers was since she had more bottles of that than any other.

"You're going to get cold," she said. "You need to get in the tub with me."

And finally he did, lowering himself into the water with her, his legs on the outside of hers, rubbing against them. He was so big that water sloshed over the rim onto the marble floor.

But she didn't care. She launched herself at him then, winding her arms around his neck. And she kissed him, rubbing her breasts against the hair on his slick chest.

He groaned, and his cock pulsated against her. "Wynona, I didn't bring a condom."

"I have an IUD," she said.

He tensed for a moment then chuckled.

"You thought I said IED." It shouldn't have been funny, not after the explosion in the warehouse. But she giggled too. "No. That wouldn't make me safe at all to have sex with you. But I am safe. I've been checked recently, and I'm fine."

"Me, too," he said.

She reached down and guided him inside her as she straddled his lap. As she rode him, he played with her hair and her breasts and kissed her over and over again.

She came once, softly keening his name.

Then he reached between them, caressing her core. And the pressure wound up again. He moved, thrusting while she arched. More water sloshed over the rim, pooling on the floor around the tub. And she came again, the orgasm so intense that it shook her.

He tensed then uttered something like a growl, and his big body shuddered as he came, too. "Wynona..." he groaned her name like he was in pain.

Maybe pleasure this intense was painful, especially when she was so worried that it wouldn't last. That eventually the saboteur who kept coming after them was going to succeed.

Or Mack was going to leave. Either way she was going to lose him.

Braden should have been relieved he heard from Mack, even though the text had been short and hadn't provided much information. Unfortunately, Ethan and Rory had just filled in the rest, and Braden was reeling now. And it wasn't just because he had that damn feeling, that sizzling of his nerve endings, that tightening in his gut, like a fire was starting.

His senses had to be all out of whack, though. He hadn't predicted that fire last night at the warehouse or the incident in the showers. Or even what had happened now with the latest attempt on the lives of Wells and McRooney.

"Hey, boss, this is good news," Ethan said. "They're all right."

"And we can write Trooper Wells off the suspect list now," Rory said, "since someone clearly lured her out there to try to kill her."

Ethan shrugged his broad shoulders. "I could point out that we all had enemies of our own in addition to the saboteur. Someone could be going after the trooper for another reason. Like how she could afford the place we followed her to?"

"Says Mr. Moneybags," Rory teased.

"Yeah, family money." His dark eyes widened. "Oh…"

"Brittney did some digging," Rory said, referring to his reporter girlfriend who was also his fellow hotshot Trent Miles's sister. "Wells is an older rookie because she spent a lot of time going from fancy college to fancy college. She doesn't have as much money as the Canterburys, but she inherited a lot when her parents died a few years ago."

Braden felt a pang of sympathy for her. His parents were alive and well and hopefully safe in Florida because he was worried that nobody close to him was safe. Hell, nobody in Northern Lakes was safe. He really needed to send Sam back to Washington to stay with her dad until the saboteur was caught. But he'd learned long ago that Sam wouldn't go anywhere she didn't want to go or stay anywhere she didn't want to stay. All the McRooneys were like that.

Trick hadn't intended to stay either. But he wasn't going anywhere now. Mack…

He was the one who was least expected to stick around anywhere. Hell, none of his family even knew where he'd been for the last twenty years, and, from what Braden had heard, Mack's visits home had been few and far between over the years.

"Did Brittney find any enemies in her past?" Braden asked, but he knew he was clutching at straws. He would still rather hope it was Wells or anyone else not on his team that was attacking the others.

Rory shook his head. "No. I think it was the saboteur that went after her. She hasn't been a cop long enough to make enemies here. Though her boss wasn't too warm to her when he took all our statements for the report."

Braden groaned. "If this person is brazen enough to go after a cop…"

"Nobody's safe," Rory finished for him, confirming his worst fear.

And that feeling intensified. A fire was starting…

Chapter 18

Mack awoke with a start and cough, smoke burning his nostrils and drying out the back of his throat. "What the hell..."

For a moment he was so disoriented that he didn't know where he was. Which mission was this? What country was he in? What war?

Then everything came rushing back to him. He reached out and touched the bed next to him, looking for her. But there was nobody lying beside him—not like she'd been when he'd fallen asleep with her curled up against him.

"Wynona!" He coughed and sputtered again. Something was burning. Her house?

Fully awake, he grabbed his clothes and pulled them on, his heart hammering in his chest with the panic gripping him. How the hell had he fallen asleep?

He knew they were in danger. He'd stayed to protect her, and now he didn't even know where she was. Had the saboteur gotten past her security system? Had he abducted her? Or worse...

Was she already dead?

Panic gripped him so tightly that he could barely breathe. He gasped for air and coughed some more as smoke filled his lungs.

Mack flipped on lights in the bedroom, which made the smoke hovering in the air appear dusky.

"Wynona!"

He coughed again and it seemed to echo, coming from somewhere else in the house. He pushed open the door of the en suite bathroom, but it was empty, the floor still slick with water. He picked up the towel that was lying in the water and pressed it over his mouth to block some of the smoke. Then he turned toward the hall, moving through the smoke toward the main living area.

"Wynona!" he shouted.

He heard a cough. Was it hers? Or was someone else inside the smoky house with them?

Someone who'd already hurt her?

He needed his gun. But he'd left it in his truck earlier, beneath the seat. He'd been so worried about her injuries from the ravine that he hadn't thought to grab it. And while he'd checked her house for her, he hadn't believed that anyone else was able to get inside.

But now...

Unless the fire had started outside, someone must have gotten in somehow. Then he heard a gun cock, and he knew that someone else had found their way inside despite that damn security system.

They must have already gotten rid of Wynona, and now he was going to be next. But he wasn't going out without one hell of a fight. And hopefully he could find Wynona, get her out of the fire, and get her medical help.

Wynona uncocked her gun just as Mack lunged toward her. "Stop!" she said. "It's me." With all the smoke and her eyes watering because of it, she hadn't been certain the big shadow moving toward her was him until he got closer.

"What the hell is going on?" Mack asked.

"I heard something and got up to check it out. There

wasn't any smoke then. I don't know where this is coming from." She coughed.

"We have to get out of here," Mack said. "Now."

She pointed at the cat carrier on the ground. Harry was already listless which had made the cat easier to catch and put in the carrier. And she'd draped a wet towel over that, but the smoke just kept getting worse and worse. "But the fire…"

"What fire? I don't see any flames. I don't feel any heat," he pointed out. Then he tensed. "Oh, my God…"

"What is it?" she asked.

"Smoke bomb. Somebody set off a smoke bomb in here," he said.

There could only be one reason for that, which Wynona voiced aloud. "To get us out…"

"It's going to work," Mack said. "We can't stay in here." He coughed again.

But the minute they stepped outside a door, Wynona knew what would happen. And Mack had to know, too. The saboteur was going to shoot at them like he had outside Mack's cabin that first time Wynona had followed him home.

But Harry emitted a pitiful, weak cry, and Wynona knew she was going to lose her cat and maybe her own life if they didn't at least try to escape the smoke.

"This way," Mack said, his voice gruff.

He took the cat carrier from her and headed through the kitchen to the French doors that opened onto the brick patio that stretched nearly to the sandy beach.

"The lakeside will give the saboteur fewer places to hide," he said. "And we can take cover behind the outside fireplace and kitchen."

It was like he'd already assessed the situation, like it was one of his military missions. And it did feel to Wynona like they were at war. She didn't want her pet and her house to be casualties of it, though.

She knew they had to get out of the smoke-filled house. Her lungs and throat were burning, and her eyes kept watering. She had her weapon in one hand, but she wasn't sure she would be able to see well enough to shoot anything, especially since it was so damn dark outside. After the long, dangerous day they'd had, they'd fallen asleep after making love, and must have been out for hours, long enough for day to slip into night.

The saboteur could be out there now, waiting to shoot them even through the glass. Mack must have thought the same thing because he pulled her down so that they were crouching lower to the hardwood floor as they crossed the kitchen to the breakfast area. He passed a wet towel to her. "Put this over your mouth."

Then he opened one of the French doors. As the fresh air came in through it, the smoke billowed and seemed to thicken around them.

First, he slid the carrier outside through the patio door, using the long handle of a broom that she hadn't even seen him grab. He pushed Harry across the patio behind the outside fireplace.

Hopefully the wind blowing in off the lake would clean out the cat's lungs. Wynona lowered that damp towel from her face, but no fresh air reached her yet. A cough racked her.

And somewhere, too close to them, a gun cocked.

Wynona tried to raise hers, but with her coughing, she couldn't even hold the Glock steady with just one hand able to grip it.

"Let me have the gun," Mack said. He took it from her hand.

But the saboteur had already started firing, and bullets

struck the house and the patio doors, shattering glass all around them. She felt something nip at her skin and flinched at the sting.

Mack fired her gun with one hand while he used his other to pull her through those shattered doors and into the shadows of the fireplace and the outside kitchen. Bullets pinged off the built-in grill and stainless-steel counter.

No matter how good a shot Mack was, Wynona wasn't sure he would be able to save them. That he would be able to stop the shooter before one of his bullets struck them instead of the house.

So much gunfire went back and forth, and then all of a sudden Mack crumpled forward and collapsed onto the patio bricks.

A scream clawed up the back of Wynona's throat. He must have been hit!

Getting the gun from the patsy's truck again had been the smart thing. He should have had it earlier, at the ravine. But it worked now.

The saboteur was pretty certain he'd hit one of them, maybe even both of them. But the problem was that he had been hit, too.

He didn't think the wound was bad. He hadn't even felt it until he saw the blood. Would anyone else notice it?

Could he cover it up? Keep anyone from seeing that he'd been hit?

Chapter 19

Mack awoke again with a start and no idea where he was. Bright lights blinded him, and he tried to talk, but something was covering his mouth. What the hell had happened? He reached up to push at it, but someone caught his hand.

"No. You need that oxygen."

The sight of the blonde peering down at him rattled him more than not knowing where he was. He pulled off the mask. "Mom?"

"Not yet," Sam said with a heavy sigh. "But hopefully soon..." Then her face flushed. "Oh, you meant...you thought I was..."

"No, no," he said when he could tell that he'd hurt her feelings for thinking that she was anything like their mother. He was the one who was most like her, just as Trick had accused him of being.

Then Trick leaned over Sam and asked, "Are you all right, big brother?" Instead of the usual resentment, there was affection and relief in Trick's green eyes.

Just like he'd thought Sam looked like their mom, Mack murmured to Trick, "You look so much like Dad..."

Tears glistened in Trick's eyes for a moment before he blinked. "You're the one who's the most like him," Trick said. "You're so damn tough. And I'm so damn glad that you are. I don't want to lose you."

Was this his brother? The one who'd been acting so resentful since his arrival in Northern Lakes?

Mack touched his head again. He hadn't hit it. Why the hell was he so confused? "What happened?" he asked his siblings.

"You passed out from that smoke bomb," Trick said, his voice gruff.

Then he wasn't that damn tough. He'd needed to stay conscious. For her. To protect her.

He jerked upright on the hospital gurney and looked around. "Where's Wynona?" Because if he'd passed out, she must have too.

"I think she loves another more than you," Trick said, but he was grinning and teasing him.

Did his younger brother know how Mack felt about the state trooper? Did Mack know? With the way his heart was pounding with fear for her, he suspected he knew, but he didn't want to face it yet. Not until the saboteur was caught and they were out of danger.

But maybe even not then because despite what Trick had said, Mack knew he was more like their mother than their father. He wasn't the McRooney that could be counted on, he was the one who would probably run.

"Where is Wynona?" he asked, his voice gruff as his concern for her choked him. "Is she okay?"

"She will be if her cat is okay," Trick said. "She insisted on taking it to the animal hospital before she would come here to get stitched up."

"Stitched up? She got hit?" And she'd gone to the veterinarian first? But that was just like her to think of others before herself, like when she'd urged him to let her go in that ravine.

"Just with some broken glass Owen told us," Sam shared. "She isn't hurt badly at all. You're the one who passed out."

He remembered firing her gun into the shadows. And then…nothing. "Did I hit him?" he asked. Or had the shooter kept firing after he'd passed out?

"Who?" Sam asked.

"The saboteur," he said.

"Who was it?" Trick asked. "Did you see who it was?"

He shook his head. "I don't know. I didn't see him. Just his damn shadow…" But he was pretty sure he'd hit him, or the person wouldn't have stopped shooting and he and Wynona would probably be dead.

"Did you hit him?" Trick asked.

Mack shrugged.

"There are troopers out at her house going over the scene right now," Sam assured him. "If someone else is out there, they'll find him."

"He'll only be there if I did hit him," Mack said, and then he started coughing again. But it felt more as if his lungs were clearing the last of the smoke out.

"You have to put the oxygen back on," Sam said, mothering him now as she reached for the mask and tried to pull it over his mouth and nose again.

But he resisted her efforts even as he coughed again. "The smoke was so bad…"

"Those bombs are brutal," Trick said. "Somehow the saboteur got his hands on some of the training ones. Braden went to check at the firehouse, and he confirmed that a couple of them are missing."

Somehow…

The saboteur had to be one of them or at least someone who had free rein to the firehouse, like Stanley or one of the volunteers. "What about the cameras? Did he see who was hanging around? Who could have taken them?"

"He checked the footage," Trick said. "But there were a lot of people coming and going. He couldn't see anyone actually holding one of the smoke bombs, but that didn't mean one of them didn't take it."

"Who?" Mack asked then coughed. "Who was there? Stanley?"

"Stanley's always there," Trick said.

Mack nodded.

"No," Sam said. "I suspected him once of being the arsonist, but that kid loves everyone too much to hurt anyone. And just suspecting him nearly destroyed him. So don't go there, Mack."

"You're getting soft," Mack mused. Must have been love that had made her less cynical than she used to be.

She flushed and touched her belly. "Yeah, I am. I'm also worried. My husband shouldn't be off on his own," she said, her brow furrowing with concern. "Not with how all these attacks have been stepped up."

The saboteur was getting more and more dangerous and more and more determined. What was his end goal? To kill Mack and Wynona or all the hotshots?

"Your husband is already on his way back," Trick assured her, sliding his arm around her shoulders.

Mack envied them that closeness. They clearly had a tighter bond than he had with any of his family. With anyone except maybe for...

"Wynona," he said, rasping out her name. "Somebody needs to check on her. See if she made it to the hospital yet."

The smoke could have snuck up on her the way it had him. It could have damaged her lungs.

What if she collapsed somewhere on her own? And there

was no one there to help her like when she'd been hanging off the side of that ravine.

"She shouldn't be off on her own either," Mack said. After nearly getting killed so many times, she should have realized that. He wanted to be angry with her over taking chances, but he was too scared that she was hurt.

"She's not alone," Trick assured him. "She's with Owen. He wanted to keep an eye on her, so he used the rig to drive her cat to the animal clinic. They're probably on their way back here now."

He hoped so because he didn't like being separated from her. Every time they had been, something happened to her. Something bad.

Wynona pushed down the oxygen mask Owen had put on her and asked, "Can you drive faster?"

He glanced across the console at her. "You told me you were feeling fine."

"I am." The oxygen had cleared the smoke from her lungs. And the emergency vet at the animal clinic had assured her that Harry's lungs looked good as well. She was worried about Mack, though. He was the one who'd passed out. But his siblings were with him and would make sure he was being taken care of. Even Trick had been so scared when he'd shown up with Owen. Mack had family to care for him. Harry only had her.

And she only had Harry like the stereotypical crazy cat lady she had vowed to become after she'd realized what a narcissist Jason Cruise had been. Wynona wasn't crazy, she was just cautious now after that near miss with a would-be killer. And if she gave her heart to anyone, it wouldn't be someone like Mack. Clearly, he wasn't going to stick around once the saboteur was caught. He was only here on a mission for his brother-in-law, and then he'd be off somewhere else. Probably back to the excitement of his old life and new missions.

But first he had to survive this one.

"I just want to get to the hospital," she said.

"Eager to get those stitches?" Owen asked.

She reached up and touched the bandage he'd affixed over some liquid bandage. "I don't need any. You took care of that cut."

"You're not worried about having a scar?" he asked.

"I'm not worried about that." She wasn't worried about herself at all.

Owen smiled as he must have figured out whom she was worried about. "I checked on Mack while you were back with the vet. He's fine," he assured her. "His oxygen levels are back up. He'll be released soon."

But that worried her even more. "I don't want that shooter trying for him again."

"Was he after Mack or you?" Owen asked. "You had that close call by the ravine."

Too close.

"You know he's gone after Mack, too," she said. "That warehouse fire had to be a setup and then the live wire in the showers…"

Owen groaned and pressed his foot down a little harder on the accelerator, but as he rounded a corner, bright lights flashed in their faces. Owen cursed then twisted the wheel as that vehicle headed straight at them, right in their lane.

The paramedic rig bounced off the shoulder of the road and into the ditch. Airbags deployed, but Wynona hadn't buckled up after she'd crawled into the passenger's seat from the back. She went flying.

Then everything went black.

* * *

Braden was in a hurry to get back to the hospital. While he knew that Mack was tough and would undoubtedly be all right once his oxygen levels were brought back up, he was more worried about Sam.

She should have stayed home with her feet up, resting. But she'd sworn she wouldn't be able to relax until she saw for herself that her brother was all right. And so she'd insisted on going to the hospital.

But Braden wanted to get her home to rest. She was going to go into labor soon—he didn't need a sixth sense to know that since she was already overdue. And the added stress of the saboteur going after her brother wasn't helping the situation at all.

With as worried as he was about his wife, he pressed his foot down harder on the accelerator and sped toward the hospital. He was drawing close to it when he saw the lights.

Off the road.

In the ditch.

One of the paramedic rigs.

Owen. And he wasn't alone.

He had Wynona in the rig with him on the way back to the hospital. But they hadn't made it. And Braden was concerned that now it might be too late to get them there.

Chapter 20

"Where is she?" Mack asked Trick. "You said she needs stitches." How badly had she been hurt? Or was it that her cat wasn't okay?

God, he hoped she hadn't lost her cat, too. Not when she was still hurting from the loss of her parents. He knew Wynona cared about that cat. Hell, he cared about the fluffy little ball of affection. If something happened to her, Wynona would be upset.

And she would be even more alone than she already was. Maybe that was why he'd been so drawn to her from the first moment they'd met. Not because she was aloof like he was, but because she was lonely like he was.

He hadn't even realized how lonely he was until he'd started spending time with her and with his family. He'd been alone too long. And while it might have been safer for him and for the people he cared about, it had been...lonely.

"Where the hell is she?" Mack repeated the question, his voice getting gruffer with the frustration and the fear that were overwhelming him.

Trick wasn't answering him. He was staring down at his phone instead and the color drained from his face as he read whatever text he received.

Dread settled heavily in Mack's stomach. Sam must have

noticed his reaction too because she pressed up against their younger brother's side and tried to read his phone. "What is it?" she asked. "What's going on? Is it Braden?"

Mack shook his head. He knew from the way that Trick glanced at him and then quickly looked away.

"The text is from Braden," Trick said. "Nothing happened to him. *He's* okay, Sam."

"But Wynona isn't," Mack said, that dread so heavy that he struggled to sit up. But he managed and then swung his legs over the side of the gurney.

Sam rushed forward and tried to shove him back. "You shouldn't be up."

"I'm fine," he said. But he coughed again. That might have been more with panic than anything. "What the hell is it, Trick? What happened?"

Instead of answering him, Trick glanced at Sam. She sighed and nodded. "Tell him."

"Braden just found the rig in the ditch."

Mack gasped now, and it wasn't for air. It was with concern for Wynona. He knew it. He knew something had happened to her, that she shouldn't have been off on her own. Well, she hadn't been quite alone—she'd been with Owen. But she hadn't been with *Mack*. "Tell me everything you know!"

Trick shrugged. "I don't know much more than you do. Owen said some vehicle came straight at him. He went in the ditch to avoid a head-on collision."

"So he avoided the head-on crash," Mack said. "That's good."

But Trick looked away from him again. "Wynona wasn't belted in."

"No!" Mack yelled. Because now he didn't want to know. If she was gone, if he'd lost her, he didn't want to know.

"They're on their way in now," Sam said, her voice soft with sympathy for him.

Like he was the one hurting. But he was hurting over just the thought of her being hurt. She had to be okay, she had to be...

And then he heard them, the commotion outside the curtained-off area where his gurney was. He heard the nurses and doctors rushing around, and he knew it was bad.

Hands came out of the darkness, grabbing at her, trying to get to her, trying to pull her even deeper into the abyss. But in that all-encompassing blackness there were rocks and boulders with jagged, sharp edges and Wynona could feel herself plunging toward them and then breaking into little pieces.

She awoke with a scream. The darkness was gone, replaced with lights so bright she flinched, and her head pounded.

"Are you okay?" a deep voice rumbled.

She turned her head to find Mack seated beside her, his hand on hers. But it wasn't his hand she'd felt in her dream. He'd held her up, he'd saved her.

"What happened?" she asked, her voice a rasp.

"Owen said—"

"Owen!" Everything rushed back. "Is he all right?"

Mack nodded. "Yeah, he was wearing his seat belt." He reached out and touched her forehead. "You weren't. You're lucky you didn't go through the windshield. The airbags saved you from any more cuts and bruises than you already had. But you have a slight concussion. That's why you've been unconscious."

"Are you okay now?" she asked. He had dark circles beneath his eyes, and his face was tense. "When you passed out, I thought you were shot…" Her voice cracked as it trailed off with the fear she'd felt then. How scared she'd been that he was gone.

He smiled at her. "Nope. I'm just a wuss who passed out," he said with self-deprecating humor.

But she felt compelled to defend him to himself. "Because your lungs were full of smoke."

"Well, my lungs are fine now," he said. "Yours are too. They checked them. They did all kinds of X-rays and MRIs on you."

She glanced down at her body then and saw that she was wearing a hospital gown beneath the sheet covering her. She patted her sides. "Where is my gun?" She remembered those hands tugging at her.

"Your gun?" Mack asked, his voice cracking a bit with alarm.

She nodded, and pain radiated throughout her skull for a moment. Spots danced in front of her eyes, and she had to hold her breath for a moment until it passed. Until her vision cleared again.

"I'll find it," Mack said. He reached under the gurney, probably where his stuff had been stored, and pulled out the bag that held her clothes and her belt and holster. But the holster was empty. "Maybe the staff took it and locked it up somewhere safe. Or Owen or Braden took it from you in the ambulance."

She closed her eyes, trying to remember, but those hands came back to her again, reaching out of the dark. When she opened her eyes, Mack was gone.

She felt a flash of panic because she knew. Someone had taken her gun, but not Owen or Braden or a hospital staff person. The saboteur had taken it.

She looked at that empty holster, and she saw the blood

on the snap that had held it shut. Maybe it was hers. The glass from the broken patio door had cut her. But that had been on her head, not her hands. And she hadn't even been aware of the cut until Owen pointed it out.

So she couldn't imagine that, when she'd taken her weapon from Mack after he'd passed out, she would have gotten blood on her holster. She wouldn't have had any blood on her hands then. So where had the blood come from?

Unless Owen had been hurt worse than Mack had admitted...

She remembered the lights coming right at them, in their lane, forcing the ambulance into the ditch. But Owen had been wearing his seat belt whereas she'd just switched from the back to the front.

But that didn't mean Owen wasn't hurt. Or maybe something else had happened to her gun. Maybe someone else had taken it. That thought scared her so much she forced herself out of bed. The room tilted despite the fact that her feet were flat on the floor. The blackness threatened again. She gripped the side of the gurney, riding out the wave of dizziness. Then she grabbed her clothes Mack had dumped out of the bag, and she dressed quickly. Before she could pull back the curtain around her area in the emergency room, Mack was back, and he wasn't alone.

"I'm sorry, Trooper Wells," Owen said. "I didn't know how to avoid that vehicle heading right at us."

"Did you see it?" she asked him. "Do you know what kind it was?"

He shook his head. "The lights were so bright, they were blinding."

She nodded, and her head pounded harder. "I know. I couldn't see anything either. Just that it was big." And coming right at them.

"But then whoever was driving it came up to the rig," Owen said. "They got the back doors open somehow, and then I think they were trying to get you out of it."

Mack cursed.

"Did you see them then?" she asked.

He shook his head. "With the airbag and all the stuff from the back flying around, I couldn't see anything but a shadow. Then there were lights coming up behind us, and whoever it was ran off."

"With your gun, Wynona," Mack said, stating what she'd already deduced for herself. "Neither Owen nor Braden saw it on you, just the empty holster."

"I didn't see him take it, but I figured he might have been grabbing other stuff out of the back, maybe trying to steal drugs. But then it didn't make sense that he was grabbing at you in the passenger seat," Owen said with a slight shudder. "I thought he was trying to pull you out of the back with him, so I held onto you."

Mack squeezed the paramedic's shoulder. "Thanks, man. You did good. You kept him from abducting her."

"Why didn't he just kill me?" she asked. "That's what he's been trying to do."

"Has he been trying to kill you or scare you off?" Mack asked. "Gingrich said something that day I visited him—"

"You visited Marty Gingrich in jail?" Owen asked, sounding horrified. But then Gingrich's mistress had tried to kill Owen, and Marty had probably helped her with some of those attempts.

Wynona chuckled. "He was trying to find out if I was working with the creep."

While Owen stared at her with wide eyes, Mack just shrugged. "Anyhow, he said something…"

When he trailed off, she finished for him. "Something I'm probably not going to like."

"He didn't think you'd last as a police officer, that you'd be too soft for the job."

"Because I'm rich and spoiled," Wynona said. Then she sighed. "He's not wrong. I am rich and spoiled."

Mack snorted. "You work damn hard and you're pretty fearless."

Owen nodded. "And relentless. You don't give up no matter how much crap we've all given you."

"But is that what someone is trying to do?" Mack asked. "Get you to give up? Could they just be trying to scare you off the case?"

"Why take my gun though?" she asked. "What reason could he have for doing that? Unless…"

"What?" Mack and Owen asked at the same time.

"What if he was shot?" she asked. "What if you hit him, Mack? That could have been why he was going through the back of the rig, too. Getting stuff for his wound."

Mack tilted his head as if considering it. "I hope like hell that I did hit him, but why take your gun, especially since he has his own?"

"It was the gun you were using…" Maybe he'd seen that, had seen Mack take it from her and when she took it back.

"But still…why?" Mack asked, his brow furrowed as he tried to figure out the reason.

"I don't know," she said. "But we better call and report all of this to Sergeant Hughes."

"Braden already called him," Owen said. "I gave him my statement a while ago."

How long had she been unconscious?

Mack nodded. "I did, too. He's probably around here somewhere waiting to take yours."

"We need to find him," she said. "To warn him about that gun…"

Because she had a feeling that something very bad was about to happen. And after everything that had already happened, that was saying a lot. But why else would the saboteur have taken her gun unless he intended to use it?

But on whom?

He sat in that corner booth laughing and joking with so many members of his team. And maybe he should have felt guilty for what he was about to do or for the things he'd already done, but all he felt was…

Rage.

The rage that had been driving him for over a year. And after getting shot earlier that night, the rage was even more intense. He didn't just hate Braden Zimmer anymore. He hated all of them.

And they all deserved what was about to happen…

But he smiled and joked around, like he always did. They didn't suspect anything.

None of them had.

And none of them would until it was too late.

He wasn't sure if they knew that he'd left or if they thought he was in the bathroom. None of them knew he was waiting for them outside the door of the Filling Station until he started shooting them as they walked out.

And one by one, they dropped to the pavement.

Chapter 21

Wynona would have preferred to take a report rather than giving it, but since she was a victim now, and stuck yet in the ER bay until the doctor released her, she had to answer her boss's questions.

Heat flushed her face because it was clear from his smirk that he knew why Mack had been at her house earlier that night. And he probably also thought the only reason she'd lost her weapon was because she was a girl, not because she'd been unconscious at the time.

Fury bubbled up inside her over that smirk and over his entire treatment of her since he'd taken over for Gingrich. She was flushed with anger, not embarrassment.

"Sergeant Hughes, I have some questions for you," she said. "Like, why was I the one you sent out to that ravine? Why not another trooper? I wasn't even on duty yet. And since you and Gingrich were so tight for many years, how the hell didn't you know what he was up to?"

The smirk slid away into a tight-lipped grimace. "I would be very careful, Trooper Wells."

"I have been," she said. "And I've had to be because I can't trust anyone I work with. I just started at this job. But you were doing it for a while. How the hell did you not know what your friend was up to? I want an answer."

"You're being insubordinate, Wells. I'll allow it this once because I can tell you're overwrought—"

"I'm furious," Wells said. "And if I were a man, there is no way in hell you'd be calling me overwrought."

Which reminded her so much of what Michaela Momber's co-worker Donovan Cunningham had said to her when the female hotshot had encouraged her boyfriend Charlie Tillerman to press charges against Cunningham's teenage boys for breaking into his bar. She and Michaela had both wondered if those teenage boys and Cunningham himself might have been responsible for all the horrible things that had happened to the hotshots.

"And you haven't answered her questions," Mack pointed out as he pushed back the curtain around her gurney and joined them.

She was glad she'd gotten dressed even though the doctor hadn't actually released her yet. Dr. Smits wanted to make sure that the follow-up CT scan she'd ordered after the initial one showed no swelling or bleeding on the brain. But it seemed as if the doctor had forgotten about her since Wynona had been back from radiology for a while now.

"I'm taking a report, not giving it," the sergeant remarked.

"I'm sure we can find out from the jail just how often you actually have been by to talk to your friend."

The sergeant shrugged. "Go ahead. I haven't been there. And I can admit when I've misjudged someone, like I misjudged Marty." He turned back to Wynona then. "And maybe you, too. Maybe you are tougher than I thought."

She was battered and bruised nearly from head to toe. So she wasn't feeling that tough at the moment.

"She is damn tough, or she wouldn't have survived the crap she's been put through," Mack said.

"But she lost her weapon—"

"While she was unconscious!" Mack shouted. "Are you a moron? How can you hold her accountable for that? Or are you just looking for a reason to harass her? Because I've found one to har—"

Wynona jumped up from the gurney and stepped between them. She didn't want Mack to get arrested, and she had no doubt that her sergeant would book the hotshot for assault if Mack so much as laid a finger on him. But before either of the men could say anything else, a commotion outside the curtains drew all their attention.

And the sergeant's radio started squawking at him.

"Déjà vu," Mack muttered. "This is what it was like when Braden brought you and Owen in. I wonder what the hell happened now."

"I guess we know where your gun turned up, Wells," the sergeant said. "Someone used it to shoot a bunch of hotshots as they were coming out of that bar they all hang out at. They're being brought in now."

"Oh, my God…" Wynona murmured. "Are there any casualties?"

"All I know is that the gun was recovered at the scene and the serial number matches yours."

Son of a bitch.

While Mack said the sergeant couldn't hold her accountable for it being taken, Wynona would hold herself responsible if anyone was killed with her gun.

From the way all the color left Mack's face, it was clear he was worried about a particular hotshot or two. His brother and brother-in-law. And probably all the others. Even though he hadn't worked with them long, he had already formed a close connection to a few of them, like Rory VanDam.

Like he'd formed a close connection to her. So close that Wynona could feel his distress.

Mack felt like he was trapped in a nightmare that would never end. Even during wars, he would have more of a break between battles than he'd had here in Northern Lakes. And the fear was overwhelming.

Not for himself but for those he cared about. Trick and Braden had left a while ago with Sam, making sure that she got safely home. But what if, instead of heading straight back to their house, they'd all stopped at the Filling Station first?

Sam was hungry all the time. She could have wanted something to eat. Then she would have been there with the hotshots.

And if something had happened to her and her baby...

No. He couldn't even let himself think that. His whole reason for coming here had been to protect his siblings, but his arrival in town had done the opposite. The saboteur had gotten even more dangerous.

Wynona pulled back the curtain of her area of the ER to watch as the others were brought in.

"I'm sorry," a nurse said as she noticed Wynona and Mack. "You two are free to leave. You're fine."

And they probably needed the bed.

But Mack wasn't fine.

Wynona squeezed his hand and used it to guide him away from her area toward the door that marked the exit to the waiting room. But Mack stopped. He wasn't going anywhere until he saw who'd been hurt.

Or worse...

"Were there any casualties?" he asked Sergeant Hughes who was leaning against the wall near where they were. He was listening to his radio.

The sergeant shook his head. "No. Doesn't sound like anyone was seriously wounded either. A couple shoulder wounds and a couple of leg wounds. Sounds like whoever was firing wasn't trying to kill."

"Thank God..." Mack murmured.

And then he saw Trick...

He wasn't on one of the gurneys, thank God. He was pushing one with Owen on the other side of it.

"Who is it?" Mack asked, trying to see around them to who lay on that stretcher.

Braden?

Sam?

"Carl," the man on the stretcher answered for himself. "Like I told you, McRooney, I should have retired, too. Don't tell my wife she was right, though."

"You'll be back fighting fires in no time," Owen said. "You've gotten hurt worse shaving your head bald."

Carl chuckled then grimaced.

Another stretcher came in behind him with one of the young guys, tears trailing down his face. "It hurts so bad!" he said, his voice cracking.

Was it Howie or Bruce?

Mack wasn't sure yet who was whom, but they were usually together. And sure enough the other one followed, grasping his bloodied shoulder as he cursed. "Son of a bitch."

"Did any of you see the shooter?" Wynona asked the question that her sergeant should have been asking, but he seemed a bit overwhelmed at the moment. Fortunately, there was a crew of officers and crime scene techs back at the Filling Station where the shooting had happened. She'd managed to get that confirmation out of her boss before he'd clammed up.

Maybe she and Mack had put him on notice regarding

his harassment of her and his lack of judgment regarding his friend Marty, and he was being more careful now. At least he couldn't be the shooter unless he'd left the scene at the Filling Station in a hell of a hurry to get to the hospital.

It was probably possible. And maybe that was why he held back. Either way, Mack didn't trust him. And he would definitely be making some calls to Hughes's superiors.

"There was no time to see anything," the other young one said, his words a bit slurred.

Mack wondered if he was sober enough to be able to identify anyone.

Two more stretchers came in, and more color drained from Wynona's already pale face. She closed her eyes for a moment, and Mack was worried that she was blaming herself for this. But he noticed something when he identified the new arrivals: Donovan Cunningham and Ed Ward.

Like Bruce and Howie, one had a shoulder wound and the other a leg wound.

But all five of the injured hotshots were the ones whose names were already circled on his suspect board. His gaze met Wynona's, and he knew she'd noticed that, too. Had the saboteur seen his board?

It was possible. After following them there, he knew where Mack lived. And maybe he'd made certain to hurt them all so that they would have no more suspects.

Sergeant Hughes finally spoke again. "You're not just on desk duty anymore, Wells. You're going to be suspended until this can all be figured out."

"You're really not going to try to blame her for this," Mack said. It wasn't a question, it was a warning. He wouldn't let that little weasel get away with pinning this on Wynona.

"I don't want her getting killed," the sergeant said.

"Maybe you should take a vacation for a while, Wells. Leave town." He met Mack's gaze. "You, too."

Was that what this all was? An attempt to get him and Wynona to drop their investigation?

From the look on her face, she had no intention of doing that any more than he did. But she smiled at her boss and replied, "Thanks for the time off." And she started walking away.

Mack followed her. He would talk to the other hotshots later, when the sergeant wasn't around. But for now, he didn't intend to be separated from Wynona again. He wasn't letting her out of his sight until the saboteur was caught or killed or…killed Mack.

Braden knew how Sam must have felt with her morning sickness. Because when he learned what had happened at the Filling Station, he got physically sick.

"They're going to be fine," Sam said. "All of them. Owen said the injuries weren't life threatening."

"This town wanted the hotshot headquarters out of here," Braden said. "And now I understand why. I guess I always understood why. We just seem to attract danger and are putting others in it, too."

"Only hotshots were harmed," Sam said. "No innocent bystanders."

That was the problem. It didn't feel like the hotshots were innocent anymore. It definitely felt like it was all about them. At least all about one of them.

"I should have stepped down months ago," Braden said. "This is probably about me. Somebody wants me gone."

"Nobody's even tried to come after you," Sam said. "Or after me. You're taking responsibility for something that isn't your fault."

"Your brothers have both been in danger because of this saboteur—"

"That's just because they're trying to figure out who he is," Sam said. "People will take drastic measures to protect themselves."

"I can't imagine anything much more drastic than tonight," he said.

But he was worried that it was going to get even worse before it got better. If it ever got better...

Chapter 22

Mack's intent for bringing Wynona home with him was to make sure she stayed safe. And that, with the concussion she had, she needed to rest. But the minute they walked into his house, she headed for the suspect board.

"You narrowed it down to these guys," she said. "And all of them were shot tonight. That can't be a coincidence."

"It wasn't me," he said, trying to lighten the heaviness gripping him. And that must have been gripping her, too, because her shoulders were bowed as if she carried a heavy burden. Guilt. "And it wasn't you," he added.

"But it was my gun," she said. "You heard Sergeant Hughes. They confirmed it with the serial number."

"Why take it when they had a gun of their own? They used it to shoot at us," Mack pointed out. "And then why shoot so many people with your gun?"

"It has to be one of them," Wynona said.

He tensed. "What?"

"You shot whoever it was who threw that smoke bomb into my house," she said. "So to cover up the fact that you'd shot them, with my gun, they had to shoot more people with my gun." She pointed to his board. "Maybe they saw this or heard about it somehow. Maybe they knew who all your suspects are. Why are the names of these guys circled on the board?"

Some of the others, like her and Stanley, were off to the side. Sergeant Hughes's name was on the board, too, but like hers, it wasn't circled like those five.

"They've consistently been in the area or at every scene of sabotage. The night Rory was hit. The night that Molotov cocktail was thrown at Michaela and Tillerman and things dating back even further than those incidents. While some of the other hotshots or you or Hughes might have been in the vicinity of one incident or another, these five were the only ones that were at all of them."

"And tonight, all of them were shot," she said.

"He must have gotten a look at the board, or maybe he heard Ethan and Rory talking about it after we filled them in," he said. "But either all of them are working together or you're right and one of them is trying to cover up getting shot tonight."

"And they could still all be working together," Wynona said.

He shrugged. "I don't know. Then I think they wouldn't have all been a possibility for every incident. They would have split up the sabotage. One does one thing, one another…" He shook his head. "No, it's one of them. Just one of them working alone."

"They're all in the hospital for tonight," she said, and she yawned. "We can interview them tomorrow."

"You're suspended," he reminded her.

"You're a hotshot," she said. "You can talk to your own team members."

"And what about you?"

"I can go with you when you talk to your team members," she said.

"As my what?" he asked. After what had happened, after

he nearly lost her, he wanted to know what they were. What he would have lost…

He had a feeling that he knew, though. His heart.

She shrugged. "I don't know, Mack. I don't even know if you're sticking around Northern Lakes after you catch the saboteur."

Neither did he really. He wanted to make her promises, but his mom had made those promises to his dad. And she'd broken them and his heart and his and Sam and Trick's when she left.

"Hell, I don't even know if I'll be sticking around," Wynona said. "Maybe the sergeant will make my suspension a termination."

"He'd be an idiot if he did."

"Why?" she asked. "Gingrich told you that I'm not cut out for this job. And I bet you didn't argue with him."

"I didn't know you then," he said. "Now that I do, I know how tough and determined you are."

"But I still haven't caught the saboteur."

"Nobody has," he said. "He's been messing with the whole team for over a year and nobody has caught him."

"They're firefighters, not police officers," she said. "Except for you. Or maybe you are. It's not as if I really know you."

"Yes, you do," he said.

He was a little afraid that she knew him better than most people did. She knew how much it meant to him to be able to help people, to save them, just as much as it obviously meant to her.

"And you also know my sister Sam," he said. "She's an arson investigator, a damn good one, and she's been helping Braden look for the saboteur and hasn't succeeded."

She shrugged as if it didn't matter who else had failed,

just that she had. She was tough on herself. That was another thing they had in common. But she was too tough.

"We have to figure out which one of them it is," she said. "Because I have a feeling someone is going to die if we don't stop him."

He gestured at those five again. "They're all in the hospital tonight. So they're safe. There will be extra security there. And since they're all in the hospital tonight, we're safe, too."

"I can go home then," she said. And she glanced toward his front door.

"Your house is full of smoke," he reminded her.

"It should be cleared out by now," she said.

He slid his arms around her and said, "I don't want you to leave, Wynona." And he was starting to fear that he would never want her to leave.

But as she'd pointed out, he wasn't even sure he was going to stay in Northern Lakes. He wasn't sure what he was going to do after this mission, after finding the saboteur.

But for tonight...

There was no place else he wanted to be but with her, reminding himself that she was alive. That he hadn't lost her. And she must have felt the same because she closed her arms around him and kissed him. Then she started tugging at his clothes but flinched.

He remembered that she didn't have her brace. She must have left it at her house, after he'd taken it off her, so she could relax in her bath. But they hadn't relaxed. They'd made love.

"You have to be careful," he said.

Her lips curved into a slight smile. "If I was being careful, I wouldn't be here."

But she was. They'd had to borrow Trick's truck to get back here, but she hadn't protested. And with the way she tugged at his clothes, she wanted him as badly as he wanted her. But maybe that was the reason she didn't think she should be here with him.

Maybe she knew him too well, and she knew that it wasn't in him to stick around. That he was too much like his mother, that he would let down the people who loved him like she had let down the people who'd loved and depended on her.

He had already let down people he loved, his dad and his sister and his brother.

"I don't want to hurt you," he said as he drew back slightly.

She smiled. "You're the one who told me I'm tough," she reminded him. "A few bruises and sprains aren't going to stop me."

"You have a concussion, too," he said. "You should be resting."

"I'm fine," she said. "The nurse just about threw us out of the ER."

Because they'd needed her bed. And Mack needed her, too much to deny himself any longer. But he took it slowly, trying to be as gentle as he could be with her. He undressed her, kissing every silky inch of skin he exposed.

And the marks on her skin, the scratches and bruises, had his heart clenching with regret over the pain she'd endured. He didn't want her to feel anything else but pleasure. So he laid her down onto the bed and he made love to her with his mouth and his hands.

Even after screaming his name as she writhed around on the bed, she reached for him, pulling him against her, into her. He tried to go slowly yet with sweat beading on his forehead and sliding down his spine, as he struggled for control.

But she kept touching him and kissing him. And his control snapped. The passion and the pleasure were just too intense. And all the feelings that pummeled him as he filled her and reached his own climax, one that shook him to his core, were too intense, too.

That climax, and those feelings, shook him more violently than any of the explosions he had been in. It was all too much, and even after his release, he couldn't relax while she fell asleep in his arms.

What was he going to do? After catching the saboteur...

That had to be what he did next. He had to make sure that all the people he cared about were safe from that bastard. But after the suspect was caught...

What would he do? Could he break the cycle his mother had started? That he'd continued? Instead of running, could he stay somewhere for once? For someone?

Right now, he intended to stay awake. He really did. But with all the suspects in the hospital, he could rest, too. And he would probably need it for the following day, for trying to figure out which one of his fellow hotshots was the saboteur. Because he had no doubt that when the guy was cornered, he wasn't going to go down without a fight.

But maybe Mack was wrong about the suspects, or at least about them staying in the hospital, because he woke up to the sound of someone messing with his door, trying to jimmy the lock.

He reached for Wynona, but the bed next to him was empty. She was gone.

Guilt weighed heavily on Wynona over losing her gun and over leaving Mack so early this morning. But with all the saboteur suspects in the hospital, he had to be safe. She had left him without a vehicle though, since she'd taken his brother's truck.

But she'd awoken with such a feeling of panic to find

herself naked in his arms. He was like an addiction to her, something she just couldn't resist no matter how much she knew it was going to wind up hurting her. Like alcohol or sweets. Wynona wasn't addicted to either of those things though. But Mack...

He might prove worse than any sweet, than any spirit or drug. Maybe if she wasn't so distracted by the desire she felt for him, she might have figured out who the saboteur was, especially since he kept trying to hurt her.

Like last night.

She'd turned over her holster to her sergeant to have forensics check that blood on it. And even though the techs had been all over her house and the grounds, too, she wanted to look for herself to see if any of the techs had marked the area and found any blood around the vicinity where the saboteur would have had to be standing last night when he'd fired all those shots at her and Mack.

It was probably a miracle that they hadn't been hit except for the shard of glass that had nicked her face. And Mack passing out from the smoke inhalation.

He'd been fine last night, though. Once he'd gotten the oxygen. He'd been better than fine later when they'd made love. At least that was what it was beginning to feel like for her. She wasn't sure how he felt about her, if he even really liked her all that much, at least enough to stay.

Of course, she didn't know if she would stay either. The new life and career she'd wanted for herself in Northern Lakes hadn't turned out like she'd hoped. But she couldn't think of anywhere else she'd rather be now that her parents were gone. This was one of the few places she hadn't traveled with them, so it had felt like she could make a fresh start here, a new life for herself.

Instead, she'd nearly lost her life too many times. After

taking his truck, she'd stopped in town to replace her phone, but she hadn't called him yet to let him know where she'd gone. Or that she'd left.

She hadn't called anyone else either.

When she pulled up to her house, there were more vehicles than hers and Mack's parked in the driveway. There was another US Forest Service vehicle. She automatically reached for her weapon, but it wasn't on her belt. She didn't even have the empty holster anymore.

Nothing to defend herself.

Mack had a gun in his truck, though, stowed under the front seat. If she could get into the locked vehicle...

She jumped out of Trick's truck and headed toward Mack's. But just as she reached the door, she heard a gun cock. She was too late.

"I'm sorry," a female voice said. "I wasn't sure who had driven up..." Sam McRooney-Zimmer stood between Wynona and the house. The arson investigator re-engaged the safety on her gun and dropped it into her cross-body purse which rested on the big swell of her belly.

The woman had treated Wynona as coldly as most of the hotshots had in the past, so Wynona wasn't particularly happy to see her here. At her home.

"What are you doing here?" Wynona asked the arson investigator. "There wasn't a fire last night." *Thank goodness.* "Just all that smoke..."

"From the smoke bomb," Sam said. "I know it wasn't arson, but I thought maybe I would find something else here, some clue..."

"That would lead to the saboteur," Wynona finished for her. "I was thinking that, too. I think Mack hit him last night. I think that's why..."

"Some of them were shot last night," Sam finished for

her and shuddered. "Braden was so upset about so many of his team getting hurt. He's blaming himself."

And that was obviously the reason his wife was here, trying to help her husband.

"It's not *his* fault," Wynona said. "None of this…but especially not that…"

"It's not your fault either," Sam said. "I've tried to catch this person for a long time, and while I've never not caught an arsonist, I haven't been able to figure out who the saboteur is." A grimace, probably of frustration, crossed her pretty face.

"I hope to find something here that might lead to him, too," Wynona said. "If Mack hit him, there might be blood where he was standing when he was shooting at us."

"Where?" Sam asked. "And wouldn't your techs have found it?"

"I don't know what all they found and didn't find at the scene," Wynona said. "Mack and I were at the hospital. And then, after I lost my weapon, Sergeant Hughes suspended me, so I can't get an update on the investigation directly from the techs."

"Hughes is an idiot then," Sam said, and she grimaced again. "What happened last night wasn't your fault. Any of it."

Wynona wanted to believe that, but she couldn't help but think that she could have done more. "I need to make it right," she said. "No matter what."

"We'll find this saboteur," Sam said. "We will." She glanced at the truck Wynona had driven here and asked, "Where is my brother? He's usually not far away from you lately."

Heat rushed to Wynona's face with embarrassment over how far she'd crossed the line with Mack. Not that he was a suspect but he had suspected her at one time. "I left him sleeping at his cabin."

"Don't be embarrassed. You have no reason to be," Sam assured her. "I totally understand that sometimes we get caught up in the adrenaline and the danger and the love."

Wynona shook her head as panic gripped her. "I barely know your brother. I don't think anyone does. Maybe not even him."

Sam sighed and nodded. "You're right. I just hope..."

"What?" Wynona asked.

Sam shook her head. "No, I'm sorry. It's not any of my business."

"I've learned in Northern Lakes that everyone's business is everyone else's business," Wynona said. There had certainly been a lot of gossip and speculation about her. Unfortunately, most of that had more to do with Gingrich and how much she'd known and how involved she'd been with the evil, little man.

Sam sighed. "True. Small towns. And family..."

"And family," Wynona repeated wistfully. She had no family anymore.

"With me and Trick, sure," Sam said. "We've always been in each other's business. But Mack has always been a loner. And now..."

"Now what?" Wynona pressed. "You obviously want to warn me or something."

"I don't know if he'll stick around," Sam said, and she flinched again as if the thought caused her pain. "And I know that there are people who want him to un-retire. They've been trying to find him."

"Do you think someone else could be trying to find him?" Wynona asked. He'd assured her that nobody was looking for him for revenge or whatever, but how could he know for certain? "From that old life of his, from whatever he did that had all those high security clearances?"

Sam smiled then, but even that looked a little pained. "You don't know any more about that life than the rest of us, huh?"

Wynona shook her head. "No. He just assured me that whoever was after him here wasn't from his previous life. That everybody he'd encountered back then had no idea who he was." Which was kind of how she felt now. Like she had no idea who he was.

"But his superiors know," Sam said. "And they want him back. They tracked him down through my dad."

A heaviness settled on Wynona's heart with the certainty that he would probably un-retire just like Sam seemed to suspect. "I had no expectations that he was going to stick around. I knew he was just here to help your husband. The only thing we really have in common is the same goal." And their inability to resist their desire for each other. "We both want to find and stop this saboteur."

"Is it a competition?" Sam asked. "Since you're here without him?"

"I just… I needed some space…"

"I get that," Sam said. "I had to get away from Braden for a while when I first fell for him, clear my head before I figured out what I really wanted."

"It's not like that," Wynona insisted. She was not falling for Mack McRooney. He was just a distraction. Like Sam and this conversation was, too. "And I need to check for that blood—"

Sam reached out and grasped her arm, squeezing, and a low growl slipped out of her mouth.

"What?" Wynona asked with alarm.

"I'm… I'm in labor," Sam said. "I think I have been for a

while now but I was thinking they were just Braxton Hicks contractions again. And now my water just broke..."

The grimaces. Sam hadn't been making those faces over their conversation, the arson investigator was having contractions. Ones that were close together from how often she'd flinched.

Wynona pulled out her cell phone to call for help, but she had a feeling it wouldn't get to them in time. That, with as close as those contractions were, the baby was going to beat the paramedics. And Wynona had to figure out how she could help Sam so that neither the mother nor the baby was lost.

The plan had gone to hell, just like where he was probably going to go as well. But at least he wouldn't go alone.

The saboteur had a backup plan to his original one, which had been to get Braden fired in disgrace. So that everyone would know that he hadn't been the best man for the superintendent job. When that hadn't happened, the plan had escalated.

And so had his rage. He was so damn angry that he didn't feel any remorse anymore. He didn't feel anything but that rage. And it was in that rage that he'd made his backup plan.

When it looked like the authorities, or Braden, were finally closing in on him, he wasn't going down without one last fight.

Without one last act of sabotage...

Chapter 23

Mack glanced across the console at the person who'd tried breaking into his cabin. "I can't believe you're here."

"You thought I would miss the birth of my first grandchild?" Mack Senior asked from the driver's seat of his pickup truck.

"No." His dad was always there for his family no matter how busy he'd been with his career. He'd always made his kids a priority. Unlike their mother...

Unlike Mack himself. That was why he'd come here, to help his siblings, to try to make up for all the years he hadn't been there for them. Trick had seemed to thaw the night before. Hopefully he was ready to forgive him. But if he did and Mack left again...

There would be no hope for their relationship. But that wasn't the only relationship Mack was concerned about ruining. Not that what he and Wynona had was a relationship. He wasn't sure what they were to each other, especially since she'd slipped out while he was asleep.

"I would have been here sooner," his dad said. "But I was busy fielding all those calls and visits from people looking for you." He arched his reddish brows over eyes that were the same green as Trick's. "A lot of very official looking people."

Mack shrugged. "They're wasting their time. I'm not going back." Especially now, not when Wynona was in danger. And even when she wasn't, Mack wasn't sure he would be able to leave her. "It's up here..." He directed his dad to drive toward her house, which was easy to find because of all the flashing lights and emergency vehicles. He cursed.

The police should have finished up at the scene last night, especially after the shooting at the firehouse. There should have been no need for an ambulance now. Unless...

Had Wynona been attacked again?

"This is the state trooper's house?" his father asked.

Mack didn't know if it was because of the house or because of the emergency vehicles that Mack Senior was questioning him.

"Yeah," Mack said. He knew for certain that he had to stay in Northern Lakes and as close to Wynona as he could because lately it seemed that if something bad happened, it happened to her. Or around her...

"She has to be okay..." he muttered. Because if she wasn't, he wasn't sure that he would be okay.

His dad barely braked the truck when Mack threw open the passenger's door and jumped out. His heart hammered in his chest as he ran toward the paramedic rig parked near Trick's truck. People were crowded around the back of it, and he shoved through them to see inside where he expected to find Wynona. But the woman sitting on the stretcher was blonde, her hair so dark with sweat that it took him a moment to realize she was his sister. "Sam?"

Then a cry filled the air, and he noticed the blanket-wrapped bundle in the arms of the man kneeling next to the stretcher. It wasn't Owen or Dalton, who were the paramedics, it was Braden.

"Sam!" Mack exclaimed now. She'd done it, his sister had become a mother.

"Sam!" Their dad echoed his shout, his voice cracking with emotion.

"Dad, you made it!" she said.

"Just a few minutes late, it looks like," the older Mack murmured, his eyes glistening.

"We were late, too," Trick said, his voice gruff. He was one of the hotshots standing around the open doors at the back of the rig.

"What do you mean?" Mack asked. And he looked at the bundle in Braden's arms. His brother-in-law's eyes were damp, too. "Who was late? What happened?"

"Your girlfriend delivered our nephew," Trick said.

"What?" He glanced around, looking for Wynona again.

"Thank God she was here," Sam said. And his sister, who was always so tough, started crying now. "I was so damn scared."

"Wynona called you a beast," Trick said, his voice warm as he spoke of the trooper. "That you were tough as hell."

"You both did well," Owen said. "But we still need to go to the hospital and get you and the baby checked out." He waved everyone back and began to shut the doors on them.

But Mack caught the edge of one of them. "They're really okay?" he asked through the emotion clogging his throat.

Owen grinned. "Yeah. I think your girlfriend might be more shook up than they were."

"Where is she?" Mack asked.

"She already headed to the hospital," Trick said.

"Why? Was she hurt again or did she reinjure herself?" he asked. "Her wrist is already sprained and she also has a concussion from when she and Owen crashed last night."

"She's a beast, too," Trick said with respect. "We all really misjudged her. She's super tough and super determined. That's why she went to the hospital, to talk to the wounded hotshots. We should have brought her into the investigation sooner. She probably would have already caught the saboteur."

Or the saboteur would have killed her by now. While he might have started out just trying to scare her off the investigation, once the perp realized that wasn't going to happen he would try harder to get rid of her.

That was why Mack had been so determined to get to her as soon as possible. He had to make sure that she stayed safe. And even though she was suspended from duty, she was obviously still working this case.

Like Trick said, she was determined to catch the saboteur. But once she did, the man wasn't going to go down without a fight and maybe not without taking her down, too. Mack had to make damn sure that didn't happen. Because if he lost her...

He wasn't sure what he would do.

Wynona couldn't stop shaking. She had helped deliver a baby before, during a ride-along while she was in the police academy. She'd helped then, but she hadn't been the only person responsible for the well-being of the mother and baby. And because of who this mother and baby were, Wynona had felt extra pressure.

She hadn't wanted anything to go wrong with Mack's sister and new nephew. Tears stung her eyes, but she blinked them back as she pulled into the parking lot of the hospital. That baby made her even more determined to catch the saboteur. That child was too young, too innocent, to lose any of his family now. He deserved to have his mother, father and uncles around to watch him grow up, and to support and guide him. Like her parents had supported and guided her.

Maybe too much since she'd felt so lost without them. She knew now what she had to do, though. She had to catch a very dangerous man.

Because with the saboteur on the loose, the Zimmers and McRooneys were all in danger, probably even the baby. As well as the rest of the hotshots and even townspeople. So screw her suspension, Wynona wasn't going to sit around and do nothing. Not when she knew she was capable. She'd saved Mack McRooney more than once, and she'd just delivered a baby. She was stronger than she'd realized she was, and she was smarter. She could take care of herself and this town. And she intended to stay…even if Mack left. But she wanted him to have the choice to leave or to stay. She didn't want that choice and his life taken from him. She cared too much.

Once she parked in the lot at the hospital she made a call on the cell phone she'd bought to replace the one she'd lost in the ravine.

"Sergeant Hughes," her boss answered.

"This is Wells."

"Not sure why you're calling me, Wells, you're suspended right now."

"If that's the case, then you'll be hearing from my lawyer," she said. "And I have a very good one who will make a case for discrimination and lack of support and resources, and you damn well know I have a case and I have the documentation to win that case."

She could hear the breath the man sucked in then released in a ragged sigh. "What do you want?" he asked.

"I want to know if any blood was recovered from the scene where the shells were found outside my house," she said.

"That's—how do you—why do you want to know?"

"Just tell me."

"Yes, is that all you want?"

"Of course not. This has been my case, and I want to close it," she said.

"You're too involved."

"And that's why I'm the only one who can close it." She suspected Mack could as well, but he wasn't a cop. She was, and she wanted to prove to everyone, including herself, that she was a good one. And she was beginning to believe that she was. She just had to finish this now. She had to put the saboteur away, so he couldn't hurt anyone else.

"You're hurt, and you don't even have a weapon."

"Who do you have stationed at the hospital for the hot-shots who've been shot?"

"Ford."

"Tell him he's working with me," she said. "But I want the arrest."

"It's going to take a while before the DNA comes back on that blood, and we have to get samples to match it to—"

"I'll get a confession," she said.

"What? Do you think you're Columbo now? Or what was that TV show with Kyra Sedgwick? *The Closer*?"

Wynona smiled. "Yes." She wanted to be a badass like that. "I'll get a confession."

The sergeant chuckled now. "I was wrong about you, Wells, and so was Gingrich. You just might make it yet."

She felt a rush of pride.

But then he added, "If you don't get yourself killed first."

"I just want to interview the hotshots who are in the hospital right now," she said.

"I already did that last night," he said. "Nobody saw anything."

"Somebody did," she said.

The saboteur.

And she was going to let him know that it was over, that the DNA would prove what he'd done and that an arrest was imminent. Whichever one of the wounded hotshots it was…

But she wasn't sure when she talked to them. She talked to the younger guys first before the older ones. Their reactions ranged from amused to annoyed.

But as she spoke to them, Ford was listening to something on his radio. When they stepped into the hall, he shared what Sergeant Hughes had just told him. "The casings and bullets from the first scene, the one at the cabin McRooney is renting, came back from ballistics with a match."

"Who?" she asked.

"Donovan Cunningham."

Armed with that knowledge, she went back to the hotshots, but one of them was already gone. It didn't matter that he'd run, the saboteur wasn't getting away.

He wasn't going to stay on the loose and harm other people. Not anymore.

He'd already hurt too many.

Braden had never felt such happiness and such fear in the same moment as he had when he'd showed up at Wynona Wells's house to find that his wife had delivered their son all on her own. Well, just her and the trooper.

He was so happy and so relieved that they were okay. A doctor just confirmed it. But after that confirmation he had to step outside the door where his father-in-law and brothers-in-law were waiting in the hall. He told Sam he was going to update her family, but he really just needed a moment to himself, a moment to regroup.

"Is something wrong?" Mack Senior asked with alarm. "Is Sam and the little guy all right?"

Braden nodded. "Yeah, they're both doing great."

Sam needed some stitches and would need some iron for the blood she'd lost at the scene. Remembering that had Braden feeling queasy again.

"Sam is so damn tough," he said with pride and awe in his wife. "And our son is strong and healthy, too."

"Of course he is," Mack Senior said. "He's a McRooney and a Zimmer."

"You're going to have to wait a few years to get him into hotshot training, old man," Trick said to his father with a teasing grin.

"I got the cigars!" Cody Mallehan announced as he came down the hall, leading a group of other hotshots.

At least the ones who weren't injured. They were still here, still in the hospital. And the thought of that made Braden feel sick all over again.

Hands slapped his back and shoulders while Hank gave him a big hug. And Cody gave him a bigger hug then handed him a cigar. "Congratulations, Daddy!"

Hank studied his face and cocked her head, making her braid swing over her shoulder. "What's wrong, boss? Is everything okay?"

Braden nodded. "I just…it's hard to be as happy as I should be without feeling guilty that some of the team is here, is hurt."

Cody cursed. "I know. This is crazy. Worse than the arsonist. Matt Hamilton just picked a few of us to go after. Now it feels like nobody is safe."

"What?" Younger Mack asked the question. "Why just a few of you?"

"Well, four of us," Cody said. "He went after Wyatt because Wyatt had been his mentor but didn't help him get on the team. And then Dawson for getting attention for saving some of those boy scouts. And me because I took the last open spot on the team. I got hired right after Bruce and Howie."

"You were supposed to stay with my team," Mack Senior grumbled. "Be a smoke jumper."

"You wanted me to have more experience as a hotshot first before you took me on as a smoke jumper," Cody reminded him.

"Yeah, you weren't supposed to stay."

"This town makes a person want to stick around," Cody said with a grin at Trick and a speculative glance at Mack Junior.

The younger Mack ignored the comment, and asked, "Who was the fourth? Who else did the arsonist go after?"

"Me, for not hiring him," Braden said. And he could just about see the gears turning in Mack's head. "What?"

"So Cody took the guy's spot. Have you taken something from someone, Braden?" Mack asked.

Braden tried to think, but Sam hadn't been involved with anyone when they met. She'd been like Trick and like he suspected the younger Mack was, unwilling to risk any relationship after their mother's desertion. He shook his head.

"What about your job?" Mack Junior asked him.

Older Mack chuckled. "You're one of the youngest hotshot superintendents."

"Gingrich said something about that," younger Mack said. "Like you just got the job because of that sixth sense thing of yours about fires…"

"Bullshit," Cody said. "He's good. That's why he got the job."

And lately that sixth sense hadn't been very reliable.

"Who else was trying for it?" Mack Junior asked. "Who else applied? There had to be someone else on the team who would have wanted to take it over and might have thought, because they were older and had more experience, that they were entitled to it."

Braden's head pounded as hard as his heart was suddenly pounding. "No..."

It couldn't be this simple. This basic. Because if it was, he'd been a fool not to realize sooner what the motive was for trying to hurt the team. To hurt him...

"Who?" Mack asked.

Braden swallowed hard, feeling like he was betraying them for even saying their names. But this had been his problem all along; he was too close to every team member to suspect any of them of being the saboteur.

"Who?" Mack prodded again.

"Donovan Cunningham, Ed Ward and Carl Kozak."

"And all three of them have gunshot wounds," Mack remarked. He was already walking away from them, already going off to talk to them.

"No," Braden murmured. He couldn't believe that it was one of them. Not guys he'd worked with for as long as he had. But part of him wished that it was one of them and that it could be proved because he wanted this all to be over. He wanted his family to be safe.

But that wouldn't be possible until the saboteur was caught.

Chapter 24

Wynona was supposed to be here. That was what the others had said, that she was heading to the hospital. Apparently, it didn't matter to her that she was suspended, she still intended to investigate.

Mack should have looked for her the minute he got to the hospital, but he'd wanted to make sure that his sister and nephew were all right. He'd wanted to be there for his family like he hadn't been in the past.

But if something happened to Wynona...

He would never forgive himself for not being there for *her*. Where could she have gone?

He got the room numbers for the three guys who'd wanted Braden's job, who might have started the sabotage to get Braden fired or at least to prove that they would have been the better choice for superintendent of the Huron Hotshot team.

He headed to Donovan Cunningham's room first. Wynona had made her opinion of the guy clear after the way she'd seen him disrespect Michaela Momber. He figured if she wanted to break anyone it would be Cunningham. But she wasn't in his room. Mack wondered if she was even in the hospital.

"Hey, how are you doing?" Mack asked.

Donovan flinched as he sat up. "I'll be better when I get the hell out of here."

"Any news on when that will be?" Mack asked.

Donovan shrugged then flinched. His wound was to his left shoulder. "Why? Are you missing me?"

"It's just been chaos over the past several days," Mack said.

"Yeah, ever since you showed up in town."

"This has nothing to do with me," Mack said. "Bad things were happening long before I came to town."

"Like some crooked FBI agent going after Rory Van-Dam," Donovan said. "You showed up then. What's your deal, McRooney? What do you really want?"

"What we should all want," Mack said. "The saboteur stopped."

Donovan flinched again, but he didn't move otherwise. "It's not me. I don't give a damn what she said about that ballistics report. She knows that I was framed."

"What?" Mack asked, his heart pounding heart. "What ballistics report?"

"The one that said my gun was used to shoot at you," Donovan said. "Anybody could have grabbed it out of my truck. I leave it in there all the time."

"But you didn't use it to shoot at me? At us?" Mack asked, fury building inside him. "Why the hell should I believe you?"

"Your girlfriend figured it out," Donovan said. "Didn't she tell you?"

"What?"

"Trooper Wells was already in here, grilling me, grilling all of us, and even after that report, she didn't arrest me. She knows it's not me."

Mack narrowed his eyes and studied his face, skeptical.

But he couldn't imagine her not arresting him unless she'd figured out who it really was.

"You doubt her?" Donovan asked, and he almost sounded hopeful.

Mack felt sick. "No. She's smart." She would have arrested Donovan if she'd really thought he was guilty.

"She had some bullshit story about finding blood at her house, swore it would get matched to whoever it was, the shooter that went after you and her..." Donovan shrugged again and flinched. "I told her it wasn't mine."

"And?"

"I think she went from room to room and then she came flying back in here. And it wasn't just about that report."

"Why?"

"Because Carl's gone. And she knows that he would have known about my gun. Hell, he might have been the only one who knew about it."

"Kozak?" Mack shook his head. "All he talks about is retiring."

"His wife talks about it," Donovan said. "It's why they split up. He's been staying at his pop's cabin out in the woods. I don't think it's far from your place."

Mack's stomach dropped. "Damn it." That was why Wynona wasn't here. "Did you tell Trooper Wells that?"

Donovan nodded.

"Where is it?" Because Mack had no doubt that was where he would find Wynona even though she had been suspended.

Donovan gave him directions, and Mack started for the door. "Wait," the older hotshot called him back.

Mack thought about ignoring him.

"You have to know something," he said. "Kozak's kind of a prepper. Guns. Rations. He's into the militia and protecting his place from trespassers or anyone else might try to tell him what to do."

Dread gripped Mack. "Protecting it how?"

"He's got stuff set up. Stuff that will go off if someone trespasses."

Mack cursed. "Did you tell the trooper that?"

Donovan closed his eyes and shook his head.

Mack cursed him. "You better hope like hell nothing's happened to her." He ran out then, and he hoped like hell that he got to her before something did.

It wasn't a confession. Wynona knew that. But Carl running after she'd told him about the blood at the scene was the same as an admission of guilt to her. And that ballistics report had made him look guiltier to her than it had made Donovan Cunningham look.

Sergeant Hughes was taking a bit more convincing. She was on the radio with him while Trooper Ford followed the directions that Donovan Cunningham had reluctantly given her. Obviously, he didn't want to believe that his buddy could have shot him or the other hotshots.

Carl hadn't reacted when she'd told him about the blood at her house. He'd just grinned and shrugged...while the others had actually been offended. And when she'd returned to his room, it was obvious he'd left in a hurry, slipping past Trooper Ford, who should have stopped him.

She glanced over the console at the trooper before speaking into the radio again. "We're going to need backup, Sergeant."

"The guy is wounded," Hughes replied.

"And he still shot other hotshots," she said.

Ford glanced nervously at her.

"We're going to talk to him," she said. "We'll get him to

turn himself in. He obviously knows it's over, or he wouldn't have run."

Ford let out a breath. "He probably headed to the airport then."

She nodded. "Yeah, he might not even be here." But she had a feeling that Kozak had no place else to go. Cunningham admitted that the guy's wife had thrown him out because he wouldn't retire. Being a hotshot was everything to him. It was who he was.

And without it...

He had nothing left to lose.

Maybe that was why Mack had taken so many chances since his retirement. Because he had nothing left to lose... but he had everything she wanted. Family. Friends. A home here in Northern Lakes, and if he wanted her, he had her, too.

"I'm concerned, sir," she spoke into the radio, "that he's going to take his own life."

"So you're calling this a welfare check?" Hughes asked. "Because you don't have a warrant yet."

"You need to get one," she said. "You need to compel him to give his DNA so we can check it against the blood found at my house."

The sergeant hesitated for a long moment then he released a shaky sigh. "You're right. I'll call the county prosecutor. I'll get that going. But you need to be careful, Wells."

"We'll just check, make sure he's okay," she said. "He left the hospital against medical advice as well. He hadn't been released. The doctor said she wanted to watch him especially for infection."

"Why him especially?"

"She couldn't officially give me his medical information, but I was able to get a look at the chart on his door.

His wound looked just a little bit older than the wounds of the other hotshots, and she had some concerns that it was already getting infected."

Sergeant Hughes let out a soft whistle. "He's your guy. How did he get past Ford?"

"I'm sorry, sir," Ford said.

"I mean, really, the guy was shot and has an infection," Hughes said. "He can't be that strong right now. He can't be that dangerous."

Wynona closed her eyes and wished he'd never said that because even though she normally wasn't a suspicious person, she felt like the sergeant had jinxed them somehow. That saying it wasn't that dangerous was going to make it especially so.

Ford, however, looked a lot less tense than he'd been. But he didn't know everything that the saboteur, that Carl Kozak, had already pulled off.

How many people he'd already hurt...

How long he'd terrorized and betrayed his own team.

Wynona didn't trust him. And she really wished she'd waited for Mack. But Mack wasn't a police officer. Despite all his clearances, he had no authority here.

And his family needed him. He had people who cared about him.

She had nobody.

But him...

But she really didn't even have him. According to his sister, his old life was calling him back, and she doubted that he would be able to ignore them, that he would be able to stay retired any more than Carl Kozak had wanted to retire.

His determination to stay working as a hotshot had ruined Carl's marriage and now his life. He hadn't just wanted to be a hotshot, though—he'd wanted to be in charge of the hotshots. That was probably why Carl had done what he had, to prove that Braden wasn't up to the challenges of the job and to gain the respect of his team.

Carl might have begrudgingly gained that respect because he'd hurt them without them ever realizing it was him this entire time. She could talk to him about that, about needing respect and use that as a way to relate to him, to talk him down. Because, after what he'd done, he must have lost the kind of respect that mattered most: self-respect. She understood that all too well, but she was getting hers back. She felt capable and competent in a way she hadn't felt before. She knew what she was doing. She was protecting as many people as she could, even Carl Kozak if he'd let her.

"This must be the driveway," Ford said as he stopped at the end of it. There was just enough space to turn off before a gate stopped any further access to the property that lay beyond it, to that cabin in the woods.

Again, Wynona had an uneasy feeling rush over her, that uneasiness that Sergeant Hughes had jinxed them.

"Stop here," Wynona said. "Out on the road, and let's make sure we're ready for this…"

"For what?" Ford asked. "We're just going to make sure that he's okay. That he hasn't killed himself or passed out from an infection, right?"

"Right," she said. That was her intention, but she had no idea what Carl Kozak's intentions were. But she was glad that she'd taken a few precautions moments later when she buzzed the intercom at the gate and a shot rang out, dropping her to the ground.

More bullets pinged off the car, striking the metal, shattering the glass.

Now she knew what Carl's intentions were. He wasn't

going down without a fight. And he was going to hurt as many people as he could before he was done. Probably even himself...

Trooper Wynona Wells had played him at the hospital. Carl knew that now. The sneaky bitch had wanted him to react, to run, just like he had. But the thing was, she probably hadn't been lying to him. There had to have been blood left near her house. His blood.

The blood that was seeping out of the wound he'd reopened when he'd run. He had more bandages on the kitchen table, but he ignored them to study the video playing out live on his laptop screen. Except nothing was moving. And she had to be bleeding now, too. Or maybe she was dead.

It wasn't going to end with her death, though. Others would come for him. Cops and undoubtedly hotshots, too. Especially one of them: Mack McRooney.

McRooney was more than a little attached to the state trooper, and he was going to be pissed that she was gone. That he hadn't been able to rush to her rescue this time like he had every time before.

He was too late to help her. And he would be too late to save himself from Carl's final acts of sabotage.

Carl was ready for Mack McRooney. He was ready for all of them. Just like he'd been ready for Trooper Wells.

She hadn't been ready for him, though. And she might have paid the ultimate price for her stupidity—her life.

Chapter 25

Mack drove as fast as he could to where Donovan had sent Wynona. Had the guy realized what he was doing? That he could have been sending her to her death?

Braden needed to overhaul his whole team because there was more than one person on it that couldn't be trusted. But Carl Kozak wasn't going to have to be fired. While Donovan had called him a prepper, Mack knew that it wasn't for the end of days.

It was for this. For his end...

For the moment that he was finally revealed as the saboteur. He wasn't going to surrender or risk being arrested. And he was going to take out as many people as he could on his own way out.

And Wynona, as the one who'd figured it out first, would be the first Kozak would try to take out. Just as the saboteur had been the most focused on her recently, trying to get her out of his way. Because he knew that she would be the one who would want to bring him to justice, to arrest him.

Mack pressed his foot down harder on the accelerator and gripped the steering wheel for the curve in the road. But as he rounded that curve, he nearly passed it...

The police SUV parked in front of a gate at the end of a gravel driveway. If not for that gate, the driveway wouldn't even be noticeable. It would have looked like any other two-track or off-road vehicle trail winding through all the forests in the Northern Lakes area. But that gate gave it away, that there was someone here who didn't want other people getting to him. Hopefully that had been enough of a signal to tip off Wynona to the danger.

Mack slammed on his brakes and pulled off to the shoulder of the road near that SUV, and that was when he noticed the holes in it and the shattered glass.

Pain gripped his heart, squeezing it.

"No, no..."

He was already too late. She'd already come under attack. She had to be okay. She had to be...

Mack reached under his seat and grabbed his weapon. Where the hell had those shots come from? Then he saw it, the barrel sticking out of one of the posts for the gate, the one across from the intercom. Keeping low and to the side of the road, Mack moved from the side of his truck to the back of the police SUV. He rounded it carefully until he got to the lowered driver's side window.

And a gun stuck out the side window toward him. "Don't—oh, McRooney..."

Mack recognized the trooper who'd helped out from time to time at the scene of every bad experience he and Wynona had had, every brush with death. "Where is she?"

"Wells? She's on the ground," Ford said, his voice cracking with fear. "I didn't know if I should try to get to her. Or just wait for help..."

That pain squeezed Mack's heart harder. "What about you? Are you hit?"

The young man shook his head. "She told me to take the shield."

Donovan Cunningham hadn't warned her like he had

Mack, but Wynona was so smart she'd figured out the threat. And she'd protected her co-worker.

But not herself?

That woman cared more about everyone else than she cared about herself. She was so damn incredible. And she could not be gone.

She had to be okay. He would not be if she wasn't. But the panic gripping him paralyzed him for a moment, and he could only stare at her body lying on the ground, not moving. She lay near the gatepost that had an intercom on it. An intercom that had probably activated that gun. Another trap, another act of sabotage, from the saboteur.

"I called for help," Ford said. "Officer down. They're on their way."

Mack could hear the high-pitched wail of sirens in the distance, approaching quickly. But not fast enough for him...

Or for Wynona.

He dropped down and crawled across to where she lay on her stomach. That gun would have shot her right in the back when she pressed the intercom. But he didn't see any blood on her back.

"Wynona," he said. "Wynona..." And he rolled her over to find her staring up at him.

"Stay down," she whispered back at him furiously.

"Are you okay?"

She nodded. "Yeah, but I know he's watching..."

So she'd played dead. She was so damn smart.

Relief overwhelmed him, and Mack leaned down and pressed a kiss against her lips, as he felt something stinging his eyes. Like tears.

"You're really all right?" he asked, his voice cracking with the emotions overwhelming him.

"Yeah, I'm wearing a vest," she said matter-of-factly.

"And you gave Ford the shield." She'd also been the one who had stepped out to do the intercom that couldn't be reached from inside a vehicle. Carl had set up quite a trap. And Mack suspected this wasn't the only one. "This is going to be too dangerous for anyone to go in there to try to get him."

"Sergeant Hughes can bring in SWAT," she said.

"Or me."

"What?" she gasped.

And he was worried that she was hurt. Even with the vest on, she could still have a broken rib. The force of the bullets could have caused internal injuries.

"I can get him," Mack said. After what the guy had done to her, how he'd hurt her again and again, Mack really needed to be the one to bring him in.

"I'm sure he has stuff set up to shoot or explode all over his property," she said.

"I know he does," Mack said. "Donovan Cunningham warned me."

She gasped. "But not me…"

"He's a son of a bitch, too," Mack said. "Braden's going to lose more than Carl from the team before this is all over." Those young guys had always been with Carl and Donovan, and Mack wondered how much they knew and how bad their attitudes were as well.

"He'll lose you, too," she said. "You can't go in there. You have no authority."

"I can get the authority," he said. He had no doubt about that, though he just might have to un-retire to do it. But he couldn't risk anyone else getting hurt when this was something he had experience doing, an experience that very few others had ever survived enough times to gain. "And I know about setups like this," he said. "I've maneuvered them before to get hostages out."

"I'm going with you," she said.

"You're suspended," he reminded her.

"Not anymore. Hughes reinstated me."

He could imagine how hard she'd had to fight for that. But he wasn't surprised she'd won. She was fierce.

"You have a sprained wrist," he said. He shouldn't have had to remind her of that. It should still be hurting like hell. But she didn't appear to be in pain, or maybe she couldn't feel it because she was so damn mad. Her face was flushed with anger. He felt that rage, too.

For months Carl had been putting the lives of people Mack cared about in danger. His brother Trick. Rory. Braden. And now Wynona...

And he was beginning to suspect he cared about her most of all. But the thought of that, of loving someone and losing them, scared him more than any trap the saboteur might have set for them.

"My wrist isn't sprained on my shooting hand," she said.

He smiled at her determination even while he worried that it was going to get her killed. It nearly had.

"And if you go in there without me, I'm going to follow you in anyway," she said. "I'll be safer with you than trying to maneuver my way on my own."

He cursed. "Wynona, it's too dangerous." And he'd lost too many people who hadn't listened to him. Who'd tried to follow him...

"We can get him—together," she said. "It's when we try to go after him on our own that we get hurt."

She was right about that. Or at least she was right about those times in the past. But he couldn't help but worry she was wrong this time. And that it might be more dangerous with them together.

"You would have to listen to me," he said, "and do everything I tell you to do."

She nodded. Then she called out to Ford. "Back the SUV up and block the road. Don't let anyone through and don't let anyone follow us inside."

"Wells—"

"I don't want anyone else getting hurt," she said.

And Mack knew why. She hadn't been able to save her parents from that horrible illness, so she was determined to save as many other people as she possibly could.

Even him...

That was why she was so determined to go with him. Mack wanted to believe that it was as personal to her as it was to him, that she cared about him, too. But he knew she had such a big heart, with so much love to give, that she cared about everyone, no matter how crappy they'd treated her.

She was an amazing person, a person that the world needed. That Northern Lakes needed. That he needed.

But if he didn't let her go inside with him, she would try to follow him. And he would lose her for certain. So he had to let her join him and make sure that Carl didn't succeed the next time he tried to take her out.

Because he was definitely going to try to take them both out.

For good.

Wynona trusted Mack knew what he was doing, that he'd done it before. So she followed him, stepping where he told her to, ducking when he told her to...

As they crept around the property, more shots rang out and the ground dropped away in places, and things swung out of trees and seemingly out of nowhere. But Mack anticipated every single one, like it was some live-action video game he'd played so many times that he knew exactly what was going to happen next.

He was keeping them both alive. But she couldn't believe how dangerous it was and how many brushes with death he must have had in the past to know what to look for, what not to trust, what area to avoid.

Part of Wynona wished she'd avoided the whole thing. But she hadn't been about to let him go in alone. And he'd known that, known that she would follow him regardless of the threat. Did he know how she felt about him?

How hard she'd fallen for him?

She wanted to tell him, but she didn't want to distract him. He was too focused. And his focus was the only thing probably keeping them alive at the moment.

She wouldn't have noticed many of the things that he had. While some traps had been obvious, there had been others that she wouldn't have guessed.

But Mack knew because he'd encountered them before. But what if Carl had concocted something the former special forces agent hadn't seen before?

Mack was in the lead. Whatever it was would hit him first. And she would be helpless to stop it, to protect him…

Her heart pounded furiously as they continued moving slowly through the trees. And finally, she could see the glimmer of the metal roof of a building poking out through moss and tree brush.

They'd found Carl's cabin. And then he stepped out onto the front porch. "I knew it would be you," he yelled. "I knew you would be the one who finally caught me! But it's too late now…too late for all of us!"

And then he touched something in his hand and the whole world exploded.

* * *

Leaving his wife and baby in the hospital had been hard, but Braden was glad now that he had. He needed to be here with the rest of the hotshot crew even though they hadn't been allowed very close to the scene. He needed to know how this ended and make sure that it did end.

He also needed to be here for his oldest brother-in-law because Mack had taken it upon himself to personally go after and try to apprehend the saboteur.

Before they'd left the hospital, Donovan had warned the hotshots that it wasn't safe for anyone to go after Carl, that he'd set up his place to withstand whoever came after him.

But if anyone could maneuver his way around whatever obstacles Carl had set up, it was Mack. Or so Braden hoped because his wife couldn't lose her older brother. They'd already been apart too long.

"Mack is really good at this kind of thing," Trick said as he paced the road where troopers had set up a barricade. "Or there wouldn't be people trying to get him to un-retire."

While Trick paced, Braden stood next to that barricade, trying to listen to the troopers' radios as they communicated with each other. The troopers wouldn't allow the hotshots through to the scene because it was too dangerous. Too dangerous even for the police to try to get inside, but Wynona Wells had gone with Mack.

"He knows what he's doing," Trick said, but he sounded more like he was trying to convince himself than Braden. "He'll make it out of there…"

But then a sudden blast shook the ground underneath all of them and thick smoke rolled out from between the trees. Then flames licked up, springing up all around the trees. And more explosions went off.

"We have to get back!" one of the troopers yelled.

But at that moment Braden wasn't worried about himself. He was worried about Mack and Wynona Wells. Had they survived? Had anyone?

Chapter 26

Wynona awoke with a start. But she had no idea where she was, if she was even still alive. That explosion…

And Carl Kozak. There was no way he had survived that. What about Mack?

He'd been ahead of her. He'd been closer to the cabin than she'd been when it had exploded. And she was hurt…

Her body felt bruised all over as her muscles throbbed and her bones ached. If she'd been hurt that badly, Mack had to have been hurt worse. She opened her mouth to speak, but no words came out. Her throat was so dry.

Had she survived?

Or was this some kind of hell?

"You're awake," someone said. The voice was female, so it was probably the ER doctor, Smits, or a nurse. But when Wynona turned her head, she found a familiar woman standing beside her bed.

"Sam…" she rasped. She tried to sit up, but the pain in her head intensified for a moment. "Mack…?"

Sam nodded. "He's okay. He never lost consciousness like you did. Something must have hit you…" Sam shuddered for a moment as if she could imagine how dangerous it had been and the things that had flown around in that explosion.

Wynona closed her eyes, but then she could see it, too.

What had happened to Carl. That cabin must have been full of explosives. And unable to bear that image, she jerked her lids open again. "He's not hurt?"

"Carl's dead," Sam said. "But Mack is good."

Then why wasn't he here?

Didn't he care about her at all? And why was his sister here?

"Mack warned the others," Sam said with obvious pride in her big brother. "He wouldn't let anyone else onto that property. And he carried you out..."

"Is he really okay?" Wynona asked. Because she couldn't imagine how he had survived... "Are you telling me the truth?"

Sam nodded. "Do you think you would be here in the hospital if he hadn't gotten you out of there? It was crazy for you to go in there with him. And he's blaming himself for letting you go and for you getting hurt..." Tears sprang to Sam's blue eyes then.

"It was my fault," Wynona said. "I was determined. He knew that I would follow him if he didn't let me go inside with him." She'd intended to keep him safe, and he was the one who'd saved her life.

"That's what I like about you," Sam said. "You're tough. You're brave."

"I could have gotten killed and gotten Mack killed, too," Wynona admitted. "You should be mad at me for putting your brother in danger."

Sam chuckled. "I don't think my brother has ever not been in danger. It's what he does. And I could never be mad at you, not after you helped me deliver my son."

"That was all you," Wynona said.

"I would have lost it without you there," Sam said. "You kept me sane. I want you to be his godmother."

"What?"

"My son," Sam said. "I want you to be his godmother."

"But Henrietta Rowlins…she's going to be your sister-in-law." Wynona knew that the female hotshot and Sam's brother Trick were engaged.

Sam nodded. "Yes. But even Hank admits that she wouldn't have handled that like you did. My son's name is Mackenzie Wells Zimmer."

Tears sprang to Wynona's eyes now. She'd felt so alone for so long, so unconnected to anyone. But Sam McRooney-Zimmer was the last person she'd expected to form such a connection to. "That's…that's not necessary," she said but then admitted, "I love it, though." And she would love that child. From the moment she'd helped him out into the world, she'd felt a connection to him, too.

But neither of those connections was as strong as the one she felt to Mack McRooney. But he must not have felt the same way because he wasn't even here. "He's gone, isn't he?" she asked his sister.

Sam didn't ask her who she was talking about, she just nodded. And those tears pooled in her eyes again.

Mack had had no choice. He'd had to go back. When he'd called in a favor so that he could go in with Wynona to apprehend Carl Kozak, he'd had to commit to doing a favor in return. But he hadn't been about to let her go in without him. And really, calling in a favor with Homeland Security had been the right call.

Carl Kozak had been a domestic terrorist. The worst kind. He'd terrorized the people who were supposed to be his friends, his teammates.

He was the worst kind of traitor in Mack's opinion. He'd

turned on those he was supposed to protect, and he'd tried to hurt them.

Kozak had hurt Wynona. And even though the man was dead, Mack wasn't about to forgive Carl Kozak for doing that. He wasn't sure he could forgive himself if he'd hurt her when he'd taken off. Leaving her had been so damn tough because she hadn't regained consciousness before the helicopter had come for him.

But this was seriously the last time. His very last mission. And he thought his superiors, his former superiors, finally understood. Because once he'd wrapped it up, he'd headed right back to Northern Lakes.

No. That little job he'd had to do, that hadn't been his last mission. This was...

And it might be his most dangerous yet. For more than one reason.

"Put your hands up and turn around slowly," a female voice ordered him. "Who the hell are you?"

His arms high above his head, he slowly turned toward her, and he saw the recognition on her face, the way her green eyes widened. But she didn't lower her weapon yet. "Are you going to shoot me?" he asked.

She quickly pulled back the gun as if she hadn't realized she was holding it. Then she slipped on the safety and holstered it. "What are you doing here?"

"I'm back."

"What are you doing sneaking around my yard in the dark?" she asked. "Are you trying to get shot?"

"I didn't think you would be so edgy now that it's over," he said. Or he might have come up with a better plan. As it was, he hadn't even made it into her backyard yet. She'd caught him in the side yard.

She sighed, but it sounded a little shaky. "It is over..."

And for the first time he felt a pang of concern. Was she talking about them? Now that the saboteur was caught, did she think they had nothing else in common? No reason to be together.

"No," he said with a bit of panic. Just because he'd figured out that he belonged here didn't mean that she felt the same way about that or about him. "It's not over, Wynona."

"You and I both saw what happened to Carl," she said. "The only problems the hotshots will have to deal with from now on are fires."

"I know that's over," he said. His family would be as safe as they would ever be, as anyone could ever be. "But us... I don't want us to be over, Wynona."

"Us?" she asked.

"You and me, we're a great team," he said. "We work well together."

"Are you trying to recruit me for your next mission?" she asked, and there was a trace of humor in her voice now. And her hand wasn't anywhere near her weapon now.

"No. You are my next mission," he said.

Her brow furrowed. "What are you talking about?"

"You," he said. "I just want to be with you, Wynona."

"That's why you left when I was in the hospital?" she asked, and there was an edge back in her voice again. Anger. Pain.

He had hurt her.

"I didn't have a choice," he said. "I had to pay back a favor. I never would have left you if it was up to me."

She wrapped her arms around herself now as if she was cold. He would have asked her to go inside the house with him, but he had a feeling she wasn't going to welcome him back. "I've heard that's what you do, Mack. You take off when people need you..."

He flinched. "I was worried that that's what I do. That I'm like my mother. That I'm selfish and don't care about other people's feelings. But I'm not like her." He was more like his dad than he'd realized.

"You took off," she said.

"Not because I wanted to," he said. "And I came back as quickly as possible."

"Why?" she asked, and that suspicion was still there.

"Because I love you."

She gasped.

"And I never intend to leave you again."

She snorted. "Until the next mission."

"No. I mean it, this is my last one," he said. "You. Us."

She shook her head as if she couldn't accept what he had to say or his love. "You're going to miss the adventure. The danger. You're not going to stay."

"I don't know, this town has been pretty dangerous for me," he said. "And I need to stick around and look out for my nephew."

"My godson," she said. "I just got back from babysitting him for Braden and Sam." And now there was a softness and affection in her voice. She was already falling for the little boy.

"He's my godson, too." He'd already talked to Sam and Braden and Trick. He and Trick were good, really good now. Mack had apologized to him and promised to make up for letting him down when they were kids. But Trick had already forgiven him.

Mack had saved her for last. For always...

Her brow furrowed as she stared at him in the faint moonlight. "I guess I can share him with you."

He smiled at how possessive she sounded over his nephew. But if he had his way, little Mack would be her nephew, too. "He's not all I want to share with you, Wynona." He held out his hand to her.

She stared at it for a long moment.

"You don't trust me," he said.

"I don't trust me," she said.

"You should, Wynona. You're smart and strong and so damn beautiful…" His chest ached with the love he felt for her. "I missed you so much."

She blinked, as if she was fighting tears. And he knew she'd missed him, too. "I didn't think you were coming back…"

"It wasn't a dangerous job," he said. "Nothing like what Carl put us through…"

"I didn't think you were coming back," she repeated.

"I wish I just told you how I felt, how I was falling for you," he said. "But I was so scared."

She cocked her head and eyed him with skepticism. "You were scared?"

He nodded. "You scare the hell out of me. What I feel for you…"

"You love me?" She still sounded skeptical.

"With all my heart," he said. "Will you take a chance on me, Wynona? Will you trust me to stick around?"

She shrugged and sighed. "I don't know…"

And he wondered if he'd been the only one who'd fallen. Maybe she really didn't care about him at all. He sucked in a breath. "I guess you and my brother Trick are right about me. I am too cocky. Too sure of myself. I'm sorry. I thought you cared about me, too."

He started to walk past her, back to his truck, but she reached out and caught his hand, stopping him.

"Don't run off now," she said.

"No more running," he said. "I'm too old and I'm retired. No wonder you're not interested in me."

She laughed. "I am more than interested in you, and you know it. I love you but…"

"But?"

She drew in a deep breath. "I'm afraid to lose anyone else."

"You're not going to lose me," he said. "I'm staying. You're going to get sick of me I'll be around so much."

"I will never get sick of you."

"And I will never get sick of you," he said. "But I felt sick when you got hurt, when I had to leave you. I'm so sorry, Wynona. I will never do that again."

"You might," she said.

He shook his head.

"If you have to rush off to save the world, I'll be okay with that," she said. "As long as you always come back."

He closed his arms around her then. "I will always come back to you." He leaned down and kissed her, deeply, passionately, with all the love he felt for her.

And she kissed him back for a long moment before she pulled away. Then she asked, "Where were you going? Why didn't you come up to my front door?"

He entwined his fingers with hers and led her around to the back patio which was aglow with lights and people. And as they rounded the corner, everyone applauded. All of the hotshots were there and some of the townspeople and her co-workers.

"What's going on?" she asked.

"It's a welcome home party," he said.

"For you?" she asked, and she laughed.

"For you, Wynona," he said. "I know you felt like you lost your home when your parents passed away. I know how alone you felt, so I wanted to make sure that you knew that you were home now. That Northern Lakes is your home."

She wrapped her arms around him and hugged him tightly. "No. You're my home, Mack. I love you."

Braden had wanted to step down as the hotshot superintendent, but his team had refused to let him. They'd insisted that he needed to stay on as their leader. But he knew who the true leader was.

The heart.

In the end they'd all followed it. His hotshots were all in love and happy. And with his wife and his son, he was happier than he'd ever been.

And he could see that it was the same for his brothers-in-law. Trick and Hank had finally set a date for their wedding now that the saboteur was gone. And he could see from the way that Mack and Wynona Wells clung to each other, that they would be getting married soon, too.

And he suspected there would be more kids coming along to grow up with little Mack. Little kids of his and Sam's as well as cousins and friends.

His team was a family. And now they were finally all safe and happy.

* * * * *

Romantic Suspense

Danger. Passion. Drama.

Available Next Month

Targeted With A Colton Beth Cornelison
A Spy's Secret Rachel Astor

Vanished In Texas Karen Whiddon
Christmas Bodyguard Katherine Garbera

🕊 LOVE INSPIRED
Trail Of Threats Jessica R. Patch
Unravelling Killer Secrets Shannon Redmon
Larger Print

🕊 LOVE INSPIRED
Fugitive Search Dana Mentink
Witness Escape Sami A. Abrams
Larger Print

🕊 LOVE INSPIRED
Sorority Cold Case Jacquelin Thomas
Hunted In The Mountains Addie Ellis
Larger Print

6 brand new stories each month

Romantic Suspense

Danger. Passion. Drama.

MILLS & BOON

Keep reading for an excerpt of a new title
from the Intrigue series,
RANCH AMBUSH by Brab Han

Chapter One

Can you ever go home again?

The question hit a little too close as Duke Remington parked his truck in front of the two-story farmhouse where he'd spent most of his happiest moments during childhood.

The white siding with green shutters, metal roof and wraparound country porch had seen better days, but his grandfather Lorenzo Remington was too proud to accept more help than he deemed necessary or could afford to hire.

Early October in Mesa Point, Texas, the weather was always a crapshoot. This year, the record-setting string of hundred-plus-degree temperatures fueled a drought that threatened to dry up the shifty soil and swallow homes whole.

As far as the farmhouse went, between Duke, his two sisters and three cousins, they could have the place spruced up in a couple of weekends. Grandpa Lor wouldn't hear of it.

The fact that Duke's beloved grandfather and grandmother were lying in separate hospital beds in the ICU instead of here at the paint horse ranch they loved hit him hard. His grandparents had defied the odds just by being high school sweethearts who went the distance. Could they do it again by surviving a horrendous car wreck? If ever there was a time for either one of their stubborn streaks to kick in, it was now.

Duke exited his truck as the sun began to climb. He'd driven from his home south of Austin to Mesa General Hospital the minute he'd received word about the crash. He'd been able to arrange leave from work first. He, his siblings and cousins planned to work out a rotation. Blinking through blurry eyes that had been open for over twenty-four hours straight, he caught sight of Nash Shiloh making a beeline toward him from the barn.

Nash, as they called him, had worked the ranch since what felt like the dawn of time but was more like sixty years. Hired at fifteen as a ranch hand before working his way up over the years to foreman, he'd been the only one permitted to hang around. Folks said all he needed to do was put his hands on a horse to hear its thoughts, which was a miracle in Duke's book. It was a gift he didn't have with horses or people, unless criminals counted. There, he seemed to excel at reading their minds and anticipating their next steps.

As a US marshal, Duke encountered his fair share of felons in need of capture and could hold his own thanks to his unique gift. At least, *gift* was the label his skill had been given by his fellow marshals. Was it what he would call it? No. There wasn't anything special about him. He couldn't read other people's thoughts. There was just a thin line between having the kind of mind that caught criminals and being one. A long time ago, Duke had realized he could stand on either side of that line. Doing good had been a choice, and he wouldn't have it any other way.

The older man's sun-worn skin practically hung on his bones at seventy-plus years old. Despite his age, Nash was still strong as an ox and could lift more hay bales than half the seasonal ranch hands four decades younger than him. But his age was starting to show in the slight limp in his right leg and the way his shoulders rounded on his six-foot frame.

Nash still had a full head of hair, and his mind was sharp as ever. "You're a sight for sore eyes."

Duke met the foreman halfway and brought him into a bear hug. "I should have been here so it didn't happen."

"You couldn't have known," Nash said with compassion. He was too quick to let Duke and the others off easy. Like when they'd painted stripes on one of the horses and then put a sign up in the barn that read Beware of Zebras. "Heck, I would have driven to pick up the new saddles myself, but the old man…" His eyes flashed at Duke. "Your grandpa wanted to take his wife out for a fancy lunch in town."

The words *fancy* and *in town* weren't something Duke thought he'd hear in his lifetime about Mesa Point. There wasn't much that would be considered extravagant about the small town. Not since the oil boom in the '70s and '80s when high-end stores brought merchandise to the ladies in town since most wouldn't set foot in a city.

Mesa Point had a small country club that barely survived the oil crash. Its green decor, complete with flowery wallpaper, was straight out of a different era. If the walls could talk, Duke had no doubt they would whisper scandals from back in the club's heyday. He'd heard of everything from affairs in the bathrooms to envelopes fat with cash being handed to golf caddies to "help" with a score or stand guard in front of a supply closet to make sure no one entered unless invited. Today, Mesa Point Golf and Social Club barely kept its doors open.

"How's the marshal business?" Nash asked in his characteristic excitement mixed with a favorite-uncle kind of warmth.

"Keeping me busy," Duke admitted before adding, "It's the reason I don't come home very often."

Nash shot him a look that meant Duke didn't have to explain. "You're here when it counts."

Duke nodded, trying to shake off the feeling that he'd let his grandparents down when they needed him most. What if they'd done that to him when his mother died after giving birth to Duke's younger sister and his father ran off?

Duke was the only son in a daughter sandwich, a middle child, except that he'd grown up with cousins Dalton and Camden who were like brothers to him. He and his sisters, Crystal and Abilene, were close as could be. His cousin Jules, or otherwise known professionally as Julie, was the middle child on her side of the family. Although, none of them ever thought of sides when thinking about each other. They were the Remington Six as far as anyone was concerned.

"Any change in their condition?" Nash asked, ushering Duke toward the back door of the farmhouse.

"Not yet," he responded in a voice that was probably too hopeful.

"They'll pull through," Nash said with a conviction that Duke didn't feel. "In the meantime, you should eat breakfast and get settled in." He paused, looking like he was trying to choose his next words carefully. "Have you decided how long you'll be staying on?"

"I took personal leave from work," Duke said, not loving the fact that he'd handed off several case files he'd been working on for weeks now. "I'm here to assess the situation and report back to the others so we can set up a rotation if needed."

Nash opened the screen door to the back porch, toed off his boots and then headed for the kitchen. "Scrambled eggs and sausage okay with you?"

"No. I'm fine. Don't go to any—"

"It's no trouble," Nash cut in with a hand wave, like he was batting a fly from a horse's behind.

Duke knew when he'd lost an argument, so he stopped himself from saying that he should be the one cooking breakfast for Nash.

Being inside his grandparents' home without them here sucked the air out of the room. Tears welled up. Emotion wasn't usually in his vocabulary. This seemed like a convenient time to remember he'd left his gym bag behind the driver's seat of his truck. His damn emotions had him thinking about someone else, too. But he didn't want to think about her after all these years.

"I'll eat whatever you put on the table as long as you let me clean up after." Before Nash could protest, Duke put a hand up and continued, "I need to get something out of my truck, so you're going to have to hold that thought."

Jogging out to the truck gave Duke a moment of reprieve from the tsunami of emotions threatening to suck him under and spit him out. Being home always reminded him of Audrey Smith, now Newcastle, and the summer she'd spent here. Then school started. She'd disappeared. But not without shattering his tender sixteen-year-old heart. For reasons he didn't want to examine, he had yet to forget that summer fourteen years ago.

Sure, Duke could blame his long memory on the fact a guy never forgot his first kiss, especially one that sizzled with the kind of promise that had been unmatched since. He'd chalked his past physical reaction up to teen hormones over finding real love when he was barely old enough to drive, let alone shave.

It had taken most of the summer for Audrey to warm up to him. Even then, she refused to speak about her past or what happened for her to end up needing a place to hide. He'd fallen fast and hard. And then she was gone. His grandparents had kept quiet about her whereabouts, asking him to respect her need for privacy even though he could hear the regret in their tones. They'd told him she left a message for him asking him to leave her alone. She'd said they were over and their relationship had been nothing more than a summer fling. With a nonworking cell number and no social media to follow, Duke had no choice but to try to forget Audrey Smith had ever entered his life.

A couple of years back, he'd heard a rumor she was back in Mesa Point as Audrey Newcastle. Married? Divorced?

He couldn't say one way or the other. He'd made a vow not to ask questions after her rejection.

Plus, Duke rarely ever visited his hometown except to spend an afternoon here and there with his grandparents, mainly doing work he worried they were getting too old to do despite his grandfather being too stubborn to admit it. True days off were rare because Duke loved his work as a US marshal and dedicated himself to searching for the most hardened criminals to lock them away and keep them from hurting other individuals. He sure wasn't planning to track down an old flame that sputtered out almost before it was lit.

Besides, during his visits to Remington Paint Ranch over the years, which weren't as often as they should have been, he never once ran into Audrey. Not at the feed store. Not at the post office. And not at the local diner where it seemed everyone passed through on the weekend to catch up on town happenings.

Audrey didn't want to have any contact with him after she'd disappeared, or she would have reached out at some point. She'd been clear about breaking up and there wasn't squat he could do about it then or now.

He'd come to understand she must have needed protection before. But now? She'd been back years and his number never changed.

Duke shook off the reverie. The morning sun beat down on him, indicating it would be another hot one. Texas heat had a bottom-of-his-boot-melting type of intensity. The summer had been brutal. Fall wasn't turning out to be much better. With sweat already beading on his forehead, he grabbed his gym bag and started toward the back door.

His cell buzzed. He fished it out of his pocket.

"What's up, Crystal?" he asked his older sister after checking the screen. Duke was the second born. Abilene, aka Abi, was the baby at twenty-eight years old. His sisters and cousins were US marshals. Each had their own reasons, but the seed had been planted long ago by their grandfather who'd been on the job to buy and support the ranch until he could work Remington Paint Ranch full time alongside his wife.

"First of all, how are they?" Crystal asked, referring to their grandparents.

"It's as bad as we feared," he admitted, raking his fingers through his hair. "They're both in comas and the road to recovery might be rocky."

"How soon do you need us there?" she asked.

"We can stick to the plan for now," he said. "I just updated the group chat so we're on the same page. Since we have to plan for the long haul, I think we should stick to the rotation we discussed."

That rotation would have Crystal taking leave next.

"I'll stop by as much as I can in the meantime," she stated, sounding as tired as he felt. Being physically tired was one thing. This was emotional draining, which was worse.

"Sounds good," he said on a sigh. Since he'd sent an update via the chat, this couldn't be the main reason for her call. "What else is going on?"

"Heard some chatter coming from the western district that I thought you might want to check out while you're in town," Crystal said. Her ominous tone added to the dark cloud overhead.

"What is it?" he asked, figuring he could make time for a pit stop after breakfast if work needed him to go somewhere. If this wasn't an emergency, he could use a shower and an hour or two of shut-eye.

Crystal hesitated, which caused Duke's blood pressure to rise. "It might be nothing, however..."

"Go on," he urged.

"You know the Ponytail Snatcher?"

"The guy who has been traveling around Texas targeting female deputies, and then torturing them before cutting off their ponytails, killing them and burying them in a shallow grave?" he asked. "What about him? He's been quiet for more than a month."

"An FBI agent tracked the perp down to a motel an hour from Mesa Point," she continued. "It's probably nothing more than a weird feeling on my part but I was studying the case, and the deputies have a lot of the same physical features as Audrey. I would feel better if someone checked on her. Since you're the one in town and our grandparents can't, I thought—"

"Do you have her address?" he asked, doing his level best not to give away his reaction—an emotional reaction that had no business rearing its head in connection with a work tip, no matter what their history had been. He'd heard Audrey had become a deputy and wondered why she'd chosen Mesa Point to live and work.

Crystal rattled off the location of a small cabin by the lake. He ignored the fact he'd kissed Audrey for the first time near that location before there'd been a development there. It couldn't have meant much to her, so it shouldn't make a difference to him, either.

"I got it," he ground out.

"Are you sure?" Crystal asked with more of that concern in her voice. Before he could answer, she said, "Never mind. That was a long time ago."

"Ancient history," he concurred.

"Check back in when you've had a chance to stop by?" Crystal asked, but she had to already know he would for work purposes. His sister wanted to check on him to make sure he was fine after seeing Audrey again all these years later.

He would be. No doubt in his mind. Even though a hand reached inside his chest and squeezed his heart at the thought. "Will do."

"Be careful," Crystal warned. Was she still talking about the perp?

"You know it," he confirmed. "And don't worry about our grandparents. I can cover."

"I should be able to drop in soon, but I'll have to leave just as fast," Crystal said. He could hear the guilt in her voice.

"We're a team," he pointed out. "All of us. And we got this. They won't be alone again."

Why did the word *alone* suddenly take on a new meaning to him?

LOUNGE CHAIR UNFOLDED to the perfect position. Check. Umbrella positioned to block the sun's unforgiving rays. Check. Good book to read on a much-needed day off. Check.

A sound in the tree line caught her attention, sent an icy shiver racing up her spine. Even after all these years, noise did that to her. Becoming a deputy was meant to face the monsters in the closet, as a manner of speaking. She'd taken self-defense classes to chase the nightmares away. So it frustrated Audrey to no end that her body still reacted to noises as if she was still that little girl hiding in her sister's closet being hunted by their mother.

The noise was just the wind, she determined.

Audrey Newcastle, formerly Audrey Smith, couldn't imagine relaxing after finding Lorenzo and Lacy Remington inside their banged-up truck in a ditch off Farm Road 12 yesterday afternoon, saddles splayed across the dirt. She couldn't conceive of what her life would have turned out to be without those lovely people intervening when she was sixteen years old and in more trouble than she knew what to do with. They'd shown her what real love looked like. All the credit for her turning her life around went to those two and not her pure evil mother and stepfather.

Leaving the hospital without knowing if the Remingtons would survive broke her heart, but she'd known better than to stick around and risk running into Duke. His grandparents gave her a heads-up every time before he visited, so she wouldn't accidentally run into him. They'd told her it was for the best if she stayed away while he was in town. She'd taken the not-so-subtle hint and made certain to keep out of sight every time. Even now. Walking away from Mesa Point and him all those years ago wasn't a choice she'd made lightly despite the message she'd asked his grandparents to give him. He would be too proud and too stubborn to forgive her for breaking up with him in that manner, but it had been the only way she could follow through with it.

Rather than go down the path of regret, she sat down facing the lake and opened her book. The glare from the water made her squint. The coffee she'd had a little while ago kicked in, causing her leg to twitch. Sitting still might not be her best move.

Getting up, she repositioned the umbrella but couldn't quite stop the glare from the water. This was her favorite lake, though, so she sat back down and looked across the surface that seemed to wink at her like brilliant stars on a clear night against a velvet canopy.

Audrey sighed as she picked up her book and opened to page one. Texas was known for its wide-open skies and sunsets that were postcard perfect. Today was no exception. Reading relaxed her.

The minute she got comfortable, her cell buzzed. Of course, it did. If not for the open kitchen window, she might not have heard it at all. Why did she always leave it inside?

Standing up, she debated answering for a half second. She'd lost countless days off covering for one of her coworkers while they attended back-to-school nights or last-minute trips to Galveston to get in more family time before school started. At thirty years old, she had no plans to become a mother, or wife for that matter. She involuntarily shivered at the thought. Parenthood wasn't for everyone.

Her stepfather was a prime example of that. Covering for coworkers was as close as she wanted to get.

By the time she got to her cell, the call had rolled to voicemail. The screen read Boss.

Her hunch that this was going to be a work-related call appeared to be dead-on. Rather than immediately call back, she waited to see if Sheriff J.D. Ackerman left a message.

Her work demanded her full attention. Being the only non-married deputy made her an easy target for helping out. But covering another shift for a coworker wasn't high on her list today. Not while she was still shaken from the devastating crash on Farm Road 12. After seeing the senior Remingtons in the hospital fighting for their lives, she was heartbroken.

Another noise outside caught her attention.

She surveyed the area, scanning the trees, searching for movement.

A deer? Some other wildlife? Wild animals were common in these parts.

Getting used to life in Mesa Point after growing up in Dallas was a big change, but she'd managed all right. And it mostly felt like home living here.

Audrey stared at the screen, tapping her fingers on the kitchen counter. Waiting. The voicemail icon lit up, showing the number 1. Audrey took a deep breath, steeling her resolve. She tapped the icon, then hit the speaker.

"I need to know a head count for the law enforcement versus fire department chili cook-off," her boss said. "Are you in?"

Audrey released the breath she'd been holding. That was easy enough to answer. As she started to send her response via text, a male figure showed up at her sliding glass door. Knocked.

Panic gripped her as she turned her full attention to the entrance. Had the noise in the trees been someone watching her?

She tamped down her nerves.

Someone out to get her wouldn't knock on the glass door.

She turned her full attention to the entrance. Her heart free fell the second she recognized the face. Duke Remington stepped inside the cabin.

Of course, he would show up in town for his grandparents.

But what could he possibly want from *her* after all this time?

BRAND NEW RELEASE

Don't miss the next instalment of the Powder River series by bestselling author B.J. Daniels! For lovers of sexy Western heroes, small-town settings and suspense with your romance.

RIVER JUSTICE

—R—

A POWDER RIVER NOVEL

PERFECT FOR FANS OF YELLOWSTONE!

Previous titles in the Powder River series

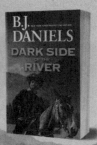

September 2023   January 2024   In-store and online August 2024

MILLS & BOON

millsandboon.com.au

Don't miss out!

Limited edition commemorative
Anniversary Collections

In honour of our golden jubilee, don't miss these four special Anniversary Collections, each honouring a beloved series line — Modern, Medical, Suspense and Western. A tribute to our legacy, these collections are a must-have for every fan.

In-store and online July and August 2024.

MILLS & BOON

millsandboon.com.au

Subscribe and fall in love with a Mills & Boon series today!

You'll be among the first to read stories delivered to your door monthly and enjoy great savings.

WE SIMPLY LOVE ROMANCE